RETURN TO LOVE

MARTHA GROSS

ZEBRA BOOKS
KENSINGTON PUBLISHING CORP.

ZEBRA BOOKS

are published by

Kensington Publishing Corp.
475 Park Avenue South
New York, NY 10016

First Printing: February, 1993

Printed in the United States of America

One

Bud stomped on the gas, pitching against the seat belt as the car surged forward. Late to his own wife's funeral? What kind of a moron was he? And drunk. Eight Scotches — or only seven? How was a two-beers-a-year guzzler supposed to keep track after the third drink — tie knots in his hankie?

Scotch had tasted like mouthwash thirty-five years ago and it still did. It had turned his head into sponge. And his legs. Smart move. Big macho move, this bender. He should have drowned his problems the way he usually did — with a macho stack of Oreos and a bottle of milk.

Would they start the funeral without him? No, wait. This wasn't the funeral. This was a wake. A viewing, they called it. Only no view. What was left of Bitsy — he winced at the thought of them scraping her up from that pavement near Fresno — would be flown up to Chicago tonight in a closed, curlicued casket for the funeral there to-morrow.

Sess had put it all together, while he, the fearless decision-maker, the crack businessman with the steel-trap mind, had totally lost it. The man who had made every decision for Bitsy for more than thirty-one years — except about her clothes and how to glitz up their houses beyond belief — had come unplugged. His decision system was down. After the call came, he could hardly get the receiver back on the hook. All he could register was this emergency signal blinking on and off in his head, "Call Sess! Call Sess!"

He couldn't even think of her number, until it caught his eye on the list of automatic-dial calls and he punched it.

Sess was on her way to Fort Lauderdale within the hour. One hell of a sister, Sess. Always was.

It was she who was now making calls and sending telegrams and night letters and everything but carrier pigeons all over Alaska to track Benjie down so he could fly home for his mother's funeral. That was the thing about Benjie. You never knew exactly where the hell he was.

All you knew was he was puttering at something or researching something — ever since he was a kid. Playing chemistry with his mother's perfumes. Studying ant hills by the hour. Chip off the old block, Benjie was. But why did he always have to trek off to some remote, untamed corner of the earth to do it? Why couldn't he tinker in some nice safe, accessible lab close to home? Like his dad?

Bud squinted at the signs ahead. Hard to see them against the glare of oncoming headlights and street signs. Hey! On the right, over there. Was that it? Riverpalm Funeral Home? He flipped the wheel, veering so abruptly into the drive that he was flung hard against the seat belt again. The Mercedes 500 sailed an arc over the lot's crunchy gravel, spraying stones as it zipped past the packed rows of cars, angling around the corner of the last full row as though it were driving itself, and sliding into the first open patch. It skidded sideways to a stop, straddling two parking places. "So sue me," he shrugged. "Charge me double."

Where'd all these cars come from, he wondered, fumbling at the seat-belt catch with fingers suddenly double-jointed. Bitsy couldn't have made that many friends in six months—not while she had been so busy "doing" the new house, crapping it up the way she always did until it made you dizzy to step in the door. Must be other wakes going on.

He leaned on the door, plunging sideways as it opened, but his flailing arm caught the edge in time. Steady there, fella. Pull yourself up. Legs like spaghetti. Concentrate, jackass! One step. Another step. One at a time. That's it.

Slowly, deliberately, his feet crunching loudly on the gravel, Bud made his way toward the carved white entrance ahead. God, he felt funny. Not ha-ha funny, Bitsy would have said. Peculiar funny.

Bitsy said that a lot. Anything Bitsy said, she said it a lot. Right is right. To each his own. That's fine and dandy. You get what you pay for. She said these things fifty times a day, day in and day out, until you wished she had a plug you could pull out, like a TV.

Well, she was unplugged now, he thought. Oh, shit. How do you get through a farce like this? The shock. The sorrow. The nagging lump of guilty relief in his throat that wouldn't go away no matter how he swallowed.

It wasn't that he hadn't loved her. You love a chair, if you have it around long enough. He had known her from the day he and Sess and their mom had moved to Arlington Heights, outside of Chicago, and rented that dumpy little cottage across the street from the Glicks' impressive, fenced-in spread. A giggly, dimpled little blonde, she had adored him from the start, and tagged after him like a puppy, as a nine-year-old sometimes will, after a thirteen-year-old. Her father, Ben, had taken a liking to Bud, too. He'd seen Bud's family's impossible money pinch, and how Bud was always hustling work—cutting lawns, weeding gardens, bathing dogs—any job he could get. And Ben had insisted on helping out—not only giving Bud work at first, but even helping with the rent or the electric bills, and just flat-out supporting him that year or so when their mother was too sick to work. And later, picking up the tuition so he and Sess could go to college.

Ben Glick, eccentric, impulsive, bigger-than-life—the Jewish version of the Marlboro man—had been like a dad to him. And when Ben's diabetes began to ravage him and his gambling got out of hand, he came to count on Bud as the one who would look after Bitsy when he was gone.

So Bud married Bitsy, the way Ben wanted. When Ben's empire fell apart and he couldn't see any answer to the mess he'd gotten into—when he put that gun in his mouth—at least he knew Bitsy would be okay.

Okay, maybe, but, God, Bitsy had missed a lot. Never enjoying sex at all. Never enjoying being touched or caressed. Enduring the efforts of a husband who simply couldn't awaken her. But then, if he had, what then? It always felt a little like incest with her anyway. He didn't much want to, either.

Yeah, Bitsy had sure been short-changed.

And so had he.

A car caught him in its beams and rumbled past on the gravel. A Buick. Next, a Cadillac. And then Bitsy's Jag rolled by.

Bitsy's Jag!

He shook his head and looked again. Idiot. It only looked like Bitsy's. Hers was scrap iron in Fresno. Remember?

Forget the cars, boozer. Just walk straight. If

they hit you, they hit you. Fool thing, running off like that—leaving Sess and Dell and Webb to cope. Slogging yourself blind in that crummy dive with the bar so sticky your money stuck to it and you had to peel it off to pay the bartender.

Some guzzler. You don't even know where to guzzle. You don't even know *what* to guzzle. God, there must be something that tastes a little better than that damned Scotch. But the one time you tried bourbon, it was even worse. And now, coming in so late. Jeez!

What was it—about seven-thirty? How long did these things last? Was it over already? Christ, better not be.

He groped for the door handle and yanked, and stepped into a blast of cool air—heavily perfumed, faintly musty. A muted roar hit him like a wave. It sounded like the noise from the crowd at a baseball game. He found himself in a kind of large, crowded foyer, being jostled from behind and the sides. Two framed signs on easels in front of him caught his eye. Harwyn Lancowicz, said one with an arrow pointing to an archway to the left. The second, pointing to the center arch, said, Bedelia Wellman.

Jesus! Bedelia? He groaned aloud. Bitsy would have had a fit! She hated the name Bedelia. Her deep secret. He'd tell the director—that little twerp with the scraggly moustache, who looked about sixteen—Simmons, that was his name. He'd damn well make him change it, right now!

Pushing one foot determinedly after the other, looking neither right nor left, muttering, "Shcuse me. Coming through. Shcuse me," he pressed his way through the human traffic jam, through the arch, into a small hall, and into the low-lit, jammed room beyond.

He stopped dead.

Hey, what were all these people doing here? No wonder it sounded like the crowd at a baseball game. It *looked* like the crowd at a baseball game. Ladies' day. The room was mobbed with women — buzzing and chattering at an irritatingly high pitch. Who were they? Was this the wrong place?

No, there were Sess and Dell in front of the grotesquely ornate brass coffin they had picked out yesterday. Only yesterday?

When they had inspected the coffin samples then, Sess had eyed all those bare-bottomed cherubs writhing on the lid of this one and asked, "You don't have something like this only with inlaid stones or handpainted flowers or something fussier, do you?"

Simmons had blinked at that, but quickly resumed his unctuous facade. "Sorry, no-o," he hummed soothingly, doing two notes to some syllables. "This is the mo-ost — uh — elaborate ca-asket, we ha-ave, on ha-and just no-ow."

"We'll take it," Sess said decisively.

Bud hissed in her ear, "Sess, are you crazy? It's horrible."

"So what?" she hissed back. "You're not going to hang it on the wall. Besides, you aren't parking in it. Bitsy is. And she would have loved it. She would have put a needlepoint cover on it."

Right. Bitsy put needlepoint on everything— including door knockers and doorknobs. One of the few big arguments they ever had was when he put his foot down at needlepoint covers for the toilet seats.

"Besides, it's the most expensive one they have," Sess added. "She would have liked that, too. And you can afford it." She also ordered the frilliest, handmade lace lining, even though no one would see it. He winced again, remembering the voice of the Santa Monica state trooper who thought his call had been switched to his wife, saying, "Don't hold dinner for me, babe. This one's going to be a mess to sort out. They hadda pick her up with a blotter."

Yes, Bitsy had adored anything frilly and fussy. Flouncy, ruffled dresses that made her look even shorter and plumper. Writhing wallpaper patterns. Ruffled curtains. When all the arrangements were completed, he had thanked his sister. "Sess, you're right. We got the right stuff."

And she had answered, "Listen, Bud, it's no secret Bitsy wasn't one of my favorite people. And I

12

know you haven't been deliriously happy with her—no, let me get this said. But she was just Bitsy. She wasn't a great brain or a great wit. But that's no crime. You did the best you could and she did the best she could. And I think it's awful for anyone to have to go that young. Anyone. Maybe I feel guilty because I used to wish she just wasn't in the picture." Sess shook her head, then went on. "So maybe you could have a little magic and electricity in your life with someone, like Dell and I have. Like with that little girl you told me about a couple of times. The one you got that sudden wild crush on back in high school. You know, the one you almost took to your prom until Ben leaned on you. With the long name that nearly rhymed."

"Pendleton. Jessie Nella Pendleton."

"Yeah, that one. And when you ran into her in Chicago that time. I could tell it really got to you. And forgive me, Bud, but I couldn't help wishing sometimes that you'd had something exciting like that.

"But I didn't want Bitsy to *die*." Sess blinked, but she couldn't stop the tears that began slipping down. "Oh, God, I should have gotten closer. They did so much for us. I guess it's too late for that. But at least I'm going to see to it that she gets exactly the kind of funeral she would have loved. Like that daughter of yours should be doing. I called your clubs and the Symphony Society and both temples and sisterhoods and everyone I

13

could think of in Chicago. I called Alaska again. They still haven't gotten hold of Benjie. There's a storm raging around his cabin at the edge of the world somewhere, and they don't have contact. So he may not make it in time.

"But Miss Mary's busy right now calling a bunch of his buddies from Stanford. So there'll be swarms of people, anyway. Bitsy loved swarms of people.

"To hell with taste. She's going to have what she would have loved, the biggest and glitziest damned send-off we can give her."

Fran made her do it.

Jessie jumped out of the way as headlights bore down on her. "That jerk's going to run me over," she muttered, ducking between two parked cars. "This place is dangerous." In the next row she dodged a zooming station wagon tailgated by a T-bird, sprinting the last few feet to the safety of the Riverpalm Funeral Home veranda.

What was this? Bumper cars at Disney World?

Her palms were clammy. God, she was nervous. Gasping. Couldn't get a deep breath. Why in heaven's name had she come? She hated funeral homes. Those smells! Like damp cellars, ammonia, industrial strength gardenias.

It was only seven-thirty-five but the lot was already more than three-quarters full. And look at that line of cars pulling in. Fran had told her the obituary said the Wellmans had only been residents for six months. So was all this for some *other* deceased?

It probably wasn't Bud, anyway. There were probably hundreds of Wellmans in the phone book, like Smiths, or Millers. Survived by her husband, Bud Wellman, the obit said. Fran had noticed it in the paper and called her at work. Sometimes she wished Fran would just stick to feeding her pepper plants, saving the planet, and tending her house-buyers. And mind her own business. But no. Having her for a roommate was like moving back in with your mother.

"Fran, I am just leaving, can I call you later?" Jessie had stalled. "I have an interview with one of Mike Tyson's former schoolmates and Pontchetrain thinks it will make a hot story and I'm going to be late."

But Fran had insisted. "You have time for this, Jessie. In today's obituaries, there was one for a lady named Wellman. Her husband's name is Bud and he's the head of some company. Medi-Quip, or some such. Isn't that the guy you were so ape for in high school?"

"Bud Wellman? Did I tell you about him?"

"Only about fourteen times. In mind-boggling detail. I could write the sit-com."

"What was *her* name?"

"Can't tell. There's a blob of ink in the middle. But I think it begins with a *B*."

"A *B!* Oh my God, Fran! But how could that

15

be? They live in Chicago. And California, I think."

"So what does that have to do with the price of oats? People move. They buy second homes. Everybody gives Florida a try sooner or later. You did. Anyway, you can check it out. The River-palm Funeral Home, on Federal Highway in North Miami. Run down after your interview."

"Oh, gosh, I can't get my breath! But what if it isn't him?"

"So? The world won't stop turning. Pretend you came to see one of the other corpses. They're sure to have some. They do land-office business in that place. Every third listing in the obits is at River-palm. You'd think they give away free shrouds or something."

"I don't know why you read those things. That's so gruesome."

"It is not. It's just keeping my Christmas card list up to date."

"Besides, what if it *is* him? After all these years. What would I say?"

"How should I know? Try 'Hello.' Or, 'Fancy meeting you here.' Or, 'Gee, don't I know you from somewhere?' You'll think of something. Every time we talk about men, Jessie, you bring up this guy. It's an absolute obsession with you. The worst scenario is if it's him and you take a look and find he isn't the hero you remember. You don't swoon anymore. Then at least you've put the ghost to rest. The *best* would be he *is* the hero you remember and he's still ape over you, too. And the two of you go sailing off into the sunset. Anyway, do what you like. But stop and pick up some skim milk and mung beans on the way home."

So here she was, her heart thumping wildly, crashing a wake. Life was strange.

Only this didn't look like any wake she'd ever been to before. It looked like Macy's parking lot on sale day. As she opened the door, a woman came charging up behind her and pushed in ahead of her. Another followed on her heels. You had to do defensive walking around here, she thought.

Inside, the mahogany-paneled foyer was packed with women. The polyglot perfume vapors were stifling. Only one man in the little room—balding, trim, not bad-looking. But he was not Bud. This man was standing next to a table and holding out a pen. For the guest book it looked like. Several women swept right by Jessie, wafting Beautiful, or Obsession or Cassini. They swept right by the man, too, ignoring the proffered pen, and through an archway. Jessie moved forward. The man held out the pen as she passed. She took it.

Looking at her face intently, he pushed the book toward her. But when she tried to sign it, the pen was dry. "Oh, wait, I'll get another," he said.

"I have mine," she answered, pulling one from

her purse. It had red ink. She shrugged and signed anyway, Jessie Nella Moore. And started toward the archway.

Then she saw the sign. Bedelia Wellman.

Oh, no! Bedelia? Not Bitsy!

Her feet stopped. Instantly a tight pulling replaced the pounding in her chest. A heavy slump of disappointment wilted her to her bones. She felt like Cinderella, as her coach turned back into a pumpkin. Fran was right. It was an obsession. She could feel tears welling. She hesitated, then turned to leave.

"You're not going in?" asked the man at the guest book.

"Oh, no. Sorry. I — I've made a mistake. The wrong Wellman. I didn't know him. I mean her." She swallowed hard, turned, and slipped out the door.

Webb watched her go. Attractive lady, he thought, automatically rating her assets. Good legs. Tight ass. Did Bud know her? Single? If so, she was probably the only single woman in Southeast Florida who would admit at this moment she didn't know Bitsy Wellman.

He'd better get inside and see if Bud was okay. He'd arrived just a minute before the lady who signed the book. Staggered in right past Webb without even seeing him. Late. And Bud was never late. And he had looked sort of tired, and messy. He'd looked, in fact, absolutely awful. He really must be taking this hard, Webb thought.

He put the book down. Hell, almost nobody was signing the damned thing, anyway. All these broads wanted to do was meet the new bachelor. Oh, well. He'd tell Bud about the looker with the red pen.

There was something about her. And why she had come, if she didn't know Bitsy? Maybe Bud would know.

Two

Cecily Lumbar spotted her brother just as he spotted her. She pushed toward him. "Bud, you're so late. Are you all right? Webb was telephoning all over trying to find you. My God, you look terrible! I knew we shouldn't have let you go off alone. You're not yourself."

"I'm awright," he answered in a stage whisper. "Thanksh for getting here early and running thingsh, kiddo. What a brawl! Who the fuck are all these people?"

"Shhh," she hushed him. Then she blinked. "You never say *fuck,* and *kiddo?* What is this? Wait a minute, is that liquor on your breath? Good grief, Bud, you're looped! But you don't drink."

"Only on shpecial occasions. Like my wife's funeral," he hissed back. "You can't get much more shpecial than that. Who the fuck are they, Sess?"

"Oh, you are drunk. I knew we should have

20

kept you with us. Who are they? I was hoping you would know. Good thing this place has adjustable walls. When Dell and I got here there was a crowd in the reception room and a mob scene in the lot, like they were waiting for a store to open at some incredible sale. Flowers everywhere. Simmons said they were all for Bitsy.

"He suggested we needed more space and said he could fold back the partition between us and the next room. He said it wasn't booked. Deaths were a little slow this week. I told him to go ahead. It only took a minute. The whole wall folded back like a fan. See? Behind that little drape? He just scooted the coffin over and rearranged a few of the flowers and one-two-three, it was done. He's a regular Mary Poppins. And they have this funeral business down to a neat little routine. Like making McDonald's hamburgers."

"Well, good for them. Now Shimmons ought to shave off that freak moustache. Looksh like Shalvador Dali. Am I supposed to do something here? Anything customary?"

"Stand at the coffin for a minute, I think." She led him over to it. Bud looked down at the ornate relief curlicues and muttered, "Ongapatchka," and turned his back on it. He didn't know exactly where poor Bitsy was now, but she sure as hell wasn't in there.

"Bud, are you okay?" Sess frowned. "How much did you drink?"

He didn't answer. He watched two women enter the room, then a woman alone. Then a group of four. "Hell, if I'd have known Bitchy had this many friends, I'd have rented the Orange Bowl and hired a band," he said. "Who would have gueshed. Ishn't there anyone *we* know?"

"A few. The Snellers were here and the Lowes. And your Chicago neighbors, the Barracks. But you know how she gets in crowds. She started palpitating so they left. But there'll be hundreds we know in Chicago tomorrow. Bud, don't lean your elbows on the coffin like that. It's not a bar."

He stepped away from it. "Shorry. I forget. I'm getting very shleepy. Maybe there's shomewhere I could shit."

"I take it you mean to say *sit?* No, don't. You can't dare fall asleep. You'd never live it down. People will understand if you're late, but not if you fall asleep. And besides we need you in here. Dell was the only man in the room at first because Webb was out there running the guest book, trying to get everyone to sign in, like at a bar mitzvah. You know—everyone signs and you look at it later."

"I'm not looking at it later."

"Yeah, Webb figured as much. And hardly

anyone was signing anyway. So he gave up. But he just said he was going out to try again a few minutes ago. Didn't you see him when you came in?" Bud shook his head. "Well, you must have walked right by him. I don't guess you're seeing any better than you're talking right now."

Bud felt a tiny tug on his arm and turned. A diminutive, sixtyish, redheaded woman with grey roots, in a bright blue print dress, was clutching his elbow. "You must be Walker, Bedelia's husband," she said in a quavery voice. Walker? Who the hell but the IRS ever called him Walker? "Oh, my dear, I am so sorry," she said. "I've never met you, but I knew Bedelia would want me to be here."

"That'sh kine of you," he said. "You musht have known my wife a long time."

"Well, uh — yes, for a while . . ."

"I mean, nobody's called her anything but B-B-Bitchy" — he tried to say Bitsy, but it insisted on coming out *Bitchy* — sinch she was a li'l girl."

"Oh, yes — Betsy."

"No. Bitchy."

"Bitchy?" the lady repeated hesitantly. "Ah, yes — sometimes I called her Bi-Bitchy, too. But, of course, I didn't mean it. Anyway, uh, I know she would want me to see that you're looked after, now. She would do it for me if my husband were still alive and I just lost him. But I already did that." She pulled a little note from

23

her bag and handed it to him. "I'm Gracie Zager. I live at Hillcrest. If you need someone to talk to, or to play a little backgammon, maybe, to get your mind off things, you just call. When you get back from the funeral, I'll make you some chicken soup."

"We'll be shitting shiva up there a few daysh," he said. What was the matter with his tongue? He pulled a hankie from his pocket, stuck his tongue out and wiped it off.

"I don't think that will help," Sess cooed at his side. "I heard that little exchange, Bud dear. Why don't you try to do as little talking as possible, the rest of this evening."

Bud shrugged and turned his back on Gracie Zager. "Heard anything from Benjie yet?"

A troubled look flitted over his sister's face. But she quickly smiled. "Not from Benjie, but Dell talked to his boss up in Anchorage. I guess the weather's pretty bad—rainstorms and all. Apparently the radios at the camp aren't working. Esme says Needle's been glued to his ham shack. He has his ham pals working on it. They'll probably have some kind of dope by the time we get to Chicago, tomorrow. Those hams could find the Loch Ness monster if they put their minds to it."

Bud started to comment but suddenly found himself facing a pair of beautiful, big-eyed brunettes—Raquel Welch and Cher knock-offs.

24

'You're Walker Wellman," gushed Welch, running her tongue over her lower lip and leaving it wet and glistening. "We're Jean Resnick and Dobie Wills. She's Jean and I'm Dobie. We had to tell you how sorry we are, just all broken up, aren't we, Jean. We feel terrible," she said with a broad cheery grin. Cher's grin, as her head bobbed in agreement, was just as wide.

"You mustn't be alone, you know," said Cher. "That's the worst. Anyone can tell you that. To get through this you need caring friends with you. To give you support. And affection."

"Yesh, well I've got my family right here. My daughter and son-in-law will meet ush in Chicago tomorrow. And my shishter is taking care of everything."

"Oh, that's wonderful," said Welch. "Bedelia always said her family was wonderful, didn't she always say that, Jean?" Both girls nodded energetically and then dug into their purses for cards which they put in his hand. "Call any time. We're always available for a few drinks or dinner or talk. Either one of us. I'm going to bring a nourishing little pot roast over next week. My late husband, before he *died four years ago*, always adored my pot roast."

"And I'll bring some potato pancakes," said Cher. "Before my late husband *passed away six years ago*, he adored my latkes." She kissed him on the cheek. Welch kissed the other cheek. "We want to help you with whatever you need or want," she said with feeling. "Anything at all."

"Anything?" whispered Sess at his side. "Ask if they do windows."

Mumbling thanks, Bud extricated his arms from their grasps and turned to flee. Oh, no! Another pair to the rear. And three more behind them. Eager smiling female faces. Good God, they were everywhere. To the right, to the left, in front, behind — walls of women. He was trapped.

Where the heck was Webb? Bud's eyes darted desperately around the room. There! Just coming in through the arch about seven feet behind Raquel Welch and Cher. Bud lunged toward him, elbowing rudely through the swarm, repeating, "Shcuse me. Lemme through," ignoring the manicured hands that grabbed his arms, and the insistent words their owners cried at him. "Oh, Mr. Wellman, I'm a friend of Bedelia's." "Mr. Wellman, remember me?" "Mr. Wellman, I'm Bedelia's friend from Coral Ridge."

He reached Webb and clutched at his arm like a drowning man at a log.

When Webb saw the look on Bud's face, he said to the women swarming around them, "Excuse us a minute, ladies; we gotta wash up," and he propelled Bud out into the reception room, down a hall and through the door to the men's room.

Once inside, he cried, "Where the hell were you? Sess was worried to a frazzle. You staggered in here like you could hardly walk, five minutes ago. Went right by me and didn't even see me. What the hell's wrong with you? You looked smashed."

"Only cuz I am. A bar on Sunrise. Or wash it Oakland Park? Or wash it . . . ? I don' know. Shomewhere. The one where the big truck crashed with a bunch of carsh a couple of hoursh ago, and made the biggesht mesh you ever shaw. It wash crawling with copsh and ambulanches and TV camerash an' tow trucksh. Did you shee it on TV?"

"I haven't been watching TV. I've been here, where you shoulda been."

"Oh. Well, anyway, I had eight Scrotches. Crotches. Scotches. Don't ask me why. Sheesh, whatsh going on out there?"

"Tell me about it. While you've been out boozing it up, I've been fending off women in heat. I keep running in here to get away from the goddamn perfume. You need a gas mask out there."

"Whoever thought she knew sho many people? Whoever thought sho many of 'em knew her name was Bedelia. I thought nobody knew that. Her darkesht shecret."

"They didn't know, genius. They got it from the paper. I'll give you odds at least three-quarters of those broads never knew her at all," said Webb.

"Yeah? Then what the hell are they doin' here?"

"Christ, for an egghead, you're so frigging dumb sometimes. They're all single. Lonely single women. Get it? That's what they're doing here."

"Huh?"

"You're a single guy now, Bud. Like me. They're getting their licks in early. A fifty says most of them never met Bitsy. They got her name from the obituary."

"The obishiary—obitchaterry? What a disgushting idea."

"And the obituaries called her Bedelia. The one in the *Herald* called you Bud, but the one in the *News* called you Walker. And I betcha half those women in there, if you talk to them, will call you Walker."

"Well, a couple did but . . ."

"Hey, come on, Bud. About fifty women tried to talk to me so far because they thought I was you, the new widower. And half of 'em called me Walker. I picked up enough phone numbers to wear out five guys for a year. A lotta dogs."

Bud looked confused.

"Don't you get it, Bud? Single guys in our age range are in short supply. And half those broads out there are so horny, they'd settle for that Simmons character. Single guys with a few nickels are even scarcer. That's the last thing you're thinking of right now, but that's the first thing those broads are thinking of. Believe me."

Bud stared at Webb as though he were talking Greek. Disbelieving.

"They're all gonna pretend they knew Bitsy and call you and invite you to dinner and bring you soup and knishes and offer to help with your laundry. Just so you won't be alone, of course. It's called solace. Consolation. Broads are not only going to be easy to get for the next few months—Bud, you're going to have to fight them off like mosquitoes."

Bud shook his head. "Sheesh, it's fucking unfair! Bitchy is the one who dies and I get the sympathy? An' what kind of husband was I? Never around. When I think of all the timesh I started to pull out . . ."

"But you didn't. You stuck. And nobody really knows about that."

"And there'sh not much I can do about it now, ish there? Except, like Shessh shaid, give her one hell of a shend-off."

"Right. You talked to Sess about Benjie?"

"Yeah."

"Well, don't get unwired. They've had mudshlides up there before. They know what to do. The cabins are very sturdy. And they don't even know that's what happened."

29

"Mudslides?"

"Oh, shit! I thought you said you talked to Sess."

"Well, she didn't get a chance to shay much."

"Don't panic. You know how Benjie is. And we'd get word through the hams if there was anything serious. Needle's on it. He'd know everything right away."

Bud digested the news and shook his head again. "Another fucking mudslide? Oh, that kid. But don' worry—I won't panic," he said. "Benjie alwaysh ties a shtring aroun' the doorknob before he headsh into a new territory. We've gone through thish shtuff before. We'll pro'lly go thru a lot more. But I sure wish he'd take up writing software or counting bacteria or shumthin' a little shafer."

Webb nodded. "Oh, yeah, I almost forgot. There was one woman who got here just a few minutes before you did. She never went in. She autographed the book, and then looked at the sign and said she was sorry, she had the wrong Wellman. Dishy broad. Kinda blondish hair. Green eyes. Something nice about her. But she looked uncomfortable."

Bud shrugged. "Whatzer name?"

"I don't know. But it's in the book. She signed at the bottom of the page. With a red pen, her own, because ours went dry. It wouldn't be hard to find. Not that many people signed. Well, are you ready to go out there and face your fans again?"

"Yeah. Lesh get it over with."

As the Scotch wore off and the relentless babble went on, Bud's head began to throb. It was a long two hours — shaking hands, being hugged and patted by dozens of strange women, turning down offers of dinners and casseroles and having cards and notes pushed at him or tucked in his pockets. At nine-thirty, Simmons and three helpers chased everyone out. Sess and Dell hugged him and left first. Webb was next. "You gonna make it home okay or should I drive you?"

"No, I'm okay."

"You're going right home?"

"Yeah. Right home. No more jerko cut-ups. Jesus, but I'm an ass, sometimes."

"Everybody's an ass sometimes. Especially when they get more dumped on them than they can handle."

As Bud went through the door, Simmons handed him the book. By the veranda light he flipped the pages toward the front. When he saw that name on page three, he almost dropped it. There, at the bottom. In red ink, in the round childish hand he remembered so well, it leapt out at him.

31

Jessie Nella Moore.

Jessie Nella Pendleton had married his class-mate, Harry Moore.

Three

Jessie dumped her purse and case on the foyer table and joined Fran and her whining Cuisinart in the kitchen. She climbed onto a stool and slumped over the counter, where her roommate was ruthlessly dispatching mounds of carrots and potatoes. "Well," Fran shouted over the noise, "Was it him?" Jessie shook her head and yelled back. "No, and I didn't even go in past the reception room. The little sign there said the deceased's name was Bedelia. It had to be someone else. Her name was definitely Bitsy."

"Who could forget a handle like that!"

"It was in the paper when they got married, and in charity write-ups later. You remembered it because they were so different, so rich. They didn't mix much. And they were Jewish. We hardly knew anybody Jewish. So was Bud. He and his sister were friendly enough. But they never had time for fun with us.

"He was a science whiz. Always busy at that or doing chores for someone. And Bitsy went to a private school in Chicago. A driver took her and drove her back every day. That big house. The servants. The four-car garage. And no vegetable garden! You don't forget the names of people like that. Especially after I met Bud and we clicked that way."

"Okay," Fran shouted. "So her name was definitely Bitsy."

"Fran, will you turn that darn thing off, so we can stop shouting."

Fran flipped the switch and Jessie slumped even lower on the stool and continued in a more normal voice. "I didn't go in. I signed the book, though, before I realized it was the wrong Wellman. But, oh, Fran, when I saw that name — what a letdown! I mean, by then I half expected to walk in and see him standing there in his cords and gym shoes. Instead I saw dozens and dozens — maybe hundreds — of pushing women. A stampede. I practically got trampled getting in the place. So I just left."

Fran scratched her nose and nodded thoughtfully. "Bedelia. Bitsy. Both begin with *B*. Hm. You know something? I think you should have stayed. At least gone in and taken a look."

"Why? I hate to look at dead bodies.

Whether I know them or not. They look so dead. I don't know that I would have recognized her, anyway, even if it had been the right funeral. I've only seen her once or twice at a distance when we were kids all those years ago. And newspaper pictures."

"I mean him, dummy. You could have at least taken a look. You know why? For one thing because you had those strong vibes. I keep telling you strong vibes always mean something. You sure are stubborn about admitting that psychic phenomena are for real."

"Not tonight, Fran. Tell it to your vegetables."

"Listen, Jessie. Nobody gets christened Bitsy. At least, I certainly hope not. What rational person would do that to a kid? Bitsy must be a nickname, probably for some name that's worse. One so awful that it never sees the light of day. One so terrible that even the name Bitsy is better. Like, for instance, the name Bedelia?"

Jessie's mouth dropped open. She put her head down on the counter and banged it twice. "Oh, lord, I never thought of that. Oh, Fran, what if it was her and I never even went in and looked! How stupid can I be?"

"Incredibly frigging stupid, sometimes," said Fran, turning to the sink to peel onions. "Add it up. Here's a guy that as far as you know, doesn't have anything major wrong with him.

Now that is a rarity in itself. Most of the guys that are old enough for you or me to mess around with—if they're single, there's a reason. I mean decent single guys in our range get snapped up so fast, and even for the losers, women are so desperate they'll marry almost anything on two feet if his signs are still barely vital. So any guy that's still single—there's usually a reason. He smells. He's a fart machine. He's gay. He's incredibly stingy. His breath is like fermenting goat's milk. He's the world's worst lover. He's totally out of commission sexually, or if his parts are still in minimal working order, he doesn't have a grasshopper's notion of what to do with them.

"So here's one that might be okay. He's the right age, three years older than you, didn't you say? He's newly single. He's got a little money. Or a lot, I gather. He's probably been monogamous so he won't have AIDS or herpes. But that can be checked. And there's reason to believe he might be very attracted to you. And you don't even have sense enough to give him a second look."

Jessie groaned and pounded the counter with her fists. "You're right. You're right. How I wish you weren't. You don't know how irritating it is to have a roommate who's always right."

"You want one who's always wrong? I'm the

best roommate you could ever have."

Jessie pounded the counter again and shook her head wordlessly.

"I took all the calls off the machine, by the way," Fran went on. "Kerry called. She will be home for the summer in approximately three weeks. She thinks she's getting all A's except one A-minus. And she said please send money."

"She always says please send money. Every note says send money. She thinks it's the same as writing, sincerely yours."

"And Emil called."

"Oh, no! Again? Was he sober?"

"Sounded almost. I thought you broke up with him."

"I did. But he's always so drunk he never remembers. I've even left the message on his answering machine so many times. Too bad he fell off the wagon. He was kind of fun while he was sober. Literate, anyway. He speaks about six languages. But when he's drinking like this—God, he's not even coherent. And dirty? What a slob."

"I wonder sometimes why we put ourselves through all this," Fran said, dumping the onions in the pot with the carrots and potatoes. "Is it worth it just to get laid once in a while? I suppose it must be, or we wouldn't do it. Anyway, back to this Bud person. All is not lost, I don't think."

"Oh, Fran, it is so. Even if it was him, he's up in Chicago."

"God, if everyone was like you, we'd all still be paying taxes to the Mongolians. Don't accept defeat so easily, Jess. He's not going to stay there, is he? The paper said they lived here for six months. That means even if he's going back to Chicago for the funeral, he's got a house or condo or something to take care of here. And it said something about the Symphony Society. You can probably get his number from their new directory. Or maybe even from the phone book. At least try."

"I can't just look up his number and call him out of the blue, Fran. What would I say? Gee, heard your wife died, Bud. Sorry about that. How'd you like to take an old flame to dinner, and see what heats up, ha-ha-ha? I'd die."

"We'll think of a good excuse. Meanwhile, this is very stressful, this stuff. You'd better keep up your strength. There's still some of my lentil soup left. We can map out a strategy over a bowl of it. You have the perfect job for this. Writers can go anywhere and ask anything."

"Well, don't make it sound so easy. It's not easy. What if it is him. And what if I meet him and he doesn't even remember me?"

Fran put a bowl of soup and a spoon on the counter. "Nothing ventured, nothing gained. Eat. He'll remember you."

"I am thirty-five years older than I was during that science fair, Fran. I'm fifteen years older than I was when I bumped into him at Marshall Field's that time. Gravity has been having its way with me. I have not been the Sleeping Beauty. Time has left its tracks. Maybe he'll take one look and be totally turned off. Or what if—it couldn't be—but what if he got all fat and bald and sloppy? How will I feel?"

"Will you stop that? Next it'll be what if he can't get it up? What if he's a lousy lover? What if he's turned to booze? It's hard enough dealing with the probabilities of disappointment without trying to deal with the possibilities, Jessie. There's too many of them. Especially with guys. Men just break down a lot faster than us women. After forty it's all downhill for them. The hearing goes down, the blood pressure goes up and sex gets so iffy that all they can do is talk about what great studs they used to be. If I never hear a fifty-year-old say again, 'You should have seen that dick of mine twenty years ago,' it'll be too soon."

"Oh, Fran, the things you say."

"Sure, this is all a long shot. But what isn't, when it comes to guys, at our age? You look great. You're trim. You've got better odds to find someone than most of the gals we know. And long shots do come in, you know." The telephone's peal interrupted her. "Now who could that be?"

Jessie grabbed the receiver. It was Kerry.

"Mom? Oh, I'm so glad you're there. Now, I don't want you to get upset, but I have something to tell you."

Jessie sank onto the nearest chair, covered the receiver and looked at Fran. "She says don't get upset she has something to tell me." And into the phone she said with deliberate calm, "What is it, honey? I won't get upset."

"Are you sitting?"

"I'm sitting! I'm sitting! Tell me. Are you all right? What's happened?"

"Well, my period is three days late. Three days, Mom. What if I'm pregnant?"

Jessie covered the mouthpiece with her hand and gasped to Fran, "Her period is three days late. What if she's pregnant?" And into the phone, "Well, baby, there are all sorts of other reasons why it could be a little late. What does Doug say?"

"He says if we're pregnant, we should probably just get married. We're going to get married anyway after he finishes his master's."

Thank goodness. Doug was a gem. Kerry was so lucky to have him for a boyfriend. With her hand over the receiver again, she whispered, "Doug wants to get married if they're pregnant," to Fran. And to Kerry, "Well, that's good. But you ought to get a test made or something first."

"The only thing is, Mom, I'm like probably going to marry Doug anyway sooner or later, but I really don't think people should get married unless they're like having great sex together. But I've never had an orgasm yet and I'm not so sure I should marry him if he can't give me orgasms. I mean like some of the kids I know are orgasming all over the place. And I never even had one. What if I never do? I'd feel so out of it. Like I missed something major. I'd be chained to this sexually dullsville existence."

Jessie's mouth dropped open and Fran hissed, "What is it? What'd she say?"

"You never had an orgasm?" Jessie repeated. "Then what do you go to bed with him for? You might as well be playing backgammon."

"Not even once?" repeated Fran. "That's terrible."

"Never. Zilch. I told you once, Mom."

"I know. I mean I knew you'd never had any before Doug, but I guess the way you two hit it off and you're planning to get married and his mother and dad are looking for a ring and everything, I just assumed that by now—"

"The one has nothing to do with the other, Mom. And it's very frustrating."

"Well, I should think so."

"Tell her not to panic," whispered Fran.

"But just don't panic, Kerry. First of all you're getting a test made. Got that?" Fran nodded vigorously at her side. "Get the test done. And second, if your period starts before you get it done or before you get results, I want to know. Immediately. Got that? Immediately. And then we can think of whether we have a problem here or not."

"Okay. And what about the orgasms, Mom? Any suggestions?"

"The orgasms? Why you don't have orgasms?" Jessie repeated, looking at Fran expectantly? But Fran just shook her head and shrugged. "Well," Jessie cleared her throat. "Uh, do you have any idea why you don't?"

"I don't know. Maybe because we don't have any privacy. I mean, these dorm walls are made of cardboard. You can hear everything right through them. Everything. When someone is doing it in the next room, you can practically see them. I know they can hear us when we're doing it. I mean no matter how wound up I get, I'm always thinking about people listening. That doesn't bother Doug. Guys don't worry about stuff like that. They'd just as soon whack off in the dorm parlor."

"Well, I guess you have to think about finding a little privacy, then. Maybe you have to go to a motel sometime. And you might also consider reading a serious sex manual and seeing if it helps."

"Gee, that's a great idea, Mom. I feel better now. I'll let you know as soon as we do the test or my period starts, whichever comes first. Talk to you, Mom."

Jessie hung up and turned to Fran, shaking her head. "Good Lord, I could never have discussed anything like that with my mother. She gave me a book when I was twelve, *Growing Up and Liking It*. I think Kotex put it out. That was my sex education."

"Yeah, well you and Kerry certainly don't have any such problems. Her channels are open. Her floodgates are open. This is the age when daughters make mamas blush. And what kids don't know about sex today hasn't been invented yet."

"Isn't that the truth? And we were so naïve, only one generation ago. After I married Harry, and finally had sex, I walked around blushing for weeks, because I knew that everyone must know what we'd been doing. Twenty-five years later people keep condoms in the glove compartment, and I'm telling my only daughter to go to a motel and have sex with her boyfriend. I don't believe I just did that."

"Well, look at what everyone is exposed to, today. TV and movies dripping sex and explicit scenes. Rock stars doing bumps and grinds.

43

Songs with suggestive lyrics. Hookers and pimps and crack dealers working right out in the open. Whenever I meet you at your office for lunch there are so many parading the street you have to look quick to keep from bumping into a couple."

"At my office? Those are hookers? Those aren't hookers. Are they?"

"Well, what do you think they're doing there? Selling Fuller brushes?"

"But how do you know?"

"The getups. The way they swish their butts like saying, 'Let me show you a good time.' Which ones are selling crack and which ones are selling sex, I can't tell. But they don't leer at you that way when they're selling brushes."

"Oh."

"Come on. Let's eat our soup before it gets cold. Between Kerry's orgasms and Bud Wellman, I have a feeling you're going to need it."

"Oh, gosh, Fran, I'm so nervous. It's thirty-five years since that science fair. I'm fifteen years older than when we met at Marshall Field's that time."

"You said that before."

"Maybe one look and he'll run in the other direction. Or maybe he'll have a red nose with little broken veins all over it. I'd hate that."

"Will you lighten up? Let's look in your Symphony Society membership book and see if he's isted. If not, call the funeral parlor. We'll find a way to check him out, don't worry. Just remember — long shots come in all the time."

Four

"Bitsy was really pulling out all the stops on this one, Bud," said Dell, waving an arm at the fussy pink and mauve chamber they sat in. Soaring beamed ceilings; pink flowered wallpaper; elaborate pouffed plum chintz-and-satin window treatments; end tables mounted on the backs of ceramic flamingos, étagères and cabinets packed with collectibles; paintings, etchings, and numbered prints on every available inch of wallspace; and crowded groupings of ornate mauve sofas and love seats strategically placed for chatting and viewing the numerous collections.

"It's Laura Ashley on speed. With a touch of Andy Warhol," he chuckled. "But I guess she was having fun with it."

"We're so hopelessly meat-and-potatoes," laughed Sess. "We'd never be able to live in one of Bitsy's museums. Where do you throw

46

your newspapers? Where do you practice putting? Where are the recliners?"

"I was teasing her that we'd better hire a couple of docents instead of maids," Bud said with a rueful chuckle. "But what could I do, so long as she left my rooms alone. You know how she loved collecting."

Webb came in from the kitchen with a red-eyed Miss Mary, the Wellmans' housekeeper for thirty-one years and Bitsy's nanny before that, pushing a serving cart laden with sandwich makings and pastries. "You guys have at least an hour before you have to leave for the airport. Miss Mary's got a bite ready for you, here."

"That airline food is made of styrofoam," the housekeeper said, shaking her head sadly and then hurrying back toward the kitchen.

"And when is your plane, Bud?" asked Sess.

"Not until almost midnight. Webb'll drop Miss Mary and me off at Delta."

"You're not going to keep this place, are you?" asked Dell, slapping a roll with tuna salad.

"I haven't thought about it," Bud shrugged. 'But I guess not. I don't even know if I'm going to stay down here or go back up north, ultimately."

"With your new labs down here, you'll probably hang around a while—at least till you've got the kinks out," offered Webb.

"But you wouldn't want to live in this house." Dell repeated. "All that fuss? Get an apartment. No headaches."

"Dell's right, Bud," nodded his sister. "I'd move out, right away. But then, I'd get terminal vertigo if I had to sit in this room for more than two hours without blinders on. Webb could find someone to help you look for an apartment. And I could help you when you find one. You sure you don't want to bunk with us tonight, Bud? Dell will run out to the airport to pick you up."

"No. I don't want either of you driving back to the airport or waiting up for us. Tomorrow will be a rough day. Let's leave all the plans as they are. I'll call you from the hotel at seven in the morning. I'm sober now. My head feels like it's in a vise but otherwise I'm okay. No more jackass moves. Esme and Needle will pick us up at eight."

"Whatever you want. You know there's always a couch at our joint," said Dell, punching his brother-in-law lightly on the arm. "We're heading out to the airport early. Gotta return the car and all that."

The telephone's loud ring startled them all. "Oh, Jeez, I hope they're not starting already!" muttered Webb.

Bud answered. It was Esme. "Hi, Daddy, is

that you? Everything go all right today?"

"I guess. Aunt Sess and Uncle Dell are just leaving for the airport."

"Well, listen, Daddy, I have some news from Alaska. There were mud slides up around Kenniak, where Benjie is. Colonel Dorrence, one of Benjie's bosses, says they still don't know too much because it's still raining torrents and there's danger of more slides so they can't get in to see how they are. But it's happened before and they're pretty safe in those camps. He says they have deep pilings and they're built to hold together—like fortresses, really. Dorrence will keep us informed. But he said not to worry."

"Cheap advice," said Bud.

"And listen, Daddy. Don't ask Aunt Sess or Miss Mary if there's anything they want, yet. In the house, I mean. Don't give anything to anybody until I get down there. A lot of that junk is very valuable, tasteless or not. So just freeze everything until I can get down and get Sotheby's or someone to look at it. Promise?"

"We'll talk about it tomorrow, Esme."

"Daddy, you know this would be upsetting to you, anyway. And you never were into collecting. So, don't make a move, not a move, until I'm there."

"I have a headache now, Esme. I'll talk to you in the morning. Goodnight."

"Esme? What did she want?" asked Sess.

"She wanted to know how you all are and she sent her love and she thanks you all for being here today when she couldn't," Bud replied hoarsely.

"Ha!" said Webb. "Sure, she did."

After his sister and brother-in-law left, Bud opened the guest book to page three. "Webb, remember once I told you about that little girl I fell for in high school, my senior year at the science fair? How I asked her to the prom? I hadn't even been thinking of going. And then how I had to tell her I couldn't take her?"

"Yeah, I think I've heard about that before a time or two. About once a month, fella."

"Did I tell you how it stayed with me?"

"Yeah, I think so. But you were kind of committed to the Glicks, and you had to take Bitsy. That one?"

"Yeah."

"Never fear. If you ever forget any part of the story, I can fill you in."

"I just couldn't do what I wanted to. I owed him too much. I worked in his office. I cleaned a couple of his buildings. One had labs for tenants. That's how I got interested in labs. But there was no way Sess and I would have gotten through school without him. I loved him like he was my dad."

"And he wanted you to marry Bitsy."

"Yeah. Not that I didn't love her. I did. Like a kid sister, or a daughter. But I loved her. I did what I thought I hadda do."

"I never figured there was any grand passion there."

"I went ahead and married her. And when Ben lost everything and killed himself—by that time I was beginning to make real money. But it was too late. I should have adopted her, instead of marrying her. But there we were."

"I guess all this has stirred up a lot of old feelings, Bud. Wait! You mean that woman at Riverpalm today . . . ?"

Bud nodded. "I think so. That handwriting. I'd bet this house it's hers. Hell, I read her whole paper on her science project. She made paints out of natural things, like berries and onion skins and leaves. And fed them to guinea pigs to see if they lived as long as guinea pigs on a regular diet, to try to prove that her natural pigments were harmless if a little kid ate them. It was a neat little project. She wasn't the Marie Curie type. And she was only a freshman. I remember that funny round hand, like printing almost."

"Then why'd she leave? If she cared enough

to come in the first place?"

"Damned if I know. But it's kind of knocked the pins out from under me. With everything else — Benjie, Bitsy, and this goddamned hangover — I'm spinning."

"It figures. Want to see her?"

"I don't know. I mean, yeah, I would, but maybe I shouldn't. Jeez, how can I even think of it now, with the funeral and all. But it was so intense, what I felt then. I felt like I was giving up everything I cared about when I told her I couldn't take her to the prom. And I was going back on my word. And when I've seen her since — just three times in thirty-five years — I take one look and I still want to grab her and run off with her. And what kind of guy am I? My wife gets killed and two days later, before she's even buried, I'm thinking about a little girl I met in the science lab when I was eighteen. And kissed once in a broom closet ten years later. Once in a school driveway. And once in an elevator fifteen years ago. What is it with me?"

"Listen, Bud, anyone you remember that clearly and think of that much after kissing her once in a goddamned broom closet, and then — okay — twice more in thirty-five years — there's something almost scary about it. So, yeah, your wife got killed. But she was never really a wife. Not a regular wife. Once you get past tomorrow and get word from Benjie, I think you gotta follow this up. Most likely, you'll look at each other now and wonder what all the fireworks were about. But you might take one look and think you've just found heaven. And if you don't check it out, you'll go bananas for the rest of your life, wondering."

"I'm thirty-five years older. She'd probably take one look and walk the other way. Or if we go out, say, and maybe even try to get it on—hell, I'm no great lover. I'd probably be a big disappointment."

"Hey, Bud. Take it from a guy who's tried it all. When you really got it for a dame, and she's got it for you, you manage. Whatever you do is better than some sexual gymnastics could ever be with some expert. 'Cause you care. You turn each other on high. And that makes the difference."

"But has she got it for me, still? How do I know that?"

"She came tonight, didn't she? So look into it. And forget that crap about Bitsy not being cold in her grave. So what? You're doing right by her. Nobody ever thought you two were the greatest love match of the century. You paid her father back in spades. How many young guys do you think were as successful as you, and could take on their whole family and in-laws, too, before they even got out of med school?

"You know what I think of true love, Bud," said Webb. "After five tries, I don't see it through the same pink glasses you do. But it happens. And when it does, it's so fucking great, it's worth a gamble."

"I guess I'll try to find her. In a while."

"What do you mean, 'You guess?' You know damn well you're going to try to find her. But even if you do and it doesn't work out, no sweat, Bud. You are going to be absolutely stampeded by women in the next few months. That's one reason you gotta get out of this house. You need a place with security. Where any broad that wants to can't just come walking into the yard or sailing up the channel, the way they can now. You're going to need protection, Buddy boy."

Bud looked at Webb as though he were crazy. "Me?"

Webb nodded. "Yeah, fella. Lots of protection. Wait and see."

The first time Jessie saw Bud after that fair was in 1967—ten years after his and Harry's graduation . . .

* * *

"I don't know why I let you talk me into this," Harry was grumbling. "Why were you so gung ho? It wasn't even your class. You didn't go to Arlington."

"But I went to grade school with them. And camp. And church. I probably knew as many of your classmates as you did," she answered defensively, stretching the truth. Her eyes darted nervously from group to group, hoping to catch a glimpse of that familiar face. And hoping not to. Ever since Harry's tenth reunion announcement had arrived, three months ago, she could think of little else. "And it's your class," she scolded. "Aren't you curious to see what's happened to him — to them?"

"What could have happened so fast? For four years everyone was in college. So it's only six years more. What happens in six years? We're all just getting started."

"A lot can happen in six years," she insisted. "Hannah Doric has had two marriages and four kids, and I hear she just ran away with some rock singer from Liverpool. That's more than just a start. And I heard Betty Whitcomb just signed for a part in some Broadway show. Remember the redhead who was always in your school plays and was already doing radio and little movie parts before you all graduated? You know — the one with the legs up to her armpits? And one of the guys in your class" — she couldn't quite bring herself to say Bud's name out loud to Harry — "is supposed to have a national company going already. Something medical." Oh my gosh, was that him in the bunch under the basketball hoop? Her heart stopped. No. Too tall. It restarted.

"Oh, you know how those things get exaggerated. Probably owns a couple of ambulances, ha-ha-ha. Maybe he's a Band-Aid distributor. Will you look at this gym? Crepe paper streamers, for Chrissake. What do they think — we're all still a bunch of kids? Well, at least there's a bar. Let's get a drink. Just like the old days, only now it's legal. Hey, there's Reggie Archibald. Come on."

"I'm going to the ladies' room for a minute, Harry," she said. "You talk to him. I'll find you near the bar. Okay?" She had to get out of there. And away from Harry for a minute. She was breathless. Keenly alert. And the air was charged. Like something momentous was going to happen any second.

She tugged one of the heavy gym doors open and slipped out into the hall. More people were milling about there. One group was hugging each other and laughing hysterically — the women, squealing. Which way were the rest rooms? She had been here for a couple of games and parties after she started dating Harry ten years ago, but she didn't know her way around. She spotted a paper sign, Rest Rooms, and an arrow painted in red. She followed it.

She didn't need a bathroom. She needed oxygen. But she walked that way, anyway, scanning the faces coming toward her, half expecting to see his among them. She was so intent, she almost bumped into him coming out of the men's room.

"Oh! Oh, I'm sorry," she said, stopping short. And then, "Oh, it's you!"

He froze, staring at her for several seconds, then breathing, "Jessie Pendleton! My God!"

"Jessie Moore, now," she breathed. "I—I got married."

"Oh," he said. "Oh, I'm sorry. I mean, congratulations. Uh, that's very nice."

"Oh, yes. You, too. I heard."

"Yes. But I—listen, Jessie, have you got a minute? Where can we talk?"

"Only a minute. Harry's inside. But yes, yes," she said.

"Bitsy's going to meet me at the dinner later, too," he said. "But just a moment to talk. Alone." She nodded.

He took her hand. It was trembling but she didn't pull it back. "I think there's a little storeroom on this floor somewhere, if I remember. This way, I think." He led her down the corridor, around a corner, and another, ten feet or so to a single door without any room number on it. He tried the knob. It turned. The door opened and they darted inside and Bud quickly closed it behind them. He felt the wall for the light switch, and flicked it on.

It was a small cubicle lined with shelves holding packages of gym suits and towels, bottles of soap and cleaner, and packages of paper goods. Maybe twenty folding chairs leaned against one wall. He opened two of them, but they didn't sit. They stood there, awkwardly, he looking down at her, she looking up at him while he held her trembling hand. "I can hardly breathe," she whispered, finally.

He nodded. "Me, too. I think of you, sometimes," he said. "More than sometimes. Oh, Jessie," the words tumbled out, "I had to do what I had to do. It was pretty rotten — just running away from you like that. Just sending a note. Not even calling or talking to you again. I didn't want to do that. God, I didn't want to. It was awful. But I had to, Jessie."

"Awful for me, too," she nodded. "I thought I had met my prince charming. It broke my heart. I was so silly."

"No. Not silly. Me, too. It was like something so—so wonderful, meeting you. A storybook thing. So wonderful that I just forgot how Ben Glick was counting on me, practically supporting us, putting Sess through college and I was next. And counting on me—expecting that Bitsy and I—oh, shit. I had to do it. If I let myself see you again, I couldn't have stuck to doing what I had to do. But I think of you. God, do I think of you. You're always there, in the back of my mind if you're not in the front. Are you happy?"

"Don't ask me that. I do the best I can. He's a decent person. I do the best I can. We're Catholic. What else can you do?"

"Listen, Jessie. We may never get another chance to say things to each other. So I'm going to tell you. I've thought hundreds of times of just leaving. My businesses are doing really well. I thought maybe I could get out of this and you—we—but my father-in-law killed himself almost four years ago. Now, Bitsy is more dependent on me than ever. We have a daughter. I'm trapped, Jessie. There's nothing I can do.

"But I fell in love with you in that lab ten years ago. You were the prettiest, sunniest, softest girl I'd ever met. You still are."

Jessie laughed sadly. "Much good did it do

me. Oh, God!" Bud took her gently in his arms and she laid her head on his shoulder. He kissed her cheeks softly, her eyelids. She reached up and wrapped her arms around his neck and they kissed on the mouth. Gently at first, so tenderly, and then with such deep feelings — love, hunger, desolation. Harder and harder until she broke away. "Oh, gosh, we fit together so well. But we can't do this. It's so wrong."

"If only we could just see each other once in a while. So I'd know how you are."

She shook her head. "We can't. You know we can't. It would just keep us hurting. And thinking of each other. Oh, it's so unfair. Life is so unfair. I would give anything if we could change it. But we can't, Bud. All that fluff about guardian angels. Where was mine when he let me meet you? I hope he's satisfied. He let me mess up my whole life."

Bud took her hand again and kissed it and held it to his cheek. Jessie felt tears welling but she pulled away and reached for the doorknob.

"Don't go yet, Jessie," he cried.

She shook her head. "I have to. I love you Bud. But I have to go. I have to do what I have to do, too."

* * *

That was twenty-five years ago. She had opened the door and marched out, closing it after herself. She had retraced her steps, blotting her eyes as she went, around the corner, down the corridor, back to the set of double doors.

Back to the gym. And Harry.

Five

Bud passed through most of the funeral in a daze. It was supergloom—everything—the sky, the almost-naked trees, the rain. That was probably why he wept.

The grey of the dawn had never faded that morning. The city was still wrapped in its murky blanket at 9 A.M. when the sky turned even heavier and more misty. And then it began to drizzle. Cars pulling up to the Lakeway Funeral Home were shiny wet, and when they pulled away an hour later, after a service of which Bud later could remember little, they were still shiny, still wet, and their wipers were swishing busily.

At the cemetery, as during most of the funeral itself, the sky barely lightened. But roiling charcoal clouds scudded across it, and everyone emerged from their cars under umbrellas—into long anonymous queues of black umbrella tops and raincoat bottoms rippling solemnly down the squishy paths toward the extended canopy and the grave.

Sess walked on one side of him. Dell on the other.

And behind him, Esme and Needle, whispering and hushing each other, and the cousins. They couldn't put aside their excitement about their new business adventure, even amid these crushing moments. "I told her they may not, under any circumstances, hand out samples here in the cemetery," said Sess. The new line of "one-serving" sizes of face makeup, eye shadow, little swabs covered with lipstick, vitamins, sun screen, toothpaste, disposable toothbrushes, etc., was a great idea. "But this is not the place," she grumbled. "I think they would have been hanging ads on the canopy, if I hadn't scolded them."

Bud's finger joints ached. He had never shaken so many hands in his life. And there were always a few hearty types who had to grab your paw in a death grip to prove they really meant it. Or squeeze your fingers like they were milking a cow. Even some of the women. Especially some of the women.

They took their places under the vast triple canopy, in the first row, at Sess's nudging.

"Why can't we sit in the back," he whispered to Dell.

"Do what Sess tells you," Dell whispered back.

He did. He turned around once to look back and see who was there and Sess hissed at him. "Don't turn around, Bud. You look like you're counting the house."

There certainly was a huge crowd. All the movers from the Symphony and the ballet and the Art Institute and Bitsy's other causes. Policemen everywhere. Two women in blue raincoats and matching rainhats scurried up to Bud before anyone could stop them, smiling eagerly. "So glad to meet you again, Mr. Wellman," said the first, squeezing his hand. Bud winced. "I'll bet you don't remember me, do you?"

"Uh, well, I—" Bud sputtered.

"Summer, two years ago, the Officers' Club at Great Lakes?"

"Uh, I—"

"I was in this pink dress with a handkerchief hem and you said . . ."

"Sorry, we'll have to play twenty questions later," said Sess sternly, nodding to one of the policemen nearby and grabbing the woman's hand to disengage it from Bud's.

"Would you please go and sit down, now," said the policeman, politely but firmly, taking both women gently by their arms. They yipped protests and apologies and finally shrugged as he led them out from under the canopy and around toward its back.

"Next thing they'll be asking for your auto-graph. Or inviting you to lunch," grumbled Sess. "Hang in there. Nothing lasts forever."

The rites went quickly. Bud watched the skies grow darker as the rabbi intoned. The strong smell of the damp earth grew fainter as the winds heightened. The trees began writhing as if in agony and the thunder broke just as they started to lower the coffin into the carefully shaved pit that would be its final resting place.

"I could manage everything but the weather," Sess said, choking. "I got her the crowd. I got her the press. But I wanted sunshine for her, too, dammit. She was so afraid of the light-ning." She sniffed and fumbled for her hankie. Bud reached over to pull her to him to hug her just as the first shovels of dirt thudded on the coffin. Lightning lit the sky and thunder crashed again and again, like blows to his heart.

That was when he came unhinged. "You did the best—" he blurted, choking. He tried again. "You did the best—" and choked again. And

65

dropping his head he began to sob—heaving, tearing, but almost silent sobs. Sess and Dell both put their arms around him. They tried to pull him to his feet. He sagged. A policeman rushed to help. And another. They supported him on the slippery ground, moving him towards the path to the limo.

The people under the canopy all began talking at once. Some murmuring, some shouting over the thunder, while the winds whipped at the canopy, threatening to tear it loose. Through the roar of noise and the confusion, they heard Esme call, "Daddy, what's the matter with you?" And then she shouted over the noise, "This is all very difficult for my father. He's so upset. I couldn't even ask him any questions about business since he got here."

The lightning spat more jagged light across the darkened sky. Thunder crashed and rolled while the seemingly endless rows of umbrella tops and raincoat bottoms began rippling hurriedly back to the cars and limos they had come from.

"So many cars. From where? Who are they?" Bud mumbled as Dell and the policemen helped him into the car.

Sess climbed in after them, first whispering to her husband, "Let Esme and Needle take another car, honey." He quickly flagged Needle

66

over to the window and whispered tersely and Needle nodded and hurried off. His and Esme's limo led the long, somber chain of wet cars that drove slowly from the cemetery and headed for home.

Bud sat with his head in his hands until the other cars were gone. Then he crawled out of the car and stood near the door, looking over towards Bitsy's grave. After several minutes, he sighed, shrugged, and got back into the car.

"Well, at least that's over," he said.

Sess nodded and patted his hand. She told the driver it was time to go.

Bud leaned back and stared silently out the tinted windows all the way to Esme's.

For three blocks before coming to the wide, intricately scrolled iron gates that led to what once had been Bud and Bitsy's home, the limo drove between queues of parked cars.

"I think they're all for us," said Sess. "Are you okay, now, Bud?"

"Yeah."

"When we get there, you go upstairs with Dell and relax a bit. Esme and Needle and I can handle it. We've got enough help to run a coronation."

Actually, Esme had not been eager to have

the shiva here. "Oh, Daddy," she had protested when he and Sess had called her from Florida after making the other arrangements there. "There is so much going on here right now. You know how a new business is, all meetings and decisions. Otherwise Needle and I would be down there. We can't just cancel all this."

"It was your mother's house, Esme," Bud had reminded her. He had deeded the large pillared brick colonial to their daughter when he had decided that he and Bitsy would move to Florida. "I think she would want it done there."

At that point, Sess, who had been standing next to him, had grabbed the phone. "Essie dear, Dell and I would do it in a shot, but Bitsy wasn't my mother. And you know how people are. They expect a daughter to do it. And if Dell and I did it in our place or a hotel, they'd wonder why it wasn't in Bitsy's old house. And they'd talk. I'm not going to let that happen to you, dear. But I know you're swamped. So would you like me to run things, sort of behind the scenes, you know? In your house and you just take as much part as you can manage. Talk to a few people — that kind of thing."

"Oh, Aunt Sess, that would solve everything. Will Daddy want to stay here?"

"I think that would look best, dear. And Webb will come up after the funeral. You know how he can't handle funerals. Just do this. Have your secretary call my caterer, First Cabin, and ask if they can do it. Or yours. Or whoever she can get that's good. She should tell them it'll be a mob and they have to do everything. Have her call me back and tell me who she got and I'll take it from there — the valets, food, flowers — the works."

So when the car pulled through the gates, Sess directed the driver past the valets and around to the back entrance. Dell and Bud slipped up the back staircase — Miss Mary's stairs, they used to call them — up to the second floor and to what had been his rooms. Miss Mary went into the kitchen, and Sess hurried out to the foyer to help Esme and Needle shake hands with people as they arrived.

"I don't know what happened," Bud said, staring out the window to the barren rock gardens below. "Something just let go. It was — I don't know — like this sudden massive regret. I gave her things, lots of things. I tried to make her life easy. Whatever she wanted, she got. Because it made me feel better. That was all I could give her. Things. And then when it rained. God, you know how terrified she was of lightning. She was ready to crawl under the bed during a storm. Miss Mary used to have to hold her hand. Why the hell did it have to rain today? I couldn't even give her a good funeral. Hell, I didn't give her any funeral. Sess did it all. Even Esme is just coasting."

"Don't be too hard on her, Bud. Or so hard on yourself. It will sink in for Esme soon enough. She's so wrapped up in her business schemes right now—maybe it's a good thing. Maybe it's the best thing that could happen. It can keep her from looking at it too closely until she's able to."

"Shit, how I hate all this. Webb's got the right idea. Just don't go. He hasn't been to a funeral in ten years. Says he just can't take them. Now I see why. I don't know if I can handle this one, either."

"Hang on. The worst is over. Sit shiva for a couple of days and it's done with. You want some Valium?"

"What would I want that for? I never take any of that garbage."

"Never say never. And don't be so indignant, Bud. Nobody's offering you grass or crack. Just something to blur the sharp edges downstairs. Doc Bauer sent it over when he heard what happened. Said you might need it. It's here if

70

you do." Dell put the small vial on the dresser.

"Nah, I'm okay now." Or he would be if he could just stop trembling.

Downstairs, more than a hundred people had already arrived and more were pulling up. A butler, Esme's idea, stood at the front door letting them in and directing them to the glassed-in sun porch, which was serving as a cloakroom, and thence to the living room and library. Sess and Esme were standing at the other end of the long foyer, chatting with arrivals. It looked remarkably like one of those cocktail parties Bitsy used to give here for the Symphony or the Art Institute, except that the foyer was so much sleeker now than during Bitsy's tenure. Esme was not into fuss and ruffles. Esme was into lean and clean.

"Good thing we got all those valets," said Sess. "Oh, look, more trays. And another basket. No, please have those taken around the back," she directed the butler. "Cook will save the cards."

"Isn't this crowd incredible, Aunt Sess?" said Esme. "It looks like one of Mother's charity parties." She turned to a group that had just stepped inside. "You can take your coats and umbrellas to the sun porch," she suggested.

71

"And please then go on into the living room and have a drink or some coffee and a bite."

"Very good, Es," nodded Sess. "It's nice to know that if you or your Dad ever go broke, you could wing it as a top-notch usher."

"Only, Needle and I have a meeting at four with the Estée Lauder people," Esme said, frowning.

Dell and Bud made their way through the crowded living room and sat on the piano bench. "I think Webb was right," observed Dell, glancing about the room. "All these women. And how many of them do you know?"

Bud followed Dell's eye. "I don't know that I know any of them." Six or eight of them closed in on the bench. "And I brought you some nice chicken soup with my homemade noodles," one was saying.

"A little something sweet is what you need," said the dumpy lady who was elbowing in front of the first.

"And if you'd like to make a donation that really matters, you could underwrite a ballet in her name," a third was explaining. How could he hear when they were all talking at once?

"There's someone we know!" whispered Bud excitedly, as a familiar couple edged closer. "The Orinths. They lived next door when we had the house in Barrington." He greeted them.

"Good to see you, Ned, Dana. You know Sess's husband, Dell."

"I've never seen so many people sitting shiva," said Dana. "It's a tribute to Bitsy. Listen, we want to have you to dinner one night. How long are you staying?"

"Just a few days, Dana."

"Well, you say when. We could bring Ned's sister, Yorrie, along. Remember her?" Yorrie? Did he remember Yorrie? Wasn't she the one with the pleated skin?

Dell saw Bud's stricken look and interrupted. "Oh, gee, Bud. Isn't your cousin Escoria coming in tomorrow?"

"Escoria? Oh, yeah, cousin Escoria," Bud nodded gratefully at Dell.

"I'll have to see what time is open and get back to you," he said.

"Escoria?" he repeated under his breath to Dell a moment later. "Where did you get that name?"

"It came to me," shrugged Dell. "Far out enough to sound real. If you're gonna lie, you should be creative."

Another faintly familiar looking couple squeezed in front of the Orinths, practically falling into Bud's lap, the lady gaunt and intense, in flowing black, leading a short, wizened-looking man. Wasn't she president of some organization of Bitsy's last year? "I just wanted to tell you, Bud," the woman chanted in rich, resonant tones, "that I think it was mahrvelous that you wept today. Absolutely exquisite, darling. Men, too often, are not in touch with their feelings. They're afraid to feel. You, Bud, know how to feel. You are in touch with your feelings. It was absolutely touching when your heart and your eyes flooded. And you blew your nose, unself-consciously."

"Why doesn't she just give you the Nobel Prize and get it over with?" whispered Dell.

"Uh, thank you," said Bud, trying to ignore the ring of people, mostly female, pushing at them, all talking at once. "Is it just me?" he hissed to Dell. "Or does this feel a little like Alice in Wonderland, Dell? Or like I just stepped into a movie or something."

"Jesus, it's wild, isn't it?" Dell whispered back. "And it's all so fucking phony. I bet half the women in this room didn't even know Bitsy. I'll bet ten percent of them never met her."

"I never realized before how intimidating women can be in hordes. Damned frightening."

"We're going to play it scarce, here, and let the girls handle most of this, the next couple of days," Dell said.

"I can't dump everything on them."

"It's easier for them. They don't have a hundred lonely widows nipping at their heels."

Seeing the two men talking to each other, several women seemed to redouble their efforts. One reached out and grabbed Bud's sleeve. Another tapped Dell's shoulder. Dell abruptly stood up and pulled Bud up with him. There was no way to push forward, so they backed up, letting the surging wave of females back them toward the open doors to the foyer. There they turned and bolted for the kitchen door, shot through it, and closed it behind them.

Bud leaned against it, shaking his head. "They're crazy! Two more days of this?"

"We'll take breaks. And we won't sit down again. That was our mistake. Too easy to get surrounded. And Webb will be here this evening to help."

"Maybe I should just go play golf for the next couple of days," Bud said.

Dell laughed. "Like the guy in all those golf jokes. They'll gang-rape you if they get a chance. I'm no great stud but I feel bound by the ties of brother-in-law-hood to offer some help. Only with the dishy ones. Of which there weren't many."

"Well, I'm no great stud, either, Dell. And that many would probably make the old dick shrink up with fear," chuckled Bud. "It might disappear altogether. I think it would be a case of never have so many been so disappointed by so little." And the two men roared and slapped each other on the back.

"I guess we better go out there again for a while," said Dell.

"Okay. But no sitting. And first let's go upstairs and get me a dose of that calmer-downer. I just might not make it without some."

Six

"I don't know why I let you talk me into this," grumbled Fran, as she and Jessie walked down the darkened street between the silhouettes of parked cars.

"I told you, I want you to meet the Montkeiths. Anything they don't know about real estate hasn't happened yet. Lally gets the big listings. Everyone wants a chance to work with her office. They open doors. It's a prestigious thing to be with them. It sure can't hurt you to know them. It might lead to something. And besides, you might meet someone here. A guy."

"At one of these creepy singles affairs? Get real, Jessie. You know who goes to these things. Losers. That's who."

"But this is for the Opera Guild. It's a classier bunch of singles."

"Okay, so I'll meet some rich losers. I don't even like opera."

"So what? Neither do half the people who support it. They do it for social credentials."

"And I don't see why you can't stay, if I have to."

"I told you, I have another party after this. A *chaîne* dinner and I'm taking Emil. So I can get it through his thick, boozy brain, sometime during the evening, that we are kaput."

"Why didn't you ask me to go to the *chaîne* dinner instead?"

"One, because the Montkeiths won't be there, and two, because it's not a singles thing. I'm supposed to bring an escort. Besides, you don't even like rich food. You're just being difficult, Fran."

"I guess you're right. And I hate having to wear stockings and makeup and do my hair up like a Junior Leaguer."

"I'd take you to my dinner if you had a long, long limo and a driver in uniform, like Emil," giggled Jessie. "It's so much more fun to arrive at these things in a limo with a driver. The valets fall all over themselves helping you in and out. You feel so pampered. But from tonight on, no more Emil for me. So I might as well enjoy his car this one last time. Too bad I can't enjoy him, at the same time. He was really so much fun to talk to, before. But now! Gosh, he doesn't register a word you say, anymore."

"Where are you meeting him?"

"I told you. Here. His driver will pick me up and then we'll go back for Emil and then go to the dinner. I'll get my story, tell him again, and go. One, two, three. Wait, this is it. Turn in here."

A hand-lettered sign hung on the oversized, carved front doors of the antebellum style house. "Opera Guild. Come in." They stepped into a large dimly lit, high-ceilinged foyer with marble floors and a mirror-and-hammered-copper wall. A tall, willowy woman in a flowing Donna Karan creation, and pearls the size of chick-peas detached herself from a small cluster of women and flew over to give Jessie a hug.

"Jessie, dear, how are you? And this is your friend. The one who saves all the plants, and knows all about healthy food."

"Fran Dimitri," smiled Fran, offering her hand.

"Lally Montkeith," said the thin lady, squeezing Fran's hand. "Your fame precedeth you. I'm sorry my husband isn't here. Herbie abhors single women en masse. He says he feels like the fox at a hunt—and hopelessly outnumbered. You're all signed in already. Just go through there and out to the Florida room. Get something to drink and find someone to dance with."

They passed through the dining room and family room and out to the Florida room where a combo was playing "String of Pearls," and perhaps forty or fifty people were gathered in small clusters. Mostly women. No one was dancing.

"Well, that was a big contact," said Fran. "I'm sure she'll remember me forever. Probably in her prayers every night."

"Will you stop that?" Jessie scolded. "She has to stay there and play hostess a while longer. She'll be back. Don't be so impatient."

"And we're supposed to find someone to dance with? Who? The bartender? I don't dance with girls. It's hard to tell in this dim light, but I think I count approximately eight men in here."

"Better than none."

"They all look like the kind that cha-cha to everything. I refuse to do the cha-cha. All that damned counting and show-off stuff. Oops, I may have miscounted. There are two huskies in the shadow over there that could be men, too. Or the kind of woman who likes to lead. Hard to tell. Why do they keep the lights so low?"

"For wrinkles. Lally says that low light—candles or pink bulbs—hides about one wrinkle in two, and everyone is more attractive in soft light. She says she wishes you could buy ten- and twenty-watt bulbs to fit her lamps, so she wouldn't have to fool with candles all the time."

"First sensible thing I've heard all night. You trip a lot, but you look a lot better in case a man should come to pick you up. Let's get a Coke or something. It shouldn't be a total loss."

"You go ahead. I've got to take a few notes and names. Soon as you get your drink, tag around after me. I'll introduce you to anyone I know."

Jessie moved off to check names, asking everyone what they thought of this event as singles events went, taking notes. Of all the many kinds of social and community events she covered, singles affairs, she had found, were the hardest to write about. There was a sameness about them, and a sense of unease and desperation. But she had learned from experience that when she couldn't think of any way to inject a little fun into her report, she could always pack her copy with quotes. If she collected enough of them, a few were bound to be provocative.

When Fran reappeared, Coke in hand, she told her, "I'm going to check out the men. But first, wander around the room slowly — make a circle and end up back here."

"Yeah? And then what? You want me to stand on my head? Or recite 'Trees' in pig Latin? Or why don't I do a somersault? That'll get their attention."

"Fran, if a man wanted to ask you to dance he might be intimidated if you're with another person or a group. But if you're just strolling alone — he might not be so intimidated."

"Listen, dear, if he hasn't got the balls to come after me, tough. I've been married five times. I've had my share of guys. I'm getting serviced regularly. I don't need 'em. If they show up here, they're probably losers, anyway. It's a seller's market out there for guys. Besides, with all these things you go to, if there was someone out there worth finding, you'd have found him already."

"Except that Lally specially invited a couple of real men to this last time. Guys that never come to singles things. They don't even belong to that fancy singles group, Who's Who."

"Well, maybe she does get some real men. I'll say one thing for your friends, no junk on the bar. And those hors d'oeuvres are the good stuff. Poached salmon. Smoked fish. Minicroissants."

Just then Lally descended on them. "Are you having a good time, girls?" she asked.

"Oh, marvelous!" said Fran. Jessie poked her.

"Did Laurie say you're in real estate, dear?"

"Up to my ears. In Ella Pinon's office."

"Excuse me, I'm going to check if Emil's car is outside yet," said Jessie. "I'll be right back."

"You do things over west?" Lally asked Fran.

"Mainly."

"Well, do give me your card, dear. This is the funniest coincidence. This friend of ours, Weston Webber—we call him Webb—has done all kinds of things in real estate. He has an office in Chicago doing clubs, restaurants, and hotels. And he does commercial stuff all over Texas and so on. But not houses or apartments. He has a friend from Chicago who just settled down here and now wants to unload his new house and get an apartment. The house is over here on the water. We can handle that, although whoever gets it will probably want to completely redecorate it. It's just been done but it's—a bit busy, shall we say.

"But he wants his apartment out west. He's open to any condo. Just wants it big. Maybe a double. Webb mentioned a couple of places that are west. The Hammock, Green Arbor, Royal Oaks. Do you know of them?"

"All of them," nodded Fran. "Two of them have a couple of outsized apartments. I know of several tenants who have joined two apartments in those buildings and others. It's like living in a house. All the room without the headaches."

"Exactly," said Lally. "Well, if you could look into what's available. It must be large. Good security."

"Does he have a big family?"

"No, he's alone. Except for the housekeeper. He just lost his wife. That's why the house is for sale. Too bad. They only had it about six months. Webb would probably like to talk to you sometime in the next couple of days. He's coming back tomorrow I believe, from Chicago. So is his friend, tomorrow or the next day or two."

"I'd be delighted to help. I'm quite familiar with the buildings. Let me give you my card, Mrs. Montkeith." She pulled one from her bag.

"Just call me Lally, dear. Everyone does. And I'll give you one of mine, and Webb's number. We could do this through our office, but we don't really know that territory. So we're better off with someone who does. Someone who'll know if there's something special that hasn't been listed yet, perhaps."

Jessie returned. "The car's here. Gotta go," she said.

"Jessie, something interesting has come up here—" said Fran.

But Jessie shook her head. "I have to hurry.

We're a little late now." She hugged Lally. "See you tonight, Fran. Tell me then." And she was gone.

Fran turned back to Lally and grinned. "She never walks, trots or canters. Her only gait is a gallop. I'll get it all together for Mr. Webber. I can think of one in our building that was beautifully decorated and I think it has vacancies on either side. Or maybe one of them is on the floor below. It hasn't been formally listed, but it's available. It's expensive, though."

"He can afford whatever he likes, Webb assured me. About Webb — he's the salt of the earth. We've known him forever. He can be gruff. He's tough in business, but he's one hundred percent honorable."

"And the other man, the one who wants the apartment?"

"We've met him. They moved down from Chicago six or seven months ago. His wife got involved with the symphony immediately. Donated to the scholarship fund before she even moved down here. And the Community Foundation and Miami City Ballet. No meetings. She was too busy doing their new house. But she underwrote a lovely new grand piano for us right off the bat. And lovely refreshments at the membership tea just six weeks ago. He owns some company. Something scientific. And holds a lot of patents, I understand. The name is Wellman. Her name was Bitsy."

"Bitsy?" Fran repeated in a tight voice.

"Yes, that's it. Somehow they put her down as Bedelia Wellman in the directory. I think that's her legal name. How could one person have two such impossible names? She was very upset about it. Said she was never called anything but Bitsy. Bitsy Wellman."

Seven

Bud's jaws ached from the forced smiling. Didn't these people ever go home? Didn't they ever stop eating? Or drinking? Of course, so many of them had sent food platters, and food baskets, and wine and even liquor, that yesterday afternoon Esme had called the caterers and asked them to cancel whatever food they could, and just send the help and any additional workers they could spare. But still, there was more food around than anyone knew what to do with, despite the fact that a couple dozen of their larger female guests were making a valiant effort to see that none of it went to waste. And more platters and baskets were arriving all the time.

It was better now that they were doing shifts. Only one or two of them downstairs at a time. Esme and Needle took turns. And Dell and Sess. Bud and Miss Mary. And Webb helped everyone.

The way to survive it, Webb advised, was to tune out. "You turn on your tape of social drivel and fly on automatic pilot," he said. But no matter how he numbed out, Bud found, he couldn't get away from the fear grinding away at his insides.

Benjie. Why hadn't they heard? Just that there had been mudslides. Was he buried in one? Had they found him at all? Had he been hurt? Or had he—? No. Don't think of that.

It was all the secrecy that mucked it up. He had long suspected Benjie was doing some other work for the government, too. CIA or defense or something. The way he would never talk much about the specifics. Bud knew how that was. He had developed several defense products and procedures on government contracts. Everything was secret. Everyone had to be cleared. You didn't chat about it to your friends. You pushed it into a corner of your mind marked No Trespassing.

He was upstairs when the call came, just after breakfast, the third day. He heard Esme's piercing scream. Seconds later, his door flew open and she dashed in, shrieking, "It's Benjie! It's Benjie! He's safe, Daddy! Pick up your phone and don't talk until I get back on." She dashed out again back to her own phone. Bud grabbed the receiver. "Benjie?"

"Hi, Dad. Gee, I'm sorry if this caused you guys any worry." A heavy gasp and then Esme's voice, breathy. "I'm back on. You can talk, Benjie. What happened to you?"

"Just a little slide. But all the lines went and the weather was so bad and we just had to wait it out. If I never see another can of condensed milk, I'll cheer. That was pretty much what we ate for the three days. That's all we had in the office where we were caught."

"You weren't hurt?" asked Esme.

"Nah. A few bruises. Stiff neck from the way I was positioned, and my legs still ache a little from being pinned. But nothing much else. I really don't know why they let you know. I mean, slides are one of the things we're here to study. So, of course, we hit one now and then. But we're ready for them. We know what to do."

"Where are you now, Benjie," Bud asked.

"Well, actually, the hospital in Anchorage, but that doesn't mean anything. They always take you in and check you out. They learn a little more each time something like this happens. I'll be out in a day or so. Just doing a lot of tests. They shouldn't have called you."

"Oh, Benjie," Esme wailed. "They didn't call us. We called you. We tried everything to get to you in time."

"In time for what, Esme?" Benjie's voice

tightened almost imperceptibly. "Why did you call me? What's happened?"

"Oh, Benjie. It's — Mother," she gasped.

"Your mother was — she was killed in a car wreck near Fresno on Thursday, Son," Bud blurted. "The funeral was two days ago, here in Chicago."

Silence. And then the sounds of stifled weeping. Benjie had adored his mother. "She — she didn't suffer?"

"No. It was instantaneous."

"Was anyone else hurt?"

"No. She was alone."

"Then she was driving. Jeez, I always tell her not to drive." True. Benjie always told his mother she was a terrible driver. Too distractable. He tried to get her to quit. To use a driver. He would often tease her when she would run a stop sign or grind her gears excruciatingly, "Get a bicycle, Mom."

"But she loved her cars," said Esme. "Remember the little T-bird? And the Mustang? And the red Porsche? Oh, Benjie, hurry down. Please."

"I'll catch the next plane," he said.

"No. You won't, son," ordered Bud. "We've just had one tragedy and we've been out of our minds with fear that something had happened to you, too. We're not looking for more trouble. You're going to stay in that hospital until you are released by their judgment, not yours. We can talk on the phone until then. And you are not coming down until your doctors think it's all right. I mean that, Benjie."

Esme sniffed. "Dad's right, Benjie. Be sure you're all right, first. What are all these bruises?"

"They're checking them out. Nothing. My one foot went asleep where it was caught. I'll tell you when I see you. You all okay?"

"Needle and I are right in the middle of our new business. We'll tell you all about it when you get here. But Aunt Sess was wonderful. She put the shiva and the funeral and the wakes together."

"Listen Es. I have to hang up now. They don't want me to talk too long yet. I'll call as soon as I can. But I'm—I'm—I wish I could have been there with you."

"Son?" Bud said. "You're sure you're okay?"

"A-okay, Dad." His voice broke again. "I—I love you both."

"We—we love you too, son," said Bud, hanging on to the receiver until he heard the click on the other end.

Benjie was alive! He could have six broken bones for all they knew. He wouldn't tell them on the phone. But he was alive. And he sounded good. Tired, but okay.

Maybe it was just as well he had missed the

last couple of days. They would have torn him apart. And when Benjie got down, they would find out what had happened to him in that mudslide. Soon enough.

Eight

Emil signaled the waiter for another refill of the Bordeaux. His eyes were half-closed. Bits of stuffed potato daubed his chin amid a glaze of saliva. Lally had sure been right about Emil.

Jessie had met Emil at several events she had covered in Miami. Metrozoo fundraisers. Benefits for AIDS or for Miami City Ballet. But she hadn't really talked to him until a few months ago, when he had apparently begun another of his drying-out spells. And so when he invited her to dinner after one event, she accepted. She found him to be delightful company — witty, urbane, literate, well-dressed. He had a dry sense of humor, and he not only spoke several languages fluently, he could make himself understood in others. Jessie was impressed.

But then he started drinking again, a pattern he had apparently repeated over and over again in the past, and he became, overnight, this

93

foul-mouthed, fumbling, vulgar wretch sitting next to her.

Lally had warned her. "He's done this over and over, dear. Dries out. Becomes charming, witty, delightful. Then goes off and becomes Mr. Slob again. I don't know how he maintains that empire of his in that condition except that he hires the best people. Once at a New World Symphony ball he became so drunk he asked little Hazel Warner—she was sitting next to him—if she wouldn't like to sneak out to the parking lot and f-u-c-k a little. Have you met Hazel? Young and sweet. Her husband owns several hotels, on the South Beach and elsewhere. Anyway, Emil started telling her in lurid detail what he planned to do to her, and halfway through, he suddenly pitched forward and passed out with his face in his plate.

"Hazel had only been married about three months. She wisely didn't tell Carl until much later. He'd have killed Emil."

"But he's not that way at all, now," Jessie had said. "He's a nice date. A little self-centered, but beautiful manners and he's certainly bright enough. I really like him, Lally. He's so nice to me. Always sending his limo for me."

"Well, dear, let's hope that this time it takes. But I just felt I should warn you. Don't count on it."

Lally had been right on the mark. But Jessie was the incurable optimist. She had finally succumbed to Emil's urging, and stayed overnight with him. And then again. Emil was an enthusiastic lover. But after the fourth time, he began drinking again.

Exit gentleman.

Enter slob.

Exit relationship.

Only Emil couldn't read the exit signs. In the car on the way to Le Dome, she had started to tell him once more but he had shushed her because he was watching the news on TV. He was nursing a tumbler full of Absolut and who knew how much he had already put away. He had tried to paw her breast during the commercial and when she slapped his hand, he simply looked at her blankly, shrugged and asked how her week had been.

And now, here he was making a perfect pig of himself at this Chaîne des Rotisseurs dinner, quickly dismantling each beautifully presented plate—poking and stabbing it into a disgusting batch of litter because he could hardly handle his knife and fork. "I'm going to fuck you to pieces tonight," he was mumbling into his venison. "Til you beg me t' stop. Fuck you and eat you and fuck you s'more."

Obviously, it wouldn't do much good to tell

him anything just now. She hoped no one else could understand his fuddled words.

"Good stuff," he mumbled, slurping the wine loudly and letting a trickle run down his chin to stain the potato dabs and then his dress shirt. He didn't notice.

Mattie Zerlopps smiled sympathetically at Jessie. She and Dan had been friends of Emil's family for thirty years. Dan's law firm did work for him. They were especially close to Emil's three dignified sisters and had seen Emil in all stages of drunkenness and sobriety.

Jessie leaned over and whispered, "Can you watch him for a minute? I'll go out and get his driver. I think we'd better leave." Mattie nodded and Jessie went outside to find Yver, who would be waiting at the entrance by then.

When she and Yver got back to the table, Bavarian crèmes had replaced the cheese and fruit, and the waiters were pouring a sauterne. "Let's go," Jessie said. Emil nodded and tried to struggle to his feet. Yver put a practiced hand under his arm and hoisted, then held him firmly, steering his stumbling path to the door. Jessie said hasty apologetic good-byes and followed them out.

Emil was snoring before they pulled out of the hotel drive. He snored all the way to Miami Beach and his bayfront home.

At his house she helped Yver bring him inside, drag him to his room, dump him on his bed and pull up the blankets. None of the live-in help so much as came to see what was going on. They were quite accustomed to Yver's delivering Emil unconscious. She and Yver slipped out. He locked the front door and set the alarm. And then she climbed back into the limo for the long drive home.

Fran was still awake, sitting on the couch, pouring over a stack of papers. Other piles of papers and envelopes littered the coffee table, her end of the couch and the floor.

Jessie pushed a pile of her own printouts off the other end of the couch and flopped. "What are you doing up?" she asked. "Nothing's wrong, is it? Kerry okay?"

"She called. She's not pregnant. Her period started and she wanted to let you know right away."

"Well, that's a relief."

"She said she and Doug got a little weepy over it. So he went right out and bought her a little guinea pig and a little cage and she's keeping it in her room even though that's strictly against the rules. They'll feed it salad and leftovers they'll sneak out of the dining hall. And don't worry, no one will tattle, because everyone thinks it's so darling. Are you sure this kid has all her marbles?"

"No. Sometimes I'm quite sure she doesn't. I'll call her now."

"No, wait. No emergency, and I have more to tell you. Big news."

"Oh?"

"Nothing wrong. Just good stuff, I think. First, you were right. Lally is okay and I'm going to help a friend of a friend of hers find just the right apartment—a big expensive one—big commission—and it could lead to something more. I'm not sure what. But any connection there can't be bad."

"I won't say I told you so."

"You just did. But that's the least of it. Wait till you hear."

"Hear what? Tell me."

"Guess who has a house to sell and who it is who wants to buy a big apartment. Just guess."

"Robert Redford."

"Close. Try again."

"Douglas Fairbanks, Jr.? I'm tired, Fran. Couldn't you give me some choices?"

"No, but you're getting warmer. Here's a clue. It's someone you've known for over thirty-five years?"

"Oh, really? Sister Marie-Claire left the convent? She ran away with Father Paulson? I always thought they had something going."

"Cold. It's someone you were mad for once. And never got over."

Jessie slid off the sofa and onto the floor and buried her face in her hands. "Don't do this to me. Fran. I can't breathe. Who? Just tell me who."

"Well, a man named Webb is the one who called Lally for help finding an apartment in the west. And he has this waterfront house to sell, too. But the friend he's scouting for, who just moved here six months ago from Chicago and who is in Chicago now for a funeral but who will be back down here in two days, and whose wife was just killed in a car accident in California, is one Bud Wellman. She couldn't remember his first name so we looked it up in the Symphony Society directory which his wife joined last year before they moved down."

"And her name. What was her name?"

"In the directory, it was Bedelia Wellman."

"See? Bedelia."

"But Lally said her name is really Bitsy and she was very upset that they used Bedelia in the directory."

"Oh, my God! Then it *was* him?" Jessie grabbed her head in her hands and pressed. "And her. Oh, and I didn't have sense enough to check it out at the funeral parlor last night!"

"Easy. When you hyperventilate like that you blow my papers all over. And I haven't even told you everything yet."

"Don't tell me any more. My head is pounding. No. Tell me, but fast. What more could there be? We won the lottery?"

"One of the buildings where this Webb person wants me to show him units is right here — the Hammock — 'cause he wants a huge apartment, probably a couple hooked together. And he heard about the Montmorency here. So I think the thing to do is to arrange for you to meet him, just casually bump into him or something, here. Provided this Webb likes the place."

"What wouldn't he like? Who's this Webb again?"

"Bud Wellman's close friend. And if Bud Wellman comes to look here, if Webb recommends it, I'm sure that one way or another, we can figure out some way for you to bump into each other." Jessie groaned and buried her head in a couch pillow. "Oh now, don't do that, Jessie. This is great news. You did me a favor, even if you had to practically drag me there kicking and screaming, and it turned out to be bread cast on the waters. You may end up hooking the very fish you've been dreaming of all these years."

Jessie groaned again and poked her head out from under the pillow. "A fish? You call Bud a fish? Hooking? Boy, you really have a way with words, Fran."

"You know what I mean. You're heading towards a happy ending. And who gets happy endings today? That's an endangered species."

"Wait a minute. Not so fast. That was all a long time ago. Look what I look like, now. If he remembers me at all, he'll have to be disappointed. And what if he's forgotten me altogether? He probably has."

"After that reunion at your school?"

"Almost twenty years ago."

"And that time you ran into him in that department store?"

"Marshall Field's — fifteen years ago. It's all just a crazy dream in my head, Fran. My little fantasy. Even if it's him, he could be short and fat by now."

"Fat, maybe. Not short. You said he was tall."

"He could be a terrible bore. Or a lush like Emil."

"No one could be a lush like Emil. He's in his own class. Did you tell him?"

"I tried again. But he was drunk. I'm going to hire one of those airplanes with a banner. Or how much does it cost to have a message flashed on the Goodyear blimp?"

"Well, anyway, make up your mind. I'm getting all the poop together. Wanna come with me when I go to take a look at their house, or not? Lally said I should go, just in case we get anyone in our office who might be interested.

We won't. But I couldn't turn down a chance to see it. Wanna come?"

"Yes. No. Oh, dear. It would be like peeking into their diary. I have to think about it. Let me call Kerry, and then I'll decide."

Her daughter answered on the first ring. "Did Fran tell you everything, Mom? Aren't you glad?"

"Yes. Well, relieved, anyway," Jessie said. "What is all this about a guinea pig?"

"We're calling him Pooper, 'cause all he does is poop. He's such a little cutie."

"How can anything that does nothing but poop be cute? And someone might report you, Kerry."

"No, everybody loves him. They're going to bring me lettuce for him."

"I'm sure he's darling. But you can't bring him home. We're not going to get thrown out of this building over a guinea pig. And they could do that. You better find a place for him before you come home for the summer."

There was a long pause on the other end of the line. Then a heavy sigh. "Mom, do you mean that?"

"I'm sorry, honey. But that's the rule here and they're very strict."

"Sometimes, it's a cruel world, isn't it, Mom?"

"Yes, darling. And sometimes it's kind of wonderful." After she hung up, Jessie went to her bathroom for some aspirin. Her head was throbbing.

Bud Wellman. It was him. After all these years.

1972

That was the year Jessie next saw him, at a Holy Savior High School general reunion, of all places. She had decided to attend it while she was visiting Chicago to see her ailing grandparents, Nana and Poppy Eldridge. Who knew when she would get another chance to go to one? Harry hadn't come with her. He wasn't into reunions—certainly not hers—and he was tied up at work. Waste processing and disposal had become a sophisticated business. Management was constantly changing the way things were done. Harry had been shifted to different positions twice in the last three years. He was uneasy about being away just now. So she came alone. And when she walked into the auditorium of the new school, there he was, big as life, standing in front of the models of the convent's soon-to-be-built retirement homes.

"You!" she cried as he hurried over to her. "What are you doing here?" She laughed in spite of her shock at seeing him. "This is an all-girls school."

"Not after next year," he said. "It's going coed. Don't you read your alumnae news? I wondered how many more of these things I was going to have to come to before I bumped into you," he said. "You don't usually show up."

"You've been here before? You're kidding. This is my first."

"It's my fourth. It dawned on me one day that this was one place where I might run into you. I gave them some money, for a grotto or a stained-glass window or something. And I think I underwrite the refreshments. So I'm always invited, even though I'm male, Jewish and not an alumnus."

"You must really have wanted to see me," giggled Jessie.

"Yeah, I did."

"But you know that I—that we—"

"I'm not up to anything. Except I'd like to talk to you. Know how things are going with you. If you need anything—"

"You make it harder, Bud."

"Can we go somewhere and just talk?"

"The cafeteria? They're serving a buffet. I can't go anywhere else with you. I just can't. We might lose our heads."

"Okay. The cafeteria."

* * *

They passed through the line, taking only coffee. He carried the tray to a table. "You actually came to three of these?" she asked as they sat down.

"I came in the middle, so that if you were late or left early I wouldn't be likely to miss you. And I didn't stay long."

"But what a crazy, beautiful thing to do."

"Yeah. Crazy, anyway. But I think about you. A lot. And I wonder. I thought that this way, if you never came—no harm done. If you did—I'd get to talk to you. Tell me about your life now. In Florida, right?"

So she told him—about walking on the beach, hunting shells, and eating her first mango and loving it, and the hurricane's near miss soon after they moved down. He told her about Esme and Benjie. She told him how much she wanted a child. How she was still hoping. He told her about his hillside home outside of San Francisco, with its sweeping view. They didn't mention Bitsy or Harry. Then he said, "I've pretty well resigned myself to the fact that this is it. I'm stuck. And I've messed up both of our lives. We would have had one heckuva good time together, I think."

She nodded. "The saddest words are: might have been. Who said that? Charles Lamb?"

"Shakespeare's always a good guess. He said

most of the things people quote. It's like osmosis. I had a biology professor once who said whenever you don't know the answer on a biology exam, put down osmosis. So many processes depend on it that you'll have about an eighty percent chance of being right."

Back in the auditorium he followed her around as she looked for her classmates and he stood nearby as she talked briefly to the five or six she found. And the several nuns. And then he walked her to her car. There in the dark, he kissed her — one gentle, bittersweet, heartsick kiss.

When she began to cry, he held her tightly, patting her back like one might a baby. He took her key and opened her car and helped her inside. And before he closed it, he bent and kissed her ever so tenderly once more. "Oh, Jessie," his voice broke. "I'm so sorry."

And then in December, in 1975.

That was the last time. She was standing at the tie counter in the Marshall Field's in downtown Chicago, stomping her feet every few seconds because they were so cold. And wet. Her Florida pumps weren't much help in the snow that was blanketing the streets outside. Harry had to come up for a convention and the company had chartered planes and brought the wives along, too. She had ducked out on the wives' activities, which never interested her that much, to take advantage of the opportunity to do a little Christmas shopping.

She was comparing two ties when she suddenly felt that prickly awareness that meant someone was standing next to her. And staring at her. She turned to look.

It was him.

"Oh, hello," she said.

"Hello," he said. "Remember me?"

"Not likely to forget," she said, breathlessly. "I'm in shock."

"You're always in shock when we meet."

"Because you turn up at such unlikely places. Uh—well, make yourself useful. What do you think of this stripe," she held up a tie. "As opposed to this print?"

"Yes," he said, studying the two carefully. "I'd say it's pretty well opposed to that print."

She laughed. "But do you like it?"

"Depends if you're getting it for an enemy or a friend," he said. "You came up from Florida, and there isn't even a reunion."

"I'm allowed. Who told you there's no reunion?"

"I get the alumnae/alumni news, remember?

And I know some of the same people your husband knows."

"Oh, yes. Then do you know I have a child? Finally. A little girl. Born about a year after that reunion, when I saw you last. Kerry."

"That's wonderful. Just one?"

"Yes. And you?"

"The same two. I think that'll be it. Are you up for Christmas shopping?"

She nodded. "And Harry has a convention. You too? I heard you live in Texas."

"Well, we kind of split our time between Texas and California and here. New York, sometimes. It's so good to see you. Could we go get coffee somewhere?" He looked down at his watch. "Or lunch?"

She looked at her watch, too. "I have an hour. I'm meeting Harry and Kerry back at his mother's." She put the ties back on the counter and tucked her arm in Bud's. "I know we shouldn't do this. But dammit, we've been so good all these years. I don't guess God will send us to hell if we go to lunch."

"Where?" he asked. "Your choice."

"How about the Stop and Shop, upstairs. Are they still open? I remember having egg-salad sandwiches there. The best. And we're not likely to run into anyone."

He took her arm and led her out of the store.

They kissed in the elevator, on the way upstairs. They held hands. And over egg-salad sandwiches hardly touched, eyes locked on each other, they talked.

"Would it be so wrong to see each other once in a while?" he asked. "Bitsy and I live in the same house sometimes. We go to a few parties together. But we lead two different lives. I've wondered a dozen times why we're still together. Except I know. She falls apart at the least hint of our splitting. And there's the kids. Esme is very independent. She doesn't seem to need either one of us very much. But Benjie's different."

"I've had thoughts like that, too, Bud. I think of that science contest. The reunions. It's like they were yesterday. A couple of times I've thought of getting in touch with you. But Kerry loves her Daddy. He adores her. And he needs me. I actually separated from him a year ago. He's always so down and grumpy. But he was devastated. He wept. He begged me to come back. And Kerry was lost. I just couldn't do it."

"I understand."

"Funny how this has lasted, isn't it? Maybe if we actually lived together for two weeks it would all be over." She laughed ruefully.

He didn't laugh. "I don't think so, Jessie. Maybe someday—when our kids are grown—

anyway, I—I want to send you something. A ring, a bracelet, anything you'd like."

"You can't, Bud. I'd love to have something from you but Harry would wonder where it came from. He never buys me things like that. And he knows I wouldn't buy them for myself."

"I need you to have something from me that is with you all the time. Don't wear it then. Keep it close to you. Your daughter. Let me get her something. A little ring. She might have been our kid, Jessie. Please."

Jessie sighed. "All right. Sapphire is her birthstone. I'll give it to her for her next birthday and pretend it's from me. She doesn't have a birthstone ring. But it has to be small. Otherwise he'll know I didn't buy it. We can't afford fancy jewelry."

"It will come in a package from Medi-Quip. Addressed to you."

"You know, Bud, it's not like we never had anything together. There's something so wonderful about knowing that someone cares. And that the feeling lasts. I'm glad we did this today, no matter how it hurts. But before it's over I want to tell you how much I love you. I do. We'll probably never see each other again. This was a fluke. But I want you to know—I can't run off with you. I'll never know what it would be like to make love to you, and sleep close to

110

you every night. But I would give anything to. I love you, so much."

"God, but you are the dearest person that ever lived, Jessie. I love you, too. I only wish I could show you one day how very, very, much."

Nine

The dining room faced the club's croquet lawn, which appeared unusually bleak and bare, for late in spring. Freezes had put the greening back over a month.

"You sit there, Daddy," ordered Esme. "I thought this table was better than a booth. So we can talk. I mean, there are things we should discuss. That's why we wanted you to come up."

"I don't know why Sess and Dell couldn't have joined us though," Bud shrugged as they took their chairs. "We have no secrets from them."

"On the other hand, Daddy, there's no need for everyone to know our business."

Bud sighed. It was their club. Their party. He couldn't tell them what to do. A waiter appeared with trays of drinks. His Perrier. Their martinis with the double olives. Esme must have called ahead. "Did you order dinner, too?" he asked. It irritated him when she did that.

"I thought that would expedite things and give us more time to talk," she said.

"About what, Esme?"

"Well, Dad, it's just that you're sometimes so naïve and trusting. And I am not."

"True, my darling daughter. No one would accuse you of being naïve and trusting. I don't know that I am, but we'll let that pass for now."

"Shrewd, fair, but not naïve," interjected Needle. "Esme is a good businesswoman."

"No question," Bud nodded. "I am astounded at the success you two have had. It's reassuring to think that if I lose everything, I can still count on you to look after me in my old age."

Esme sat up at that. "Why, uh, of course — you know, Dad, we — "

"Esme was thinking more about right now, sir," interjected Needle hastily.

"We're wondering about the wisdom of your staying down there in Florida," began Esme. "You could get a little place up here close to us — " He noticed she said nothing about giving his house back, or about his moving in with them, which he would never do anyway. What she said was, "We're all you have left."

"Except for a son, several cousins, my sister and her husband, a couple of aunts and assorted friends," said Bud.

"Needle and I expect to have or adopt a couple of children, probably in about three years."

"This is the first I've heard of it. Congratulations. Three years?"

"Schedulewise that seems to work out best, sir," said Needle.

"And how will you find time to raise children when you are so involved with your business? Kids take time," Bud said.

"You did it without spending much time with us," said Esme coolly.

"I was busy getting us set up financially," he retorted. "I just couldn't be everywhere at once. But your mother was always there."

"When she wasn't at one of her luncheons or meetings. But certainly she was there more than you. Yes, you took us with you on trips sometimes, but you really weren't around much, Dad. And Benjie and I survived."

"We plan to hire the best help. Really nurturing people," said Needle over a mouthful of bread. "And we may not be able to give them large quantities of time. But we'll give them quality time. We'll do much of our work at home, via computers. We will not be absentee parents," he added. "We've examined all these issues carefully."

"Dad, we thought perhaps we should talk a little about inheritances and taxes and things.

Our man says that sometimes it's best to dispose of things early, living trusts and other devices, to avoid heavy taxation."

"Are you suggesting I hand everything over to you now, Esme, and check into a home?"

Esme and Needle broke into peals of laughter. "Oh, of course not, Dad. We know you have to keep busy. But we just want you to know that we'd be ready to and happy to take over anything you want us to. And we're saying that we should all three put our heads together and formulate a plan. So we don't find ourselves wishing later that we had taken different courses than we did."

"And we think we should all stay close," said Needle. "And it would be better if we know what's going on with you and your business. So if ever we're needed, we can step right in."

"Don't you think I should learn all about your ventures too? For some time I've had a few good suggestions to make on your tape and cassette service, that I think would open up a wider customer base. And your helicopter bank service—I don't know why it couldn't be franchised. But I have tactfully refrained from offering suggestions until I was asked. Because these are your businesses. Not mine."

But Esme looked right past the dig. "Oh, Daddy, we're not the ones who need someone in the wings. We're young. We've got a lot of time to work everything out. And there are two of us."

The waiter brought lump crabmeat cocktails with the extra horseradish Bud preferred. Esme was thorough, no question. Bud dug into his food with gusto, suddenly feeling almost relieved. If this little meeting had revealed a heartbroken Esme, he would have shared her pain. He would have felt compelled to spend time up here, help her whatever way he could to get through her loss.

But no. Her mother's death seemed little more to her than a bookkeeping entry. From the living column to the dead. Bitsy had been spoiled, and a little self-indulgent, and not very quick, but she had a big heart for her children and her causes. She had adored Esme and been so proud of her. And Benjie. How could Esme be worrying about dollars and cents now when they still didn't really know how badly Benjie had been hurt? When although his son made light of his injuries, they wouldn't really know until they saw him?

He flagged the waiter. "I'll have a Scotch and water," he said. "Dewars." Dewars was what Dell drank. It must be okay.

"Daddy! You don't drink. And I heard you got smashed at the Florida wake, too. What are you starting here?"

"Just felt like one, honey," Bud nodded.

Esme gave Needle a meaningful glance. "Well, Daddy, now about Florida. I can come down and go through the house next week. As soon as we get the contracts signed here on our Bitty-Pax line of cosmetics. I'll arrange to ship up whatever—"

"No need, Es," he said firmly. The waiter brought his drink and he took a long swig. "I'm staying in Florida. And I'm taking a lot of things from the house into the apartment I'm renting."

"How much can you fit in a little apartment?"

"Oh, well, I'm not getting a little one. I'm getting a big one. A double or triple. And you don't have room for much of anything anyway."

"But Dad, they were my mother's things."

"And they were my wife's and I'm not dead yet, Es. I'll bring you all the jewelry when I come back. I know that's what's important to you."

"Well, of course it is, Dad." The waiter placed Caesar salads in front of them. Needle and Bud dug in but Esme just stared at hers with her hands in her lap. "Do you mean," her voice went suddenly small and hesitant, "that I can't have the little armoire from the hall? The one that used to be in Mommy's dressing room? I remember that from as long as I can remember anything. Mommy pulling lollipops out of it when I was really little. And my first white gloves when I was about four. And all the charms you got for my bracelet. She always put the fun little presents in there. I used to think it must be full of such good things.

"But once I snuck in there when she was at a meeting and looked and there were just a few boxes of her chocolates. And her gloves and hankies and things like that. I guess she put things in there just before she gave them to me, to make it more fun — like she was finding things in the shelves. Can't I even have that, Dad?"

Was that a small tear in the corner of his daughter's eye? Bud relented. He had not seen Esme shed a tear in twenty years. Even at the funeral itself. Worry over Benjie seemed the only thing that could force normal sympathy or compassion from that calculating mind. But there was the tear. What kind of schmuck was he that he could only see her hard side, when this soft side was there, too?

He coughed and cleared his throat. "Well, sure you can, honey. And the rest of the stuff — come down like you planned. Take anything you want. I don't really need any of it. I can always call a decorator. I might even find something furnished. You're right. She was your mother. Just see that Benjie — that Benjie gets whatever he wants, too."

* * *

Just then, Bud felt a hand on his back, and several people crowded around them. Old friends, the Schwartzes and the Berkens. Ed and Debbie, Art and Carol. They had been at the funeral. And at the house, after. They were with another woman. Bud and Needle stood. "Oh, no, sit," said Art. "Awful sorry about your loss, Bud, Esme, Needle. How you doing? Getting through it all okay?"

"Oh, I guess you don't know my sister-in-law," said Carol. "Janie Novack. Bud Wellman. Esme and Needle Pearlman."

"I'm glad to meet you all," said Janie Novack, smiling broadly at Bud. She was attractive, fiftyish, with the tanned, somewhat leathery skin of one who spent the winters in sunny climes, and the wiry build of a tennis player.

"You staying up long, Bud?" asked Art.

"No. Heading back tomorrow night." Carol Novack's broad smile collapsed.

"Janie will be down in Boca Raton in November," said Carol, hopefully.

Bud didn't pick it up. "That's a nice area," he said. "Nice of you to stop by."

"Well, enjoy your dinner," said Art, patting Bud on the shoulder. And the five of them moved off toward their own table.

Six times more during dinner, friends stopped by to say hello. Most of them seemed to have an extra lady in tow. A guy who was into that kind of thing could make out like a bandit, Bud reflected as they sipped coffee afterward, while Needle attacked the desserts.

A single guy.

Hey, wait a minute. *He* was a single guy now.

Ten

Fran banged on her door. "Get up. You're coming with me."

"What time is it," mumbled Jessie. "Good grief, it's only seven. Isn't this Tuesday? I don't have to get to the office until ten. I want to sleep."

"No. You've got to come with me. I'm meeting the Webb person for coffee at Pomperdale's at nine for a rundown on what Wellman's looking for. You could take a look and see if you know him."

"I can't do that, Fran. I already told you I don't know the name. There's got to be a better way. You do it. Please. Find out all you can about this Wellman and call me as soon as you leave."

"You know it's him. How could there be two Bitsy Wellmans? It's remarkable that there's even one. I just have this feeling that this

121

Webb person should see you. You know how psychic I am. What about if you come in like by accident, to buy some bagels around nine-thirty or ten like you had no idea I would be there. I'll say, 'What do you know. There's my roommate!' Let me notice you instead of you noticing us. So it won't look set-up. I'll introduce you and mention Wellman's name and you can say, 'Isn't it a small world. I used to go to school with someone named Wellman, blah, blah, blah.' "

"It's probably not him."

"It is! I'm positive. Anyway, he won't be there. But if this Webb goes and tells this Wellman he saw you, and mentions your name, twenty to one he arranges to see you."

"And what will he see? I don't look like the yearbook anymore, Fran. Look at these wrinkles."

"Don't worry about them. No one sees them. That's why God makes everyone's eyesight start to get lousy at forty. By fifty these guys can hardly make out which is your front and which is your back, so how can they see wrinkles? Besides, you look terrific. Plenty of forty-year-olds would love to look as good as you do. Put on that blue vest with the black pants. And your boots. Look a little sexy. See you at Pomperdale's at ten. No, make it nine-thirty. It might not take us long to talk. Make it nine-twenty."

He was waiting out front. "You're Fran Dimitri?" he asked, reaching to shake her hand. He was about five-eleven. Firm handshake. Compact build. Weathered skin. Strong jaw. Balding. She saw his eyes dart quickly over her and then peer intently into her own.

She nodded. "And you're Mr. Webber."

"Webb's good enough. Let's go in." He held the door. As usual, the tiny deli was crowded. There was one table free against the wall. He grabbed it. "Here. Sit. Whad'ya want? I'll get it while you hold the table."

"A salt bagel with tuna salad," she said. "And coffee. Straight."

"Gotcha." She watched while he ordered at the counter, then made his way down the narrow aisle to the coffee-makers in the back, poured two cups and brought them to their table. While he picked up their orders—bacon and eggs for him—she got her papers out.

He shook his head. "Eat first," he ordered.

She started to ask why, then thought better of it. She'd tell him that she didn't take orders, thank you, after she found the apartment and got the commission check. After Jessie met her Bud. Then, she'd really tell him.

"Lally tells me you know the west," he said, downing half an egg in one bite.

Fran nodded. "Pretty much. Tell me just what you're looking for."

"Lots of room. He doesn't need waterfront. Bud's not into boats; he gets seasick in the shower. He has a couple of labs and an office he just opened out west. One way out around Rock Creek. The other out there past State Road Seven, off Stirling, near Davie somewhere. About halfway to Tampa, it seems to me. He wants to be handy to his work. And he wants to escape that social circus in Fort Lauderdale. He's not much into that stuff. That's why he's selling the waterfront house. They'd only been in it a few months. His wife was just finishing decorating it when she was killed."

"I'm sorry," said Fran. "I don't know how much you know about the real estate market down here, Mr. Webber—"

"Just Webb. I do commercial stuff, not housing, which is why I asked Lally to get me someone when Bud asked me."

"Well, there are the horsey, ranchy places way west, the houses and apartments on the canals and the ocean, and a lot of condos, town houses, villas and houses in between."

"Condos. That's what he's looking for now. An apartment or town house maybe. With security. It's gotta have good security."

"What price range?"

"Like I told you, he's used to room. He needs an office, a bedroom, a small room for a lab. A guest room or two. A room for a live-in housekeeper. He'll pay what it's worth but he doesn't want to be taken."

"I wouldn't think of it," Fran couldn't resist murmuring. He looked up from running a chunk of bagel around his plate to sop up the last of his eggs. His eyes narrowed but then he shrugged.

"He can use about 3,500 feet. Up to maybe 4,500 I figure."

"Which means custom. Running a couple together. They don't have any apartments out west that big. But I know of a couple of doubles. There is one in my building, the Hammock, 2,600 feet, next to a smaller apartment on the north. They'll sell them together or separate. There's a vacant one on the south. And I think one below. The big one is all decorated and furnished. It's not listed yet. There are several other buildings that have a double already put together, that's for sale. But only one, Green Pond, has anything with terraces like those on the Hammock Montmorency — 800 feet. Not those narrow little porches, but big screened-in rooms. All tiled."

"Sounds good. Oh, yeah, he likes a place to jog, under security. And a gym on the premises, if possible. Let's go through what you have here. I can probably eliminate some without going to see them. I don't want to waste his time or mine either."

"Does he plan to live in it full time?"

"For now. Ultimately, who knows?"

"You said Mr. Wellman is from Chicago?" asked Fran.

"Yeah. And he had a home there until last year. When they moved here. But he also has places in Texas and New York. And California."

"What business is he in?"

"Labs, lab construction, disposable medical and health products, real estate — several things. Why do you ask?"

"Well, my roommate — we share an apartment at the Hammock — knows Lally. That's how Lally happened to ask me to help. And when Lally mentioned Mr. Wellman, Jessie said she used to know a boy with that name way back in high school. He went to Arlington Heights High School I think."

"Near Chicago? Could be. I'm not sure what his school was. But I think that might be it. I knew his father-in-law long before I knew Bud, and Ben Glick did live in Arlington Heights when I first knew him. Small world."

"Oh, and would you believe this — there's my roommate now. At the counter. Jessie," she called. "Over here."

Jessie turned, looked properly surprised, and

headed over. "Fran," she cried. "If I'd known you were coming up here, you could have picked up the bagels." Webb turned to see who Fran was talking to and he stood up so abruptly he knocked his cup over.

Jessie's eyes grew wide. "You," she said. "At the wake."

"Mr. — I mean Webb, this is —"

"I know," he interrupted. "Jessie Nella Moore. Née Pendleton. You came to the wake. And left right away."

Fran grabbed a bunch of napkins and mopped Webb's coffee while Jessie nodded and blushed. "I saw the obituary, but it was all inked up in my paper. And I was going to be in that area so I decided to stop in. Just an impulse. But the name Bedelia. I never heard of any Bedelia. So I didn't think it was the same Wellman."

Webb leaned back against the wall and cocked his head sideways, frankly staring at the lady standing before him. "Well, Jessie — it's all right if I call you Jessie? The papers and the funeral home used her legal name. But nobody ever called her anything but Bitsy." He grabbed an empty chair from the next table and slid it behind Jessie — just as her knees turned to jelly.

She was so flustered she could hardly talk. "You mean that was Bud's wife who died? And they — he's down here?"

"I'm picking him up at the airport tonight. He was in Chicago for the funeral and sitting shiva. Do you know what that means?"

Jessie nodded. "After a funeral, I think. Everyone comes to your house and—and—gives their sympathy."

Webb nodded. "Right. When I tell him about this, he'll be amazed. He'll want to see you, I'm sure."

"See me? Oh, maybe," said Jessie. "Or maybe not. I mean I'm not even a classmate, actually. And he was three years ahead of me. In a different school. I went to an all-girls school, Holy Savior. We lived in the same town," she finished lamely. "He might not even remember me."

"I have a feeling he will. Maybe we'll all arrange to meet here tomorrow and then I can lead Fran off—"

"I am not easily led," said Fran.

"And let the two of you catch up on old times while Fran and I get into some kind of trouble."

"Surely you can offer better than that," said Fran.

"Listen, Mr. Webb—"

"Just Webb."

"Webb, then. I think it would be very nice if you would mention to Bud, to Mr. Wellman, that you—uh—ran into me, and then just—

uh—see what his reaction is. Certainly, if he'd like to see me again, I would be happy to see him again. But who knows? Maybe he's very busy or whatever. Maybe he has a f-f-friend he's busy with—"

"Bud? Straight-arrow Bud? When his wife just died a week ago? No chance."

"Oh, I didn't mean that. I meant—I don't know what I meant. But you two go look at your apartments. I'm going to go somewhere— uh—I have to put these bagels away at home and then go to the office. I'm very busy. My car needs washing. I have to pick up the cleaning and things. I—I—well—I'll see you later." She stood up abruptly.

"When we come to the Hammock, why don't you come around with us?" invited Webb.

"Oh, no! I mean, I've got to get to the office, now. If I can leave I will, but probably I won't be able to get away." And she fled from the deli.

"She seems very nervous," said Webb.

"I think it's called scared. I don't know how she got to this guy Bud, but I think he really got to her when she was a little teenager. I think she thought of him as a knight in shining armor, until he let her down. No way to treat a lady."

"He's regretted it all his life," said Webb. "He's talked about it to me a few times, too.

Isn't this interesting. I can't wait to see how it comes out. Meanwhile, what time do we meet this afternoon, and where?"

"Why don't we just take a run through all these possibilities. Then we can start with the Hammock. We can go from here if you like."

"I'll follow you."

"If I lose you—"

"I'm not easy to lose," he said, grinning.

"But if I do, meet me in the lot of the Hollywood Federal at 46th Avenue and Sheridan. It's only about eight or ten blocks from the Hammock, and a little closer to Royal Oaks."

Webb paid the check, walked her outside to her car, and helped her in. She watched in the mirror as he climbed into a Mercedes 500. Jeans and a sport shirt. Nothing special in the clothes department. And he drove a Mercedes. Maybe he had borrowed it. Maybe it belonged to Wellman.

She pulled out of the lot and headed west on Commercial. The taupe Mercedes was right behind her.

"It's nuts for you to do this, Webb. I could have gotten a cab or a car," said Bud, dumping his bag in the back seat and sliding into the front.

"No, I got stuff to tell you and I didn't want

to tell you on the phone and have you stewing all the way back on the plane." He eased out into the traffic lane and headed towards the airport exit.

"What's up? Trouble with those Yancy County leases?"

"Nothing like that. Two things. The first is, I got busy on the condos and found two. One double apartment. One triple. Big enough for your lab and office and Miss Mary. And room to run around in. Security, jogging. Small gyms. Pretty much what you need, and they're both in the west."

"Good. But you could have told me that on the phone."

"There's more. One thing—I don't want you to walk in your house and go into shock. Miss Mary had to hire someone to handle all the food these crazy, horny broads keep bringing and sending. Just to get rid of it and keep track of the senders. She ordered a form thank-you note. And she kept a list of all the ones from the neighborhood that stopped in to borrow a cup of sugar or the hedging shears. They can't all be from that close by. But that's not the big news either. The big news is, I've found her."

"Found her? Found who?" asked Bud.

Webb looked at him sideways. "Who do you think?"

"Keep your eyes on the road, will you? Who? You don't mean — You can't mean —"

"Oh, yes I can. And she lives in one of the two houses where you've got apartments to look at tomorrow."

"Are you sure? What's her name? What does she look like?"

"Jessie Nella Moore. Was Pendleton. There can't be two of them. She's smallish, blondish, prettyish. Good little bod. Green eyes."

"Well, she could still be the wrong one. You really think it's her?"

"I'd make book on it. This was the one that came to the wake. And signed her name."

"Oh, Christ!"

"What do you mean, 'Oh, Christ'? Aren't you glad? You've been dreaming about a dame for thirty-five years and when she turns up all you can say is 'Oh, Christ?' Don't worry, she looks good. Great, in fact. In fact if you're not interested, I think I'll give it a shot."

"Webb, hands off. Jessie's not going to be another notch in your belt."

Webb laughed. "I was only kidding. See? You're still interested."

"Listen, it's thirty-five years. I was a kid then. I looked good. I was strong."

"So what's wrong with you now? You look okay."

"Oh, yeah. Great. The waist is a little bigger,

the chest is slipping, half my teeth are capped. Otherwise I'm just the same."

"So don't tell her until after you're married."

"And what would I do with her?"

"You could start with hugging and kissing."

"Hug her? Kiss her! What do I know about hugging and kissing anymore? Bitsy and I, hell, we turned that off a long time ago."

"It's like swimming. You'll remember once you dive in."

"How did it happen? How did you find her?"

"A thousand-to-one shot. When my friend Lally Montkeith got me someone who knows the real estate market in the west, she turns out to be Jessie Nella Moore's roommate. She's the one who came to Riverpalm."

"Now listen, Webb. I don't want any artificial carryings on here. Nothing staged. I want it to be natural, our meeting. I don't want to make a fool of myself. What if she's not the least bit interested?"

"She's interested."

"How would you know?"

"I met her. For five minutes."

"She may take one look and run the other way. Wait. You met her? What did she look like? Was she all right? Did she—did she say anything about me?"

"I already told you she looked damn good. But she was upset. Scared, maybe, or really nervous. Interested, for sure. But all flustered."

"What would happen if we met again?"

"How the hell do I know? And you'll never know until you try, will you?"

At the house, Miss Mary met them at the door. "Oh, Mr. Wellman, I don't know what we're going to do. If they bring us any more food, we'll have to open a restaurant."

"What food, Miss Mary?" Bud was puzzled.

"The food I told you about in the car," Webb laughed. "I told you it would happen. Broads always think the way to your hormones is through your stomach."

"There's been women coming here for days bringing baskets and platters and bowls of food," wailed Miss Mary. "Everything you could think of. I hired a lady to help keep a record of who brought what. And what platter and bowl goes to who. Had her take things to Center One and Covenant House and Women in Distress and I don't know where all. Couldn't let all that go to waste. And no one here to eat it.

"I knew Miss Bitsy would want us to do that. These women just keep bringing things. We wrote them all thank-you notes. You can sign them or you can write more by hand if you want, but there's so many." And she hurried off to the kitchen to make some coffee.

"I don't believe it," said Bud. "It was the same at Esme's. She and Sess said they put enough in their freezers to feed the entire Peace Corps for six months. Why do they do that?"

"I told you, Bud. You don't listen. Because they think it's a good way to get your attention."

"It's enough to make you run in the other direction."

"That's something else we should talk about, Bud. You're single now. You can run around if you want. You can do all the chasing you never did as a kid. Or you can find someone and tie up again, if you're more comfortable that way. But think about it. If there's something you always wanted to get out of your system, you might want to wait a little before making any commitments or anything."

"I've done my chasing, Webb."

"You? When? Not since I've known you."

"Yeah, since we've known each other. And before. Mostly before. I was very sneaky. It started a couple of years after we got married. Bitsy never was very physical. Just not her nature. And I was hitting it big with my labs. Making a lot more money than I ever had before, traveling all over the country. Got into trouble a few times in hotels. Then Esme was born and Bitsy really turned off. For about another four years, I couldn't seem to get enough. I never fooled anyone. There was one gal I really began to get hooked on in Kansas. So I disconnected."

"I never had an inkling," said Webb.

"I don't put much faith in shrinks but I went for a little counseling anyway. And he said if divorce wasn't an option, I should try waking up Bitsy. But Bitsy just wouldn't wake up. God knows I tried. Even tried loosening her up with a little booze. Benjie was the result. But she just wouldn't waken. By that time, Bitsy'd gotten pretty hefty and she didn't like anyone to see her undressed. I gave up on the booze. She had too much of a tendency that way anyway, and it didn't really help. I tried flowers and little gifts and little notes. Nothing worked. So I looked elsewhere. Mostly I did without. But later I had an affair for almost eight years with a lady ten years older than me. That was when I knew you. A sexy teacher from St. Charles. Her husband had been in a car accident — paraplegic. Nice lady. She taught me a hell of a lot.

"You always thought I was so straight, didn't you? But for about eight years there, I had a great sex life. I don't know how good I was for her. I was pretty conservative I guess, at first. But she knew how to get around everything. I relaxed after a while. But I was very careful and so was she. I'm sure her husband never guessed. Even you never guessed, did you?"

"Never. Sheesh! I can't believe it. I kind of wondered once or twice why you didn't look for something, but I never guessed you had."

"Nobody guessed. We couldn't either one afford to have anyone guess. We met downtown at different hotels when we could. Never even once had dinner any place public."

"And didn't you ever go with Bitsy again?"

"To tell you the truth, my heart wasn't in it. I didn't have it for her that way. It was almost as bad for me as it was for her when I tried. I'd still think of divorce every now and then. I wanted out the worst way. I even kind of hinted to Bitsy a couple of times that maybe she'd be happier that way. But that terrified her. So how could I? She trusted me. Now, I've been pretty close to celibate for the last eight or ten years.

"No, I've done enough chasing. I hated the deceit. I guess what I always kind of hoped, was that I'd meet up with Jessie again someday, and make up to her for the way I shafted her back then. I kept track of her until about five or six years ago. Always knew where she was living, at least, even though I couldn't do anything about it. And then, I guess I gave up. It didn't look like there was any point in hoping. And now, look what's happened.

"But I don't want anything to be awkward or hokey. It's gotta be natural. Nothing staged. We should just — just run into each other."

"You know something Bud? For a guy that used to be as easy to be around as a coffee-pot — no waves ever — you're suddenly more trouble than all my money. But let me think about it. And what we should do. Meanwhile, we can look at the apartments tomorrow. And I'll figure out something."

Eleven

"Okay, it's 10 K?" Jessie tapped away at her keyboard, taking down the details of the Salvation Army's fundraising run. "Next Sunday? What time? Eight A.M. Holiday Park. Got it." She had barely hung up when the phone rang again. That was life at the *Community News*. The telephone fast lane. They called to say they were sending an invitation or a press release for an event. To see if you got it. To see if you were coming. To ask if you were bringing a photographer. To ask when the story would run. How any one ever gets any writing done around here, she thought, is beyond me.

This time it was Fran. "Where were you this morning when he came to see the apartments? I kept expecting to bump into you in the hall or something. Four other single women managed to bump into us."

"Wednesday is deadline day, Fran. You know

that. I had to get my stuff in. I just couldn't get away. But what happened? What did he look like?"

"Liar! Coward! He was gorgeous. Not young hunk gorgeous. Middle-aged gorgeous. Nice-looking. Quiet. Seemed a little fidgety. He's got all his parts as far as I can tell, and everything seems to be in working order. Polite. Asked a bunch of questions, and then put in a bid at the exact minimum they would have taken. Now how did he know that? Pretty shrewd, I'd say. They both thought it was wonderful that I zeroed in so quickly on exactly what he wanted. But that Webb rubs me the wrong way. Bloody outspoken. Thinks he's right about everything."

"You're saying Bud's going to be living in our building? Oh, no!"

"That's what I'm trying to tell you. So where were you?"

"Oh, Fran, that would have been so obvious. So pushy. I just couldn't. And I really had to be here. Does he know I live there?"

"Of course. That's when he seemed a little fidgety. I think he was really disappointed that you weren't there. He got sort of breathless when I brought up your name."

"Oh, don't bring up my name. Just let it happen naturally."

"Nothing's going to happen at all if somebody

doesn't bring up your name. With all the single broads here in the Hammock, one of them will snap him up if he's not aware that you're here. But if he once sees you again — just once — they'll be wasting their time. Anyway, in the course of looking at the apartments, I learned a lot about him."

"Apartments? Plural?"

"Well he's a kind of tinkerer and inventor and scientist, I gather, and he needs a place to putter. So he took the Montmorency and the Billingsgate next to it, and the Hillbourne one floor down under the Montmorency. He could put in his own bowling alley."

Jessie laughed. "Why doesn't he just buy a Ramada Inn?"

"He likes security."

"Is he so rich? I'd heard he'd done well."

"He owns a chain of labs and a company that makes medical supplies and he's in some real estate things and I forget the rest. A real tycoon. And Lally said he holds a lot of patents."

"Oh gosh, then what would he want with a poor ditz like me? I'm just one of the great unwashed masses."

"So you'll wash. And wanting you has nothing to do with being loaded. Don't hold it against him. Much money is always nicer than not so much money. Anyway, the rest of what I found out is that he jogs. Just like you. He works out a little. And he's a real golf nut when he can find time, which he apparently does in spurts and binges in between business things. And the last thing I found out is that his friend Webb is a card-carrying pain in the ass."

"Oh, Fran! He seemed nice enough."

"Except he thinks he knows everything. How to care for your plants, how to write a listing, how a woman should dress—everything. Better than anyone else."

"Maybe he's just trying to help you."

"I don't need his help. And he had the nerve to say to me, 'Wonder what you'd look like with a little makeup on. Like a real girl, I bet. I bet you'd clean up pretty good.' "

"Oh, dear. And what did you answer him, I'm afraid to ask?"

"I waited until after the papers were signed. Then I told him that I bet that if he kept his mouth shut someone might even take him for a gentleman. And you know what the smartass bastard did? He laughed, goddammit! Roared. Like I was being funny. He didn't even take me seriously!"

"Well, calm down. It's over."

"Not quite. I won't be home until late. I'm showing Wellman's house this evening. It's crazy. We don't ever get calls for that kind of

142

listing, but lo and behold, we did this morning. When I was showing Bud and Webb the gym and the billiards room, who was in the gym but Aaron Greenberg. They have a Montmorency, too, that's supposed to be simply glorious. And his brother owns half of Ohio. And anyway, his sister-in-law decided to get a place here. She's the dizzy, ritzy type and she wants to buy a home and staff it. They already have three, and from what he says, I gather she has taste like your Bitsy. Thinks it's illegal to leave one square inch undecorated or uncovered. We got to talking, and after Bud and Webb left, I called him and bullshat him a little and the result is that I'm showing his sister-in-law the house tonight. Picking her up from the plane. Webb is going to be there so I conned him into taking Mrs. Greenberg and me to dinner. And he's sending me in a limo to pick her up. He says that's how you have to do with this grade of customer. See? He thinks he knows everything. I'm going to order the most expensive thing on the menu. And I'm not going to wear any makeup."

"Shoes, at least? In a limo, you should always wear shoes."

"Very funny."

"Fran? Before you hang up. One more thing."

"Yeah?"

"Could you maybe find out when he's moving in? And what time he jogs and works out? Not that I intend to bump into him or anything. But—well, it wouldn't hurt to know."

"I'm beginning to feel like a private eye. I'll see what I can find out. So that we'll know what we're doing when we're putting together all those plans we're not going to make."

When Webb had shown her the house, Fran could hardly believe her eyes. She had walked into the mauve, pink, and plum drawing room, cringed, and blurted, "My gosh! I'd need blinders in here." She had looked at Webb apologetically, expecting a frown, but instead he was grinning.

Display cases and fancy, carved shelving loaded with thousands of pieces of Lladró, Boehm, Lalique, Daum and a hundred other collectibles surrounded them. The walls, right up to and including the beamed ceilings were covered with patterned wall-coverings in coordinated designs. The vast room was almost crowded, with little clusters of seating—sofas, love seats, upholstered chairs—grouped around various antique desks, tables and other furniture, and the displays. One wall was covered, floor to ceiling, with various framed paintings, prints, etchings, etc.

"Ain't that something? It makes me dizzy, too. All these thousands of little doodads and junk—she collected everything, and she decorated everything," he said.

"An overdose of San Simeon. I'm getting seasick."

"But somewhere there is probably a lady who suits this house and vice versa."

"Do you really think so?" asked Fran. "If there is, she's probably legally blind. Well, if I come across anyone, I'll keep it in mind."

"Wait. Let me show you the gargoyle bathroom. Wait till you see the chandelier in there. And those sconce things on every wall. Their other houses were the same way. I could never stay with them. They asked me a hundred times. But ten minutes of all that stuff always gave me a headache. She got worse and worse. Bud couldn't stand it either. He spent all his time in his rooms—and they were stripped like a monk's cell. What he needed. Nothing else. That's when he was home I mean, which wasn't all that often."

Webb took her through the family room into the most incredible bathroom Fran had ever seen. It had a twenty-foot ceiling, from which hung a chandelier right out of Donald Trump's Taj Mahal. Paneling in the walls was inset with crystal. There were sconces, and in between, more cases with collections of thimbles, antique fountain pens, deco compacts, etc.

She shook her head, speechless. He led her upstairs into the two fussy guest rooms, then into Bitsy's suite. It was more of the same — all pink and ruffles and busy prints, with full display cases everywhere. And finally, Bud's rooms. A spartan male bastion, as Webb had said. Two panelled rooms lined with bookshelves crammed with books. Three desks. Two computers. Two worktables. Cabinets. Not one trinket anywhere. "Is he that neat?" asked Fran.

"Yes, actually he is," nodded Webb. "He can drive you crazy sometimes. I always thought it must be a kind of reaction to Bitsy and her 360-degree clutter. Why do you ask?"

"Why? I don't know. I guess it's a reaction with me, too. I'm just the opposite. Congenitally messy. So is Jessie, thank goodness. So as roommates, we don't drive each other nuts. Look, there isn't even a candy wrapper or a Kleenex in his wastebasket." She tiptoed from the room. "I feel like we shouldn't be looking. Like I'm reading someone's mail," she said. "I don't know why. I've inspected hundreds of houses. But these rooms are so revealing."

Webb shrugged. "You have to know it if you're going to show it."

Fran left the house with her mouth pursed, as if she had just eaten too much sugar.

And now, here was Mrs. Greenberg going into ecstasies over the place. "Oh, how I love all those darling beams," she trilled. "And the wallpapers. Using three companion prints that way. Such a lovely touch. I simply abhor white walls. They look like someone didn't care enough to finish the job. They say it's better for hanging works of art, but that's not so. It shows a lack of courage, of commitment to a theme. But these walls are as thematic as can be. They have charm. Character. Personality."

And galloping schizophrenia, thought Fran, stifling a groan.

True to his word, Webb took the three of them to Yesterday's for dinner. Fran tried to bring the subject around to jogging, to pick up the information Jessie wanted. "Do you jog, too?" she asked Webb over their swordfish.

"I play backgammon," he said. "Tennis, when I get a chance. But I don't get much chance. I'm in and out of town."

"My husband used to jog, but his knees went," said Mrs. Greenberg. "He does aquatic exercises now, and we both get massages. I think that one bedroom upstairs would make a good room for massages. The one in mauve."

"Yes, it would be easy to convert," said Fran.

"And the house is simply made for my collections. I have so many lovely things in the warehouse because there's no room left in our other homes. I could put my doll collection here. It takes a large room, and I miss not having some of my favorites around. And my spoons. I have spoons used by the royal families of fourteen different countries. Oh, I can't wait to start planning what to put where. Can you get me some floor plans, dear?"

Fran kicked Webb, who nodded slightly, then replied, "Of course we can, Mrs. Greenberg. Sounds like you're really interested."

"Oh, yes. Do call me Amelia, dears. Everyone does. Yes, I definitely want it. I have never before looked at a house that was done just the way I like it. It's like a big load lifted. All the work I won't have to do with decorators and so on. Oh, a little to fit the collections in. But that will be such fun."

"Would you like to submit a contract, Mrs. — Amelia? I'm sure we can have something ready within an hour or two if you'll like us to —"

"Not me. My husband or my brother-in-law can handle that. But my brother-in-law has a check from my husband in case I found something. I never handle the money end of things. When you bring me back, you can talk to him. I've never had it all go as easily as this before. Isn't this simply marvelous?"

148

"And I've never sold a house so easily either, Amelia," said Fran. "I guess the two of us are just a little easy." And Amelia Greenberg went into paroxysms of giggles at the very idea.

This time when Fran got home, it was Jessie who was waiting up. "Well? Was he there? What did he look like? Did he ask about me? What was the house like? What did he say? What did he—?"

"Slow down. You sound like a machine gun. I didn't see him. Because he was apparently over here getting things started to get the place ready for him. Nobody was there but us. And the housekeeper, in her room. But I have some great news. I think I sold the house. Just like that. I never sold a house that big before. Or that expensive. Or that idiotically decorated. You have never seen such a madly busy place so garbaged up with tons of little so-called treasures. Talk about overkill. And yet I sold it, just like that."

"Oh, that's wonderful! How much money will you get? Wait! He wasn't there? He was *here?*"

"I don't know. I haven't formally signed with anyone on it. On the apartments, I'm covered. But this all happened so fast. I don't know if they'll give me the full commission or take out a lot. We didn't talk price. It's their listing.

Either way, with a house going for over a million and a half, it'll be a chunk."

"Here! I could have run into him! I mean, uh, if I know Lally, you'll get every penny you're entitled to. That's how they get the best people. They take care of them."

"This Mrs. Greenberg went into raptures over the place. Absolutely orgasms. And Jessie, it's so terribly, unbearably, fussy and busy, it would be like living in a strawberry milk shake. Everything is painted and printed — fussy wallpaper all the way up to the skylights. It looks like it's trying to crawl right off the wall. Painted designs on the beams. Only his suite is simple and comfortable."

"You saw his suite!"

"But this Greenberg nut likes it. Likes it? She loves it! It's her kind of decorating. The two were made for each other. She could have been Bitsy's best friend."

"Well, I'm thrilled for you. But — ah — you couldn't find out anything about when he's moving in here?"

"Yes, Webb mentioned it. You won't believe this, but next week. He has Paola Smith poking through all the furniture and stuff at the house and what's in the apartments and he told her just what he wants and needs. You know Paola. She can get anything done yesterday. And they were already doing the joining work today. He hired a couple of his own truckers to move what he wants moved and put where it should be put. Even if everything isn't quite finished, he wants to be in here in a few days. When he moves, he moves. He wants to get out of that house because he's getting all these calls from women. He'll have an unlisted phone here."

"He's bringing a housekeeper?"

"Yeah. Apparently she's been with his wife since she was a little girl. Must be a hundred years old. I met her last night. She's spry and fit. Kind of feisty. She's overseeing a lot of the move. And his sister is coming down next week."

"How was dinner?"

"Okay. Of course it's all poison in those places. Swimming in cholesterol. They can't put a green bean on a plate without slathering it in butter. I made them change my fish to a dry plate. That fooled them. So it was surprisingly pleasant. Mrs. Greenberg chattered nonstop. And Webb is the ultimate egomaniac. But it was fun. Even though he thinks he knows everything there is to know about wines and food. With a lot of men, that means the sex has gone. They have such fragile egos, they need something to give them stature so they become experts in wining and dining."

"But what did you find out about Bud's

151

jogging? When? How often?"

"Well, I couldn't just flat-out ask him, Jessie. I snuck into it by a side door. I talked about how many walkers there were in the building. I brought up about how nice it was at the Hammock for joggers except that it gets a little crowded with walkers, about nine in the morning. And he said Bud wouldn't have any problem because he was usually out by six or six-thirty at the latest."

Jessie groaned. "I have to get up that early? Oh, and maybe I'd better get a new jogging outfit. Mine is so old and ratty."

"Oh, Jessie, don't be silly. No one expects you to look like Grace Kelly when you're jogging. Everyone gets messy and sweaty. And by the way, have you been out on the terrace at all, today? The peppers and green beans and tomatoes are all blooming at once. I have to get out there and pollinate."

"How can you even think of that farm of yours at a time like this?"

"How can I forget it? This planet is dying, Jessie. It's an emergency. Plants for the Planet has about ten people growing these special green beans, and the survival of that species depends on us. The responsibility is awesome. If we don't keep it going, it will die out forever. And all the future generations of that particular green bean, will never see the light of day.

Suppose they find that there's something in that particular strain that will cure AIDS or prevent osteoporosis. Or stop Alzheimer's. And it's too late. It's extinct. What a tragedy. And things like that are happening in the rain forests right now. Different species are being wiped out right and left."

"Oh, Fran, I'm sorry. Don't mind me. It's so wonderful that you care about the plant life. You should have been a scientist. But right now I'm exhausted. I'm going to bed and dream about jogging. Maybe it's just as well I wasn't there this morning. I don't want to look too eager. I don't want to scare him away. I'll bump into him jogging. By accident. That'll be a better way."

But at six-thirty in the morning? She'd have to get up at six!

All night long in her dreams, she was jogging eagerly on the Hammock's perimeter road. And knowing that any minute, she would run into Bud Wellman.

Twelve

Bud picked her up in a limo. That was one way Esme certainly took after her mother. She, too, loved the pretentious trappings. Bitsy had adored her Rolls. Until she had finally learned to drive, more or less, at forty. From then on she preferred smaller, sporty cars, always in the brightest colors.

That was probably the only taste or trait mother and daughter had had in common, and Bud obliged it. Bitsy had been short and round. Esme was tall and angular. Bitsy procrastinated. She hated making decisions. Esme was quick and decisive. Bitsy was vague and disliked considering the whys and wherefores. Esme always ferreted out the facts and reasons, evaluated them, and never forgot them.

And their clothes. Bitsy was usually cushioned in layers of fluff, frills and ruffles. Esme preferred the clean and lean. Stark but smart.

He spotted her coming past the security check and he hurried up to kiss her and take the package she carried. "You didn't have to come. You could have just sent a car, Daddy. Those are bagels from Emory's. Aunt Sess sent them. She froze them and put them in a thermal pack so they'd keep. Just pop them in the freezer."

"Good. I still haven't found a bagel place here as good as Emory's," he said. "How are you doing, Es? You okay?"

"Yes, Daddy. I'm indestructible. I think we're getting close on the Estée Lauder deal, and Needle will probably wrap up Cover Girl while I'm down here."

"Wonderful. And I've got some other good news for you. Benjie is coming in, too. Now. We have about thirty minutes to kill before his plane gets in."

"Tonight? Benjie? Oh, that's wonderful Daddy," Esme smiled broadly. Esme's affection for her brother, unlike that for the rest of the family, had always been without reservation. And he was probably the only family member who loved Esme the same way, wholeheartedly — without reservation. "I was so frightened this time. It was worse than that time in the Amazon. After those slides in California, I knew what could be happening. And missing for three days! He could have been dead. Oh

Daddy, why does he have to keep doing such dangerous things?"

"He's like Webb. He's afraid the planet is going to hell. And he feels someone's got to try and save it."

"I have nightmares that one of these times, he's not going to make it. If there's a dangerous bit of research to be done, Benjie finds it. Studying those high altitude plants in Peru when there was practically a shooting war going on. And that time on the oil platform. Sometimes I think he has a death wish. How did he sound?"

"Pretty good. I gather they still don't want him to travel. And I guess the leg is still giving him some pain. You know Benjie. It's hard to get him to admit anything hurts. I guess we won't really know what condition he's in until we see him. But he's just going to stay at the house and do nothing for two days. Miss Mary can't wait to get her hands on him. Here we are going crazy trying to sort everything for moving over to the new apartments, in some kind of organized way, and in the middle of it all, she's been baking Benjie's cookies and banana bread."

"Listen, Daddy, the best way to do this is for you to tell me what plane. Then you go and bring my things to the car, while I go to meet Benjie's plane — as soon as it comes in, of course. Then Benjie and I can claim his luggage, and you can pick us up at the curb."

Bud nodded. That was exactly what he had already outlined to the driver. And certainly, it was the logical way to organize the double pickup. But it always amazed him when Esme's mind would work exactly like his. Of course, that was the only way, he told himself, in which they were remotely alike.

He had been parked in front of the Delta arrivals for about five minutes when they came out. People turned to look at the pair. Esme with her model's figure and her sleek, put-together look, and Benjie, so tall and lanky, with an actor's chiseled good looks. Benjie toted a hand-carry under his right arm. His left was in a cast. "We don't have to wait for his luggage, Daddy," Esme called as he got out of the car. She pointed to the hand-carry. "That's it. He's still traveling light."

Bud hugged his son hungrily. Benjie's good arm wrapped around him and he kissed his father's cheek. The boy had never been self-conscious about showing affection.

"I see we've had your usual edited report on your physical condition," said Bud. "What's with the arm?"

"Well, Dad, it's only a hairline and you know

if I'd mentioned it, you'd both have been sure it had been amputated or something."

Bud laughed. "Only because of previous editing, son."

Miss Mary met them at the door, laughing and weeping at the same time, reaching up to hug each in turn. "Oh, children, I'm so glad to have you back for a couple of days," she cried, pulling a hankie from her pocket to blot her eyes. Esme quickly extricated herself from Miss Mary's hug. Esme was not demonstrative. But Benjie hugged the housekeeper back, dancing around the entry hall with her. "Can't pick you up and swing you this time, Miss Mary," he explained. "This darn cast. And the legs are still a little wobbly. We'll do two swings next time. Hey, is that Scotchies I smell?"

Miss Mary beamed. "I knew that's why you came home," she said. "I just took the last pan out of the oven. I made enough so you can take a big parcel back up to Alaska with you."

"I'll get the bags up to your rooms, kids. No one here but Miss Mary and me tonight. And you, son," Bud grabbed his son's arm as Benjie started back toward the front door, "you just sit there. The old man can still lift a couple of suitcases."

Miss Mary wheeled a cart in from the

kitchen, laden with a pot of coffee, cups and a plate of Benjie's favorite butterscotch chip oatmeal cookies. He grabbed two in his good hand but Esme only sniffed them, then shook her head and pulled a little tablet out of her handbag. "I'm going to make a list, Daddy, and I'll put little yellow stickers on everything I want, too, so the movers won't make too many mistakes. Needle pulled a few wires and they'll be here the day after tomorrow before noon. Is that time a problem?"

"Not for me," said Benjie. "I'll be heading back that morning. Gosh, these are good! No one makes cookies like you do, Miss Mary," he said, grabbing another pair from the plate.

"Don't you just want to sit for a while after that trip, Es?" asked her father, dumping her bags on the stairway.

"Well actually, Daddy, I might as well be going over the jewelry while I'm sitting here. Why don't you run up and get the stuff from the vault. Is there any still in the bank?"

"No, I got it all out this morning. I'll bring it down."

"So the businesses are going well, Es?" Benjie asked, as their father headed upstairs.

"Incredibly," said Esme. "We're going to franchise the gourmet food shops. And our Bitty-Pax—our line of one-application packets of cosmetics and such—is sailing. It will mean megabucks. We have some patents on the packets. Looks like we're going to start off with a couple or three big cosmetics companies right from the beginning."

"Gee, that's wonderful, Sis. You're really having fun with it, too, I can tell. You're going to end up being a female King Midas. Everything you touch turns to gold."

"And Mom always thought I should take up something like selling gifts in a museum, or being a receptionist for the Historical Society," Esme sighed. "Something where I could support myself, but just barely. I think she thought that my thinking big and aiming high and wanting to make things work was a fault. A grievous fault."

"She would have come to understand in time, honey. You were two very different people but she would have understood in time. She was trying."

"Yes, we certainly were different," nodded Esme. "Look at this room, Benjie. I don't know what she was thinking of."

"Well, you know what she used to say: To each his own."

Bud returned with a large tray of jewel boxes and cases and set them on the coffee table. "This is it, Es."

Esme opened the top case and peered inside. "Actually, Daddy, the best thing for me to do is to just take it all back and go through it at home."

"I don't think you should try to carry all that. It might be dangerous," Bud said.

"Nonsense. No one knows it's jewelry," replied Esme. "I'll take everything out of the cases and wrap it in tissue. I can fit it all in my ostrich overnight case and keep it with me. I'll send all the boxes up with the movers and decide later which to keep. No problem."

"No. I'm sending a bodyguard up with you. And no arguments," said Bud.

"Dad's right, sis," Benjie said quickly. "Why take any chances. There are crazy people out there who would kill someone for just one of those pieces."

Esme shrugged.

"And save some things for Benjie, here. He might want to give them to his kids or his wife. If you ever marry, Son," he added.

"I can pick out things for Benjie, Daddy. I know what he likes. But I think I should keep it all until he does marry someone—I'll have a better idea which pieces might do. And if we give him anything now, he'll just lose it in a jungle river or a mudslide somewhere."

"True," laughed her brother.

"Oh, and I think we should give your mother's smaller opal ring to Miss Mary. She always admired it and your mother used to kid her sometimes and say she'd leave it to her in her will."

"Whatever you say, Daddy," Esme nodded. "I'll pick it out before I go. Are you going to take any of the crystal or the Limoges or anything to your apartment?"

"Take whatever you want," Bud said resolutely.

"Then I'd better get started," she said. "It's a lot to go through in just two days." She got up and took her pad and stickers into the dining room and began ticketing the antique secretary, the huge marble topped dining table, the Chippendale chairs and the china and crystal — and making little entries in her notebook.

"I don't know what her hurry is," Bud grumbled.

"Well, you know, Dad — she's probably still pretty upset. And it's easier to just keep moving." Benjie always stuck up for his sister. Always explained away her impatience or seeming greediness or thoughtlessness. She was his sister. He loved her. That was enough.

"So tell me exactly what happened up there," Bud asked.

"Oh, there was a storm that lasted five days. Really heavy rain. And then the slide came slathering down. Actually a few of them, right around us. They found one of our outbuildings half a mile down the mountain. The cabin stood, but part of it was crushed and part of the roof caved in. When we heard it coming we all ran for the middle room—it's the sturdiest. Jim Noonan and I were out in the yard. We sprinted like roadrunners and slammed the bar in the door. Jim grabbed a couple of cases from the pantry and threw them in the room and I grabbed a couple of cases of the bottled water and then we hit the floor—just in time. Everything went crunch and fell in and I went out. When I woke up, I could hear Jim and Bill Murray moaning but I couldn't see much at first. It must have been at night. I could see more a few hours later. I felt irresistibly drowsy though. And I was trapped. My legs. And without being able to see anything, I was afraid to try and move anything. So I just caught up on my sleep at first. Not many other choices that I could think of."

"At least you had food and water handy," Bud answered.

"No, the food cases both turned out to be little tins of condensed milk," Benjie said. "And that was all we had to eat for the three days we were trapped. I can't recommend it for a steady diet. It was like eating syrup. And Bill Murray was closest to the water but he had a broken leg, broken shoulder and a bunch of cracked ribs and he was so out of it. For the first day and a half, he was delirious. Didn't know where he was. And we couldn't get him to understand about the water. Late on the second day he came to. He was pinned down. But darned if he didn't manage to wriggle his good arm loose and slide a couple of bottles over somehow.

"And we rolled the milk tins around. We were all trapped, one way or another. Jim didn't have any bones broken, but he did have a slight concussion and he was vomiting for hours. That place smelled to high heaven. The radio was crushed but we weren't near enough to reach it anyway. The mud was right up to the eaves, and oozing in over the kitchen wall. We had air, though. And they knew where we were, so we knew we'd get help as soon as the rain let up and they could get in. Trouble was it was still storming that first couple of days, too."

"You're lucky to be alive," Bud said.

"Nyah. It's not that dangerous, Dad. This one was just a little atypical. But we're finding out things. Big things. Little things. Like those pop-top cans. If the milk hadn't been in pop-top cans, we'd have had a lot of trouble getting it out. So that's something to think of. Put all the food you possibly can in a station like that, in pop-top cans. And have a little food and water in every possible room. Things like that, you learn."

"You know, son, whatever you want from this

house, you'd better tell Esme now. Before she disposes of it. Speak up or forever hold your peace."

"Oh, let her take it Dad. You know I'm not big on owning things. Easier when you travel light, in my work."

It was good to be with Benjie. They made a couple of trips over to see the new apartments and check on their progress, suggest changes, and be sure where all the personal things — clothes and toiletries — were going. Miss Mary would see to it there weren't too many glitches. They drove around the perimeter road past all the walkers.

They tore Esme away from her tags and lists long enough to eat dinner with them at the Rustic Inn. Bud and Benjie banged on the newspaper-covered tables with their hammers, like everyone else, and ate stone crabs and garlic crabs and sang "Happy Birthday," to various customers. Esme ordered halibut and picked at it as usual. Benjie finished it. Bud noticed how several women at nearby tables kept eyeing his handsome son. Benjie was oblivious.

And on Monday morning he took Benjie to the airport. The good-byes were not easy. "Come up soon, Dad," Benjie urged, hugging his father tightly.

"I will son. As soon as I can," Bud promised. The movers' truck pulled into the drive an hour later. And Esme spent the rest of the day orchestrating the dismantling of her parents' newest home, seeing that all the right things were loaded, the collections packed with infinite care and marked clearly, the expendables gathered in one place and marked with pink stickers, giving the movers advice on pieces that required special care. A Salvation Army truck arrived at noon and whisked away three wardrobes full of pink-tagged clothes and miscellaneous items, and several pieces of furniture. The movers helped them. There were twelve of them, which meant that Needle certainly had pulled the right strings. The job was done by seven in the evening, and by eight Bud and Miss Mary were delivering Esme to the airport. By nine, they were at the Hammock, Bud's new home.

As he put the key in his new door, he felt like he was closing a long and involved novel. One from which the characters would probably linger with him for some time.

Thirteen

Tuesday, 6 A.M.

In G770, Jessie woke before her alarm went off, slid reluctantly from her bed, and padded over to press the button before it buzzed. Such a jarring buzz. Someone ought to invent an alarm clock that began with the softest of muffled chimes, which gradually evolved into a favorite bit of music — one where the buzzer buzzed only as a last resort. It would be like being wakened by a kiss from your mother instead of being dragged from sleep by the scruff of your neck.

Lord, this is ridiculous, she whispered to herself, eyeing the almost black sky from her windows. Six-fifteen. She'd better move it if she wanted to get down there before he finished. If he was there.

Slipping into her grey jogging outfit, she

grabbed the shoes with the Velcro flaps — no time to waste on laces — brushed her teeth, washed off the Retin-A, smeared on sunscreen. Pancake, a bit of rouge, eyebrow pencil and a bit of liner. No way she'd let him see her the first time in fifteen years totally *au naturel*.

Keys, big hankie and sunglasses — for what — looking at the stars — in hand, she headed for the door.

Downstairs it was not only dark. It was wet. From the covered parking lot she could hear it. A soft pattering of rain. Not a heavy downpour. Just a soft pattering.

Was it winding up or barely getting started?

And would he be out running in the rain?

Yeah, probably. A little rain didn't bother a man. They could get soaked and all they did was jump in the shower afterwards and they looked fine. For a woman it meant hairdo meltdown, mascara rivulets down the cheeks, and hours of putting herself back together.

With her luck, if she decided not to jog, he'd be out there this morning. And if she did jog, and got soaked and had to spend two hours redoing her hair, he wouldn't be there anyway. She would compromise — do her running in the covered parking lots under the building as she often did on rainy days. She would run a few circles in one lot, and then the next, working her way around the U-shaped building. And keeping her eyes on the exits to the perimeter road, hoping to catch a glimpse of him jogging by. If she did, then she could run out, and accidentally bump into him. Mission accomplished.

If she didn't find him in thirty laps, equivalent to her regular three miles, she'd give up. She'd run under the F and E buildings. From them she could see the F, E, and D elevators. If he came down, he was likely to use one of the three. I wonder, she thought, if General Eisenhower took this much care planning the Normandy invasion.

In E770, Bud looked up from the financial pages to check his watch. It was 6:47 A.M. He got up and let himself out onto the terrace for the fourth time. No, it wasn't easing up. If anything, it was raining harder. And it was still so dark that when he looked downstairs, he wasn't sure if the road was empty or not.

She should be coming out in fifteen minutes or half an hour. But would she jog on a day like this? Women weren't fond of rain. Then again, down here, he had learned, that rain could dry up in the next five minutes. It probably wouldn't. He would probably miss her and his golf game, too. Damn! Oh, well, look on the bright side. He could do some more work on the new Band-Aid wrapper he was developing. He went back inside and poured himself another cup of coffee.

Jessie didn't much like running in the parking lots. The concrete floors made her feet burn after a couple of miles. But on days when she started late and the sun was already up too high, or when it was raining, like today, the covered parking lots were handy. Five laps in one section equaled one lap on the perimeter road. The sides were open, so she could enjoy the smell and sound of the rain and the freshening gardens without getting drenched.

She was running under E—his building—now. Flump, flump, flump, flump, her shoes slapped the pavement as she threaded her way at a trot between two cars, between a car and the wall, between rows, past the elevator, past the bicycle stands and the exits—closing her crude circle and starting around again.

The rain was really coming down, now—gusting through the open sides, spritzing her as she ran. She could hardly see the road, but she could tell the low spots outside were already underwater. Surely, if he were running, she'd have seen him by now. But so far she had seen no one. The regular walkers didn't come out in this kind of weather. And the E entrance door had opened only once. An elderly man had shuffled out to his car, opened it to dig a package from the glove compartment, and shuffled back through the entrance door again.

One more lap and she'd give up.

At 7 A.M. Bud finished the paper. No point in going out on the terrace to look again. Anyone jogging in that downpour would have to be part frog. He sighed. Oh, well, it might take a couple of days, but they were bound to run into each other sooner or later. He might as well work on the new Band-Aid package. His golf game would probably be off, too, so he might as well go over to the lab. His clubs were in the car. If it let up he could call the guys from there. He went back to his room to change into a pair of slacks.

Jessie finished the lap, her thirtieth, and instead of starting another, she headed back towards her entrance. No harm done, she thought. So I didn't run into him today. Meanwhile, I got my three miles in. And there's always tomorrow. "Tomorrow, tomorrow," she hummed, letting herself in the G entrance, "I

171

love you tomorrow; you're only a day away."

As her elevator door opened, and she stepped in, the elevator door in the E lobby, two entrances down, opened, too. And Bud Wellman, carrying an oversized attaché case, stepped out.

Thursday, 6 A.M.

She padded on tiptoe down the unlit hall to the living room. But the light was on in the kitchen. Fran poked her head out. "Good luck. Maybe this will be the day."

"The night," corrected Jessie. "This is like jogging at midnight. Like jogging through ink. Nobody out there but me and the owls. It is so black out, how will I know if he's running, too? Listen for the thumping of his feet?"

"Well, Webb said he's a religious jogger. No matter where he is. But maybe with his wife dying and moving and all that at once, he could be a little off his schedule. Don't be disappointed if you don't run into him the very first week."

"You mean I might have to do this for a whole week?" groaned Jessie. "This is my third time getting up while it's still dark and rushing downstairs to go tripping over the damn Muscovy ducks out there. Yesterday they were pooping all over the road. Gosh, it smells awful. Thank goodness, they don't do that every day.

"If he's not there this time, I give up."

"No you won't, Jessie. You don't want one of those predatory women this place is crawling with, to grab him first."

"I guess not. But six in the morning is not my finest hour, Fran. I can hardly tell my knee from my elbow. Have I got my shoes on the right feet?"

Fran nodded sympathetically as Jessie let herself quietly out of the front door.

In E670, Bud looked at his watch. it was 6:15. He didn't really like to jog any later than this. The air was cooler and fresher. Especially down here. And there were usually few runners out. He would have the whole bright new world to himself some mornings. And the words to "Morning Has Broken," would sing in his head.

But Fran, Jessie's roommate, had told Webb that Jessie usually jogged around seven or seven-thirty. He'd wait. He wouldn't want to miss her. Day before yesterday it rained. He could understand her skipping it then. And there could be a dozen other reasons why she hadn't jogged yesterday. It happened to him, sometimes, too. But if he kept going out at the time she usually ran, he was bound to run into her sooner or later. A nice, natural meeting. Nothing set up. Nothing awkward.

He turned over and tried to slip back to sleep, but thinking about Jessie was a relentless waker-upper. That she had become a jogger pleased him. But it didn't surprise him. He knew thirty-five years ago that they thought alike.

He got up and brushed his teeth and squirted his mouth with Binaca. He would squirt again just before he went down. It wouldn't do to have less than perfect breath the first time he saw her. Maybe even kissed her? He felt the blood rush to his face at the thought. And elsewhere. She was here. Somewhere probably only a few hundred feet away from him at this very moment. Jesus!

He showered quickly without waiting for the water to warm up, hopped out and sprayed with Right Guard. Showering before jogging? But what if he ran into her and hugged her and he smelled a little ripe? He threw on his jogging shoes, shorts and a shirt, went out to open the hall door. Yep, the papers were waiting. Bless Miss Mary; she had everything working dependably. The coffee-maker was ready to plug in. Bran muffins, danish, bagels and nova waited in the fridge. He sat down and unwrapped the paper.

The sky was growing lighter. Jessie loped along at her usual fourteen minutes per mile, half expecting to see him come trotting out of one of the entrances right in front of her.

Maybe he's running late today, she thought. Who's on such a perfect schedule? Especially when they've just moved in. Oh, God, the Muscovy ducks were right out in the middle of the road again. She would have to run around them. What if one flew at her? Such creepy, beady-eyed creatures. If Bud were running with her, he would chase them away. She skirted the two in her path, trying not to look at them. They hissed menacingly.

The second mile. Oh, well, if he didn't come out, he didn't come out. At least the ducks had retreated to the banks of the canal. She jogged past the Rowans walking hand-in-hand as they always did, because if he didn't hang on to her, she went wandering off. Dementia. Once she had crawled down the bank and fallen into the canal. Ferdie, the yard man had pulled her out and gotten his picture in the paper.

Two-thirds of the way around she passed Mr. Blosser, the elderly gentleman who walked early every morning with a vile-smelling cigar clamped in his jaw. His wife probably wouldn't let him in their apartment with it. Who could blame her? You could smell it for a long time after he passed. It was worse than the duck poop.

On her fourth lap, she ran into the Retzgers — him heading one way, her the other. They didn't walk together. Jim was about six-four and Joyce was about four-eleven and couldn't keep up, so they walked separately. Besides, they argued a lot, he shouting down from his height and she screaming up at him, and everyone could hear them. It was better this way. Sara Gunderson, the Condo Owners' Association secretary was walking with Joyce. Sara's right arm was pumping away with her stride, while her left arm, as usual, hung almost lifeless at her side. Jessie thought she must have had a stroke or something.

She thumped past her entrance again. Three miles. Her regular run. But if he was starting late today, it would be a shame to miss him just because she quit too soon. She'd do one more mile before heading into the gym for her regular windup, a fast and furious five minutes of pumping iron.

Bud finished the comics and the sports, checked the market and pushed the paper aside. Was it only seven? He felt like he'd been reading for hours. It was light out. He eased a sliding door open quietly so as not to waken Miss Mary, who often slept until after eight. He stepped out on the balcony and looked down on the perimeter road and the walkers below.

Three walkers trudged down there right now. Two men. One very fat lady. No runners. Maybe she was on the other side of the building. He tore a sheet from the pad Miss Mary used for her grocery lists. He wrote the apartment number and his new phone number on it and tucked it in his shoe. On the way out he spritzed the Binaca again and peered at himself in the full-length foyer mirror. He wasn't as skinny as he had been in high school, but he wasn't fat. A little huskier. More stomach. His hair was definitely thinner, but he wasn't bald. He looked his age, he guessed. He felt a tightness at the back of his throat. He was anxious. He let himself out and headed for the elevator.

Jessie slogged past her entrance once more. Her fifth mile. Where the hell was he? Her legs were begging her to stop. Sweat dripped from her face, and the sunscreen, running into her eyes, stung. God knows what she needed the sunscreen for at this hour. Moonscreen, when she started, maybe. Her feet slapped relentlessly on, dragging her along, like a floppy rag doll. The ball of her left foot was cramping. And there was another damned duck in her path. She'd like to give him a good, swift kick, the fat, arrogant, patriarch. Or matriarch? How do you tell on a duck? And who cared anyway but another damned duck?

In fact, they were so repulsive-looking, she bet the ducks didn't care much, either. How would you like to wake up in the morning next to something that looked like that, she thought? Probably the only reason they ever got together and made babies at all was that no other birds would do it with them.

God, she was going to have to stop. She just couldn't make another lap. He must not be coming out. Maybe he was avoiding the chance of running into her. His wife was only gone a couple of weeks. Probably the last thing he wanted at this point was to be reminded of some high-school romance.

Oh, darn. Just a look at him — that would be enough. A peek. The suspense, knowing he was there and not knowing when or if she might bump into him was almost unbearable. Damn her bastard boss, Ponchie, for making her stay and do all those cutlines last week. Dick the Prick the girls in the office called him, and they were right.

No. She simply could not jog another foot.

She turned and walked, slowly, panting heavily, toward the gym.

It was empty. She flopped on the first bench and began pulling the weights. Sweat was making her hands slippery, and she felt tears of disappointment welling. No. She wouldn't cry. Not one tear. Maybe tomorrow, she told herself. "Tomorrow, tomorrow, I love you tomorrow —" she hummed. No, she would not cry.

Bud sprinted through the first lap. Nobody walking that road faintly resembled her. Well, come to think of it, maybe Jessie didn't resemble Jessie anymore, either — not the one he knew. Maybe she was an ungodly mess. It happened to some dishy ones. But, no. Webb had said she looked great. He loped around three broad-beamed women in pastel exercise outfits and matching shoes. They were ambling slowly, gabbing, gesticulating, squealing and laughing — and taking up half of the road. They smiled and waved at him. "Are you the new man in E770?" called the tall, horsey one in the middle. "There's an association coffee for newcomers on the first and third Mondays. In the game room. Eight o'clock. Chance for you to meet everyone. Us, too."

Bud smiled politely, nodded and ran on. He sprinted through the second lap until he began passing the same walkers. The three women again. "Hi, handsome," the tall one called. She was walking on the outside now. "Don't forget the coffee. I'm bringing noodle pudding. We're all dying to meet you!"

Bud didn't smile this time. Don't encourage them, he thought. He sprinted past quickly, as though he hadn't heard.

She wasn't running. Or surely he'd have spotted her. Damn!

Or was she in the gym already? Maybe sometimes she hit the gym first? Why not take a look? Now, where did that lady, Fran, say it was again. Oh, yes. North side of the lobby. "And your lobby entrance keys unlock everything," she'd told him. He stopped at one door, unlocked it, poked his head in and saw billiard tables and bookcases. Obviously the game room, not the gym. But down about thirty feet from it was a little alcove with a bulletin board in it and with doors facing each other on either side. One said Women. One said Men. That was probably it.

He crossed over and was just fitting his key in the lock in the Men's door, when he heard a click and a swish as the women's door behind him swung open.

He caught his breath. He felt the hair rise

on the back of his neck.

He turned around. And he saw her step out and stop. Saw her mouth make a silent, "Oh!" And those familiar grey-green eyes grow huge, staring back at him.

Fourteen

"It's you!" cried Jessie. "You're late. I mean, I thought you ran at —"

"Late! Where were you?" cried Bud. "I looked all over the road for you! You're supposed to run at —"

"I ran early. Just to —"

"I ran late. Just so I could —"

He stopped and reached for her just as she reached for him. Their arms tangled, but they quickly reached again and she felt his arms wrap tightly around her. "It's okay. It's okay," he said, kissing her hair and pushing his cheek tight against hers. "Oh, God, you feel so good, Jessie Nella Pendleton."

"Moore. I'm Jessie Moore," she corrected, squeezing against him, feeling his chest hard against hers. She lifted her face to his, then abruptly pulled back. "Wait! Not out here. In the gym," she whispered quickly. They broke

182

apart, each spinning around toward their appropriate entrances, and fumbled with their keys. Hers turned and she ran in and his turned and he did the same. Inside, they raced through their separate outer rooms and dressing rooms, and into the coed gym proper.

He lunged at her but missed as she sidestepped towards the floor-to-ceiling windows. "The verticals. Close the verticals," she said, tugging at the rope that pulled them across the windows and then at the loop that swung them closed. And then she turned to him and he lunged again, connected, and swept her into his arms, and they kissed.

"Oh, gosh, I don't believe this is happening," she whimpered. "I'm such a mess. All sweaty. Oh, kiss me again. Oh, gosh. I just ran five miles. I never run that far. Oh, hold me. Don't let me go."

"Never. Never."

"Oh, Bud, where can we go? Someone will come in here. Fran's upstairs in our place. But she's usually out by nine the latest."

"My housekeeper is in my place."

"Our luck, we won't be able to think of anyplace. Better come to mine. G670. I can call you when Fran leaves. Not that we want to do anything. Oh, I mean, just to be alone for a little. To talk and to—"

"Right. To talk. We have so much to talk

about. But I don't know my phone number yet. Wait. I've got it in my shoe." He pulled out the scrap. "Here," he said, tearing it in half and keeping the scrap with the apartment number. "I'd never find my way back without this," he laughed.

"The apartments Fran showed you? The two big ones next to each other? I know which ones they are. On the same floor as ours, the seventh. I think it was E770 and the one next to it on the other side. And one on the next floor down, but I'm not sure which one."

"Right."

"That's an awful lot of room."

"I use up a lot of room. I need an office and a big lab workshop. And rooms for my housekeeper and for my kids when they visit. My son and daughter were both just here. And sometimes I just need pacing space, when I'm working on an idea. God, Jessie, you're so pretty. I think you're even prettier than you were. You look wonderful." He ran a finger over her cheeks and chin.

"So do you. All grown up. I can't believe we're here. What time is it?"

"Almost eight."

"OK. I'm going up to take a shower. I'll call you. Do you have Fran's card? Our number is on it. In case you need it."

"And I'll take a shower, too."

"Yes."

"We'll both be squeaky clean."

"Yes."

"But I love to hug you sweaty, too," he said, giving her another long tight squeeze. The door on the women's side opened and they broke apart as Belle Dinnisman, a fiftyish widow from the B building, came in. She smiled broadly at Bud and said, "Well! Hello!"

"Uh, hello," answered Bud. He turned back to Jessie and said, "Well, I'll see you around, then." He took her hand and shook it formally and each of them nodded at Dinnisman, turned toward their respective doors and marched out. Outside, Jessie said, "Let's not walk up together. Everyone will see us and talk."

"Right," agreed Bud. Then he frowned, puzzled. "Uh, what will they talk about?"

"That one will tell everyone she found us making out in the gym. And then heading for your apartment together? They'll add two and two and get a hot romance."

Bud nodded. "Gotcha." He waited a moment, then followed her, about five steps behind, across the courtyard and up to the door of the G building. In front of it, he looked stealthily around, grabbed her and quickly kissed her once more. "Jessie, I'm overflowing with feelings," he whispered. "I could leap ten feet in the air."

185

"I'll leap with you," she said, giggling. "Take your own elevator up. That way," she pointed.

"How can I wait until nine when I've already waited for thirty-five years?" He reached for her again and gave her a very long and tender kiss. "I've wanted to do that again, and again, and again. Ever since we kissed in that broom closet."

"We have a rule, Fran and I. Neither of us ever brings anyone into the apartment," said Jessie. "Or we could go there and we wouldn't have to wait."

"Wait. I know. My downstairs apartment. The one on the sixth floor. It's not knocked through yet but it's partially furnished. And Miss Mary doesn't have the key. It's the one directly under my other two. We'll go there. I'll turn the air on."

"That would be E670, I think. I'll bring a pot of coffee and some cups."

"How long will it take you to shower?"

"Twenty minutes."

"I'll leave it unlocked," he said, squeezing her hand, and he quickly strode off toward the E building.

Upstairs, Jessie let herself in, leaned against the door and listened to her heart pound for a few moments. No other sound. She called out, "Fran?" No answer. The apartment was empty. It was sublime, savoring this bliss all by herself.

Yes, she could leap ten feet in the air, too. "I am in love with Bud Wellman," she said out loud. "And I always have been. I've loved him for thirty-five years."

Fifteen

The phone rang just as Jessie stepped out of the shower. With a towel flapping around her like a toga, she ran to grab it. A man's voice answered her. "Hello, Jessie?" It was Emil Worth.

"Oh, hi, Emil. I'm glad you called. Listen, I haven't time to talk to you now but I've been telling you for weeks that I—well, that I'm not going to date you any more. But you don't listen. Or you're too bombed to register it. Please, Emil. I shouldn't have to keep telling you. It just makes it so much harder. Please, Emil. Listen to me. It's over. You and me. It's over."

"Say what?" Emil sputtered. "Jessie, what are you talking about?" Emil was not accustomed to receiving Dear John messages. Women didn't often give them to a fellow whose family owned half of California, a luxury cruise line, mining operations all over the world, three newspapers and God knew what all else. A man who had settled big millions on his first four wives. No matter if he had four brothers and three sisters to share it all with. They were all very rich already. There was enough for all of them. Not too many women—those who could put up with his drinking in the first place—had walked away from Emil. He walked out on them.

"It's over, Emil," she said as gently as she could. "I'm really sorry. I've been trying to tell you. But you're always so drunk. You don't hear what I say to you."

"But to just tell someone on the telephone—"

"I didn't want to do that. And I didn't. I've told you in person three times, already, Emil. Or tried to."

"Oh. Well, if you're sure that's what you want—"

"Yes, Emil. That's what I want. I—I'm sorry. I have to go now. Good-bye."

She started back to the bathroom but the phone pealed again.

"Jessie? It's me," said Bud. "Listen, I went to turn the air on in the apartment downstairs but it's a mess. The furniture is all stacked in the living room. Come here, instead. We have nothing to hide. It's not like the only thing we're thinking of is jumping into bed right away."

189

Jessie frowned. Did that mean he didn't want to? Had that first look at her disappointed him? He hadn't seemed disappointed. Did he think there was something wrong with jumping into bed right away? The way they both felt? Talking, they could do later. "I have to be at the office by ten-thirty," she said.

"On the other hand, if we do want to, you know, do anything—we can go to a hotel. It might be nice to do that anyway. But we don't have to. Whatever you say. Only for now, come over here for breakfast. Then when you get home from work—I can drive you there and pick you up this evening—let's go out on a date. A real date. Dinner. Dancing if you like. I have two left feet but I took lessons a long time ago. We could try. And then . . ."

"I'll be there in ten minutes. E770."

"How do you like your eggs? Miss Mary will fix them."

Eggs? Who wanted eggs? She wanted to hug him and kiss him, and touch him and feel him touching her all over. His hands on her. She wanted to cling to him for dear life. Who needed all this dancing and dinner stuff? Maybe he thought she did.

"One poached on toast," she said.

"Can you make it any sooner?"

"In five minutes if I just wear this towel. The neighbors might talk, though. If you'll get off this phone I'll climb into some jeans and throw on a little makeup."

"You don't need makeup. You don't even need . . ."

"Neither do you."

Miss Mary was frowning. She put the eggs and coffee and grapefruit halves down with a definite bump. She poured the coffee with a kind of swagger of the hand, so it sloshed in the saucers. "Miss Mary, this is Jessie Nella Moore, an old schoolmate of mine," said Bud. "From thirty-five years ago."

"Glad to meetcha," mumbled Miss Mary, looking over Jessie's head at the breakfast room moulding.

"I don't think she likes me," whispered Jessie, after the housekeeper had returned to the kitchen.

"It's not a matter of liking. She doesn't know you yet. But she's almost eighty and she took care of Bitsy from the time she was a kid. She was very loyal to her."

"I don't know if I should eat these eggs," giggled Jessie. "Wanna trade?"

"You'd kill me off before we even got to—do anything?"

"I suppose she thinks we already have."

"I wish she were right."

191

"If we'd had a place to go, I—I think she would have been," said Jessie, blushing.

"About tonight. Where do you want to go? How about the French Quarter. What hotel is close by, just in case my some mad impulse should overtake us?"

Oh, I hope so, thought Jessie. "The Riverside—right down the block."

"I'll put a suitcase in my trunk. Just in case."

"Yes, you never know," she said, blushing even redder.

"Too tell you the truth, Jessie, I don't know what we'd do if the mad impulse won. I've led a celibate life the last couple of years. I'm not some young stud. You might be awfully disappointed."

"Do you think I've been messing around with young studs? Listen, Bud. Just to be together. Kissing. Holding each other. Like in the gym just now. God, that was wonderful. I was so afraid to meet you again. I wanted to desperately but I was terrified, too."

"You, too? I was so sure that you'd take one look and keep on walking. Or you'd tell me to grow up. That was just kid stuff all those years ago. Maybe I was blowing something up in my mind bigger than it ever was."

"No, you weren't. I've fantasized, too, Bud. I thought what if you took one look and realized that I've grown a lot older? Fran had to talk me into this."

"I knew there was something I liked about her. Remind me to send her flowers."

"That's why I went jogging so early. She said she thought that's when you jogged. I went, but I was so afraid."

"Oh, Jessie! You're just as lovely now as you were then. The sweetness is all still there. But you're a woman now. Forget the French Quarter. Let's just go to the Riverside. Now, finish your eggs. You're going to need your strength to cope with this old man."

The kitchen door opened and Miss Mary minced into the breakfast room, with her apron removed, wearing a cardigan and a hat, and carrying a purse. "I'll get those dishes later, if you don't mind, Mr. Bud. I'm going to do the shopping and then I'm going to pick out the tiles for my bathroom and then I'll take those pictures you wanted framed and get them ordered. I should be back by two. There's a gefilte fish plate in the refrigerator, in case you decide to lunch in. Enough for two," she added stiffly.

Bud looked up from his eggs and sneaked a quick glance at Jessie. "Isn't that a lot for you to be doing in one day, Miss Mary?"

"No, Mr. Bud. I feel rather spry today. And I ordered a car like you said. Pampered like a princess. Now don't try to pick these things up yourself, Mr. Bud. You know what a mess you make. I don't know how you can be so neat everywhere else and such a terror in a kitchen. You can't pour dishwasher soap without getting it all over the floor. Although it won't matter now if you wreck the dishwasher. We've got two backups with all these kitchens."

Jessie had stopped midchew. She looked up and her eyes locked on Bud's during the housekeeper's speech. When they heard the front door click shut, she swallowed her bite of toast whole. His hand groped across the table for hers. She clutched at his. When they heard the lock turn, he stood up abruptly and pulled her to her feet. "Call in sick," he said hoarsely.

Jessie nodded. Cynthia could proofread for her. Someone else could do the cut lines. The calendar could run as it was. And that dumb interview . . . "Where's the phone?" she asked.

"There's one in the kitchen I think. And one in my bedroom."

"I'll use the kitchen," she said breathlessly. "Once we get into your bedroom—" He nodded and opened the kitchen door for her.

Jessie dialed with shaking hands. "Hello, Heloise? Listen, I'm—sick. I'm not going to be in until—this afternoon sometime. Stomach virus. I can't leave the bathroom. Yes, I'm taking something. That story Pontchy wanted me to do on the lady who won't get out of the hot

194

tub? If she's been there for four days now, I think we can assume she'll still be there this afternoon. Can you call and change it for me, Hel? At the Banyan Club. Don't even mention to him that I'm not there. Unless he asks." Bud tugged at her arm. "Oh, sorry, gotta run. Yeah. I will. Bye."

"What'd she say?" Bud asked, putting his arm around her and walking her back out into the breakfast room, into the living room and down a long hallway.

Jessie giggled. "She said to call the drugstore and get some milk of magnesia."

"It just dropped in our lap," Bud said, pushing open the door to his room.

"Should I run to my place and get a nightgown or something?"

For an answer, he pulled her hand down to feel his urgency. She jumped as though she had touched a live wire. He led her to his freshly made, king-sized bed. Jessie quickly kicked off her shoes and pulled her shirt over her head, where it got stuck. She'd forgotten the sleeve buttons. "Dammit," she mumbled, dancing with impatience and pulling the shirt down again to unbutton them. Bud's shirt and pants were already on the floor. As she tore off her shirt, he tore off his shorts. He turned to her and

195

yanked the zipper on her jeans and in one deft move peeled them and her panties down to her ankles. Squatting down, he kissed her calves as he lifted her feet and slipped her panties off.

"Last one in is a rotten egg," she cried, tearing the spread back and letting herself flop onto the sheets, while Bud was still nibbling at her knees. He turned her over and quickly unhooked her bra, then turned her back again and whispered in awe, "My God, Jessie. I can't believe you look like this!"

They fell on each other in a ravenous frenzy of hugging, kissing, licking, tasting whatever parts they could reach, opening their mouths so wide their teeth scraped. "I can't wait. God dammit, not so fast. No, I can't wait!" cried Bud. In two seconds he was on top of her, and his finger had slipped in and then behind it, *him*—hard, pushing—pushing.

But not quite all the way. Should she help him? She licked a bit of saliva onto her fingers, reached down and wiped him, lifting up, and there! He plunged in—ahhh! He held her so tightly she could hardly breathe and then she cried out, "No-no-no-no, not-so-fast, not-so-fast, not-so-fast!" He thrashed, grinding into her and half-stifling her guttural cries—grinding, groaning—until he fell limply against her.

* * *

They lay there, gasping, feeling each other's hearts thudding, thudding, and then easing slowly to a softer beat.

Bud rolled over, reached for her and drew her into his arms. "Jesus, I'm sorry, Jessie. That was the most wonderful thing in the world for me. And nothing for you."

"Oh, no. Just being with you and having you hold me and touch me and seeing you go crazy like that. I'm flying higher than I've ever been before." He held her for a time, saying nothing.

"It's not surprising you couldn't wait the first time, Bud," she whispered. "Feelings build up. Fran is very smart about these things. She's been married five times and had a lot of different — you know — close friends. And she says that first times never work very well. All those stories where everything is perfect and everyone comes together are hogwash. Hardly anyone ever comes together and it usually takes practice to work out the details. That's what she says."

Bud shook his head. "I'm amazed. It's been over a year. I was worried that I wouldn't be able to — "

She stroked his face. "Bud, darling Bud. It's all right. Just hold me. Touch me." He pulled her close and mumbled into her neck.

"When I first got married — I have to tell you this, Jessie — I often just let myself explode like that. Bitsy hated sex. She tried to put up with it. She thought of it as a wife's job. But I always felt I should get it over with in a hurry. And I did it so seldom, I guess I was always ready to explode.

"Harry was a decent man, Bud. Kerry thinks her dad was a saint. You knew him — sincere, hardworking, honest. But — dull, I guess. No sense of humor. And sex was something *he* did. It wasn't something *we* did. I was just something he used when he did it, like you use a Kleenex to blow your nose. I used to ache to be touched all over and kissed all over and to feel excited. I was so naïve. I thought oral sex meant talking dirty. But just being here with you is so very much better than that. I'm so — so — elated. On a cloud up there somewhere, where I know only wonderful things are coming."

"I want to make you happy," he whispered. And he began kissing her shoulders slowly, licking, tasting them, and then her breasts — wet, loving, stroking kisses — more and more of them. And touching with warm fingers. Her delight was almost unbearable. And when she thought she couldn't stand it another minute, he turned her over and began licking the back of her legs, kissing them — and her knees, and thighs — and then her inner thighs. And he turned her again and lifted her pelvis like a cup of fine wine, and drank—kissing, caressing and exploring her lovingly with his tongue. "Come for me Jessie. Come for me."

She was moaning with delight. She couldn't help it. Lifting, straining, to be closer and closer, for more and more. Gasping for breath, as the sensations overwhelmed her—building, building and suddenly exploding into a long spasm of ecstasy that tripped into another. And another. She shivered and shivered through echoes of her peak, finally slumping with a languor that drained her to her bones.

Bud moved up beside her to hold her tightly, murmuring into her hair, "Oh, my Jessie, my little Jessie. Be happy, my little Jessie."

Tears slipped from her lids. He kissed them away. "That's crying for happy," she whispered. "Oh, my God, Bud! Oh, how could anything be like that? Nothing's ever been like that . . . in my whole life . . . God! I never knew I had so many hot spots. Every place you touch me . . ."

"You were worth waiting for, Jess. I knew. All this time, I knew it would be wonderful. That we belonged together."

"I'm a rag doll," she said slowly. "I think my bones have melted. Funny. There's no way you can imagine some things, is there?"

"And I loved being in you, honey. The next time I'll stay in you longer. And feel you around me." He lifted up on one elbow. "But we have to work out a place. We don't want to have to always wait until Miss Mary goes to the store. She's like my mother, Jessie. She's retiring soon. We've been talking about it for months. But until then, I can't just chase her out, and we can't make love while she's here. Not for a while, until she gets used to the idea. But I'm going to get that apartment downstairs fixed up right now. For us. I could put my workroom there, too."

"Whatever you say. Whenever. Wherever. The back seat of your car, if you say so. I just want to be with you."

"For tonight, let's settle for a hotel."

"Okay. But for now, I've got to get out of here," said Jessie.

"Can't you stay," he begged. "Just a little longer."

"I can't. My job. There's tonight." Leaping from the bed, she caught sight of herself in the dresser mirror, shrieked, grabbed her shirt and threw it over her head as she raced for the bathroom.

Bud followed her. "What was the shirt for?" he yelled through the closed door.

"Because I look terrible—like I do when I get up in the morning, and I don't want you to take a really good look and scream," her muffled voice came through the door.

"Don't be silly. You look fine. And I wouldn't scream. Open the door. Let me take a good look at what you're like after making love."

"No."

"Please."

"No. You'll scream."

"No I won't. Open the door. Let me see."

A pause. Then the door slowly swung open half way and Jessie's face appeared.

Bud looked and yelled, "Agh!"

A wet washcloth came flying out and hit him in the face.

He laughed and she ran out and hugged him. And he led her back to the bed.

"No, I can't get in there again. I've got to get out of here. I have an interview. I'll see you tonight."

"I want to love you again, before I let you go," he said, walking her back to the bed and pulling her down with him and nuzzling her neck. "Now. Just once more."

"I don't have much time," she began, "and I have to get dressed—"

He began licking her breasts, pushing them together with his hands and lapping at them rapidly, all over, squeezing them gently at the same time. She felt herself melting. It was so good.

"Oh, well," she murmured, leaning back slowly, languidly, sensuously savoring his touch.

Oh, that wonderful feeling. The warmth. She let her eyelids close and she slipped into a dream of very real delights. And she purred, "I guess I've got a few more minutes."

Sixteen

"I knew you'd ask that," pouted Melodie Drimple, the shapely young woman sitting in the Big Banyan Club hot tub. She twisted a strand of bright orange hair around a pink-taloned finger. "For one thing, I'm not in the water all the time. I'd shrivel up like a prune. Sometimes I'm only sitting on the edge. And this cabana," she pointed to the little stucco building behind the tub, "has a bathroom. I mean, what do people think? That I use bedpans? I mean, we're trying to set a record here, and even if you don't eat or drink much, you have to go once in a while. But don't put that in. I mean, who cares about that? Everybody has to go to the bathroom. The interesting part about this is that you can practically live your life in a hot tub. Eat, make phone calls, order groceries. Other things, of a romantic nature. You know what I'm saying?"

"How old are you, Miss Drimple?" Jessie asked. She looked like a nubile fifteen. A slightly over-the-hill Lolita.

"Ax me no questions, I'll tell you no lies."

"How tall?"

"I'm five-three and I weigh 108. My waist is twenty-two, bust thirty-six, and I duck into my cabana every two hours and change into another gorgeous suit."

"When you change suits, is that when you — er —"

"Go to the bathroom? Yes."

"Tell me, Miss Drimple. Just why are you doing this?"

"Like, it's a promotion. The club wants everyone to know they now have seven hot tubs and seven cabanas. You can entertain in them just like you would take a table in the lounge. They have their own nibble-and-nosh menu. They'll serve drinks."

"Their own menu? What's different from what you can get in the lounge?"

"They have all the pretzels and chips and dips and stuff. I think anything that melts if it falls in the water is okay. But they don't serve peanuts, or fried cheese or like that. Nothin' that would clog the plumbing. You know what I'm saying?"

"One last question, Miss Drimple. How do you keep from getting wrinkled like a prune? You're not wrinkled at all."

"I smear myself from head to foot with Vaseline. It's the only thing that works. I'm a little slippery, but otherwise, by now I wouldn't have any skin left."

Before she left, Jessie talked to several Big Banyan members who strolled past the tubs with a remarkable lack of interest. It didn't look as though they were going to be a big hit among this rather conservative bunch. She grabbed a PR kit on the way out.

Back at the office, Richard Pontchetrain looked up as she logged on at her terminal. "Believe it or not, I have more important things to do than play your secretary, Jessie," he snapped. "Weren't you supposed to be in earlier? You've had a dozen calls."

Heloise, standing behind Pontchy, gave her a quick wink.

"Well, the hot tub interview took forever, Mr. Pontchetrain," Jessie ad-libbed. "She kept disappearing into the cabana. And it was pulling teeth to get any kind of answer from her when she came out. Not much of a story, but I'll manage to make something of it." She had learned early on at this job to let Richard think, as often as possible, that it was taking a heroic effort to turn a given assignment into readable copy. He thought heroic efforts were part of a normal work load.

"Well, hurry it up. Cynthia is waiting to get that page laid out." Behind his back, Heloise shook her head, then gave the boss the finger.

Jessie began rapping out her story. "Slippery Siren Tries For Hot Tub Record." Twelve column-inches later she messaged Cynthia, "Save fourteen inches for hot tub story. Plus picture." She would write two inches of ending later. First, the messages.

One from Bud. He would call again at three.

One from Kerry. She dialed her daughter's dorm number. "Oh, Mom, I've had another fight with Doug. About my not having orgasms again. Everybody has them but me. It's not fair. I come so close sometimes. But not quite. I don't think so, anyway."

Jessie digested that statement. "If you had, you'd know," she said. "Have you tried a book on — on the subject?"

"It didn't help, but we're going to try another one. And Doug is going to talk to his godfather."

"His godfather!"

"Well, he says he could never talk to his father about anything like that. But he's very close to his godfather. Oh, and Mom, if Doug can come down this summer for a week, could he stay with us? I know your apartment rules and I know what a prude you are, but I'm a different generation and otherwise how can he come? I won't see him all summer. Please, Mom."

"I'll see what Fran thinks," said Jessie.

Next, she returned Fran's call. "Did you do it? Did you run into him jogging? Was the third time lucky? Did you run upstairs and screw your heads off?"

"Sort of," Jessie laughed. "I ran until I was exhausted and then collapsed in the gym. And when I gave up and I was leaving to come back upstairs, I bumped into him. And we had breakfast at his place. His housekeeper was giving me such mean looks, I was afraid to eat. We didn't know where to go, but his housekeeper went out shopping so we stayed there. We're going to a hotel or his apartment on the fifth floor tonight. I told him he couldn't come to our place. That we have rules and it's sacrosanct."

"I think this is one time we could make an exception. When I'm not there."

"No, let's leave it this way. It's always such a mess, and I get the feeling that he's completely organized. I don't want to scare him away."

"You're probably right. Webb said he was, anyway."

"Well, let's let him learn about my congenital sloppiness gradually. I don't want to turn him off. If we're going to make any exceptions, let's make one for Kerry and Doug. She wants him to visit this summer for a week and stay in her room."

Fran thought about it for a few seconds. Then

said, "Listen Jessie. They're young. They're in love. A week wouldn't kill us. If having me around would make them nervous he could come when I'm in Georgia visiting my mom. But otherwise, any time's okay."

"Oh, Fran. You are a peach of a roommate."

"I know. So back to the romance. The magic was still there?"

"And how! He's perfect. Just perfect."

"Wait a couple of weeks. None of 'em are perfect."

"Well, maybe he's a teensy bit too neat."

"In case you get in early—not likely—but in case—I might be out. I'll be having dinner with what's-his-face—Webb. Now he wants to pick my brain about a couple of new developments west of Pine Island Road. It's always something with him. And he'll nag at me if I don't wear lipstick. Is that nerve! I won't be real late, that's for sure."

"Gotta hang up, Fran. I have a call waiting."

She clicked the receiver and took the next call. *Community News,* Jessie Moore."

"Well-Tech Labs—Bud Wellman," said Bud. "Hi, honey."

"Hi. What's up?"

"Don't ask. But I called to tell you that I love you. In case I haven't told you."

"Me, too. But I can't talk, here."

"I just want you to know I'm on top of the situation. Had my lab manager get me a couple of men to pick up and deliver mattresses, kitchen stuff, linens—the necessaries. I'm having champagne sent over. That caterer, Word of Mouth, is filling the fridge with God knows what. And I've having the deli send over dinner. Roumanian steak, gefilte fish, matzoball soup, salad, baked potatoes, bread and cookies. How's that?"

"Gosh, that's a lot of food. We're not staying for a week. I'd settle for an egg-salad sandwich."

"Okay. I'll get one, but I'm ordering the rest too, or you'll probably be picking at mine, and I think I'm going to be very hungry. What time will you get there?"

"As soon after six as I can."

"I pulled a TV from upstairs. And if there's something else we need, at least all we have to do is run upstairs for it."

Jessie cupped her hand over the receiver and whispered into it, "I wish I could be there right now."

"Hurry, as fast as you can. I'll get there about five or five-thirty. We'll make love all night long. I love you."

Jessie hung up and turned to the hot tub story, but she could almost feel Bud's tongue on her shoulders.

This was going to be the most wonderful night of her life.

Seventeen

Fran tasted the lentil soup, then shook in more curry. When you didn't use meat you had to do more with the seasonings. And after Webb's cracks about vegetarian food being "so much garbage," she planned to give him a jar of soup to show him how wrong he was. So this batch had to be perfect. She heard a key in the front door and came out to greet Jessie. "Oh, yeah, I remember you. Didn't you used to live here? And where have you been for the past three or four days, as if I needed to ask?"

Jessie dropped her purse and briefcase on the foyer floor and followed Fran back into the kitchen. "You are absolutely glowing," grinned Fran. "For God's sake, don't go near the heat alarms."

"I know this is wild. I haven't been in here for more than half an hour at a time since Saturday. Long enough to change or grab a few

210

clothes or do the mail. I've been with him every minute I'm not at work. And if it was up to him, I'd never get to work."

"So why'd he let you off the hook tonight?"

"He had to go to Chicago. His daughter heard about us and was all upset. Plus he had some business to attend to. He's moved two of his labs and the headquarters down here, but some company is still up there, I'm not sure what. He referred to all that so quickly I didn't get it all sorted out. And I had other things on my mind. Ahem. He wanted me to go up there with him, but I really can't just walk out on everything like that. I've got major events to cover Saturday and Sunday. And Monday is deadline day. He wasn't too happy about it. But to tell the truth, Fran, as glorious as it all has been, I'm almost glad I can't go with him. I need a night's sleep so badly I can taste it. I've lost three pounds, just like that. Oh, does that soup smell good!"

"I baked a couple of potatoes, too, just in case. I figured if you didn't show, I could dice up the extra one and throw it in the soup. And I peeled some kiwis." She dished up big bowls of soup and put them on the counter with the steaming potatoes, mashed chick-peas with grated onions, and the fruit.

"My gosh what a potful. You expecting company or are you going in business?"

"I made enough so I can give a big jar to Webb. To prove to him that he's wrong for once. That low-fat stuff can be scrumptious."

"If he doesn't love this," said Jessie, tasting the soup and sighing, "something's wrong with his taster. It's your best ever."

"So the story's having a happy ending. You and Bud. And you were afraid to meet him again."

"So was he. And he was afraid that when we made love, nothing would work because its been so long for him and because he'd be trying too hard because he wanted me so much and maybe I'd be disappointed. He was so nervous."

"Well, at his age, I don't blame him. At his age, men have more problems with their peckers than Carter has pills. We women may be slower to get the hang of sex, but once we do, we can go on forever. The only thing that stops us is we keep running out of men. They start dropping like flies around forty and pretty soon there aren't enough left to go around."

"Oh, Fran!"

"It's true. And men are the opposite of women. They're so oversexed when they're young, but they poop out early. Some break down altogether. Some have these malfunctions. Premature ejaculation is more common than you'd think. I was a receptionist for a shared doctor's waiting room when I first came down here, for about two months—the only work I could get. There was a urologist, a psychologist, a psychiatrist, and a proctologist, and believe me, between them I saw it all. A lot of men, even if they're not out-and-out preemies, are so fast the woman can hardly ever have an orgasm.

"And one of my husbands was one. He could get hard again another time or two, but he'd just do pop goes the weasel again. So what good was it?"

"No, Bud wasn't like that. He was wonderful. And the second time we took forever. My gosh, I've never had such a lover. Now let's change the subject. I don't know how I'm talking to you about such things. But you're like Kerry. You can say anything that's in your head, anything. And somehow I just join in."

"Well, it all sounds pretty damn good to me."

"The only problem is, he doesn't understand how busy I am. We don't have a housekeeper here and a company full of people to do what we ask like he does. Oh, and did I tell you, he's a doctor, too. But he never practiced. Because his business had taken off by the time he got his degree. Say, this soup is fantastic, Fran. And it smells so good, too."

"Webb better like it. He's such a nut for ecology and preservation organizations, you'd think he'd realize the planet would be better off if everyone went vegetarian. When he heard about my plants and how Plants for the Planet is trying to save all the different varieties, he got all excited and wanted to learn all about it. That's why I went to dinner with him again. And sure enough, now he's joining up. He obviously doesn't think anything like that can be successful without his sterling touch."

"Really? He seemed nice enough to me. Bud says he's the best guy but he marries the worst women. And in between he has droves of girl friends. Webb knew Bud's father-in-law before he knew Bud. I gather Webb was a gambler, too, when he was younger. But one day he was thinking about Ben and what happened to him, and it got to him so that he just quit. Cold turkey."

"Interesting," said Fran. "Only it doesn't change the fact that he's bossy. A lot of women like being bossed. But some of us don't."

"Do I detect a little interest there, Fran? I hear he's a sexy guy."

"Hell, no. I don't need those complications in my life anymore. All he's looking for is another notch on his bed post. And I think hit-and-run sex should be as illegal as hit-and-run accidents on the highway. I'm keeping my mouth shut now. Until I get my Greenberg money and see if Lally wants me to work for her. She values his opinion, so I won't make any more waves till then. He can call my veggies rabbit food or garbage until then. But I don't need any more heartbreak. I get laid once in a while. That's all I need. And Stash has an inexhaustible sex drive. There's a lot to be said for that."

"And you said Clark was impotent."

"So what? That doesn't stop him from taking care of a woman better than some of these so-called potent pricks who only think of themselves. Pleasing you is his mission. He knows more tricks than a card shark. Of course, he lies and he cheats. But only with high-class women. And if he's seeing you, he might be seeing another woman too, but that's all. He's never messing around with so many he can't keep their names straight like some of these jerks. When I was first dating him, he was also seeing Iva Dorain, the eye doctor. While she was separated from her husband. At the Tower Club a week ago, there were three of his past lovers sitting at the same table when in he walked with Dilly Bingham. They're separated, you know, the Binghams. And someone at the table noticed her and said, 'Now, what would a nice girl like Dilly, with a lovely husband like Bobby, want with a roué like Clark Curley?' And the three of us caught each other's eyes and had to look away. We were all grinning wildly. We knew exactly what she wanted from

Clark. And he'll deliver. We could all tell you that."

She refilled Jessie's bowl, and then her own. "Stash doesn't have a lot of money, so you just go to his place. But Clark does it first class. Champagne, fancy hotel room, room service."

"It all sounds so depraved and yucky. I keep thinking I'm all grown-up now. I've had several affairs, and I don't expect a scarlet letter to pop out on my forehead anymore. I don't even feel guilty. But I still have to really like the guy. I need a relationship and I can't handle more than one at a time. And there's no way I'd ever share someone like that."

"Never say never, Jessie," said Fran. "You never know. Oh, maybe you want to check the phone messages. I didn't do it when I came in. I'll go ahead and put these in the dishwasher."

The first call was from Emil again. "I take it we're still going to the Salvation Army thing at Le Dome Saturday night? I have it on my calendar. I'll pick you up at seven." She had forgotten. Way back months ago, before he went off the wagon, Emil had suggested they attend this dinner together. Well, she would let him pick her up, but she would cab home. And this time, she would make sure he got the message.

The second call was from Bud's sister. "Jessie Moore, this is Cecily Lumbar, Bud's sister. I picked him up at O'Hare and in the car he told me all about you. And what's happening. It's beautiful. He looks marvelous. Ten years whisked off. He had told me a little bit about you years ago. In fact, he's mentioned you several times. My husband Dell and I are coming down next week and I'm dying to meet you. Oh, and don't worry about Esme. She's just very—analytical about things. It's really none of her concern. See you next week."

Then two calls for Fran. One from Lally. One from a client. And one from Bud. "No hijacking, no fuselage flew off. And we landed in the right airport. Dull trip. I love you. I love you. God, do I love you."

Then four or five calls about social events.

And the last call was from Kerry.

"Mom, you won't believe this but I had an orgasm. About three of them, in fact. Last night. And one this morning. Boy, they're neat! Now I see what all the fuss is about. Thank Doug's godfather. When Doug talked to him he said we needed privacy. And he gave Doug the money to take me to a nice hotel and get room service and everything. We did it last night. And it worked like a charm.

"We tried another book, too, before that. It didn't work but it was funny. Doug said we had to try some of the things, so we'd get in some utterly weird position and he'd say 'Excuse me a minute.' And he'd pull the book out from

217

under the pillow and say, 'Now, how does that part go again?' He had me in stitches. I guess we'll go ahead and get married. Not soon, you know, someday.

"I'll be in Doug's room tonight if you call."

Eighteen

Emil's stretch limo, probably the longest one in Miami, pulled up to the guardhouse at seven. Jessie had forgotten to call down to tell the guards to expect him but they waved him in anyway. Guards, she had found, rarely stopped a limo or a Rolls. "If I were a burglar, I wouldn't have any trouble getting past any guardhouse in town," she once told Fran. "I'd just rent a limo or a Rolls."

That was one reason she had agreed to go on that first date with Emil. He intimidated her. He lived in a world of wealth and connections she knew little about. But he was very pleasant the few times he had talked to her — at Dade county assignments she was covering. Then he asked her to that Forum luncheon at which Diane Sawyer was speaking.

She hardly thought there was much point in accepting. Surely the fact that they lived in different counties made her Geographically Undesirable. And why would a man like him be interested in a nobody like her? But she had enjoyed talking with him. And she couldn't resist the idea of arriving at the Forum in that limo. He was able to arrange for her to have a few minutes of private interview time with Sawyer, whom he knew slightly, and he had turned out to be a smart, courteous escort. But he was on the wagon then. And she had not yet seen him up close when he wasn't.

Fortunately, the guard did call up to tell her the limo had arrived. Yver followed the perimeter road around to the G building, pulled into the underground parking and waited, while Jessie hurried down. She had told Bud on the phone that she was taking Emil to this party. Bud wasn't exactly thrilled with the idea, but she had explained that there were several men in town with whom she had no romantic relationship, but whom she used as escorts as needed. "This will kill two birds with one date," she said. "I can't get Emil to accept the fact that we're kaput. He gets drunk and makes these terrible calls. Crude. So this will take care of some unfinished business. I'll give it to him very bluntly and get him out of my hair for once and for all, I hope."

Emil appeared to be relatively sober. "How are you, tonight?" he said, reaching over to kiss her. She pulled back. He frowned, slumped back to his side, and asked his routine question, "Have a good week?"

"Marvelous. I ran into an old flame," she answered, knowing Emil would register little of her answer. "And we picked right up where we had left off thirty-five years ago."

"Busy at the office, too?"

"When I got there. I played hooky to spend every minute I could with Bud."

"Well, you do have such a busy schedule. What was that about hooky?"

"From the office. To be with my friend."

"Well, seeing friends is important. What friend was this?"

"From back in high school. I was madly in love with him."

"Old friends are the best," he said, reaching for his glass and the decanter of Scotch to splash another hefty belt into his glass. He turned on the limo's small TV, to catch the news.

"So this is our swan song tonight, Emil. Are you listening to me? I have found another love."

"They still haven't got channel six coming in right, but it's amazing how well that Fox Network has done. It's a performer." He reached down to pat Jessie's thigh, and when she pushed his hand away, reached for her crotch. Jessie slapped his hand, hard.

"Now what was that for?" he cried, looking confused.

She grabbed his glass and set it on the bar, then flipped off the TV. "That's to get your attention. You never listen to what anyone says, Emil. You ask me questions and then never listen to the answers. So listen now. Do you hear me."

"There is no need to behave this way, Jessie. I'm listening."

"I just told you that we are through. Over. Kaput. I am not going to see you or talk to you any more. I have told you and told you and you don't hear me."

"I heard you. I didn't think you meant it."

"I mean it. I will enter that party with you tonight and I will sit with you, but I am not staying very long. And I am never going to see you again. Do you understand what I'm saying?"

"I am not an idiot, Jessie. You make yourself perfectly clear."

"I am seeing someone else. It's serious. I am committed to him. So do not grab me. From this moment forth, hands off. Do not call me. We have nothing more to say. I hope you get your drinking under control again. You're such a nice person when you're sober. Special, even,

Emil. But you are a slobbering, repulsive lout when you're drinking. I'm so sorry to tell you that but it's a fact and somebody should."

She clicked the TV on again. "Now watch the news and leave me alone until we get there."

Emil picked up his glass and drank half of it in a long swallow. And stared, frowning, at the news.

He behaved himself well enough at the Miami Beach restaurant, as far as Jessie knew. She didn't see much of him. They walked in together but she immediately began moving around alone, her pad in hand, first checking with the benefit chairmen to get the essential facts—headcount, profit to charity, the spelling of the chairpeople's names, etc.

And then working the crowd, chatting with this one and that, picking up anecdotes, opinions, notes on dress. She peeked into the dining room and scribbled the details of the decor—pink tablecloths, pink and white flowers, donated by Birmingham, probably. Tiny crystal boxes for favors.

But by the time they took their places at the table, she could see that Emil was already losing it. In garbled speech, he ordered another double from the waiter, sat down and began butchering his seafood appetizer before the rest of the table were seated, spattering cocktail sauce every which way. Jessie gave him an elbow jab and hissed, "Wait!" He looked around, dropped his fork with a clank, and swiped his water glass which crashed over, dumping its contents in his lap.

"I've got to get him out of here," she whispered to Sally Martin on her left. "God! And we just got here." Sally, who had done the party seating, nodded. "Make our good-byes, and apologize for me, would you, Sally? I've got what I need for the paper."

She took Emil by the arm. "We have to go out to the bar, for a minute, Emil," she whispered in his ear. If she had told him they were leaving, he would have started long, incoherent good-byes to everyone at the table. He pulled himself unsteadily to his feet, finished his drink with a long, loud slurp, gave her his arm and staggered towards the bar. Once there, Jessie just kept him going. Out the door. Onto the sidewalk. Luckily Yver was already waiting right down the street and he spotted them walking toward him. Together, they helped Emil inside. He flopped limply into his seat, his head fell back, his mouth fell open, and he was out.

"Take me home first, please, would you, Yver? He'll never know the difference."

Yver nodded, drove around the block, and

then headed west on 41st street, towards the causeway to I-95. At the Hammock, thirty-five minutes later, she thanked him. "I won't be riding with you any more, Yver. Remind him of that in case he forgets. Thanks for everything. Take care of him."

She felt relieved. And sad. Emil was such a waste. That first two months of dating, while he had been on the wagon, had been fun. Even sober, he was accustomed to having people cater to his needs, wants and opinions. Sometimes he was inattentive. Sometimes he made her feel like an afterthought. But drunk, he was impossible — sloppy, clumsy, crude. And sometimes, like tonight, a zombie.

The phone was ringing when she let herself in the door. Did it ever stop? "Where were you honey? I've been calling for an hour." It was Bud.

"I told you I had this thing to cover tonight. The only reason I'm home this early is because Emil was so drunk he barely made it through the cocktail hour. And tomorrow, I've got the Single Sugar Daddies dinner up in Boca."

"I don't like the idea of you dating anyone else."

"Just escorts. Nothing romantic."

"To tell you the truth, honey, I don't much like the thought of you spending time with another man when you can't find enough time for us. And you work too hard. Too many hours. How are you going to fit in time for us?"

"I managed this week."

"But you couldn't come here with me. I think you'd better quit that job. What do you need it for? The one thing I can do is support us."

"But I can't give up my whole career just like that, Bud. You're here today but where will you be tomorrow? And I've wanted to be a writer all my life. I know I'm going to get an offer from a real daily here, soon. I've already had a nibble from the Boca paper. I can't just throw that all away."

"I'm not here today gone tomorrow, Jessie. How can you think that? I love you. You love me, don't you?"

"Do you have to ask?"

"Then we should be together. Life is so short. We should be — you know, a couple. With each other all the time. Married."

She caught her breath. "Married?"

"Well, yes. That's what people in love do, isn't it?"

"Sleeping in the same bed together every night? Eating breakfast at the same table together every morning? If this is a proposal, Bud Wellman, you snuck it in the side door."

"It's what I should have said to you thirty-five years ago, Jessie. But I couldn't. Or I thought I couldn't. I was stuck."

"Tell me why, Bud. You've never really told me all of it."

"Now? Over the phone?"

"Yes. I need to hear your voice right now. And I want to know."

"Well, when we moved to Arlington Heights, the Glicks had that big place across the street. Acres of lawn. Fences. My dad had died and we were broke. Mom worked as a nurse and I did lawns, walked dogs, whatever I could. Sess baby-sat. Bitsy got this crush on me first time we met. I was thirteen. She was nine, a chubby little princess. She was my shadow from then on. I did yard work for her father, Ben, and cleaned his buildings. He took a liking to me and my family and he hired me often, and then just began helping us out. Maybe because we were the only other Jews in that neighborhood, although God knows neither one of us was very religious. We just kind of understood each other.

"Bitsy always said she was going to marry me and everyone kind of assumed after a while that she would. Ben planned to send me to medical school. And Sess to college. He paid to straighten Sess's teeth, and for my appendix operation. And when my mom got sick, he supported us."

"I can see how you felt obligated."

"He was a maverick, with a heart of gold. But an incurable gambler. I really loved him. He became like a dad to me. Taught me to play golf. Even took me fishing in Canada once. Yes, I was indebted to him. I was a science nut. I had already invented a couple of things, looping test tubes, stuff like that, and Ben helped me apply for patents. I started making a little money on that stuff my first year out of high school.

"I had no time to mix with the other kids much in high school. I was working or puttering or with the Glicks. And then at the science fair when I met you and I came home and told Ben I was going to take you to the prom, he was hurt. He was having a lot of trouble with his diabetes by then. And I guess he'd felt at least he didn't have to worry about Bitsy. I would marry her and take care of her. He talked about those plans and then he said, 'Bud, you just can't do it. Go to that prom with this girl and you'll break Bitsy's heart. You gotta take Bitsy if you go.'

"I realized he was right. And I owed him. And that Bitsy would be devastated if I took you. I guess he could tell how much you'd gotten to me. So I listened. I sent you that note. Only Bitsy and I didn't go anyway. On prom night, Ben rented a big car and a driver and took us out on the town. All dressed up. He knew you were from a different school. I guess he didn't want to chance us seeing each other again and he knew that my prom was the only place it was likely to happen.

"Ben put me through premed and the start of med school. By then I started making real money and I took over. Bitsy and I got married when she was eighteen. Ben got sicker and sicker. Emphysema, too. And the sicker he got the more he'd gamble. Out to Las Vegas all the time when he could barely breathe. By that time I'd set up several labs in or near doctors' offices. And my patents were bringing in more money all the time. By the time I was twenty-five, I had the medical supply company started and was consolidating the labs. It seemed like everything I touched turned to gold. And everything Ben touched was a disaster. When Ben died — he killed himself, you know — he owed money all over the place. I took care of all of it.

"The marriage was a disaster right from the start in a lot of ways. She thought of me like Prince Charming in a fairy tale. Not a man. To me she was like a pet. Like my kid. Hell, I always say I should have adopted her, not married her.

"Sex was an ordeal for her. She hated it. I tried to make it better. But what did I know,

229

then? Esme came along and later Benjie. And you don't walk out on kids."

Jessie sighed. "You know, Bud, mine wasn't great either. Harry was just the guy I went to that prom with. After you couldn't go with me, I felt I had to go with somebody. But he was a decent person. And he kept hanging around. I kept hoping you, or someone like you would happen in my life. Meanwhile, Harry hung in there. And finally after going with him for so many years, I married him.

"I got through life with him. I thought of leaving him a dozen times. But it wasn't his fault. He didn't do anything wrong. It was me. So I stayed. We didn't have Kerry until we had been married for eight years. He was a devoted father. Just not very interesting. And then when he got so sick—how could I run out on him then?"

"We're so lucky, Jessie," Bud said. "We're still young enough to enjoy each other. To eat each other up. We have so many plans to make. If you really feel you have to write, I guess we'll work it out. I know that my flying off to Chicago and California all the time isn't so great. Especially if you can't come along."

"Sometimes I probably can."

"But whatever it is, your work, mine— let's work it out. We'll figure a way. Nothing's going to keep us from getting married and being together."

"Oh, Bud, hurry home. I need you."

"Soon as I can, honey. Keep everything warm."

"Any warmer and I'll go up in smoke. Goodnight, my love."

When she hung up the phone, she did a little dance around the room. Married. He wanted to get married! It was too good to be true.

Something would probably come along and mess it up.

"Daddy, are you sure you realize what you're doing?" Esme's voice dripped with deliberate patience, as if she were talking to a child. "Mother, your wife of thirty-four years, is barely cold in her grave, and here you are womanizing all over Florida like a dirty old man."

Bud was taken aback. What the hell was this? "Hardly womanizing, Es, although I thank you for the compliment. One woman at a time is probably all I can manage, if that. And I haven't had her out of Fort Lauderdale."

"You think it's funny, Father? Something to joke about?" When Esme called him Father instead of Daddy, he knew she was really tied in a knot.

"No, Daughter. I think that at this time of

my life, women are to be taken very seriously. Calling me a dirty old man is like calling cutting your fingernails an operation. But flattery will get you nowhere, Daughter. And where did you get the idea that I am 'womanizing' as you put it?"

"It was Webb, sir," volunteered Needle, putting down his fork for a moment to answer. Esme wasn't eating. She almost never did. He had never seen her take more than four bites of anything since she was twelve years old, so strong was her determination not to become fat like her mother. Esme, as a result, always looked emaciated. Her cheeks caved in, not out. Her hipbones protruded from her skirts. Her sternum protruded farther than her minimal bosom. But she did look very smart in an almost tubercular way.

In restaurants, it was Needle, who had no such compulsions, who finished both their plates. "I had called to ask about those North Carolina properties," he explained. "Near Yancy, sir. Land values have taken off so in the past five years in that area and we thought that if perhaps you and Webb still had some of that property, we should talk to you about it. And we would have talked to you, but because of your—bereavement, we thought we would check the status with Webb first and then—"

"You're veering, Needle," Esme interrupted.

"We can bring that up another time."

"And he said why didn't I talk to you and I said I hadn't been able to reach you for a couple of days and he laughed and said probably because you were too busy womanizing down there. And that half the females in Florida were after you."

"And it never occurred to you two that Webb might be kidding?" asked Bud.

"True," Esme conceded. "Webb does fancy himself a humorist. But he is a womanizer himself. And I remembered the old adage, it takes one to know one."

"Well, I'm sure that's an accolade Webb does not usually apply lightly. But this time, it was like calling Bess Truman a flirt. He was only kidding."

"Not altogether. I called Aunt Sess and asked her if she had heard anything and I told her what Webb had said and she said she only had heard of one woman, but it might be serious. All right, one. But I still say, how could you?"

The waiter began clearing their plates. "The dessert specials tonight, lady and gentlemen are—"

"Just coffee," said Es.

"Same," said Bud.

"Just a little coffee ice cream for me," said Needle. "With a little fudge sauce. And maybe a little whipped cream. And bring us a plate of cookies."

"Esme," said Bud when the waiter departed, "How could you, during your mother's funeral, sit there and chatter and giggle with your cousins about your new damn business? Why couldn't you make it to Florida for the viewing there? Why did Aunt Sess have to make all the arrangements. She wasn't related to your mother. You were."

Esme turned white. Needle grabbed her hand and said, "Now, wait a minute, sir—" But Bud went on.

"Those were questions I didn't ask before. I figured we each have to find our own way. Although it didn't seem to me that you were looking very hard. Let me make a couple of points very clear, here. One, what I do with the rest of my life is my choice. Not yours. You don't even get a vote. Two, if I decide to womanize, I will. If I decide to see one lady only, I will. If I decide to get married again, I will. I have not even considered the idea of asking your advice or permission."

Esme seemed to flounder, groping for the right words. "Well, I—it's just that—don't be upset. It's just that when I see you acting strangely, it worries me."

"Afraid that I might blow my lid and lose everything, Esme? I don't think it likely. And even if I did. You already have the trusts you got at twenty-one and thirty. And you and Needle are building your own empire. You don't really need any more help from me. If I gave everything to charity, you'd never miss it."

Both Needle's and Esme's heads jerked up at that, and a look of horror flashed over both faces.

"Your brother, Benjie is the only one we should worry about. He has no business sense. He keeps giving his money to his causes—trying to save the planet for you and me, and planet-saving doesn't pay very well. With him I have no choice. I've had to set up some kind of an income trust or he'd be out in the street one day. Something locked up so he can't give it all away to the Sierra Club."

"Daddy," cried Esme in terrified awe, "do you mean to say that because Needle and I have worked hard and achieved a certain success, that you would punish us by cutting us off?"

"Your idea, Es. Not mine. But I'll consider it as I do all your suggestions. I don't know where this preoccupation with my business and my money comes from all of a sudden."

"Because I care what happens to us and to our children," she cried.

"What children?"

"When we adopt them, and their children, and Benjie's if he ever gets married to a woman instead of his work."

"I just don't understand all this insecurity, Es. You've never wanted for anything. Never known anything but comfort and plenty. Where is this coming from?"

"I know all about insecurity," Esme retorted angrily. "Don't tell me I don't. Mother told me all about Grampa Ben. How he lost everything. She told me all about you and Grandma Letty. How Grandpa Wellman left you destitute and Grampa Ben had to pay for everything for you and send you and Aunt Sess to school or you couldn't go."

"To college. We made it that far. He didn't totally support us except for a short time. I always worked. My mother worked. Sess baby-sat."

"But Mother told me over and over how rich they had been. And how Grampa Ben still lost a lot in business and then he gambled the rest away. How horrified he was to realize they had nothing. Absolutely nothing. They were poor. And he couldn't face it. And that's why he killed himself."

Bud was jolted by her words. "I didn't know you knew that, Es," he said heavily.

"Mother always made us promise never to tell you we knew. Benjie knows, too. She said it was so horrible. To have to move from the big house into that little one you had been brought up in. She had to make her own bed and she didn't know how. She used to laugh at that part. And when she talked about going to the supermarket herself, instead of just letting the cook take care of everything.

"She said it was only about six months before you managed to move back into the big house. But no maids at first. Only a cook because that was the most important. You were all getting pretty tired of Kraft Dinner and grilled cheese sandwiches. And that's all she could make. And Mother said that your labs and Medi-Quip were so successful that you were a millionaire before you got out of med school. But if it hadn't been for you, she would have been desperate like Grandma Letty. Worse. Destitute. She wasn't a nurse and couldn't do anything to earn a living. She would have ended up on the street. That's why she wanted me to learn some kind of work. So I could make a living for certain if you ever lost everything. Deep down, she didn't trust business."

"But her father was a gambler. It was a sickness. That's how he lost everything. That's what killed him, really. I'm not a gambler, Es."

"No, but what about alcohol? I heard about how you were drunk at the viewing down there."

"One bender does not an alcoholic make."

"And you were acting so strange while we were sitting shiva."

"Dell got me some tranquilizers and I took them. I was a little discombobulated, you're right. But I'm not likely to jump off a building tomorrow."

"And all those women. At the funeral and my house the next couple of days. And Sess said something about so many women coming to the wake down there. Who were they? What was that all about?"

"Damned if I know. Ask Webb. He says it happens to all widowers."

"No, things are definitely not adding up, Daddy. And I happen to think that a family owes its future generations the obligation to take care of what it has. So nobody ends up in need. Or in the street."

"That's very considerate of you, Es."

"I'm never going to end up one of those people in the street, Daddy. It could happen to anyone. You don't care what happens to me. But I do. I am never, never going to be poor and homeless. I'm not going to let my children or their children be poor and homeless. And if you won't see to it, then I will. Needle and I will."

The waiter finally served the coffee. Bud watched this daughter of his meticulously add sweetener and about four drops of cream. Where did she come from? She was totally unlike Bitsy. Totally unlike Benjie. Unlike Ben. Certainly not like him or Sess or his mother. Not like any of the cousins or Ben's devil-may-care brothers, who still went scuba diving at eighty.

Her hair was straight and black, like Ben's. Bitsy's had been curly and blond. She had Ben's nose until she was sixteen, when it was redone. Bitsy's skin and eyebrows. His own business drive. Only she was more fiercely determined than he had ever been. She had her own personality. And, it now appeared, a streak of insecurity a yard wide.

"Now what was this about North Carolina?" he asked, firmly changing the subject.

"Well, sir, it was—"

"No, Needle, dear," Esme interrupted. "Don't bother Daddy with that. He's made his position perfectly clear. Anything we want, we can get for ourselves. So we will." The waiter brought a tray of chocolates and began refilling their cups. Esme stood up. "Don't bother. We've had enough. Quite enough."

Needle quickly gobbled the last of his ice cream, stuffed two little cakes in his mouth, and swept the wrapped chocolates off the tray into his pocket. Then he stood up, too. "Goodnight, sir," he said stiffly, taking Esme's arm. And with Needle chewing vigorously, they marched disdainfully out.

Nineteen

Fran swung the door open so hard it smashed against the doorstop. She marched in and bawled, "Jessie, are you here? Where are you?" She slammed the door with a crash that shook the wall.

Jessie ran to the foyer to see her roommate dumping—practically throwing—her purse, umbrella, sweater and briefcase on the cluttered foyer table. "That son of a bitch," she snapped. "Who does he think he is?"

"Who?" cried Jessie. "What are you steaming about? What's the matter?"

"That friend of a friend of yours. Weston Webber. Webb. That's what!"

"My friend? My gosh, what'd he do?"

"He just invited me on a two-day jaunt with him, that's what. Told me to get my hair done. Said I should lop off the braids and put on some makeup and not wear tennis shoes. The fucking nerve."

"You're right. That's certainly nervy. And rude. I mean, I tell you that all the time, but that's different. I'm your friend. I tell you because I think you'd do better in business, and be more likely to meet someone worthwhile, if you didn't always look like one of the Bobbsey twins at camp."

"Are you on his side?" Fran asked.

"Why would you think that?"

"Because he said almost the same thing. Except he said I look like one of the Rover Boys."

"I'm on your side, Fran. You know that. Come on, make yourself a cup of your camomile tea and calm down and tell me about it." Jessie led Fran into the kitchen where the counter was littered with packages and with bowls of oatmeal, rice cereal, raisins, almonds and such. "My gosh, what's all this out for?" Jessie asked.

"I thought I'd get everything ready to make granola before I went over to meet him, so it wouldn't take long when I got back. I mean, all he was going to do was pick my brain about those two new developments. Only he also said he had a proposition for me. Ha! I'll say!" She put the kettle on and dug two camomile tea bags out of the tea caddy.

"None for me," said Jessie. "I'll have a nice depraved diet Coke. I need a saccharin fix."

"No, have the tea. It'll do you good."

Jessie said nothing. When Fran was in a state like this, you didn't argue with her.

"It was at the deli," Fran said, pouring the contents of the largest package into the largest bowl. "I met him there and he already had a booth. Just because he drives me nuts being so bossy and he didn't ask me where I'd like to eat, I ordered the most expensive thing in the house—the mixed smoked fish platter. Enough for two people. And without even looking at the menu, he says to the waitress, 'Bring me the same thing.' She says, 'It's very big, sir, enough for two.' And he tells her we're very hungry. Can you imagine if I did that to Stash, he'd march out and let me pay for it."

"Sounds like he's a sport, at least."

"Or showing off. Anyway, he tells me that he has several properties he's considering upstate and in North Carolina. And he'd like me to go with him on a two-day swing to look at them. He says I have a good feel for what the lower income buyers will go for. I almost choked on my whitefish. And he goes on about my having a good feel for the market here. These properties are not all exactly in my area of expertise. But he says he'll pay me a consultant fee of two hundred a day, and expenses. Meals and that."

"Well, what are you screaming about? I think that sounds terrific," said Jessie.

"And I said, 'What if I don't have any invaluable comments to make?' And he says, 'Well, then I'm no worse off than I was. But I think you have a good insight. You sure picked up on Bud's house. Houses like that don't usually sell in five days,' he says. 'You have a touch,' he says. 'You could probably be selling a more lucrative market, if you'd dress like a grown-up and fix your hair and wear a little makeup. What you do on your own time is fine. But when you're selling, you have to think of your market,' he says. 'Some people will back off from someone who runs around in jeans and sneakers and braids. They don't buy expensive properties from people who look like field hands, blah-blah-blah.' Can you beat that?"

Jessie shook her head sympathetically.

"He told me Lally's interested in working with me, too. She thinks I'm straight and dependable. But she wants to be sure I can cut it in the class department. He says he knows I can, if I just will, but why do I run from it? I tried to tell him I think all that's superficial and women shouldn't have to do that to get ahead. And he says what should be is one thing. What is, is another. I was ready to slug him. He's so damned logical. You can never win in a discussion with him."

Jessie studied her friend. Then frowned. "Maybe because sometimes he's right. Maybe you ought to take a few bucks from the fat commission you got on the house and invest in a few really smart outfits from Neiman's and a day at Elizabeth Arden."

"And then he says," Fran continued, as though Jessie hadn't said a word, " 'I don't know why you're so determined to look ugly. You couldn't, if you tried. Even if you took ugly pills. You're basically a good-looking woman. Good figure. Good bones,' he says. So I said, 'Not that it's any of your business, but I don't care about such things. Women use them to catch a man. I've had five husbands. I'm not interested in another. The only reason I listen to you at all is the money. The commissions on Bud's apartments and house are more money than I've made all year, so far.'

"So he says, 'Good. Now you're making sense. Don't you see? You could be making that kind of money all the time. And I'm not bringing any consultant along who looks like a camp counsellor. We go the day after tomorrow. Pick you up at seven in the morning.' So I'm going. But I tell you, if the S.O.B. makes a pass at me, I'll rent a car and split so fast his head will spin off."

"Wanna borrow anything of mine to wear?" asked Jessie.

"No, I've still got a bunch of fancy clothes in the back of my closet, from when I used to dress that way. And I'm going to get my hair done and my nails. Disguise myself as one of the ladies who go to lunch."

Jessie left Fran busy with her granola and went to check the answering machine. It was blinking. A call from Kerry, of course. That kid spent more on phone calls than she did on food.

"Oh, Mom, I'm so glad you called back," said Kerry.

"Don't I always?"

"Mom, don't say I told you so, but it's this stupid guinea pig."

"I told you so."

"Mommy, it's growing before our very eyes. I had to get two bigger boxes for it, already. All it does is eat and shit. Talk about boring. And when I let it out of its box—"

"Oh, honey, should you?"

"—it shits all over the room. You'd think it would be grateful to be let out and it would wait until it gets back in. He hops around from one end of the room to the other, dropping turds wherever he pleases. And he's not easy to catch anymore."

"Just be glad you don't have another one around or he'd be doing something else, too and you'd soon have more guinea pigs than you know what to do with."

245

"One is already more than I know what to do with. But I can't just turn him loose. What would happen to him?"

"Well, call all the grade schools and nursery schools around and ask if they can use him. Some schools have little petting zoos."

"Mom, you're a genius. I'll do it first thing tomorrow."

She went back in the kitchen and told Fran. "Yeah, that's a good idea," Fran nodded. "It's probably too big to flush down the toilet by now."

"Oh, Fran!"

"Well, I guess I feel better now. The granola's made. I drank my tea. And I'll see what happens on the trip. You never know what men are up to. They usually have an angle. Something on their minds. And most of them think with their pricks."

"Maybe it's just that he likes you," suggested Jessie.

"No, I don't think so. He's the type that goes for bimbos and ditzes with round heels. The kind that don't wear panties. Lally said he's been married five times, too. I'd say that between us we've exhausted the marriage possibilities. But if he can give me a leg up into the real estate fast lane, I'd be grateful enough to put up with him temporarily. There's so much money to be made there. He's right about that. It's like shoveling it up in the streets."

"Uh-huh," said Jessie. "I heard that slip by. You'd be grateful? How grateful?"

"Well, how do I know? Everyone seems to think he's a very sexy guy. I don't see it myself, but who knows?"

Jessie grinned knowingly. She opened her mouth to say something, then closed it. She wouldn't confide in Fran yet about what Bud had said about getting married. She didn't want to until she was really positive it would happen. It was too wonderful. A fragile, lovely dream. Talking about it might scare it away.

Twenty

The plane was late. Passenger pickup was a snarl of honking cars three-deep, shouting travelers and exasperated airport police threatening tickets to those who dallied. Jessie had to maneuver the labyrinth and circle around the airport three times but she was too elated to care. Even when a BMW driver gave her the finger for cutting into a lane he apparently considered his private domain, she only laughed, instead of pointedly taking down his license number. Not that she ever reported such gestures but it made her feel better if the driver thought she was going to.

Her heart was still thumping wildly. It had started when Bud called at eight to say he was coming in tonight instead of tomorrow morning. She pulled the draft of the story about Sugar Daddies from her briefcase to proof it while she waited, or until a policeman made her move again. That should calm her down. It had been a boring affair. Her escort, Charlie Able, couldn't hear, his hearing aids were useless, so he interrupted constantly because he never realized you were talking. And he never heard your comments. You both did monologues. You might as well have never said a word to each other all night.

Amazing how many men in their fifties and up were essentially deaf. Fran was right. She said men's ears usually went even before the sex. And it took a long time for guys to admit either. But Larry was a willing escort. Socially, he was impeccably acceptable. And he was content with a sterile relationship.

Her story concentrated on what made a good Sugar Daddy. She peered at the printout, but the words wouldn't register. Her eye-to-brain connection kept shorting out. Interference from a competing signal. The words, "He wants to marry me! He wants to marry me! I love him so much!" kept dancing blithely across the page like subtitles in a foreign movie.

"I'll call as soon as I get in," he'd said.

"I'll pick you up. What airline?" she'd replied.

"I don't want you driving that time of night."

"I do it all the time and I really want to. Fran is out of town. She and Webb went to tour some properties together, and she gave me a special dispensation. You can stay here tonight."

"I can't wait. I've just had the most ridiculous visit. My daughter is behaving like a jackass."

Jessie's heart sank. "Because of me, you mean."

"Because of a lot of other things, too. I'll tell you about it when I get home. Delta 406, 11 P.M. Keep the car doors locked. Just be at the curb. What's doing with Webb and Fran. Anything?"

"Go catch your plane. I'll tell you when you get here. It's so much like a soap opera around here, I keep expecting someone to break in with a commercial."

Too bad she wouldn't really have time to pick up the apartment. Oh, well. He'd just have to understand.

Ah, finally. The automatic doors swept open and the first passengers strode out. Two couples. Then three teenagers dragging dufflebags. A redcap with a cart followed by three women. Then a whole string of passengers toting bags and hand-carries.

The man in the car in front of her got out and opened his trunk and the three teenagers hoisted their dufflebags into it. They all scrambled into the back seat and the car pulled out of line.

Where was he? Oh, if he missed the plane she'd have a tantrum. And after she'd torn through her room shoving things in drawers and under the bed and emptying the waste baskets and garbage and cleaning the toilets at the speed of light. She had taken a quick shower, squatted over the bidet, dusted herself with talcum and swabbed her neck with Joy.

She was ready. Boy, was she ready!

Without her glasses, Jessie could hardly make out the passengers coming through the door. But she didn't want to have glasses on when he saw her. Wait, that one in the duck pants and the jacket and the single suitcase. It was him! "Mister, you sure look gorgeous in duck pants," she said aloud, rapping her horn lightly. He spotted her and broke into a run. She opened the door; he threw his case in the back seat, climbed in the front and reached for her just as she reached for him. They bumped noses, cried ouch together, tried again, hugging each other tightly. "Oh, I'm so glad you're back. So glad, glad, glad." His lips found hers. They kissed.

"Blat!" the car behind them honked. Bud broke away. "Get us out of here."

She squeezed his knee and took off. While she navigated the airport exit, wallowing in togetherness, they didn't say a word. Radio WLYF was playing, "Just Call Me Angel of the Morning." At the end of the song he said "I will call you angel in the morning."

Jessie squeezed his knee again. It seemed the

loveliest thing to say.

When she pulled into her Hammock parking spot, she asked, "Do you want me to take you back to your building, first? Do you want to check in with Miss Mary or anything?"

Bud shook his head and laughed. "And ask her for permission to sleep over?"

In the elevator he took her into his arms and held her tightly. "Ah, bliss," she thought, feeling him so close. At the third floor the elevator stopped and they broke apart guiltily. The Glovers from five got on. "Oh, hello, Mrs. Moore," said Mrs. Glover. "Back from one of your parties?"

"No," said Jessie. "I mean, yes. I had a couple of things to cover today."

"You do lead an interesting life, dear." The elevator stopped at five. "Well, time to call it a night." Her glance moved to Bud. Jessie's eyes followed. Oh, dear. Lipstick on his mouth. Mrs. Glover looked pointedly down at Bud's suitcase, then gave her husband a knowing glance. "Well, you have a nice evening now," she said sweetly as they got off.

"Nasty lady. I think we just made the Hammock Gazette."

"What's the Hammock Gazette?" asked Bud. The elevator moved up.

"That's what Fran calls the gossip and news network here. I think we just hit the front page.

We'll be all over the building by tomorrow."

The door opened at six. Standing there, waiting for the elevator, were Monty Mover from across the hall, and his latest live-in, an exotic Latin with a few wrinkles on the face but a waist like a young Elizabeth Taylor's. "Hi, Jessie," said Monte, as they stepped off. The live-in nodded. Jessie smiled, turned right and headed through the door into her hallway. Bud coughed, picked up his suitcase and turned left and through the door into the hallway leading to the F and E buildings as Monte and his live-in boarded the elevator.

The elevator door closed.

A second later both hallway doors flew open. Bud burst from one and Jessie from the other, both laughing helplessly. He took her hand and they headed back toward her apartment. "That was quick thinking," she whispered.

"We couldn't have another reporter confirming the scoop," he said. "Sorry about that, Jessie."

"Forget the Gazette. Right now I want to jump into bed with you so badly, I don't care if they put it in the *Wall Street Journal.*"

Inside her apartment, he took her in his arms again.

"Oh, this is the nicest place to be," she crooned. "Safe with your arms around me like this. Do you want the tour before or after?"

"After," he replied. "First things first. Just lead us to your bedroom."

* * *

When he followed her into the room, he stopped short. Her bed was unmade. Four dresser drawers were open, with bras and pantyhose hanging from two of them. Her desk was a mess. "I clean it up when I get time," she said quickly and began taking off her clothes. He did the same, looking about at the sweaters and anklets piled on a chair, and the books piled everywhere. She closed in and kissed him on the mouth. That got his attention. He began kissing her back with feeling. She pulled him with her to tumble onto the bed and they began to grab at each other and touch and kiss with such urgency, that they both knew this time neither one of them could wait. And this time it was she who came almost immediately and with such a frenzy that she tripped all his restraint and his orgasm crashed onto hers, and they both cried out and clung together, straining, rocking, groaning—then easing into a delicious trembling in each other's arms.

"Jesus, babe, I just can't believe this. God, how I love you, Jessie." They lay there a long time after the trembling faded, half drowsing, half awake. After a while, he brought her hand to his mouth and kissed her palm. He rose and put his head down to kiss her breasts. With his eyes closed, he explored slowly, with the tips of his fingers, the corners of her mouth, the rise of her brow, her neck and the hollow at the bottom. And then he began tracing the path again, with his mouth.

Jessie was almost purring. How good his touch was. How sweet. Almost sweeter than she could stand. And what an incredible invention a tongue was. What a wonderful instrument of love.

He took his time. But soon she was arching toward him again, touching any part she could reach, and then they were fused once more, and she was pushing closer and closer, until they and time and space were entwined sublimely in one long throbbing burst of almost unbearably intense pleasure.

She collapsed and pushed his head away. And he wrapped his arms around her hips, and laid his cheek on her stomach.

They half dozed for a time in the comfortable stillness. And when he stirred and reached for her hand again, she said, "What is that song that says nobody does it like you do? I'm not the most qualified expert, Bud, but you've got my vote. It's too good to be real."

"And you've got mine. But know what let's do now?" he said, sitting up, abruptly. "Let's get something to eat. All this wonderful exercise has made me ravenous."

She led him to the kitchen, which was unusually neat after her hasty efforts earlier. There she mixed a can of salmon with some mayonnaise and heated up Fran's lentil soup. "No meat in it," she said as Bud praised it. "Fran won't have meat in the apartment. And she grows a lot of the herbs and veggies on the terrace. Wait till you see it in daylight. Sometimes she has a box of landcrabs out there that she's feeding corn meal or something for a while before she makes a kind of gumbo out of them. I've never quite been able to make myself taste it but it smells incredibly good.

"She grows all these different varieties of vegetables that would otherwise be dying out if some people didn't grow them now and then and save the seeds. Right out there on the terrace. Plants of the Planet for Tomorrow it's called. Your friend Webb got all excited about it and joined. And she supports all these ecological societies. She's a little like your son, Benjie, I think."

"No wonder she and Webb hit it off. He's into all that, too. Save the whales. Save the dolphins. Save the man-eating nasturtiums. So what's up with those two?"

"Hard to say. Mostly antagonism, it seems. They keep seeing each other, but there's always a business reason. She says he's egotistical and bossy. And he keeps telling her to wear makeup and get her hair done and stop dressing like a field hand. I tell her the same thing."

"She's actually very pretty," said Bud.

"But she thinks men are mostly jerks. She's been married five times. Mainly lemons. She's helping a couple of nieces through school and she says she has no time to waste on anything but working and relaxing. You have to love her for her beautiful soul. But she thinks most of us women have our priorities all messed up."

"But Webb seems interested?"

"I don't know if it's her, the woman, or her, the consultant."

"Consultant?" Bud guffawed. "He knows more about land and development potential than anyone I've ever met."

"Well, they get back tomorrow. You can quiz him then."

"No way. Webb never says a word about his women. God knows he's had enough of them but he's very closemouthed."

"Hey, I'm not so sure she'd class herself as one of his women. She says he's never made a pass. But okay. Next subject. Your daughter. Wanna talk? Or not. Up to you."

"First give me some more of that soup. Your roommate can cook for me any time. That's fantastic." Jessie filled their bowls again and sat opposite him at the counter. "Well?"

"Well, Esme's hard to talk about. Hard to figure. She's always been a curious person to me. She's a great businesswoman — tough, shrewd. She and her husband, Needle, are fast becoming tycoons. Benjie, my son is the soft one. Wants to save the world. Like Webb. Only Benjie goes out in the wilderness and risks his life for it.

"He got buried in a mudslide the day his mother was killed. Didn't make the funeral. We didn't even know if he was alive or not for three days. Broke his arm. He's the best-looking kid you've ever seen. Tall, handsome, dark curly hair. I'd say my daughter got the brains and my son the looks, but that's not true either. He's brilliant. It's just that he has no fire under him to make money or a name, like Esme does. Only to save the planet."

"I think I like him already."

"He's the gentle one. Esme's the tough one. She thinks I have no right to be seeing anyone so soon. She actually thinks I'm losing my marbles and she and Needle better take over all my businesses and money and life, and I should get a little place in Chicago and retire and moult."

"I can kind of understand her feeling about us. And that it's so soon—"

"But that's my business. Not hers. Funny thing is, she was never close to her mother. Bitsy adored Esme and Esme tolerated Bitsy. Barely. And she was apparently anything but grief-stricken during the funeral. It seemed that to her it was a big social event. She let Sess handle most of it. She was all wrapped up in her business ventures. She hardly talked of anything else."

"It may be just her way of handling her loss.

Of protecting herself, because she can't handle it. She may change after a bit."

"Maybe, but don't count on it, honey. Right now she's furious with me because I told her it was none of her business. When she finds out we're getting married, I think the shit will hit the fan."

They made love again in the morning—laughing, teasing, chasing each other all over the bed. "Whoever invented the king-sized bed ought to be knighted," sighed Jessie. "I never knew getting up in the morning could be this much fun."

"I've been imagining this scene for thirty-five years," Bud said, hugging her fiercely. "And my imagination didn't even come close."

"Obviously, all your celibacy didn't have any effect on you."

"Not since that day downstairs at the gym door," he laughed. "I've been walking around with half an erection ever since. I might end up owning a drugstore."

She looked at him blankly. "You might what?"

"You never heard that old story? This guy gets an erection that won't go away. Nothing helps. He has to stay indoors for three days. So he's desperate. That night, he puts on a baggy coat and hurries over to the nearest drugstore, which is owned by two older maiden ladies.

"He goes in and says to the one sister, 'Can I

talk to the pharmacist?' And she says, 'I'm the pharmacist. What can I do for you?' He doesn't know what else to do so he tells her, 'Well, I don't know how to put this but I've had an erection for three days and it won't go away. Is there something I can do? I'll try anything.' And he opens his coat and says, 'See? What can you give me for this?'

"The pharmacist lady frowns, says, 'Just a minute,' and goes in the back for a while. Then she returns. And she says, 'Well, I talked it over with my sister. And business is kind of slow lately, but would you take fifty dollars and the drugstore?' "

"If it ever happens to you," Jessie giggled, "let me know before you go to the drugstore. I'll give you a written testimonial. You're worth a lot more than fifty dollars and a drugstore."

Bud crawled out of bed, stood up and yawned. "Thank you ma'am. My pleasure." He glanced around the room again. "Boy, this place is a mess, Jessie. I think I'd better get you a maid." He began throwing on his clothes. "I better hurry over to my place, honey, and see if there are any important messages. I'm kind of expecting a couple."

"I'll make some breakfast while you're gone," she said. "Oatmeal okay? And a bagel, if we have any?"

"Anything," he nodded. And grabbing his suitcase he headed down the hall to the front door.

She heard it open and close. He was gone.

Jessie showered. She began dressing. He hadn't called by the time she finished. She put on the oatmeal and coffee, did her makeup and her hair and took in the morning paper. He still hadn't called. She started to read and finished the whole Lifestyle section before the phone rang.

"Jessie, I'm sorry about this, but something really important has come up. I—I have to catch a plane for—San Diego—right away." His voice sounded different. Tight. Strained, somehow. "No time for breakfast. Sorry. Big emergency."

"Oh, no! You just got home. When will you get back?"

"I—I'm not certain. And I know you can't come with me."

"Not without a little notice."

"That job of yours gets in the way. We'll have to work that out somehow. I'll call from the airport if I can. Or when I have time out there. Tell Webb to call my office if you hear from him. I—I want him to get out there fast, if he can. He's not in. I left messages around for him. I love you, Jessie. I'm sorry as hell this happened. But I have to take care of it. Bye, honey."

Jessie hung up slowly. At first she puzzled over the funny sound of Bud's voice. What was he sorry as hell about. And wait a minute. "He thinks *my* work is too demanding?" she said out

261

loud. "And he's the one who has to run out of town for an indefinite stay with a big ten minutes' notice. And I'm too messy? I have to change? He doesn't have to adjust — I have to change? I think we have a couple of wrinkles to iron out, here, my love. The minute you get back."

Twenty-one

The gatehouse called up at exactly seven-thirty. "There's a Mr. Webb here for you."

"Send him around to the G entrance. I'll be right down," said Fran. On the way out she glimpsed a smart-looking woman in the foyer mirror.

Pleated cream-colored linen skirt. Navy linen blazer. Red silk shell. Navy pumps. Was that her? The halo of curls. The red lips. She felt like Cinderella. Utter nonsense. But two hundred dollars a day for what would amount to a short vacation, she supposed she could put up with it.

Webb was waiting outside the lobby door. He took one look and then whistled. "Oh, wait a minute, it's you," he said.

"Who else were you expecting?" snapped Fran. "I'm still the same old field hand."

"Yeah, but you sure clean up good," he grinned, opening the door to a teal blue Jaguar.

The first stop was a small development in West Broward. They drove up and down the three streets that were "in." "We're considering taking this one over," said Webb. "Olson, the original developer, died about six months ago. His son and daughter are running it. Right into the ground. They don't know beans about building houses. And they haven't spoken to each other in years, until this happened. Instant chaos. They'll just lose it if they don't sell it. Buyers have pulled out. Three law suits. Incredible liens."

"Is there enough potential to make it worth all the hassle?" asked Fran.

"That's why I brought you here. Houses aren't my thing. What do you think? Could you sell houses here?"

"I could sell houses on the moon if they were cheap enough, and these look to be. There's such a shortage of starter housing anywhere. No-frills stuff will sell because people are willing to go through the drag of commuting to get a place of their own. Sometimes there's no other way. That's how suburbs happen some-times. But will you be able to make enough on such cheap houses, by the time you get through with the law suits and liens and god knows what else that hasn't surfaced yet? And why did they put up this one fancy Leslie Park model in the middle of all the junk?"

"Because they were incredibly stupid," laughed Webb.

He drove up past Daytona where they looked at a beautiful six-unit building on the beach. "They're practically giving this one away. They can't get insurance," said Webb.

"Of course not," Fran nodded. "Look at the erosion. It's going to start tipping any minute. No matter how cheap you get it, you have to have your head examined, if you buy it. Unless it's for an instant turnover. And I'd never be able to let any client of mine buy that kind of trouble. One storm and no house. Just a mort-gage to keep paying on forever."

At the airport, they caught a plane for Jack-sonville. "Good timing," said Fran, when they were in the air in about twenty minutes.

"Good planning," said Webb.

In Jacksonville they looked at an office build-ing, and a shopping center. "Shopping centers and office buildings are not my area of expertise," she said. "But I never let that stop me from saying my piece. I don't know how the numbers go but I do know this is a beautiful area. That people up here have to shop, too, and that if you have a good grocer and drug-store in here, the location is so good and the natives up here have so much disposable in-come you could probably print money."

Webb nodded and said nothing.

They lunched at an unpretentious little fish place where Webb was obviously a regular. "You want the crabs or the yellowtail, Mr. Webb?" the waitress asked. "Or we have cobia today, too. You like cobia."

"I think we'll have the yellowtail, and red chowder."

"I don't get a choice? What other colors do they have?" asked Fran.

"Two. A white one and a brown one. But they're not as good. This one is practically a bouillabaisse. Trust me."

"Seems to me I've heard that phrase before," laughed Fran. "All right. It's your party. But bring lots of bread," she told the waitress.

"Bring her a little taste of the other two, Patty," he added. "And somehow, I feel like a gin and tonic. What would you like to drink?"

"I don't often drink," said Fran. "But why not? I'm not driving. I'll have the same."

When their drinks arrived, Webb toasted her.

"To Fran. The best-dressed woman in the place."

"Which we both know is an absolute hub of fashion."

"Nothing wrong in starting small," he said. They took long thirsty swallows. "I think it'll take two of these." And he signalled the waitress. Then he turned to Fran and studied her face. "You're actually a looker. When you obviously have all the raw material and you know what to do with it, why do you choose to ignore it all? You're a beautiful dame running around disguised as a dowdy one."

"It takes time and energy to look like this," Fran shrugged. "I have better uses for both. And for what? To catch another man?"

"Well, I've struck out five times, too, but I still enjoy the game. Why don't you?"

The waitress brought their refills. They drank thirstily once more and he signalled the waitress yet again.

"You're awfully goddammed nosy, Mr. Webber."

"The word is curious."

"My marriages were nothing that doesn't happen to thousands of other women. You would soon be yawning."

"Try me."

"Okay. Number one. Neighborhood hunk. Opened a gas station after coming home from the navy after World War II. Ten years older than me. Got married just as I was starting college. After a couple of months he wanted me to quit. Made fun of 'all those jerks with their little piece of paper.' Got very insistent. Pushed me around a bit. Gave me an ultimatum, and I chose school.

"Next, one of my fellow students. Intellectual. So sweet. Started coming on strong. Insisting. Pleading. Good family. Brilliant. I was on scholarship. He was doing graduate work and paying his own way. He said we'd wait about sex until we were married. Which was fine with me. I was terribly moral in those days. The honeymoon and the whole marriage was a disaster. He was a homosexual who was fighting it. He didn't mean to use me. He really loved me. But not sexually."

The waitress brought another round. "From Mr. Morrison," she said.

"Morrison's the owner," explained Webb, looking around, spotting his host and waving thanks. "Go on."

"He ran away with a psych major—a guy. He died of AIDS four years ago. He left me some money. He didn't have much. But it helped with my nieces' tuition.

"It was about five years before the next one. I still believed in marriage and love and all that. I met Chuck Metowski. Big ugly, wonderful Chuck. Not terribly erudite, but at least his ego was strong enough that my degree and my work didn't threaten him. He was a little loud and his tastes were simple but we had a great five years."

"Only five years? What happened?"

"Some kind of very rapid cancer. Anaplastic or something like that, I think they called it. It only took a couple of months from the first spells.

"Number four was the batterer. But in case you think I just married anyone who asked me, not so. There were two affairs in between. One drunk. One cheater. Very classy. He moved around in the best triangles. Quadrangles. Polygons. Both bought rings. I backed out."

"I would think with your looks, there'd be a line waiting," said Webb.

"Looks. It's amazing how much stock people put in looks instead of in important things, isn't it?"

"Whoops. Objection sustained."

"Had enough?"

"No. Go on."

"The batterer seemed as nice as Chuck. What a disguise. The first time he hit me was after I had been visiting my sister and I came home and the ash trays were dirty. They had been dumped but there were ashes in the bottom. Do you really want to hear all this?"

Webb nodded. "And he said Harry Prince had been over. I went into my bathroom and saw this lipstick on my counter. Not mine. I came out and said, 'Gene, your friend Harry left his lipstick.' I thought I was being funny. Harry could have had a girl with him, for all I knew. But he got so angry, he socked me and then grabbed me and shook me until my head rattled. Then he calmed down. I almost couldn't believe it had happened. He was so upset. He said he couldn't believe it had happened. I shouldn't have listened.

"I took a couple more good ones. The second one put me in the hospital. He tried to kill me. He would have. But I threw a skillet through a window and someone heard the crash and heard me screaming. They called the police and an ambulance. I didn't go back. But it's amazing how many women do. Now, let's talk about something else."

"Might as well finish. Only one more."

"All right. The last was the love of my life. Louie Dimitri. He was A-okay. But he had emphysema. That was where I met Jessie. Her husband Harry was getting treated at the same hospital, Miami Heart Institute. We're so different, but we became friends. We went through the same hell together. Except that Louie was my big romance, and I don't think Harry was anybody's big romance. He

270

was just a man who tried hard."

"But I still don't see why you're so against glamour. It doesn't matter in your private life. But when you're out there hustling—it can help."

"I've about decided to go that route again— for business. But it's such a chore. It's okay for brunettes. A little lipstick and they're on their way. But I'm so fair. My lashes and brows are colorless. My skin is pale. My hair is pale. My eyes are light. If I don't paint a face on my head every morning you can hardly tell which is my front and which is my back." Webb chuckled. "It saves a lot of time to skip all that, since I'm through with the boy-girl business, anyway."

"Altogether?"

"Anyone can get laid if they want to. And I do sometimes. But no relationships."

"That's putting it plainly enough. Interesting, but something's missing," said Webb. "Only I guess I'll have to find out over dinner, or we'll miss our plane to Asheville."

Fran looked down at her empty plate. "It's gone, so I guess I must have eaten it, but I don't remember a bite. I'm not used to drinking. I might be a little sloshed. Did I like it?"

"You loved the fish and you liked the red chowder best. See, I told you you would."

"Okay, so this time you were right."

* * *

They snoozed on the flight to Charlotte. And on the leg from Charlotte to Asheville. Fran had a slight headache by the time they landed. A car picked them up and took them to the vast, stone-walled Grove Inn. While Webb checked them in, she looked about the great lobby with its huge stone fireplace and the verandas with their sweeping vistas. What a place for a tryst, she thought. How could her opinions possibly be worth the cost of this trip? And if he wanted to go to bed with her, why didn't he come out and say it?

The pitch would probably come tonight. After dinner. A little rap at her door. And he would probably be standing there in his robe. He'd say, "I wondered if you were still awake. I can't sleep. Sometimes I have a lot of trouble getting to sleep at night."

And Fran knew just what she would tell him, before she gently closed the door in his face. She'd say, "Then why don't you get a night job?"

When Fran came in at ten, Jessie was waiting for her. "You're late. Have you got a note?"

"What do you mean, late," grumbled Fran, dumping her overnight bag and purse in the foyer and marching into the kitchen. "It's only ten."

"But you said you'd be here by eight. I was wondering if something happened to you. Flat tire. Kidnapping. Elopement."

"Very funny. You see how I'm roaring with laughter."

"Actually, you look very good." Jessie eyed her friend. "Skirt a bit wrinkled. Jacket the same. But linen gets away with wrinkles. The eye makeup is stunning. I've never seen you look so pretty! Do you have anything to tell me?"

"Such as what?"

"What do you mean such as what? You go off with a guy on an overnight—"

"Strictly business. And separate rooms, remember?"

"And you think he's up to something but you can't figure what—"

"I still can't."

"So what happened? Did he make a pass? Did he knock on your door late at night? Did he try to take a little grab while you were in the car together? Did he carry your briefcase? Anything?"

"No, dammit! And I had all my putdowns ready for him. I never even got to use them." She grabbed the plug for the electric teakettle and shoved it viciously into the socket. "All he did was get me tipsy at lunch and worm out of me the basic poop on my five marriages."

"And nothing else?"

"I told you, no, no and no!" She took two cups from the cabinet and slammed the cabinet door.

"Do I detect a slight note of irritation in those dulcet tones? A touch, perhaps of anger?"

"Anger is a waste of energy," Fran snapped, yanking the silverware drawer open with such force that half a dozen spoons and forks flew out and rattled across on the floor. She bent to pick them up. "It's just that I can't figure out what he's up to. Except that he's the most conceited jerk—"

"You already said that."

"Well, he still is."

"He doesn't seem that way."

"No. He hides it. But he just thinks he knows everything. Underneath that just-one-of-the-guys cover he's so self-confident. I don't know if he's really just not interested except businesswise or if he figures he can insult me about my looks and then just wait until he's ready and when he crooks his little finger I'll come crawling, the way other women apparently have. Not that I care. He's not my type. Five marriages? That says it all."

"Wait a minute, my feisty friend. You've had five marriages, too—"

"Well, I'm not proud of it. I don't exactly put it on my résumé."

"No matter what you say, I give him points. He got you to do your hair and to put on some pretty clothes I didn't even know you owned, and to paint your pretty face a little."

"Prostitution. I'm doing it for the money. I'm just another kind of hooker, so let's drop the subject."

"Sorry. I only brought it up because Bud asked me what was going on."

"Tell him to ask Webb."

"I did. But he said Webb never talks about his women. But he told me a little about Webb's marriages."

"Oh?"

"Yeah."

"Well?"

"I thought you wanted to drop the subject."

"I do. After you tell me what Bud said. It's—it's of academic interest to me at this point."

"Well, three he married when he was drunk. Showgirls. Bud says that's why he quit drinking. When he started working deals in Las Vegas, every time he got bombed, he'd wake up married. So he quit. Now he drinks almost never."

"He drank at lunch with me yesterday."

"You missed your chance. And there was another showgirl he was really mad about. But they were cheating on each other like crazy. Bud says that Webb said it was his fault as much as hers. And then, I guess he had his Louie, too. His high-school sweetheart who he was married to first. Breast cancer. That was before Bud knew him."

"Well, I suppose if I'm going to switch to Lally's office, I'm going to have to run around in these costumes for a time. Two of Lally's people pick up their clients in their Rolls-Royces. Too rich for my blood. But I'll rent a Mercedes for a month and see. If the thing with Lally works out, I should get one. Webb says there are a couple of sleaze-ball used-car dealers down in Miami where I could probably get a pretty good price on one," she shrugged, pouring two cups of tea. "He said not to go down there and dicker without him, of course. The only one who knows how to handle these people is him. And now, enough of that. How was your little rendezvous? Did you stay here?"

"Yes, but now he's gone again. San Diego. Said he doesn't even know when he'll be back. And he might not get to call at all."

"And this is the man that wants the two of you glued together at the hip?"

"And wait till you hear this: he wants to get me a maid so I'll be neater. I think he wants me to quit work. I said I don't want to. Even stranger. While he's running off, he's telling me that we have to work something out about my job so we can be together more. So I can go with him on a lot of these trips."

"I told you nothing's perfect."

"But wait. He's talking about getting married. Married, Fran! It's too good to be true."

"Not if you have to give up everything you want to do. When?"

"We didn't talk about when. But he's serious. His sister called today about rings."

"His sister? Rings? Bathtub rings or engagement rings?"

"She asked my size, what cut of stone I liked best and if I had any style preferences. I told her make it big, and she laughed. I thought she was kidding. And then she said she'll be down with some choices as soon as she can round them up. Bud asked her to help because he doesn't trust his taste in jewelry."

"Don't count your diamonds until they're on your finger."

"Oh, Fran. Bud isn't that way. He loves me. There's just that little neatness thing."

"There's always at least one little thing."

"Well, maybe that's a small price to pay for multiple orgasms," said Jessie, blushing.

"What are you blushing for, Jessie? Sex isn't something to blush about. It's damned important. Not only that, it's good for you. So healthy. Right up there with swimming when it comes to aerobic exercise. Time spent on sex is time well spent."

Jessie glanced at the clock. "Oh, gosh, how late is it? I was supposed to call her at ten. Let me do that now."

Cecily answered on the first ring. "Listen, Jessie, I'm coming down the day after tomorrow. Bud called and said he won't be back for another four or five days but he'll call you when he can. Not to worry if he doesn't get in touch with you for a few days. He might be in Dallas. Or Alaska. He's not sure. Something very important must be going on. He's usually so precise about his itinerary. But his offices can always track him down, if it's really important.

"Anyway, I'm flying down in a private jet, la-de-dah, with a friend of Bud's and they're arranging a limo at the airport for us. I'm coming with a guard because I'm bringing the rings. Bud insisted.

"Now I don't want you to tell anyone a word about this. Bud's orders. I am bringing three rings for you to look at. You can take your pick or pick none of them. If you don't like any of them, we'll talk about what you'd like and we'll have our man down there, Artie Feldmesser, find it. I don't know why Bud is in such a hurry. But he wants you to have a ring right away."

278

"Gosh, I didn't even know he was doing this. We didn't talk about rings."

"When my brother moves, he moves fast. And I said I'd be the messenger because I hated the idea of you being shown your ring for the first time by some jeweler or delivery man or someone. And Bud not even there."

"That's lovely of you."

"I have an ulterior motive. I'm dying to meet you. I've heard about you for thirty-five years. I know you must be special. And while I'm there I'm killing three birds with one stone. For Bud. He wants me to ease the way between you and Miss Mary. You can understand why she's been a little standoffish. She took care of Bitsy from when she was just a child. She was barely old enough for the job when she started. Just in her early twenties. But she's a sweetheart, even if she's a little old and crotchety sometimes now. She'll come around. She's not going to be working for Bud much longer, anyway, but it's still better to be friends."

"Yes, she did seem upset the time I met her. Bud brought me in for breakfast the morning we ran into each other here."

"And the third thing is to assure you about Esme. Esme is—different. Hard to figure. She was a pain-in-the-ass kid. Grown up to be a pain-in-the-ass woman. She has a lot of good points but sometimes they're hard to see. Miss

Mary does not like Esme as much as she used to. She raised her like a mother and then Esme just pushed her pretty much out of her life. Miss Mary is hurt. She can't get past it. All I have to do is tell her what a little snot Esme is being about you, and Miss Mary will want to adopt you. And you have never been adopted until you have been adopted by Miss Mary. She's not even Jewish but she's the classic Jewish mother."

Jessie laughed. "Well, I could use a mother. Mine abdicated decades ago."

"I expect to get in about eleven."

"Why don't you call me at my office when you land. I'll slip out and meet you at Bud's and we'll probably both get there at the same time."

"Good. Bud wants you to be wearing a ring, if possible, when he gets back. We'll try to make it."

"What a good sister you are, Sess."

"You don't know what a good brother Bud is. And he was a pretty fine husband, too, especially when you know the whole story."

When she hung up, Jessie turned to Fran, "Did you get all that? I'm going to meet her tomorrow to get my ring. She's bringing three down for me to choose from, with a body-

280

guard. On a private jet. Or if I don't like them, she'll look for whatever I want. Bud wants me to have a ring by the time he gets back. I can't believe it. Is this right out of a drugstore novel?"

"If it was anyone but Bud, I'd ask, what's the rush? What's he making up for?"

"Nothing. He just wants me to have a ring."

"And when's he coming back?"

"I told you, I don't exactly know. In a couple of days or so. He's heading for Dallas or Alaska or somewhere. And he may not even be able to call."

"Dallas or Alaska or somewhere? Are you kidding?" She frowned. "You know, Jessie, I wonder if something funny's going on. I have no idea what. But he can't even tell you where he'll be? Or call you? There's no place in the country you can't make a telephone call from if you want to."

"Well, I'm sure there's a good reason for all this," said Jessie. "I'm sure there is." But now she was frowning, too.

Twenty-two

Sess's call came in at 11:10. Jessie logged off her terminal, grabbed her purse and headed for the door.

"What are you running out for, now," growled Pontchetrain as he stomped back through the office from the men's room. Jessie ignored him. Growling was his customary vocal mode, except when he shifted down to whining, or up to roaring. But growling was his drive gear. "I have a couple of personal matters to attend to," she said to Heloise, loudly enough so he could hear. "I'll be back in time for the Holy Cross thing."

"And I want you to read the proofs after they're typeset," he called after her. "Everyone has to help proof around here from now on. We can't have such blatant misspellings like last week in every issue. Oh, how I bleed over this paper!" He smote his forehead dramatically and stalked back into his office.

Heloise didn't look up. "Tell him not to bleed on Cynthia's copy. She's writing about McArthur Dairy today."

"It's not easy to keep kosher around here," giggled Cynthia. "Especially with all that ham around. What are you running out for, Jess? A little matinee, huh?"

"No. A preview of sorts, but not the kind you're thinking of."

"Not even a tryout?" smirked Cynthia. "Just lunch? Too bad."

"You think sex is everyone's favorite pastime," said Jessie.

"Well, if it isn't, it should be. It's very good for you. It can cure anything but a yeast infection. It can even make Ponchy smile. You can always tell the next morning when he's had a pop."

Twenty minutes later, Jessie rapped on Bud's apartment door. It swung open immediately, and a long-limbed, sandy-blond woman opened it and put out her hand. "I'm Sess. You're Jessie. I'm so glad to meet you at last. Come in."

"I'm overwhelmed," said Jessie, walking in. "This has all happened so fast. I'm still pinching myself."

"I think Bud is, too. It happened fast after a wait of thirty-five years. That's life, I guess.

283

Well, let's have a look at you." She stepped back and frankly inspected Jessie head to toe. "I can see why he's crazy about you. I told Miss Mary we'd eat right away, even though it's a little early. I know you have to get back to work. But that won't be for long. You certainly won't have to work once you're married."

"Oh, but I—" Jessie hesitated, but then said nothing. No, she would work that out with Bud, not with his sister.

"Come, let's sit down." Sess pointed to a chair at the dining room table. "I told Miss Mary we'd eat in the breakfast room but after I mentioned the ruckus with Esme, she insisted on setting up in here. I think she's halfway to your side already."

"Did she tell you Bud and I had breakfast here, that first morning? I think she highly disapproved, then."

"Well, don't worry. She adores Bud. She'll end up loving anyone he loves." She picked up a large long jeweler's case next to her plate. "These are the rings. Hope you like one of them. Open it." Just then Miss Mary came through the kitchen door carrying two cups of soup. "Oh, good. Gumbo soup. Miss Mary makes incredible gumbo."

"I love homemade gumbo," said Jessie. "And this smells so good. And it looks wonderful. Nice and brown."

"If you don't get the roux good and brown, you don't have real gumbo," said Miss Mary. "You have to take the time to get it very dark—almost burnt, but not quite." And she whisked back into the kitchen.

"You're almost home," grinned Sess.

Jessie found the catch, opened the box, and stopped breathing for ten full seconds. "But—but—they're so beautiful. And so big!"

"He said nothing under five carats. That one's seven. This one's six plus. That one's about five and a half."

"The five and a half, the marquis, looks the biggest," said Jessie in a hushed tone. Such stones seemed to call for reverence.

"Yeah. Marquis cuts do that sometimes. Look big. Which do you like?"

"Well, I like the other two better. I mean I love them all."

"If there's some other style—they're doing tri-angle cuts now and hearts. And different settings."

The six-plus was an oval; the seven-carat was an emerald cut. "I love the oval," said Jessie. "I've never seen anything quite like it." Instead of a standard Tiffany setting of two baguettes, it was flanked on either side by a fan of large baguettes.

"I like that one best too. Try it on."

"Oh, Sess! It fits."

"Wear it in good health, Jessie. If you want that one, I mean. But honest, if it isn't exactly what you want, we'll find you whatever you say. You can sketch it. Feldmesser will get it or get it made."

"Oh, no! How could I like anything more than this?"

"Feldmesser will scout up wedding bands that will go with it. Or have them made. But I didn't wait for them. We'll send them or I'll bring them, however it works out, as soon as we find them."

"Wedding bands?"

"And I'm supposed to ask you subtle, sneaky questions about other stuff. Bud said he thinks some of the basic jewelry things would be good to get you for a wedding present. So what do you have and what don't you have? We don't have to be subtle. Let's be efficient instead."

"Well, I don't have a lot. I have good pearls. One long one and one short. I have a couple of gold pins, gold bracelets. One kunzita and diamond cocktail ring. Half-carat diamond studs. Everything else I have is fake. Oh, and a gold watch. And a charm bracelet."

"So you can use everything but pearls."

"I don't come with much of a dowry, I'm afraid."

"Well, don't feel bad. We never had any of that stuff either until Bud started making so much money. And Dell's done pretty well, too. He's given me a lot of stuff, but I've never been that big on jewelry. Bitsy adored it. She was always buying the most unusual things. Esme's having most of it taken apart. Her mother's taste was too fussy for her. But if you like jewelry, Bud will get it for you. He's good that way. On the other hand, if you don't like it, that wouldn't bother him a bit either. He's such an egghead. He doesn't think the way a lot of men do."

"Thank goodness," laughed Jessie.

Jessie tasted the soup. "Gosh, this is as good as it looks."

"Miss Mary is a pretty good cook. Most things. She loves to bake or cook little sweets to give to you. She still sends me cookies. And Benjie. And when my mother was so sick, she kept running over to rub her back or change her bed. She'd bring her soup and pot pies, God love her."

Miss Mary returned with plates of salmon steak, boiled potatoes and broccoli. And plenty of lemon.

"Well, Miss Mary, see the ring?" Sess took Jessie's hand and held it out to the housekeeper.

"My, it's lovely, Miss Jessie. Mr. Bud must l-love you very much." She blinked and made a teary little smile.

Jessie took her hand. "I know it's not easy

for you, Miss Mary. I'm so sorry. But I do love him, too. Very much."

"I know. He told me," she said with a small sniff. "It's just hard for someone as old as me to change so fast."

"Please, don't change at all," said Jessie. "Everybody here loves you the way you are."

"Yes, they do, I think," she said, hurrying back into the kitchen.

"I'm going to cry," said Sess. "It's so strange, this whole picture. Bitsy bored me silly. Irritated me, sometimes, if the truth be known. No brains. No taste. She never read anything except about fashion and society. But I loved her, too, in a way. She had a certain innate sweetness. Like a six-year-old. Bud loved her but he wasn't in love with her. He got trapped. And his way of handling it was just to be with her very little. Sometimes he didn't come home for a month or two at a time. But he was always in close touch by phone, directing her every move. Almost like a parent with a not-quite-bright child.

"Sometimes Esme couldn't stand her own mother. Of course Esme can't stand much of anybody who isn't brilliant and efficient. Her husband is both. But Miss Mary really cared about her. Like Bitsy, Esme was her child, almost. And Dell and I cared about her too, in our way. I can't eat all this. The gumbo is always filling."

"I can't either. Will she mind?"

"No. She's used to Esme taking one bite and saying she's through and she's used to Bitsy ordering seconds of everything. Don't worry. Do you have to get back to work, or have you got any time?"

"I've got to get back to work. I've got a Holy Cross Hospital do to cover. And I have to write it up fast enough to get it typeset by five."

"Then I'm going to check with the Spencers to see what time they're flying back. If it's not sometime this afternoon, I'll get a commercial flight. We have a museum benefit tonight. I don't go to a lot of these things, but Dell's on the museum board. Let me tell Miss Mary we'll skip dessert."

"Can I drop you anywhere?"

"No. I have the driver downstairs that Bud hired for me. Might as well go in style. Dell and I never do that. Neither does Bud, himself. But he's always doing it for us. Can I drop you?"

"Thanks, no. I'll need my car to get over to work and home. It's been wonderful meeting you, Sess. I see why Bud thinks the world of you."

"I'm so glad to do something for him. He's always taking care of the rest of us. Solving our problems. Giving us a push in the right direction when we need it." The two women stood up and Sess gave Jessie a tight hug. "Welcome to the family. Strange family, but welcome. Wait a sec and we can go down together."

Sess disappeared into the kitchen. Jessie eyed her new ring. It was so beautiful, she was almost afraid to wear it to the tea. Oh, well, no one would think it was real. Sess came out with Miss Mary, who followed them to the door. "I'll be seeing you soon Miss Jessie," she said.

"Right," said Jessie, giving her hand a little squeeze. "Lunch was delicious."

Outside, Sess hugged Jessie again. "So far, so good," she said. "Two down. One to go. Esme. The last hurdle. Only she's not a hurdle. She's more like hemorrhoid. A chronic—you'll excuse the expression—pain in the ass."

"We'll cross that one when we get to it," said Jessie. "Fortunately, we can kind of ignore the problem for now. We're here and she's in Chicago."

"Yes," nodded Sess, climbing into the waiting limo, "but you don't know Esme. That could change at any moment."

Twenty-three

Jessie had to hand it to her. Kaye Stevens was a trouper. The famous redheaded actress/vocalist/comedienne had just begun working the crowd in the Sister Innocent Hall at Holy Cross Hospital, when the threatening note arrived. One of the guests, a Sally Martinez, had been asked to deliver it by "a man in a car." She couldn't remember much about the car or its driver. The note read, "A bomb will go off in this hale [misspelled] in twenty minutes."

No signature.

No date.

The party chairman, Debbie Winters, asked her co-chairman, Julia Welt, to call the police, then hurried right over to Stevens and whispered in her ear. Stevens, without missing a beat, had raised her voice and with that seemingly effortless projection of hers, announced, "Attention, everyone. Attention! We are all going outside now for a few minutes. Don't ask why. It's a surprise. Just move it. Through that door. That's it." She herself was among the last to leave. Within a few minutes she had herded everyone well away from the building, by which time the police and a SWAT team and a bomb squad had arrived and had begun checking every inch of the building and grounds.

The verdict — no bomb. A hoax.

Meanwhile, Stevens mixed with the crowd, chatting with this one and that as she would have been doing inside. "She gave them everything but the tea," said Winters to Jessie.

And when police and the bomb squad said everyone could go back inside, Stevens got their attention again. "You're a wonderful bunch. And you're probably wondering what this was all about," she said. "Well, it was a bomb scare. A silly note. But no bomb, the bomb squad and their dogs and experts have assured us. Now, we're going back in. You can join us or not as you choose. We're going to have our tea and goodies and I'm going to sing a song or two as we planned.

"I want you to know this is my first bomb threat. I have played in a few bombs but I have never been threatened by one before." The crowd laughed and followed her back into the hall where they could help themselves to tea and goodies while Stevens did her comedy patter and belted out a few favorite songs.

Yes, she was a trouper. It would make a great story. It might even get picked up and used by some of the big local papers. And if it was, it might then get picked up on the wire and run heaven only knew where.

The office was empty when Jessie got back. She logged on at her terminal and began writing. First, a header. Hospice Tea Bombs? Or, Kaye Stevens Braves Bombs for Hospice? Yes, that was better. She was halfway through her first draft when Cynthia came in toting a huge pizza box. "Want some? I thought I'd order enough for everyone and now nobody's here to eat it."

"Thanks. I just came in from a monster lunch and then a heavy tea at Holy Cross. Enough food for a hunt breakfast."

"Did you find my note? About the calls? No?"

A note? Jessie tore through the papers on her desk, searching frantically.

"Easy. It's there. He didn't leave a number anyway. He said he'd call back."

"When? When did he say that? And when did he say he'd call?"

"Last call was just before I went to get the pizza, ten minutes ago. He just said he'd try again. He didn't say when. But probably in fifteen minutes. He's been calling about every fifteen minutes, for an hour. Ponchie was in here twice when he called and started grumbling about you getting so many personal calls on his time, the skinflint." Had it been Bud? And she'd missed him!

Jessie and Cynthia tapped away at their computers in silence. Five minutes later the telephone rang. Jessie pounced on it. *"Community News,* Jessie Moore."

"Mom? It's Kerry."

"I figured, when you said Mom, that it was you, dear. Not too many people call me Mom."

"Oh, Mom, don't make fun of me. I just wanted you to know we got rid of little Pooper. The school was so glad to get him. And I'm still having orgasms. Doug is so proud. He goes around grinning like Garfield. But I'm working on one of my important papers in criminal law so I wanted to warn you I probably won't call for a couple of days. You know how I do. Slaving day and night to make a masterpiece."

"Slaving day and night because you put it off to the last minute again, right?"

"Well, that's just the way I work, Mom. Talk to you in a few days."

* * *

The phone rang again a few minutes later and again Jessie pounced. It was Emil. "I just thought I'd call and try to straighten out our little misunderstanding the other night," he said.

"That was no misunderstanding, Emil. That was our final date. I made that clear."

"Oh, well, if that's how you want it. Whatever you say, my dear."

"That's how I want it," said Jessie. "And I don't want you to call me here, anymore. Please Emil. Let's just forget each other." She hung up without a good-bye.

The phone immediately pealed again. She thought it was Emil again. "Emil, I meant what I said. Can't you understand?"

But it wasn't Emil. It was Bud. "What's that all about?" he asked. "Who doesn't understand what?"

"Oh, nothing. Just this man I can't quite seem to get rid of. But darling, I met Sess at your place and she brought the rings," she told him quickly, "and the one we picked — we both liked it best — is absolutely beautiful. I love it. I love you. I'm in such shock. I didn't know you were even thinking about a ring."

"I didn't. Somebody at the office got engaged and was busy showing everyone her ring and it dawned on me that that's what I'm supposed to do. So I called Sess and dumped it on her. No point in waiting. We know where we're going."

"Where are you?"

He hesitated, then said, "Uh—in—Arizona. Yes, Arizona now, but I'm not going to be here long. I'm at a company where there's—uh—something going on."

"Where can I reach you if I need to talk to you?"

"Better let me call you for the next couple of days. I'm swamped. I might not even get a chance to call. I'll be—moving around pretty fast. I'll call when I can. I love you, more than I can tell you. You're my girl. We'll make plans and set the day and all that, as soon as I get back. I love you."

"I love you, too." She started to tell him more about the ring, then realized the line was dead. He must have hung up.

"My God, what's all that?" cried Cynthia who had listened unabashedly. "Hot damn! That sounded like heavy love stuff. What's been going on here right under my very nose that you didn't even tell me about?"

"Well, it all happened very fast. Someone I used to know many years ago. I think I'm engaged."

296

"Engaged? Don't you know?" She ran over and grabbed Jessie's left hand. "Have you got a—ring! Wow! What a rock! What a bunch of rocks. Jesus, who are you engaged to, Donald Trump?"

"No. Just an old friend. Maybe it's Cubic Zirconia."

"Do you think so?"

"No. But listen, please don't make a lot of fuss about this. You overheard, so I'm explaining. But something very funny is going on. He's out of town. He can't give me a number. And he had his sister give me the ring."

"His sister? Did she get down on her knees?"

"Don't be funny. And he's off in Arizona or somewhere for a few days and he as much as told me he might not call me."

"Yeah, well, I wouldn't let that bother me. He's probably got a little unfinished business with some other broad that he has to wind up or something like that. You know how guys are. Don't bug him. If he bought you that ring, he means business. Jeez, what did you have to do to get a rock like that? Tell him I'll do it, too, whatever it was."

"I only wish I knew," laughed Jessie. "I'd offer to do it again if he'd just hurry home."

"What did they say at your Kaye Stevens thing?"

"I sort of kept my hand at my side or in my

pocket and nobody noticed. Everybody in that bunch has a big diamond, anyway. And there was a bomb scare. Nobody checks out your jewelry during a bomb scare. They're too busy worrying about the building blowing up. Please don't say anything to anybody. I haven't gotten used to it myself yet."

"Does Kerry know?"

"No. But I'll tell her as soon as he gets back, I guess. Now let me get this thing finished. I want to go home and crash. This day has just been way too much for me."

Cynthia shrugged and went back to her own desk, but when Heloise came in she flew to her, crying, "Heloise. Wait until you hear! Only you can't tell anyone. Jessie is engaged and she has a ring with a diamond the size of a baseball. Show her, Jessie." Jessie sighed and held up her left hand while her right one kept pecking at her keyboard. "I told you not a word, Cynthia," she scolded.

"Well, I won't tell anyone. But we had to tell Heloise. We're all practically sisters." Heloise rushed over for a close look.

"Has he got a brother? A father? A third cousin?"

As soon as Jessie finished her story and sent it to Cynthia's queue, she headed home. She

298

would talk to Fran. Fran knew everything about men. She would know what this trip and Bud's strange call meant. The ring kept catching her eye as she drove. It made her hand look elegant. If she was going to be wearing a rock like that, maybe she ought to get a manicure. Was it insured? Maybe she shouldn't wear it to work until she found out. But she would be very uneasy just leaving it in the apartment. The bank? But what good was it if she had to keep it in the bank?

At least she would turn the stone inward when she wore it to the office tomorrow.

At home, when she showed the ring to Fran, Fran blinked at it and stared, wordless for once. But when Jessie told her about Bud's calls, Fran frowned. "I told you I thought it was a little funny when he just upped and flew out of here like that. Well let me tell you, today Webb did the same thing. We were supposed to have a meeting and he calls me from Texas, or so he says, to tell me he can't make it. Just as I was leaving the office. Left no phone number. Said he wasn't sure just when he'd be back. And he couldn't talk."

"Just like Bud. What the heck do you suppose is going on?" The phone rang and Jessie grabbed it. It wasn't Bud. It was Webb. "Hi Jessie. Fran there?"

"She's taking a shower," Jessie said quickly, winking broadly at Fran. "I'll call her for you. But where have you been?" she asked.

"Bud and I had some business that came up very suddenly. That happens once in a while. He's taking care of part of it and I'm taking care of part."

"How long will you two be gone?"

"Depends on just what he finds out there."

Jessie shook her head and said, "As if you didn't know. I'll call Fran. Just a minute." She waited ten seconds, pressed the volume button, and then handed the phone to Fran, and crowded close, her ear near the receiver, to listen.

"Oh, it's you," said Fran.

"Sorry about the appointment. I wouldn't do that if it wasn't something very serious that came up. I had no choice, Fran."

"Of course not. None of us has much choice. We're all just feathers in the wind."

"I'll be back tomorrow. Can we take a raincheck? Lunch first and then there's a building we're taking over in Hallandale. I'd like you to look at it. And if you're interested you handle the resales."

"The resales?" Fran repeated.

"Yeah. We'll inspect everything first and you can make up your mind. Meet you at the deli at Macy's at one?"

"Okay. But tell me, will Bud be back then, too?"

"I doubt it. He's got a lot more stops to make than I have. But Bud doesn't check his itineraries with me. See you tomorrow." They heard the click. And Fran slowly put the telephone back on the hook.

"He doesn't know," said Jessie.

"That's not what he said. He said, 'Bud doesn't check his itineraries with me.' He cleverly avoided actually answering the question. Hm. I'll see if I can find out anything tomorrow at lunch."

Twenty-four

Cynthia signaled to Jessie that Fran was on the other line. Jessie quickly wrapped up her telephone interview with the Museum of Art secretary and took Fran's call. "You won't believe this. I'm not going to lunch with Webb today, either. He called and said it was off again. Postponed. He said there's some real estate deal he and Bud are both involved in and it was critical to get a bunch of leases signed right away. And there was something very peculiar about his voice that I can't quite put my finger on. He said he'd call when he could. Something is just not kosher, Jessie."

"Webb's involved, too?"

"Uh-huh. You know how he always makes our appointments include lunch or dinner. He can never just tell me anything over the phone. It's always gotta be over a meal. I don't think he can stand to eat alone. You were here when

302

he called yesterday and apologized and said we'd have it today. And now he says he'll have to be out of town for a couple of days. An emergency. And he'll call. That's all. Nothing like, 'Hey, I'll be in Seattle,' or, 'I'll be in New York.' The only clue is that it's about leases. That could mean anything. What's the big secret? Are they working for the CIA? I'm beginning to think we've lucked into a pair of total flakes, here."

"Bud isn't a flake. Or at least he wasn't before. And the ring. Would a flake do that?"

"Are you sure it's real?"

"It looks real to me."

"Anyway, this whole thing with Webb has been crazy. Why is the man always having to do lunch? And the trip. I would have told him to kiss off after that, but when he set up the meeting for yesterday he said there's this building they're taking over in Hallandale and they'd like me to handle the resales. So I said okay. I'd have lunch. I'd look at it. Even though I'd miss my soaps. And then he cancels."

"What do you mean, miss your soaps. You don't even watch them."

"But if I did, I'd have been giving them up for his meeting. Same difference. So then he sets the meeting up again, for today. And lunch. And cancels again. Go figure."

"I think he thinks you have a good eye for

things and your head works pretty well. It does, you know. You don't realize how astute your judgment is."

"That's what he says. My comments are astute. Bullshit. He wants me to make a trip to California with him in a week or so. Maybe that's when he'll make his move. I was up half the night at the Grove Inn in Asheville expecting him to knock on my door and he never did. Then again, maybe he never will. He's got me going around in circles."

"Were you disappointed? In Asheville? When nothing happened?"

"No. Yes. No. Oh, hell, in a way, yes. At least then I'd have an answer. I've been blunt as hell to him. When he started sniffing around about my personal life at dinner that night, after getting me drunk and worming the story of my marriages out of me that afternoon at lunch, I fixed him. I told him about Stash."

"Oh, Fran, you didn't!"

"And he said, 'In your present state of mind, I suppose that's a logical solution.' What did he mean by that? I don't know if he's just checking me out so thoroughly because of Lally or for himself. But I sure don't think he's interested in me as a woman. If he is, he's fooled me. But enough about Webb. Now what about Bud? Where is he? What's he doing that you can't know about?"

"He's called a couple of times, but he doesn't say where I can reach him. He keeps saying he'll be moving around and may not be able to call me for a few days. And he sounds strange."

"Evasive?"

"Right. And different. When he called at the office, this afternoon, Cynthia heard us and I had to tell her about him. She thinks he probably has some unfinished business, some other woman somewhere that he's got to wrap up. But what does she know? She never met him."

"With guys, anything is possible. He could be the man in Havana. He could be a bigamist. But you know what I think?"

"No, I'm just asking because I like to hear you talk."

"I think he's used to being married to a ditz who couldn't decide which shoe to put on her left foot without asking him. The only stuff she ever decided, apparently, was about decorating, so he's used to making all the decisions. Fast. By himself. And he's used to spending a lot of time away from her and just dashing off all the time with no questions asked. Maybe he's not really hiding anything. Maybe he's just got to learn that you're not like Bitsy. And that most marriages don't work the way his did—that in most marriages, everyone wants to know what the hell everyone else is doing. And where the hell they are. All the time."

"Oh, Fran, I bet that's it. We just need to sit down and talk about it. And we will. When he comes back."

I hope that's it, thought Fran. She didn't want to worry Jessie. But she was afraid there was more to it than that.

Wednesday. No word.

Thursday morning. Early, just after she came up from jogging, the phone pealed. Jessie dove for it and caught it before the second ring.

"Jessie? It's me. Bud."

She caught her breath. Then said tartly, "Let's see. Bud. Bud. Oh, yes, I used to have this friend named Bud. I think he gave me a ring once."

"Oh, honey, I'm sorry about this. You don't know how sorry. But I had to—to take care of this."

"Where are you?"

"Uh—in—Atlanta now."

"I don't like you to be gone this long. It makes me feel awful."

"Me, too. But I had to do it."

"Do what?"

"Take care of something. It's too complicated to explain over the phone. I'll catch you up on everything in a couple of days."

"Is there somewhere where I can call you?"

"Where you can call me? Uh—I don't see a number. And I won't be here later. I'll call you as soon as—" Click. The line went dead.

Twenty minutes later, when it finally pealed again, Jessie grabbed it immediately.

"Bud? We were cut off."

"Jessie? This isn't Bud. It's Webb. Is Fran there?"

"I think she's in the shower, again. I'll call her. Where have you been?"

"Oh, I—I had a business thing come up suddenly."

"Well, FYI, I still think it's very peculiar that you and Bud both disappeared at the same time."

"Oh, Bud's still gone, too?"

"Since Sunday. Wait, here's Fran." As Fran came out of her hallway, Jessie handed her the receiver, hissing, "It's Webb!"

"Hello?" said Fran formally.

"Hi Fran. It's Webb."

"Webb. Webb," she repeated. "Ah, yes. The man who stands up field hands."

"No, technically, not a stand-up. I let you know as soon as I knew. I'm sorry. Believe me, nothing I could do about it. Perhaps you and Lally and I could lunch tomorrow, instead—with a partner of ours in that same Hallandale building. The one we'd like you to handle re-sales on."

"You sure know which carrot to hold out in front of me. Do I have to comb my hair and wear lipstick and shoes?"

"Yes."

"If you like, I'll just put a bag over my head. When and where?"

"Down Under. About 1 P.M. Figure on a couple of hours and then another hour or two at the building inspecting everything and talk-ing over our approach."

"I'll be there. All cleaned up like a city gal. And then will you tell me anything about where you've been and why you disappeared? I'm not your mother, but it seems the thing to do when you break appointments."

"Maybe sometimes. Not in business. In busi-ness there's no point in telling anyone anything unless they have a need to know. That's my M.O., Fran. All that loose information flying around out there can get you into trouble. And you have no real need to know. Like you said, you're not my mother."

Fran's head snapped back as though she'd been slapped. She could think of no retort to that. He was right. It was none of her busi-ness. Why had she even asked?

After a lengthy pause, Webb said, "Sorry. That wasn't a fair shot. I've been caught between a rock and a hard place, Fran. I'll explain it all. Soon. But not tomorrow. Okay? It's called compromise."

"Fine with me," said Fran as unconcernedly as she could manage. "See you tomorrow."

She hung up and she turned to Jessie. "Lunch tomorrow. And the meeting. With Lally and someone else. And he said he would tell me where he was. Soon. But not tomorrow. Last week it felt like we were living in a soap opera. This week it's a damned Agatha Christie novel."

Bud called twenty minutes later. He sounded more like himself. "Good news. I'm coming home on Monday," he said. "Tomorrow's Sunday, so that's just two days."

"Can I meet you at the airport?"

"No, honey. No need."

He called Sunday morning, too. "Just had to hear your voice. You don't know how I miss you."

"Then why aren't you here? I miss you, too, you know."

"Listen. I changed my mind. I do want you to come to the airport, if you can. Webb might come, too."

"He's having lunch with Fran and Lally to-morrow."

"Yeah. I heard."

"Bud, he really has Fran in a tizzy. She can't figure out what he's up to. She usually reads men like so many grade-school primers. But not him. I thought maybe he liked her but she doesn't think so. She says he's really insulting sometimes, although I must say I've never seen it. But she's getting some peculiar vibes. She can't figure him out."

"I think he can't quite figure her out, either. But we'll talk about them, too, tomorrow, if you want. Webb will come for you about nine in the morning. Is that okay? No interviews or parties?"

"Monday's a deadline day this week, but I'll go in tonight and get some of it written up. I'll be ready."

Twenty-five

Jessie dumped her large, heavy carry-on next to the kitchen door. Why couldn't she ever pack for even just one night without taking enough junk to start homesteading? Fran was up, she knew, because she heard her shower running. She would find the note Jessie had left on her door when she got out.

Sure enough, a minute later, Fran came stomping out into the kitchen, Jessie's note in hand. "You're still here. Now just what is this all about, Jessie? Are you going to disappear, too? What is going on here?"

"I was going to tell you last night when I came in, but you were already asleep."

"For this you could have wakened me," Fran said, pacing the kitchen reading from the note. " 'Fran, I won't be home tonight. Bud's coming this morning. Webb and I are meeting him at the airport. Will spend the night with him. If Miss Mary isn't off and we have to stay in a hotel, I'll call and give you the room number.' Then Webb is back. They sneak out of town, like a mystery. And come back separately. Two of you to meet Bud at the airport. What is all this? I sure hope you ask him to explain it all, and I hope he has a good story."

"I don't know what it is, but I'm sure he has an explanation. Anyway, I've got a full day at work. An interview. A ribbon-cutting. And Webb will be here any minute to pick me up."

A loud insistent thumping on the front door interrupted her. The doorbell rang briskly three times in a row. "That wouldn't be Webb," said Fran and Jessie together. "He'd call from downstairs."

"You expecting anyone?" asked Jessie.

Fran shook her head. "Someone must have the wrong apartment."

They both went to the door. Fran unlocked it and pulled it open.

The lady standing there was tall and thin with brown hair styled in a sleek bob. She wore a simply cut but clearly expensive brown crepe suit with a cream-colored blouse and ropes of small, irregular opals. "You are Jessie Moore, I believe?" she asked crisply.

"Yes, I am," said Jessie. "And you're—"

"My name is Esme Elizabeth Pearlman. Bud

Wellman's daughter. And I think you'd better tell me, where is my father?"

Jessie stared. Fran, standing behind her, gave her a poke in the ribs and said smoothly, "Oh, what a lovely surprise. Won't you come in."

"Uh—Bud's daughter," Jessie repeated awkwardly. "I'm so glad to meet you." She put her hand out. Esme ignored it.

"I'm Jessie's roommate, Fran Dimitri," said Fran.

"Roommate? How nice," said Esme, stepping in carefully as though she feared she might put her foot in something on the floor.

"Jessie and I were just making coffee. You sit right there and we'll have it in no time." She gave Jessie a meaningful look. "Your turn to make the coffee, Jessie. I'll get the cups. Excuse us for just a moment, Mrs. Pearlman. *Faites comme chez vous,*" she crooned with a saccharin smile.

Once in the kitchen Jessie whispered, "What was that you said? French? You?" She grabbed the coffee and the pot.

Fran whispered back, "I said make yourself at home. It's the only French I know except how to ask for the check. I learned it at a realtors' conference they had in Montreal once." She took the pot from Jessie and began filling it.

"Fran, I'm not going to talk to that crazy woman. She asked where Bud is. That means she doesn't know. That means Bud doesn't want her to know. And I'm not going to be the one to tell her anything he doesn't want her to know. She obviously doesn't know he's coming back today, either."

"But how can you avoid telling her? She's in our living room, Jessie."

"And I don't want her to know Webb is picking me up. I'm sneaking out of here. Out of this door. Tell her—tell her I remembered an assignment. Just stall until Webb and I can get out of here."

"Oh, how do I let you get me into these things!" cried Fran. "But you're right. Go." Fran plugged in the coffee-maker, filled a plate with cookies and carried it back out to the living room while Jessie hoisted her hand-carry's strap on her shoulder and let herself out into the hall.

Downstairs she saw Esme's white stretch limo waiting near the entrance to the E-building. She turned and headed the other way, through the covered parking, across the courtyard, into the main lobby and out the other side, and over to the main gate, where she waited anxiously.

Two minutes later a navy blue limo pulled in and as the guard stepped out to query the driver, the door opened and Webb poked his head out. "What are you doing here at the gate, Jessie? We'd come around and get you." Jessie handed him her hand carry and quickly climbed in after it.

"Esme's here," she said.

"Esme's here?" he repeated.

"Oh, boy, is she! With smoke coming out of her ears. Let's get out of here. I'll tell you on the way."

Upstairs, Fran flipped on the TV and tuned in the Channel Seven morning news. "Here. You can catch the news while we bring the coffee," she said.

"I want to know about my father," said Esme, deliberately turning away from the TV.

"Don't we all," said Fran, running back to the kitchen. What could she tell her? She had to think of something. Oh, well, nothing would do much good probably anyway. She put cups, spoons, sugar and milk on a tray and carried it back into the living room. And braced herself to face this smartly dressed, angry woman who was sitting, stiff-backed and frozen-faced, staring into space just to the left of the TV, tapping her foot impatiently.

"Where is Mrs. Moore?" Esme asked.

"Mrs. Moore? Oh, you mean Jessie. Oh,

she's gone to work. She didn't realize how late it was. And—uh—she has an appointment for an interview. She works for a paper, you know. They're not very understanding if she's late. So I told her to run along and I'd make her apologies. That you'd understand. So she did."

"You what? She what? You mean she's gone? She's not here?" Esme cried indignantly.

"Yeah. I think that's what I just said."

Esme stood up, seething with fury.

"Well, I'm sorry you're so upset about your father," Fran said. "We've all been extremely curious too. Except that we know he's a big boy and he can take care of himself."

"I'm not so sure, Miss Dimitri," Esme's words dripped icicles. "And I think I probably know my father better than you do. He has sustained a terrible trauma. The stress can be very unsettling. I am very concerned about his condition and about where he is."

"Yes, I understand. But I don't know if anyone knows. Did you try asking his office?"

"My dear Miss Dimitri," said Esme in a voice that could curdle milk, "I always call my father's office to find out where to reach him. I have been doing that all my life. I do it several times a week. And they always give me a number. Until now. And I want to know why they've been so vague. Is it because they don't know either and they don't want to worry me?

Has something happened to him? Is it because he doesn't want me to know where he is? I want to know where he is and why. And I want to know now!"

"Well, you could probably call Mrs. Moore at her paper later if you'd like, and if she's out you could leave a message."

Esme was fuming. "How stupid do you think I am, Miss Dimitri? Mrs. Moore has flown the coop as it were, to avoid talking to me. And you are nothing but an accomplice. When I find my father, I'll tell him exactly what the two of you have done here this morning. If I don't have some substantial information about him, if I have not talked to him within the next twenty-four hours, I am calling the police. Kidnapping, I would remind you, is a capital offence."

"Oh, I'm sure no such drastic steps will be necessary," began Fran. But Esme swept past her, let herself out the door, and slammed it behind her.

While Fran stood there, wondering just what to do next, Esme stalked down the hall, looking for E770, her father's apartment. When she found it she knocked loudly on the door, waited two seconds, then knocked again. In a moment, Miss Mary called "Who's there?" and opened it. She stared, wide-eyed at the woman

317

before her. "Well, land sakes, Miss Esme! What are you doing here? I didn't know you were coming."

"I didn't send out announcements," Esme snapped. "I'm looking for my father and I've been getting a runaround from that common little snip down the hall."

"Down the hall? You don't mean Miss Jessie? Do you know her?"

"I do now."

"And you don't know where your father is? Is that what you're saying?"

"No, I don't know. But I'm going to find out, I promise you. And whoever is playing games with me will get just what they deserve."

"Games?" Miss Mary stepped aside so Esme could enter the apartment.

"I haven't been able to reach him for several days. Something is going on. And don't tell me he's in Alaska. I was just talking to Benjie and Benjie hasn't seen him since he came down here a couple of weeks ago. So he's not there."

"Maybe not now, but he was. He said he was there when he called a couple of days ago. Alaska's a big place. He didn't necessarily have to be seeing Benjie there. I don't know where he is right now, either, but I'm sure I'll hear from him soon." Esme strode angrily over to a phone.

"Now, what are you doing, Miss Esme? Are

you staying here, tonight? In case your father calls."

"I'll stay a couple of days. I have to call down to the limo and tell the driver to park. And to bring my things up. Would you please make me some coffee. Strong."

At the airport, Bud was one of the first off the plane. He spotted the car and hurried to it, pulled open the door, climbed in and took Jessie into his arms for a long, tight hug and kiss. When they broke apart, Jessie pulled back and said, "All right. Now what was this all about?"

Bud looked uncomfortable. "Jessie, I — just business. I told you. Very important." He turned to Webb, shook his head and mumbled, "Some leases."

Webb interrupted. "Esme's in town, Bud. Came to Jessie's a few minutes before I did. Angry. Asking where you've been."

"Oh, Christ," said Bud. "Did you tell her?" he asked Jessie.

"No. I snuck out the kitchen door and let Fran stall her. I didn't want to tell her anything if you didn't want her to know. And I didn't want to lie to her. I didn't know if you wanted her to know you're back."

"No. Definitely not."

"So I panicked. I just fled to the kitchen and

picked up my bag and headed downstairs. I knew Webb would be there any minute and I didn't want her to see him. Fran said she would tell her I had an assignment. Pretty lame excuse for running out, but we couldn't think of anything better on the spur of the moment like that. Maybe I should have stayed."

"I've put you all in impossible situations," said Bud. "But who expected her to come down here? I called Sess last night and she said Es was on the warpath. But I didn't think she'd get so crazy."

"Well, if she calls me at the office today, what should I say?" asked Jessie. "Do you want to see her?"

"No," said Bud. "I've had it with her attitude. I'm her father. Not her child. Okay, if she calls the office, you know nothing. She'll probably stay with Miss Mary tonight or maybe a day or two. We'll stay in a hotel."

"And you don't want anyone else to know where you are. Right?"

"Anyone who wants to reach me, including Es, can do so by calling my office. My office will pass the numbers on to me. I'll call whoever I think really needs to talk to me. Or whoever I want to talk to. But not Esme, yet. I'll talk to that kid of mine when I'm darn good and ready."

"Bud, what is this all about? What is the big

mystery here? If you don't talk to Esme, she's going to be sure it's my doing. She'll blame me and we may never be able to work out a decent relationship. And I don't like the idea of you just disappearing the way you did. You'd be very upset if I ever did that to you, wouldn't you?"

Bud shrugged. "I suppose so. But I hope I'd trust you, no matter what. And I have had a bellyful of Esme's attitude. How to handle it is my problem, not yours. So let's drop the subject, for now."

"Meanwhile," Webb interrupted tactfully, as the car sped down the exit road, "the driver is going to head for the Hammock. I suggest we go have breakfast somewhere instead, figure out where you want to stay tonight, and make a reservation. Driver, don't head south on U.S. 1, up there. Take the lane that gets us on U.S. 1 going north. We're not going to the address I gave you before. We're going to a deli called Pomperdale's. Near Bayview. Know the one I mean?"

"Yes sir," said the driver, switching lanes adroitly.

Bud fished a portable phone out of his bag and pressed an automatic-dial button. "Cromwell's probably in already," he said to Webb. "Hello, Edgar? . . . Yeah, I'm here. Complications. My daughter Esme is here and I don't want her under any circumstances to know that I'm back. I'll stay in a hotel a day or two till she leaves. Call and get me a room where I can check in now—in half an hour, maybe. Marriott, 110 Tower, Crown Sterling—a suite. Stock it. Send over a couple of changes for me. Report any calls to me there, including Esme's if she makes any and I'm sure she will. Don't let anyone else know I'm there, or back for another day or so. They can deal through you. Call me on my portable. Any problem with the portable, for the next half hour or so I'll be at—what's that place Webb?"

Webb grabbed the portable. "It's Pomperdale's deli on Commercial near Bayview, Edgar," he said. "We'll be there in about five minutes."

"I have a brunch to cover at ten, Bud," Jessie said. "Remember?"

He nodded. "Don't worry. It's only about nine, now. We'll take you there, first."

"But I don't have my car. I was thinking we'd be taking you back to the Hammock and I'd take my car from there."

"We can probably have the driver here pick you up after your brunch and take you back to get your car," said Webb. "No problem. Where is it?"

Jessie pulled her assignment book from her purse and flipped through the pages. "At 110

Tower," she said.

"Okay. Now who wants what for breakfast? So we can expedite that."

At Pomperdale's they found a table near the back and Webb went up to order their breakfasts. "Be patient with me, Jess," Bud said, patting her shoulder and giving it a gentle squeeze. "I'm handling things the best I can. We'll talk when I can. You know I love you."

Jessie nodded, patting his hand on her shoulder. He was right. She trusted him. She was probably making much ado about nothing. And he knew best about Esme. She went to get their coffee. "Webb takes it black," he called after her. She brought their cups and went back for Webb's. And she then went to help Webb carry their food over as the chefs slapped their orders onto the counter.

Jessie told Bud in more detail about Esme's visit that morning. And she was just about to remind him that she was now wearing his ring, when the call came in from his assistant, Edgar. "Yeah," he said into the phone, grabbing a paper napkin to scribble on. "There's a what? All over town? . . . Three of them? . . . What about up here? No, Boca's too far . . . 110 Tower?" He looked at Jessie. "Well, if that's what we can get, that's what we'll take. And we can check in now? . . . Right . . . Tell them we'll be there in about fifteen minutes . . . Call Miss Mary. Don't tell her I'm here but see if there's anything she needs. See if Esme's staying there, but don't ask. She'll probably tell you. Talk to you after we check in." And he hung up.

"You're staying at the 110 Tower," Jessie said.

"Only place we could get a suite. Someone canceled just before he called. There are three conventions going on in town, he said. Some lawyers' thing. Some diet thing that's drawing doctors, nutritionists, dieters, diet clinic experts—half the country apparently. And some women's thing."

"That's where my brunch is," said Jessie.

"Well, at least it will save you one trip."

"And if we don't have to go any farther than that," said Webb, "we've all got time for another cup of coffee."

Twenty-six

The acrid gas-station smell from the dozens of cars clogging the 110 Tower drive-through made their eyes water. It was a Hadassah donor brunch. Webb and Jessie hopped out first. Bud crawled out last. No bellhop out front. So Bud and Webb grabbed Bud's bags and the three of them hurried into the ground floor lobby where the air was better, and toward the elevator.

At the check-in desk at the seventh floor lobby, they handed over Jessie's bag, and Bud's suitcase and garment bag, but hung on to his carry-on, which contained his portable phone, important papers and two portable computers. The room was ready. Bud asked for two keys and slipped one into Jessie's hand. The suite was one floor up.

They stepped into the lounge for a minute so Jessie could look it over. It was full of women, already, though it was barely ten. "Is that the thing you're covering?" asked Webb.

She nodded. "I'll come back as soon as we're all settled upstairs and I'll make a quick job of it. Too bad your computers can't talk to ours at work, Bud. I could just write it here and send it."

"Why didn't we think of that before?" Bud said. "We should do that. Let's get one that can. You could spend more time with me."

"Well, we use those portables—Trash 80s we call them. They're Tandys. And that's what we take when we have to cover something out of town or when we have to stay somewhere a long time and we need to file while we're there. I have to clean up the copy at the office, but I can write almost finished stuff."

"Good idea. We'll get one. We might even have one somewhere at the office or the labs. Damn, I wish there weren't so many people around here. But Edgar said the Marriott and Bahia Mar and the Pier were worse."

"And at least here I can make short work of the brunch," added Jessie. "Oh, dear. Look who I see. Daniella Larkin and Devi Talker from the Hammock. Oh, darn, they saw me. Here they come."

"Why, hello, Mrs. Moore," trilled Dannie Larkin. "You're covering this? Isn't that nice." She put her hand out to Bud. "I'm Daniella

Larkin and this is Devi Talker," she said. Bud shook their hands.

"And this is Bud Wellman and his friend, Mr. Webber," Jessie said.

"Bud Wellman. Glad to meet you," the women said together. "Mrs. Moore, would you like us to tell you who else is here from the Hammock?" asked Talker.

"Oh, yes. That would be nice. But I—I have a few calls to make first. What table are you at? I'll find you later."

"Six, I think," said Devi. "Aren't we six, Dannie?"

"I'll find you," said Jessie, quickly. She turned to Bud and Webb and gave them a look. "Well, nice to see you, Mr. Wellman. Mr. Webber." And she headed toward the special elevator that stopped at the hotel floors, only. Bud and Webb glanced at each other, waited a moment and then followed, a few feet behind. Jessie stepped into the car alone and the doors closed. She rode it to the floor above, then sent it back to the seventh. After a moment, the doors opened again, and the two men emerged.

"I don't know if we fooled them or not," said Jessie.

"To the room. Quickly," Bud ordered. And they hurried down the corridor to Bud's door. He slipped his key in the lock and tried to turn it. It wouldn't turn. He jiggled it. The elevator doors opened and another couple stepped off and headed toward them. Bud jiggled the key once more and it turned and the door opened.

The couple approached. It was the Glovers. From the Hammock. How many people were here from the Hammock, today?

"Oh, hello, Mrs. Moore," called Mrs. Glover, spotting Jessie immediately. "I guess we took the wrong elevator. I think these are the hotel rooms, don't you? Are you coming to the brunch, too?" she asked, taking in Webb and Bud, the carry-on, and the open door.

"Yes, I'll see you there," said Jessie.

"See you later then," said Mr. Glover herding his wife back towards the elevators from whence they came.

They ducked into the room and closed the door. Jessie leaned against it and laughed ruefully. "Oh, the hell with it. So much for my good name. I don't guess anyone thinks I'm a virgin anymore, anyway. But I'd better get back down to that brunch or they'll all be sure we're having a wild, wild orgy in here. See you later."

By the time Jessie could sneak back upstairs an hour and a half later, Bud's office had made their deliveries. The desk in the sitting room was set up with a full-sized computer. A pot of coffee, a tray of sandwiches and a basket of fruit waited on the bar. "Well, this is cozy," said Jessie, eyeing a crate of books and a stack of stuffed yellow envelopes. "Where's Webb?"

"He's making another quick run up to North Carolina. Important. A land buy we're working on."

"You two do some curious chasing around. Do you want to talk about this one?"

"I—I—when it all works out, I'll explain it," he said lamely. "No big deal. Nothing to worry about."

Then why couldn't he tell her, Jessie wondered. Well, apparently he planned to, sometime. Until then, she had best simply put it out of her mind. "I've got to go to the office, too, in a few minutes," she said.

"I know, honey. The driver will take you. I had him wait."

"Oh, no. I can't get dropped off there in a limo. But if he'll take me back home, I'll pick up my car and I won't have to cab around."

"Now, wait a minute, Jessie. You said you have another thing to cover this evening. I really don't like you driving all over by yourself at night like that."

"But if I'm coming and going in a limousine, everyone will notice it and start poking around. I don't like everyone to know my business, Bud. Our business. In fact, if I can walk over to the courthouse and he can pick me up there, that would be better."

Bud shook his head. "Okay, I'll tell him on the car phone."

"You haven't even asked to see the ring," she pouted, thrusting her hand in front of his face. "It's so beautiful. But so many people have asked questions."

"Do you like it?"

"I love it. How could I not? It's just that this is all such a change in my life. Harry and I weren't poor. But we weren't rich. And it almost all went while he was sick. No insurance. And I've really had to be careful since. Limos and diamonds haven't been my lifestyle, Bud. That's another reason I work so hard. I have a kid to educate. And I have almost no backup."

"Well, you don't need the job now. Whatever happens, you won't starve."

"But Honey, it isn't only that I need to. I want to. *Community News* is just a little piece of junk, but I've freelanced a dozen pieces the last few months. I'm doing features. I'm getting nibbles. I just have to follow it a while and see how far I can go."

"Jessie, I had a wife for over thirty years who stayed put while I roamed all over the country. The world. We grew further and further apart until we could hardly say ten words to each other. I don't want that again. I want you with me. I want us to enjoy each other. Make up for all those years. Do you understand?"

She nodded slowly. "But Bud, don't you understand, too? That could never happen to us. I love you so much. I want you. Diamonds and limos are nice but I don't need them. What I need is you. But don't try to make me quit this. Please. Don't try to take it away from me."

Bud shook his head and sighed. "We'll talk about it another time. Hurry back as soon as you can."

"You keep mighty strange hours around here, lately," snorted Pontchetrain when Jessie finally got to the office after picking up her own car at the Hammock.

"I had that Hadassah brunch. A madhouse. Had to wait forever for my car," she lied blithely, mentally squashing a tiny twinge of guilt. Lying to Dick the Prick didn't count. It was vital to survival at this job. She quickly logged on and found the usual queue of messages. One from Kerry. "Will arrive home this afternoon if the car makes it. Which it might.

Can we order Chinese take-out for dinner?" Oh, dear! What bad timing. Now how could she spend tonight with Bud?

One from Peg Bush over at Club 110. Jessie called back.

"I wanted to give you the month's charity schedule," said Bush. "Hey, someone said you arrived here this morning in a limo."

"I'm not much into limos," said Jessie, side-stepping the question. "Maybe someone needs their glasses checked." She took down the schedule and hung up.

"What's that about limos?" asked Pontchetrain. "I heard you arrived at that thing this morning in one. I'd better not see any limos on your expense chits, Lady Jane. When you've got car trouble you can take a bus. We're not made of money. I'm working on the budget this afternoon. No calls." And he disappeared behind his office door.

"I hate it when he hovers out here like that, eavesdropping and sniffing for trouble," grumbled Jessie.

"Did you arrive in a limo?" asked Heloise.

"I haven't got time to go into it now," said Jessie.

"Then you did!" squealed Cynthia. "What'd you have to do for a limo ride, kid? Whatever it was, tell him I'll —"

"I know, Cynthia," interrupted Jessie. "I'll

tell him." She quickly dialed Fran at her office. "So what happened after I left?"

"The roof is still on, but then again, I always said that was a very sturdy building. I think the lady's unhinged. She threatened lawyers and kidnapping charges and then stomped off. And guess who called me here just a few minutes ago? Webb. He said he's been very tied up with Bud and that *you* could explain it all, and that he was now heading up to North Carolina for a couple of days, but that when he came back perhaps the four of us could have dinner. Because if they go ahead with this deal I might help organize the sales force. It was one of the properties we looked at on that trip."

"That sounds like fun. By the way, let me warn you that Kerry's coming in today sometime. Home for the summer. Two months of rock and reggae. Get your ear plugs ready."

"Maybe we can talk her into getting a job. In a summer camp in Canada."

"And here I'm supposed to stay with Bud tonight. He's not letting Esme know he's here. He's furious with her. So he's staying in a hotel, because she's probably bunking here in his apartment. Gosh, but life gets complicated."

Esme called around two. "Mrs. Moore?" she said coldly. "This is Esme Pearlman."

"Ah yes, Esme—Mrs. Pearlman. First, let me say that there's no way I can explain or excuse this morning. I'm really sorry, but I had to leave right then. I didn't have time to explain. My ride was waiting. And I—I had an assignment," she finished lamely.

Silence on the other end of the line. "If it's any consolation, your father didn't tell me where he was going," Jessie added. "And I couldn't call him either."

"I find all this secrecy almost amusing. You'd think he was having a face lift."

"Well, all I can say is that he can, and I'm sure he will, explain everything to you soon. Uh—and to me, too."

"He's just not behaving in a responsible way," said Esme.

"But your father is a very responsible person."

"Well, will you please take a message to him for me?"

"I—I'm not sure when I'll be able to deliver it"—another fib, another twinge of guilt—"but I will as soon as I have a chance."

"Tell him that I will be staying here with Miss Mary for a couple of days. I think I'm getting a colitis attack. And I would appreciate talking to him."

* * *

Jessie gave Cynthia the Hadassah write-up at three, spent fifteen minutes tapping out a couple of brief fillers from press releases and was just cleaning off her desk when Kerry called. "I made it, Mom. By the skin of my hubcaps. I just brought everything upstairs and dumped it in the foyer, without even turning off the motor—I was afraid it wouldn't start again if I once turned it off—and drove it over to the Citgo. It was practically Dead On Arrival. It's in intensive care now, Mom—the alternator. Very serious. Gloomy prognosis. Like, even if it survives, I have no wheels until at least the day after tomorrow. I walked back from Citgo. And here Becky and April and I were going to hang out together tonight. There's a party. And I was going to drive us."

"Oh, dear, that's too bad. And it would have worked out so well, because I'm supposed to see Bud tonight."

"Bud? Who's Bud?"

"My new interest. I was going to see him tonight, after this ribbon-cutting party I've got to cover."

"Maybe one of the other girls can borrow a car," said Kerry.

"Wait, honey. I don't know if I can do anything but I had a thought. Let me try it out and I'll get right back to you."

She called Bud. "Darling, Kerry just got

home. And she had plans for tonight, so that worked out fine except that her car broke down."

"Give her yours and use the limo. I didn't get rid of it yet. I sent him out for a couple of things I needed, and over to my office for some disks and a head cleaner from Edgar. I was going to let him go when he gets back but I'll send him over there."

"Except that I don't want to come and go at that party tonight in a limo."

"Then let your daughter use it. Same difference."

"Oh, Bud, could she? She'd be in seventh heaven."

"I'll send him over to the Hammock as soon as he gets back."

"Wonderful. I have another bit of jolly news but let me call Kerry and tell her about the car. And then I'll call you back."

She hung up and dialed the apartment. "Kerry? I've got wheels for you. Very spiffy wheels."

"Oh, Mom, you don't have to give up yours. How will you get around?"

"Not mine. Much, much spiffier. You've got a limo."

"A limo? Like in limousine? Okay, sure, Mom. With or without champagne?"

"Without," laughed Jessie. "But with a

driver. I mean it. Bud had it rented for the rest of the day and he thought I would use it but I can't be seen coming and going in limos. Everyone starts wondering what's going on."

"And what is going on?"

"Plenty. A romance. His daughter is trying to sabotage it, but he won't even talk to her." She told Kerry briefly about Bud's able and difficult daughter. "So this is a confusing, strange and wonderful romance."

"Oh, that's the best kind. About time. So am I really getting a limo for the night?"

"Yup. With a sun-roof. The driver will call up when he gets there. Soon. Maybe a half hour or an hour, I'd guess. He'll take you and your pals anywhere you like. Only no funny business. Just you and Becky and April. There's a little bar, so you might want to bring some diet Coke or something along."

Kerry squealed. "I can't believe this is happening! We'll have such fun! I think I like this Bud already."

She called Bud back. "Listen darling, the jolly news is Esme did call here. She thinks I'm trying to hide you from her, somehow. She seems very — hostile. Suspicious, as though there's something sinister going on. She kind of suggests that you have been behaving

337

strangely. She wants to talk to you and she says she's staying with Miss Mary for a couple of days and she thinks she's having a colitis attack."

"She always has a colitis attack. If nothing else works try colitis."

"Well, the ball is in your court. I didn't tell her you're back. I didn't know what else to say to her."

"Don't say anything. I'm sorry you got caught in the line of fire. If she gets really sick, I'll have Sess call Needle and tell him to come and get her. I simply am not going to back down. She's been behaving like a greedy, impossible witch ever since Bitsy—ever since the funeral."

"Well, sometimes people act badly because they can't handle grief. Or they have fears. She may fear losing you."

"Only the black ink. I don't know how Bitsy and I ever had a daughter like her."

"She may just be so worried, she's not behaving rationally."

"Esme never worries. She analyzes. Her primary concern is Esme. Benjie once in a while. But mainly, herself. I'm sorry, Jessie. I'm afraid we haven't seen the worst of this. I got drunk at the Florida wake. And I took a tranquilizer when we were sitting shiva. And my lovely daughter has been hinting ever since that I'm growing incompetent. That perhaps she and Needle should take over all my affairs."

Jessie gasped.

"No," Bud shook his head. "I don't think we've seen anything yet."

Twenty-seven

"Boy, is this the life?" cried Kerry, letting the breeze whip through her hair as they headed down Sheridan. "I never stood up in a limousine with my head sticking out of its sun-roof before."

"Move over," said Fran. "Neither have I."

"I've never even been in a limo, before, period," giggled Kerry. "Wait till we drive up to Wan's to pick up our chow mein. They'll choke on their egg rolls."

"I'm so glad you thought of this," said Fran.

"Well, Mom said we could get Chinese tonight. And I'm not picking the girls up until seven. And when will I ever have a limo at my disposal again? A limo? Usually I drive a car that can hardly even get into reverse. So it seemed like such a total waste not to take advantage of every minute."

"Good thinking," said Fran, closing her eyes

340

and letting the wind ruffle her hair, too. "This is fun. I think your mother lucked out."

"Yeah. I think she got herself the right guy this time," Kerry giggled. "I thought maybe it was going to be Emil. He came on so strong. And she kind of liked him. I did, too, at first. He was awfully smart. He had a car and driver, too, but I never got to ride in it. And I guess after I went back to school after spring break, he started drinking again."

"Like a sponge," said Fran. "Too bad."

"We've still got lots of time. Let's not go to the restaurant yet," said Kerry. She ducked down inside the car again. "Hamilton, don't pull in at Wan's yet, okay? We'd like to go over to Federal Highway for a while. Down to Hollywood Circle. Then over to the beach and back by Sheridan. And then we'll stop and pick up the Chinese. Okay?" The driver nodded and they sailed right by the restaurant.

"Where are you going to take your friends, later, Kerry?"

"There's a party at Calie's. But now that we've got this, I think we'll go for a ride first. We can stop in Bennigan's for a while. Or the Beverly Hills Cafe. If it was daytime I'd drive by Hollywood Hills High School, but no point at night. Nobody I know there anymore, anyway, day or night."

"We ought to do the drive-through at Burger

341

King. And just order one small Coke," grinned Fran. "The sublime doing the ridiculous."

"And McDonald's. They'll go ape," roared Kerry. "I'll bet Hamilton's never done a ride like this."

Before Jessie entered the Pier 66 Panorama room for the symphony's underwriters' cocktail party at five, she turned her new ring around, to hide the diamonds. Inside, she was immediately surrounded. That in itself was not unusual. Chairpeople at such affairs were usually right there to help reporters get their facts straight, and to point out the workers who deserved mention. And the publicity addicts always made sure the reporters knew, they were there. Some gave her bright, quotable quips. Jessie never minded being used that way. A good quote, as far as she was concerned, earned its donors a bit of space.

But this time, there was another reason. Five people during the first half-hour asked her about Bud Wellman. "You know that new lady in town? The one that was killed in a car wreck in California? Well, I heard that her husband lives in your building," said Joy Lewes, a pretty divorcee from Coral Springs, who had just recently become active in the PACERS, the American Heart Association and the Symphony

Society. "Have you met him? If he ever comes to one of these things, would you introduce me?"

Bunny Berwitz said almost the same thing. "Maybe I could take him to an event or two—I always buy two tickets anyway—just to be nice and help him get acquainted."

Cora Maynard was a jump ahead of them. "I went to the viewing, here, and I saw him, Jessie. It was really disgusting. There were so many people there—maybe twenty or more who are here tonight—so you couldn't get near him. I at least had met her—his wife, I mean. But I don't think most of those women knew her at all. He was nice-looking. I hear he's loaded."

And Debbie Buchan was there. "Who are you with, tonight, Jess?" she asked. "Anyone new?"

"No, I came by myself. I wanted to get in and out. I have a lot of stuff to take care of at home."

"Or a heavy late date?" teased Peg.

"Don't I wish," said Jessie, feeling her diamond push reassuringly against her palm as she made a fist with her left hand.

By seven-thirty she was on her way back to the 110 Tower.

When she put her key in the lock to Bud's room, Bud himself swung the door open. "Come into my parlor, little girl," he said.

343

"Wipe that lecherous look off your face," she giggled.

"I thought you liked it."

"I do. But you'll send me home glowing again and everyone will know I've been up to something with someone."

"Then again, maybe if the room-service guy sees you glowing, he'll let me alone."

"What do you mean 'the room-service guy?' "

"I got a little excited while I was talking to you on the phone before about the car. And just then the room-service guy brought in the Evian water I'd ordered. And he noticed and I guess he thought it was him. He started being so solicitous, voice like honey, wanting to pour the water for me and all. He wouldn't leave. I had to practically chase him from the room. And he's called up here three times since asking if there's anything he can do for me."

"Call down and order me some tea and when he comes up, I'll be sitting in your lap wrapped in a slinky nightgown. Except I didn't bring one with me. And I don't guess I want him to see my bare skin."

"You're doing that to me again."

"Well I hope so. I didn't come over to play backgammon." She crawled into his lap and kissed his neck. But as he began kissing hers and fumbling with the buttons on her shirt, she mumbled into his hair, "Listen, darling. I'm not going to stay all night. It's Kerry's first night home. Do you mind terribly if I leave about midnight. I don't think she'll be in before then. I'll get you bedded down and thoroughly drained and then I'll skip out. I'll stay with you tomorrow night, wherever you are."

Bud sighed. "You're right. A mother should get in sometime before dawn, her daughter's first night home. Midnight's a long way off. Let's order a nice dinner. And when it arrives, I'll have you in my lap in a robe. There are terry robes in each bathroom, if you didn't bring one. You'd look sexy wrapped in a rug. I want that room-service guy to see he hasn't got a prayer."

Kerry was waiting up for her, sitting on the couch with a copy of *Harper's Bazaar* in her lap when Jessie opened the front door. "Well, Mom," she smirked, "is there anything you want to tell me?"

"No, darling, not a word," said Jessie airily, giving her daughter a hug. "And don't be a smartmouth. It's only twelve-thirty. I came home a little earlier than I planned so that I'd be sure to be here when you got in. I thought I'd be waiting up for you."

"We ran out of places. We pretty much went everywhere we could to impress people. And I didn't want Hamilton, the driver, hanging around at Calie's party. In case there were any strange types there. God knows what they might do, if they saw him sitting there in the limo all that time. So we just had him drop us off and leave and then come back for us in an hour. Then we had nightcaps at Wendy's."

"In the limousine?"

"Yeah. We drove through. Hamilton didn't want us getting out. He said that late at night, if any slum-bums happened to be there and they saw us pull up in a limo, they might think we had money or expensive jewelry and anything could happen. And then he brought us all home. Besides, I wanted to be here when you came in. In case you wanted to tell me anything."

"I do not kiss and tell, Kerry."

"Why not? I tell you everything."

"I'm a different generation."

"Well, everybody needs to talk to someone. Who did your generation unload to?"

"A diary or a priest."

"What a bummer."

"So tell me more about your limo ride."

"Oh, Mom, it was terrific. When we went to Wan's, we decided to eat inside — Fran and me. She came along. We brought back the rest. It's in the fridge if you want some. Anyway, Hamilton came in with us and ate at another table and then picked up the check. He said it was his boss's orders. We had such fun. We went through the drive-in cleaners and picked up Fran's cleaning. She remembered her tickets were in her purse. And we went through drive-through lines at Burger King and McDonald's and Wendy's and any other drive-through we could find. We got one diet Coke to go at each one. The workers stared at us like we were movie stars and did everything for us but clean the windshields. We laughed our heads off. I wonder if that's how Madonna feels.

"Then we brought Fran home and picked up the girls and did more of the same. We drove down A1A with our heads poking out of the sun-roof. That's really neato, Mom. The people in the other cars think you're freaking out. And Becky kept shouting, 'Let 'em eat cake!' And then we went to Shari's party."

"Sure does sound like fun."

"We pooled all our money and tried to tip Hamilton. We had $6.52 between us, but he wouldn't take it. He said strict orders from Mr. Wellman. It was already taken care of."

"That's the kind of guy Bud is," said Jessie. "Mr. Wonderful. He doesn't use limos much himself, but he got this one today to make it more comfortable for us, Webb and me, coming to pick him up at the airport."

"Fran says he's awfully nice. Not too old. Not

a boozer. Not fat. And rich. Maybe you better grab him."

Jessie laughed. "I just might."

"Has he got a son?"

"As a matter of fact, he does. Terribly handsome, I hear. He's doing some kind of research up in Alaska. He's single, but he's not into limos. He's like Fran. He's busy saving the planet."

"I guess someone's got to do it," yawned Kerry. "And it's usually kind of nice to talk to people who are deep into something that important. They usually have done a lot of thinking and learning. And they're caring people, even if they're a little nuts sometimes."

"How did Fran like the limo ride?"

"You know Fran. She really loved it. But what she said was she could probably get used to driving around like that if she had to. Especially standing up with her head out of the sun-roof." She yawned again. "Well, if you don't have anything to tell me, Mom, or anything to talk over, or any questions, I guess I'll crash."

"Have a good night's sleep, Dr. Ruth. See you in the morning."

Twenty-eight

The G elevator was on the blink again. Kerry walked over to the F elevator. A tall, thin, handsome brunette was searching her purse for her key. "It's okay. I've got mine," said Kerry, opening the door.

"Thank you, that's very kind of you," said the brunette. She was thirtyish, Kerry judged. A chiseled face, with the kind of hollow cheeks Kerry had longed for since she was fourteen and figured she would probably never have.

"I rang and rang upstairs, but my father's housekeeper is apparently out. Or napping. She's rather elderly." She pressed the six button.

"Oh, my goodness, are you on the top floor, too?" asked Kerry.

"Yes. My father is."

"And he's Bud Wellman?"

"Yes. How did you know?"

"Because my mother and your father are seeing each other. My mother's name is Jessie Moore. I'm Kerry, her daughter. And she told me Bud's housekeeper is elderly." She put her hand out. "I'm so glad to meet you. I've heard so much about you and how smart you are and what an amazing businesswoman you are." Tactfully, she picked out only the good things her mother had told her about Esme. "Mom said your dad says you've been starting businesses since you were a kid and you made your first million dollars before you were twenty-five. Gosh, how did you ever do that?"

Esme hesitated, then took the proffered hand and shook it. "Who told you all that?" she asked.

"My mom. I haven't met your father yet. Hardly anyone has. But my mother says he's so proud of you and he says" — she stretched the truth a bit again — "you're even a better businessman than he is."

Esme smiled faintly. "I had a good role model," she said generously.

"I'll say. But my mom says you did it in totally different businesses. All by yourself."

Esme smiled again, graciously.

"Say, listen, are you doing anything for lunch? I mean, maybe we could talk. I wish I knew what was going on here. I mean, I don't understand why your father disappeared last week. My mother doesn't know why. What's the story with these two? Fran, my mom's roommate, tells me a little and my mother tells me a little but what's the big picture?"

"I've been wondering myself," said Esme. "I'm interested to learn that I'm not the only one kept in the dark."

"Maybe if we put our heads together we could figure out a little more. Or at least narrow down the possibilities. I mean, you imagine all sorts of things when you don't have any hard facts. It's like a spy movie around here."

"That's very true," said Esme. "In fact, that's why I'm here. To find out. And I have to go back to Chicago this afternoon. I can't leave everything on my husband's shoulders indefinitely. But I felt I had to find out what's going on. Where would you like to have lunch?"

"Well I've got some leftover pizza in the fridge we could warm up. Or we could go over to the deli."

"Let's do that," said Esme. "Is now okay?"

"Right," said Kerry. "Let's go."

Over thick corned beef sandwiches—Esme nibbled, Kerry tore into hers—Esme began asking questions.

"How did this all happen so quickly? My mother only died a few weeks ago."

"My mom told me they met in high school and they had fierce crushes on each other."

"In high school?" repeated Esme.

"Yeah. They were mad for each other but they never really dated. It was at some science project. Your dad was already committed, I guess, so she married my dad, and he married your mom. My mom says they never thought they'd ever see each other again. But they did. Three times. And each time it was a big emotional pow! Really heavy. The pull was still there. But they were both married so they just walked away from each other. Three times! Isn't that an incredible story? It would make a great movie."

"It certainly has suspense."

"I just found all this out from Fran. My mother and I talk a lot, and I tell her everything, but she doesn't tell me everything."

"You tell her everything?"

"Sure. I figure there's probably nothing I can tell her that she hasn't heard before. And if there is, it's time she did hear about it."

Esme laughed. "But she doesn't bare her soul to you."

Kerry shook her head. "No. She's kind of square for one thing. It took her a long time after my father died before she even went on a date. And I don't think she got really involved for another year or so after that. She was busy working, too. I don't see as much of her as I did when I was little. Because she's gotta work. I mean, she loves it, but then again, she doesn't have much choice."

"I never did see much of my parents, either," said Esme, taking a tiny nibble of her sandwich. "My mother was busy with her causes. And my father was always wrapped up in business. We would be in Chicago and he'd be in California. We'd be in California and he'd be in Texas. My parents never argued. They were just never together. I felt more like his daughter than my mother's. I wanted to be close to him but how could I when he wasn't there?"

"So what did you do to make up for it?"

"To make up for it?"

"Everyone does something. I got into school work. To get Mom's attention by pulling the grades."

"I suppose I did the same thing," said Esme. "I was always starting businesses. Other kids baby-sat. I started a sitting agency when I was thirteen. And a delivery service when I was fifteen. They got me a certain amount of approval from him, but not much more time or affection."

"I think it was Fran who helped get them together. Mom's roommate. And Webb. Your dad's friend. I like him. And it was only about a week or so after your mother's funeral. Fran says it was another thunderbolt, just like in high school. Only now, they're both free."

"Why didn't they just get married way back then, if they were so crazy about each other?" asked Esme, puzzled, taking another small bite of her sandwich.

"Your dad was already spoken for. Your grandfather was helping support him and his mother and sister. He was planning to put them through college. So your dad did what he thought was the right thing. And we wouldn't be here if he hadn't. We'd both be somebody else. Or not here at all. Did you ever think of that?"

"It's not a comfortable thought," said Esme. "Well, of course, I wish my father every happiness," she went on. "But I do think he might have waited a little. Out of respect for my mother. I mean she wasn't cold in her grave—"

"Oh, I don't know," said Kerry. "At their age . . . I mean, people don't live forever. And how long do they enjoy sex and like that? They might be pretty platonic already for all we know. I think that at their ages they have to move fast. Of course, I don't know if I could have handled all this as easily right after my father died. But I didn't understand things then. See, my dad was a swell dad. But I don't think they were the great romance of the century. I mean, my mother has never once blushed when she was talking about him. But she blushed last night when she was talking about your dad. I think they might be crackling with current."

"Well, now that you mention it—I don't know about my father and mother, either. I don't suppose they ever—crackled. Otherwise he'd have stayed around more, I would think. And the one time my mother tried to explain life and so on to me, I got the distinct impression that she felt sex was a rather nasty obligation."

The waitress dropped the check and Esme grabbed it.

"Let's go Dutch," said Kerry.

"No. This is my treat. It's been a very enlightening discussion. I still think my father has behaved very badly. To me, I mean. But I suppose one can understand to a degree when one knows the background facts. I'm sorry I'm leaving today. I would have liked to talk more to you. Perhaps I could call sometime. Better yet, I don't want to call here, or your apartment. Too many strained feelings involved. My father has certainly managed to stir up a hornets' nest," she laughed ruefully. "But take my card."

She handed it to Kerry. "Would you call me collect? Only collect or I'll hang up. I insist. If you would let me know how my father is, and that he's okay and what's happening. And I'll tell you anything I learn, too, although I don't suppose that would be much at my end. But I'll talk to Aunt Sess. She's the sort of person people confide in. She often knows what's going on when no one else does."

"Sure thing. If they tell me anything I'll tell you, and vice versa."

"At least you're talking to your mother. I'm not even getting to see my own father. It's unconscionable. He's cross with me for even worrying about him."

"Listen Esme, you're older than me, and it's probably been longer since you were under your folks' thumb. But remember, parents are total dingbats sometimes. They expect you to be reasonable and logical, but they do some of the weirdest things themselves. There's no rhyme or reason. But don't be upset. Don't worry. I'm keeping on top of the scene and I'll call if there's anything to tell you."

"No matter how trivial. If there's nothing much, just call anyway and tell me there's nothing much. Collect? Will you?"

"I promise. You're okay, Esme."

"So are you, Kerry. Let's get back to the

apartment. I've got to pack. And go home and rethink the problem, with all this new input. And maybe rethink what I should do about it."

Twenty-nine

The room was a bower of flowers. The table was beautifully set. The napkins were folded to look like birds, and tall sparkling goblets stood like guards at each place setting. Yesterday's really knew how to lay on an elegant little dinner. This private room with its rich green walls and its large polished table gave any meal the grace of an intimate dinner party in a grand private home.

It was so nice of Webb to do it. And to pick a date when Sess and Dell could be here too. And so thoughtful of him to include Kerry and Miss Mary. Jessie was finding herself liking Webb more and more all the time. Hard to figure out what it was about him that turned Fran off so.

The only thing that kept the evening from being absolutely perfect was that feisty little conversation they'd had this morning. They'd spent the night in the fifth floor apartment. She had been so tired after working late the night before that she had barely managed to shower and eat a bagel before she had to fall in bed and crash. Bud hadn't wakened her, but the next morning, after they woke and made love, he had started in on her job again. "What do you have to work that hard for? You could stay home and freelance at your own pace if you must write. And be available when I want you to travel with me."

"Oh, Bud," she groaned. "Please. I told you what this means to me. And I'm the breadwinner. I must work. Besides which, I want to. Maybe not quite this hard, but I can't do anything about that right now."

"Honey, you came in here so tired last night, you dropped your purse on the couch, your shoes on the floor. You didn't rinse out your plate and cup after your bagel. You didn't even hang up your clothes; you just dumped them over a chair."

"That has nothing to do with my being tired, Mr. Clean. I do that a lot. I have never been naturally neat. And sometimes I just have more important things on my mind. And don't talk to me about how my work is so demanding, please. Look at yours. Mine doesn't call me out of town with ten minutes' notice like some

359

people's I could mention. So you couldn't even be here to give me your ring, and your sister had to do it."

"Well at least I'll be here to announce our wedding plans. Sess won't have to do that for me."

"You're going to announce what?"

"That we're getting married. In a couple of weeks. Our wedding plans. I'll do it at the dinner tonight."

"What plans?" she had asked. "We haven't made any."

"I mean just let them all know we're going to get married sometime within the next couple of weeks. That's the reason Webb's doing the dinner."

"You talked with Webb about our plans that we haven't even made yet? And not me? The next couple of weeks? Bud how can we do it in two weeks? Don't we have to get blood tests or something? It's been so long since I've done it I forget how it goes."

"Don't worry. My lawyers will know. They'll tell us what to do."

"We don't have to have a big fuss, do we? Can we just do it with nobody there? Or almost nobody? And why do your lawyers have to get into it? I don't like lawyers, honey."

"Neither do I. But you can't get very far today without them. We'll talk about it tonight," he said. "There are just a couple of things I'd like and the rest is up to you."

All day at work she had been in shock. How could she keep her mind on a ribbon-cutting at the new Salvation Army building when she had just found out she would be getting married in two weeks? And why hadn't he discussed it with her, instead of just telling her he had decided that all by himself? And this neatness business. It was bad enough that Bud was ridiculously neat. But was he going to expect her to be the same way? And he still hadn't talked to her about why he had disappeared that morning. Where he had actually been, and what he had actually been doing? He said he would. What was the big deal?

When Pontchetrain called her in to discuss their coverage of the Discovery Center's Dinosaur Festival, she wondered how he would take the news of her impending wedding. She scribbled his suggestions without hearing them, nodding vacantly. She would need shorter, more flexible hours. Bud would insist. And there would be trips with him, no doubt popping up at the wrong time. Maybe a honeymoon. Was Bud thinking of one? They hadn't discussed it. She would have to let Ponchie know.

And what was he talking to his lawyers about? Couldn't they just call city hall to find out what was required? And if he was going to tell everyone their plans, shouldn't his daughter and son be there? She would have insisted on that if he had consulted her. And he really should have. It was her life, too, darn it.

But she would talk to Bud about all this later. She knew he meant well. For now, bring on the champagne!

She looked down the table at Fran and Kerry and Sess and Dell, all laughing and gabbing animatedly as the waiter passed caviar. No lumpfish for Webb. It was the real thing—beluga—with tiny, buckwheat blinis warm from the griddle. Who would have thought that Webb, who obviously had resources but who seemed to prefer the simpler pleasures, could put on a spread like this? Real caviar!

"I don't know if I'll like it," said Kerry, eyeing the dark grey blob with suspicion.

"You'll probably be wild over it," said Fran, sitting on Kerry's right. "You loved truffles, morels and saffron the first time you tasted them. You have congenital champagne tastes, my dear."

Kerry giggled. "You're just picking on me because I don't like your granola, Fran. Don't take it personally. I don't like anyone's granola."

"You have a sympathetic spirit here, Kerry," said Webb, who sat on her left. "I can't stand the stuff either. It's like eating gravel. But Fran would wear it if she could figure out a way."

Saying so, Webb stood up and lifted his water glass. "Here's to Bud and Jessie and their new life together."

"Hear, hear," cried everyone, lifting their champagne flutes.

Bud stood up as Webb sat down. "And may I announce that you are all invited to our wedding. You will probably be the only people at our wedding. Jessie doesn't want a big hoe-down. We plan to do it within the next few weeks. As soon as we can get it together."

"Oh, Bud, that's wonderful," cried Sess, leaping up to give her brother a hug. Dell reached over to slap his cheek lightly. And they both hugged Jessie.

"Mommy!" cried Kerry. "So soon! You didn't tell me."

"Because—because—we hadn't talked about dates."

Another waiter appeared, to pass menus and relate the night's special dishes. "The swordfish is particularly good tonight," he recommended. "Fresh, very tender—mesquite-grilled with an anchovy butter sauce."

"I'll have that. Sauce on the side. No butter," said Fran.

"Me too, same way," ordered Jessie.

"Me too, but with all the sauce and butter,"

said Bud.

"Same here. Give us their butter," grinned Webb.

"Give her the sauce and butter, too," said Bud, pointing to Jessie.

"No, don't. I want it plain."

"A little butter won't hurt you, honey," he said. "You don't have any weight problem."

"It's cholesterol, not weight, I'm thinking of. No butter, no sauce," she told the waiter again, firmly.

"Fran's got you brainwashed," said Webb.

"No, but she's right about that. You two worry me, the way you eat. Have you had your cholesterol counted lately?"

"Oh, that's a crock!" said Webb.

"Sure it's a crock," said Fran. "That's why men your age are dropping dead right and left, and triple bypasses are all the rage."

"With all the exercise we get?"

"Golf doesn't count as exercise. Listen, I would defend with my life your right to eat your way to an early grave, if you choose to. But we also have the right to abstain our way to a ripe old age, if we choose."

"There you go again, Fran," giggled Kerry. "You keep trying to save the world and I keep telling you, save your breath. The world—it doesn't want to be saved. Mom, is it fresh tuna or swordfish that I like so much?"

"Swordfish, Kerry."

"Okay, I'll have it, too, then. Only plain. I'm dieting."

"I believe I prefer the yellowtail," said Miss Mary. "I made swordfish myself, last night."

Sess and Dell decided to share a Chateaubriand. "We don't have meat more than once a month," she explained to Fran. "We're on your side. But when we do, we have nothing but the best. Usually Chateaubriand or a Wendy's hamburger."

"And who wants what first?" asked Webb.

"We already had the caviar," said Fran.

No one volunteered a request so Webb said to the waiter, "Bring a platter with seafood and sauces. You know—shrimp, stone crabs, oysters—and let everyone take what they want."

"A communal seafood cocktail," said Kerry. "How neat."

The first waiter came around with the champagne again and tried to pour some in Webb's flute. Webb turned it upsidedown. Looking across Kerry to Fran he said, "Not for me. Every time I get drunk, I end up getting married."

"Funny," said Fran. "For me it's just the opposite. Every time I get married, I want to get drunk."

"You keep marrying the wrong guys. You're a bad picker."

"Look who's talking. It takes one to know one. And maybe you're a bad pick, too."

Kerry leaned back in her seat so the two of them could spar more easily. "Sometimes," Webb said quietly, leaning across her toward Fran, "I wonder why I try so hard to get along with you, Fran. Why don't you pitch that chip off your shoulder just for once. Like maybe just for tonight. Relax and enjoy yourself and let everyone else enjoy themselves, too."

"Sure," said Fran, just as quietly, leaning toward him. "So long as you keep off my grass."

"Don't worry. No more slips. Strictly business. You don't have to guard your gate with a cannon and a pit bull against me, kid. I only go where I'm invited. I'm just trying to get along."

"Try harder," said Fran.

"You're right, Fran. I love caviar," said Kerry, enthusiastically cleaning the last dab of her second helping from her plate.

"You can have mine," said Fran.

"You know what I'd like, Jessie?" asked Bud, who was now on his third glass of champagne. "I'd like you to wear one of those pretty white gowns and a veil and all that when we get married."

"Oh, Bud, I thought you said we could have just a quiet little wedding. Just families and

Fran and Webb and Miss Mary."

"Yeah, thass okay. But I would like to see you come down the aisle in a white dress. I used to think of you that way sometimes."

"But darling, it's not a first marriage. And we're both middle-aged."

"For me, baby?"

"Bud, are you getting a little bombed?"

"Yeah, I guess. I bomb easy."

"Well, if you still want me to wear a white dress when you wake up in the morning, we'll talk about it. Just so I don't have to wear it in front of hundreds of people. I'd feel silly."

"Otchee kaytchee."

"Oh, you are bombed! And you're supposed to play golf tomorrow. You'll be all hung over and feel terrible. You've had too much champagne!"

"Well, take a good look 'cause I prolly won't do it again for years." He put his arm around her and gave her a loud smack on the cheek. And then he stood up and said, "Tenshun everyone. Lissen up. We have to do one more very important toast here. To our Miss Mary, who has taken care of this family for a lifetime. And who we can never begin to repay for all she has done for us. Miss Mary is retiring in two weeks. As soon as she can help Jessie find a replacement. No. A housekeeper. No one could be a replacement. There's only one Miss

Mary. She's taking a round the worl' cruise with her sister. But first a li'l Caribbean cruise here to see if she likes this cruisin' stuff. And then she's going to decide whether to retire back in Chicago with her sister or bring her sister down here. But whichever, we all love her to pieces and we certainly never plan to ever get together like this in the future without her."

Jessie stared openmouthed at Bud and then at Miss Mary during this speech. Was Miss Mary leaving because of her? Or did she think she was being retired because she, Jessie, wanted her to be? Bud hadn't said a word to her. She wouldn't make a scene now, but when they got home, she and Bud were going to have to have a little talk. A very serious little talk.

The party broke up at ten-thirty. Kerry went back with Webb and Fran. Jessie drove Bud's car, with Bud snoring in the front seat. She had never heard him snore before. When he did, she realized, he sounded amazingly like Harry!

When they pulled into his parking spot, Bud woke up. "Home already, honey?" he mumbled.

"Get out of the car, Bud. We need to walk a bit. And talk."

"Sure honey, whash up?" he asked agreeably.

"I'm really upset, that's what. Bud, why didn't you tell me anything about it or talk it over with me before you announced that we're getting married in a couple of weeks?"

"I told you this morning."

"You told me like giving me orders. You decided. That's it. We didn't discuss it."

"Huh?"

"And Miss Mary. She'll think it's my fault you're retiring her and I wouldn't chase her away for anything."

"Hell, it has nothing to do with you except indirectly. Sess and I had been planning this a couple weeks before Bitsy's accident. Miss Mary's getting too old to have that much on her shoulders. I'm gonna take good care of her. But I hadda do it now."

"Why?"

"Because I want us to be living in the same fucking apartment, and sleeping in the same fucking bed and reading the same fucking newspaper in the morning. I need you with me. And no matter how much she tries, that might be hard for Miss Mary to take, honey. We've been planning to do this for some time anyway. Now seems a good time."

"Okay. I can understand that. But why didn't you talk to me about it? Bud, you never talk to me about anything. You decide everything. You've been making plans with a lawyer about getting married instead of talking to me. I'm not a child. I'm a grown-up too. And it's my life, too, you know."

"Heck, I'm just trying to make it all easier for you. I don't want you to bother your pretty little head over things."

"But I want my head bothered. Anything we do, anything we plan, I should have a chance to add my two cents."

"Honey, I'm only trying to be a good guy and make it all easy for you. That's what I did for Bitsy."

"Well, that's not being a good guy. That's being insulting. Because Bitsy, I gather, didn't have a brain in her head. But *I'm* not Bitsy!" And she ran toward her entrance, leaving him standing there, confused.

Upstairs, in the apartment, Sess and Dell were waiting for them. When Bud stomped in alone, Sess ran to the door and looked down the hall. "Where's Jessie?" she asked.

"She went up to her own apartment. I'm in the doghouse," said Bud.

"What'd you do?" asked Sess.

"She says I make all the plans, for the wedding and Miss Mary and everything else without ever asking what she thinks. Heck, I'm just trying to save her the bother. The way I did for Bitsy."

"Jessie is not Bitsy, Bud," said Sess. "She's not

even close."

"That's just what she said. What's that supposed to mean? Boy, I sure don't understand women."

"I think that's a fair statement, Brother. If we were made of computer chips, you'd have no problem. But your brilliance, your inventiveness, your insight, do not extend to women. The answer is obvious. Talk everything over with her. Let her help decide things."

"Yeah? You think that'll do it?"

"Sure do. Well, Brother dear, we're turning in."

And Dell nodded. "Oh, Bud, maybe you better write that down. Otherwise I don't think you'll remember it in the morning."

Bud woke, started to roll over to crawl out of bed and winced at the pain that squeezed his head like a vise. Gritting his teeth, he forced himself to the edge of the bed, pulled himself upright, which felt like bumping his head on an invisible ceiling, and staggered into the bathroom. Aspirin. Advil. Something. He downed three of the little white pills, and only then realized he was fully dressed except for his shoes. Why had he gone to bed with his clothes on? Why wasn't he sleeping downstairs, with Jessie? Why this head? And then he remembered the dinner the night before.

And his drinking. And Jessie being upset.

He felt a little better after a shower, and three cups of Miss Mary's good coffee. "Sess and Dell said to say good-bye," said Miss Mary. "Their plane left at eight something."

He nodded. He guessed he could stand to shave now. As he did his head grew clearer. And the memory of last night grew sharper.

What was it Sess had said? Talk everything over with Jessie first? He dialed her office number. She answered on one ring.

"Jessie, it's me, Bud. And Honey, about last night —"

"Oh, Bud, I'm so glad you called. I was afraid to call you —"

"Why afraid to call me?"

"When I got home last night it dawned on me that I was doing the same thing you were. Instead of talking it out I was just getting upset. And that's just as bad."

"It's okay, honey," he said, relieved that she wasn't still angry.

"No, it's not. I love you, Bud. I should have talked to you."

"I love you, too, honey. Sess says I can't make all the decisions myself, anymore. I have to let you help. Let's get all that legal stuff worked out and get married as soon as we can and we'll decide everything together."

"What legal stuff?"

"Oh, my lawyers came up with all sorts of things we have to settle."

"Lawyers? Settle? Like what?"

"Let's talk about it over dinner tonight."

"Okay. I'll call you as soon as I know when I'll get home."

"Want to go out? Or should I let Miss Mary make something. She's dying to."

"Okay, then let her. It's sure to be good."

Jessie hung up slowly. What was all this with his lawyers, now? Would they make up some complicated agreement she would have to sign? Lawyers could turn anything into a confusing mess. How she wished that it was all over and done with already. But she had a sinking feeling that if Bud was bringing his lawyers into the act, nothing would go as simply and surely as they had thought.

Thirty

Bud went down for the mail at four. And immediately he spotted the pink envelope from Ginny. Now how had she gotten this address? He tore it open. A folded note with just three words inside. "Thanks! Love, Ginny." He shuddered. Jessie could have found it. He had given her a copy of his mail key. She often checked his box for him now, when she got home before him, to save Miss Mary the trouble. That's all he needed. Not that he didn't want to tell Jessie all about it. Why he had to disappear so abruptly. Why he couldn't tell her why. Why he had to do it. Why he had lied to her about where he was. Jesus, how had he botched that all up? Would she be able to handle it if he told her? He just couldn't take a chance on losing her. Would she understand that it would never happen again? That book was now closed. Surely, she would understand.

But what if she didn't? He simply couldn't take the chance. Not now. Soon, he promised himself. Very soon. Maybe right after the wedding.

He burned the note in the sink and washed the ashes down the garbage disposal.

Just as he reached for the phone to dial his office, it rang.

"Hello," he barked.

"Hello, is this Bud Wellman?" a sexy feminine voice poured into his ear.

"Yes. Who is this?"

"My name is Cynthia. I work at the *Community News*. With Jessie. This was the number she gave me once to call in an emergency. Like if Ponchie was blowing his cork or something. So I just knew it had to be yours."

"Yes. Well, what can I do for you Miss—er—Cynthia?"

"Don't get me started. We'll be on this phone all day, from what I hear about you," she giggled. "But I just wanted to tell you that Jessie would probably throttle me if she knew I called. But Hel and me—that's Heloise, she works here, too—we wanted to tell you how neat we think it is about you and Jessie. And we wanted to tell you, whatever she had to do to get that ring, we'd do it too. I mean in case you've got a friend or a brother or somebody that might be looking," and she giggled again, seductively. "Only kidding, of course."

"Of course," said Bud.

"Jessie is so lucky. She's always attracting you powerhouse guys. That Mr. Worth from down in Miami with the limo a block long. And that fancy-dancy doctor that turned out to still be married. And that real estate guy in Boca—"

"Listen," Bud interrupted, "I'm sorry I haven't got more time to talk, but I have to make some calls to my office—"

"Oh, that's okay. I understand. We're always chasing our own tails around here, too. Heloise and I just wanted to say congratulations or whatever you're supposed to say, and tell you that we hope we can come to your wedding. No matter how small it is. After all, we're all like sisters here. And you never know who we might meet there."

Bud cleared his throat. "We haven't actually made very firm plans yet," Bud said, dodging the question. "But I'll talk to Jessie."

"Oh, no! Don't tell her I called. But when you're doing the list, you could just say, like, 'Don't forget your friends from the office, honey,' or something like that."

"I'll keep that in mind," said Bud. "Thanks for calling." And he hung up. Sheesh, what kind of a broad was that? What kind of a place was that where Jessie worked? Well, he'd do something about that pretty soon. And did Jessie really attract all those men this person was talking about?

He dialed his offices. "This is Mr. Wellman," he said when the switchboard answered. "Is Cromwell there? Let me talk to him."

A small pause and Edgar Cromwell answered, "Yes sir?"

"Edgar, listen, I want you to reserve Burt and Jack's for the wedding. Make it two or three weeks from Wednesday or whenever you can get it. Get a rabbi. Reform. As close to Protestant as you can find because she's not Jewish and I don't want any objections and stuff at the last minute. Get a judge or a notary or someone as a backup. Or to marry us if you can't find a rabbi. Flowers and stuff and a chuppah and music. Whatever people do for weddings. Do it right. Dinner, champagne, fancy cake. Yeah, everything. I don't know what time. Maybe one or two in the afternoon? Have to do it in the afternoon if we want the place to ourselves. Or if they're busy, Yesterday's would be fine, too. Let me know which day and run all the details by me so I can tell you what to change and what to keep, okay Edgar? Talk to you later."

What was keeping Jessie? She'd spent last

night at home with Kerry, so tonight was his. They'd maybe play a little backgammon. Have dinner. Hold hands and talk. Make love. It would be a good evening. His doorbell rang. Probably her now. He hurried to open the door.

The woman standing there with the papers and envelopes in her hands looked familiar. "Oh, Mr. Wellman, you're home. I'm Katie Resnick. Two apartments down the hall. I'm collecting for leukemia. May I come in?"

Bud stepped back and she stepped in. She stared up at him, gasped a couple of short breaths and blushed bright red. "I'm finally getting to talk to my handsome new single neighbor," she said, gasping again and stepping past him into his living room. "What a beautiful place. I hope you don't get—uh—lonesome here. If you do—I'm right—down the hall." She seemed to choke on those last words and her chest was heaving.

"You're collecting for leukemia, you said?" Bud reminded her uncomfortably.

"Oh. Yes." She rattled off her prepared speech at ninety miles an hour, gasping every few words. "I'm going to give you an envelope and you can (gasp) give as much as you can and just leave it (gasp) in the office for me and I will (gasp) collect it there and I thank you for all (gasp) the people with leukemia and all those who (gasp) will have it in the future and the people (gasp) who are trying to help them at the Leukemia (gasp) Society."

Bud took her hand and on the last few words began leading her toward the door. She stared at him adoringly until she realized he was guiding her back out to the hall, but then her face crumpled.

"Sorry, I never invite a woman into my apartment when I'm alone here," he said. "My fiancée wouldn't like it. But do give me the envelope."

She mouthed the word "fiancée" sadly, handed him an envelope and turned towards her own apartment, as Bud gently closed the door.

Jessie arrived ten minutes later. This time Bud looked out the peephole before opening the door. He pulled her quickly inside, closed the door and looked out the peephole again.

"Don't I get a kiss?" she asked. "Darling, what's the matter? Do you feel all right?"

"Oh sure. Great. I just opened the door, thinking it was you, and there was this lady from down the hall collecting for leukemia. And she practically made a pass at me. What is wrong with the women in this town?"

"Oh, Bud, how funny!"

"Funny!" he shouted. "Why do you always think everything is funny? It's humiliating."

"Oh, darling, don't be silly. She was probably just a little bit lonesome, that's all. Maybe a tiny bit horny. It happens."

"Well, I've had enough of it."

"Don't be so impatient. Once we're married it will all stop and you'll probably miss all the attention."

"Yeah, I'll sure miss having a lot of pushy women leering at me," Bud said, reaching past her to pick up the phone. He dialed his office and asked for Cromwell again. "Listen Edgar, have you got all that marriage stuff ready to go over? The agreement stuff you said we had to talk about? Well, let's get it over with. No use fooling around. Let's get all this stuff over with. Tomorrow if Jessie can. If not, the day after. I'll talk to her, now."

"What was that all about?" asked Jessie.

"We've gotta go over some stuff about getting married. Are you free tomorrow? Or would you rather do it the day after?"

Jessie sighed. "Tomorrow, I guess. You're right. We might as well get it over with."

Jessie had never visited Bud's office before. "It's not really my office," he said as they entered the front door and were greeted by a cheery wave from the receptionist. "I just move in at any of my installations as I need to. They all have meeting rooms and stuff." Bud nodded at the receptionist and introduced Jessie. "Jessie, this is Miss Halloran. Miss Halloran, Mrs. Moore." Miss Halloran beamed.

He led her down a wide, carpeted corridor, lined with paintings and tables displaying bowls of flowers, past several closed doors and into a conference room with a lustrous burled table surrounded by high-backed, upholstered chairs.

"This is my Medi-Quip branch down here. We have big offices in about ten cities and smaller facilities in a dozen or so more," explained Bud. "The main one is Chicago. There's a room I use here but my only real office down here is in the lab out near Rock Creek. But this is closer and Edgar said he would be here this morning anyway, working on the new pension plan. I do as little as possible of that nuts-and-bolts stuff anymore. Gets in the way of my golf."

They sat down, and two minutes later a short, rather slight man in a suit and vest, maybe ten years younger than Bud, came in, followed by a woman pushing a cart holding a coffee service and a tray of Danish. "Coffee, please. That's all. We've just finished breakfast," said Bud. "The same, thank you," nodded

Jessie. "Nothing for me," said the man whom Bud called Edgar, taking a chair.

"Edgar, this is Jessie Moore. Jessie, Edgar Cromwell. He wants to go over a few things with us."

"First, you have to apply for a license and get your blood tests," said Cromwell, plunging right in. "I've made all the appointments with second choices. You can call and confirm, or we'll do it if you like. These are copies of your appointments, and a list of the documentation you might need."

"We beat you on those, Edgar," grinned Bud. "We did our tests a couple of days ago."

Unperturbed, Cromwell went on. "Fine. Now Barnett is making up your prenuptial agreements. Mr. Wellman is setting your trust, Mrs. Moore, and there is an agreement to sign which covers contingencies such as the marriage failing, Mr. Wellman's demise or yours, and his agreement to support you—that sort of thing. Standard for people in your positions. But generous. We suggest you have your own lawyer examine it."

"What lawyer?" asked Jessie. "The one I keep on retainer for all my prenuptial agreements like this?"

"Ha-ha-ha," laughed Cromwell tentatively. "And there are a few other matters to settle. For instance, should you predecease Mr.

Wellman, where would you want to be buried? And if Mr. Wellman should predecease you, he will, of course, be buried in the family plot in Chicago, next to his wife. His first wife, that is."

Jessie put her cup down. "Next to his first wife? But we've never discussed that."

"Where do you wish to be buried, Mrs. Moore?" Cromwell asked in an unctuous tone.

"I really don't want to be buried anywhere," said Jessie. "I don't like the idea of dying at all."

"Do you have a plot?" he asked.

"Well, yes. My husband—my first husband—got them. Three spaces. One for me and one for our daughter, too. My husband—my first husband—is buried there. And I'm sure that now that Kerry's planning to marry Doug, she'd probably rather be buried next to him someday than next to Harry and me."

"But you want to be buried there."

"Actually, not really. I hadn't thought of it before, but now that I do think of it, no, I really don't want to. But Kerry would probably be crushed if I didn't. I wish I had some other choices."

"If you don't want to, don't get buried there," said Bud.

"Oh, I should be buried by myself, all alone for all eternity in some strange cemetery somewhere, while you're lying all cozy next to Bitsy? That doesn't sound like any fun. It seems like after all this waiting, we ought to be able to be together."

"But what will the kids say? I'm sure Esme would raise hell, and I've got enough trouble with her as it is. She's been very quiet and pleasant on the telephone the last few calls but I think she's a smoldering volcano right now."

"And I think Kerry would be upset if I got buried anywhere else."

"And after all, Jessie. We'll never know the difference."

"No, but I know the difference now, and I'm not happy about it. Can't you think of some better solution, Bud?"

"Well if you're going to get buried next to your husband, I might as well get buried next to Bitsy. No point in my getting tucked away with strangers somewhere, either."

"Well, maybe I won't get buried next to Harry. What I really don't like, Bud is that you just assumed things again without asking me for my opinion."

"No, I really didn't, honey. This time I didn't even know Edgar was going to bring this up. Why don't we think about it for a couple of days and then decide what to do."

"The other matters we should run by you include your estate, Mrs. Moore."

"My estate? I don't think I have one. I mean, there's a little. I don't know that I'd call it an estate."

"Mr. Wellman will waive any rights to your estate, should you predecease him."

"That's not waiving good-bye to much, but whatever I have must go to Kerry, Bud. She'll need it and you won't. In fact that's one of the reasons I want to keep working. I really have to try to look after my daughter. If something happened to me, it would be terrible for her."

"Jessie," said Bud, "don't you know I would never let your child go wanting?"

"But what if something happened to us both at once and then Esme claimed whatever you should get from me?"

"Esme wouldn't do that. She has plenty of her own."

"I don't think she's feeling very benevolent towards me at the moment. It's such a little bit, but I never spent any of it. I guess I've read too much Dickens. You don't spend capital. And I think of it as being for Kerry. I'll feel better if she's protected. Things happen."

"That's why we have this waiver," said Mr. Cromwell.

"And I think you better write up something in that agreement that has me looking after Kerry then. And some kind of trust for her. Just in case," said Bud.

"Yes sir," nodded Cromwell.

"Oh, Bud, would you? That would be so wonderful."

"So then, you can quit that job."

"But darling, I've explained that to you. I don't want to quit yet. It's not a job. It's a career. It's like being a painter or a dancer or an actor. It's something I feel I have to do. Cutting back is one thing. Quitting is something else."

Cromwell began doodling on his pad.

"But Jessie," Bud countered, "we want to be together as much as we possibly can. Your time isn't your own. I want you to travel with me sometimes. That job has you shackled and chained."

"So does yours. And I told you, I'll talk to Pontchetrain about working less and having more flexible hours. So I can go with you sometimes. Even if he lowers my pay, it's okay. But I want to write, Bud. My foot's in the door. I've just got to keep that job."

Cromwell's doodling picked up speed.

"Listen Jessie. You tell me not to make decisions without getting your input first. But you've made this one without mine. And you don't want mine. You're determined to work whether I want you to or not."

"But you don't want to just give me some input. I heard your input. It's called giving orders. I don't try to tell you not to run around so much for your business. Or not to play so much golf. But you're trying to dictate to me. You know how much this means to me but you don't care. It's not that you want to be with me. Because you'll be spending a lot of time on the golf course and at work. You won't be with me then. I could be working then. But you just want me at home waiting, so that when or if you come home, I'll be there. I should just give up my dream, to spend my time waiting for you to come home."

"What about my dream, Jessie? For thirty-five years, I've dreamed about you. About us together. Now it looks like all I'm going to get is the leftovers of your time."

As the debate picked up heat, Cromwell's doodling picked up speed, until by now he was scribbling furiously, slapping his legal pad this way and that as he filled page after page with his furious scribbles.

Several times he tried to interject a comment to get their train of thought back on the track. "Mrs. Moore? Mr. Wellman? There are a few other things I think we should discuss. Just to get everything on the table. Ah, Mrs. Moore? Mr. Wellman? Ah, for instance, do you have any serious health problems, Mrs. Moore that Mr. Wellman is not aware of? Mrs. Moore? I said have you any—"

"What kind of question is that?" asked Bud.

"Well, sir, I just —"

"Well, that's none of your business, Edgar. Forget it."

"Yes sir. Then, Mrs. Moore, do you have any large debts or any legal obligations, Mr. Wellman isn't aware of?"

"Where did you dig up these questions, Edgar?" demanded Bud.

Cromwell flushed, turned the page and began doodling on a fresh one. His pencil was worn down. He threw it into the middle of the table, pulled another from his shirt pocket and began racing it over the page in bold strokes.

"I'm not trying to hide anything. Any defects, or debts, Mr. Cromwell. On the other hand, I am not a piece of sale merchandise at Macy's."

"All I'm looking to do is get this over with," said Bud. "And be a family with the lady. How did it get so complicated?"

"Don't look at me," said Jessie. "I didn't bring in a lawyer. And another thing, if we're supposed to be a family, I think Esme should have been invited to Webb's dinner. She's going to think I had something to do with her not being there."

"How could she think that? It was Webb's party. He can invite anyone he chooses. I think he didn't invite her because he thought she might make a scene. Although I guess when I said I'd rather she weren't invited, that might have affected his decision. She probably wouldn't have come anyway. She's very angry with me."

"Maybe she wouldn't have come and maybe she would have. But at least it would have been *her* choice. You can't make decisions for everyone all the time, Bud. We're grown-ups too. And you and I can't get married unless Esme and Needle are there. It would make a wall between us that we'd never be able to tear down if we tried for the rest of our lives."

"Did it ever occur to you that she might not want to come?"

The two of them turned away from each other. Cromwell stopped drawing, midstroke, cleared his throat and said, "Well, Mrs. Moore, and Mr. Wellman, I think the best strategy would be for you to discuss and resolve these three issues. Inviting your daughter, sir, to the wedding, or not inviting her. Who gets buried where. And Mrs. Moore's job. We will add the trust for Kerry Moore and your responsibility for her. And then we can set another appointment to discuss these matters."

"That's fine with me," snapped Jessie.

"And fine with me," retorted Bud. They had come in Jessie's car. "Edgar, will you show

Mrs. Moore to her car. And then you can find a company car and someone to drive me back to my apartment."

"I can certainly drive you back," said Jessie.

"I wouldn't want to make you late for work. You go ahead. I'll get a lift."

"Whatever you prefer," said Jessie huffily, standing up and marching out with Cromwell scurrying behind her.

"And give my regards to Mr. Pontchetrain," Bud called after her. He turned back to the table, grabbed his copy of the blood test schedules, and squeezed it into a very small ball.

Jessie let herself in the apartment, dropped her purse on the foyer floor, sank against the closed door and leaned there for a while, numb with despair. "How did that happen?" she mumbled to herself. "Fran? Kerry?" she called. No answer. The apartment was empty. Where were they when you needed them?

Oh, damn, the phone was blinking. "You monster," she scolded it. "I can't even be miserable in peace and quiet without you nagging at me." She watched it blink for a couple of seconds and then punched the replay button. It whirred, clicked bleeped and began replaying its calls.

"Jessie, do you have one of the new style

books?" It was Heloise. "Ponchie is having a fit because we couldn't find one here to check usage on measurements."

The door chimes chimed. She went to answer, as a call from Kerry came on. "Mom, I'm at Bloomie's and as soon as I leave I'm heading for the airport to pick up Doug. Remember? So if my door is closed when you come in, don't just barge in. Got the message? Oh, and listen. Like, I just saw this incredibly darling tie-dye outfit . . ."

She opened the door. Bud stood there, looking sheepish. She backed up and he came in.

"And if you would just give me a small advance on next month's allowance . . ."

"I'm playing my answering machine," she said.

"I'll wait. I think we should talk," he said, parking on the sectional. "I'm sorry I got so huffy. That was awful. Those dumb questions."

"I'll charge it and we can work it out," said Kerry's voice. "It's only $32.50, Mom and it was $110. No way I could pass it up."

A click and a whirr and the next call came on. "Jessie, this is Emil. Are you over whatever was bothering you?" His voice was thick and slow but the words were unmistakable. "I miss your little body. I miss your little cunt."

Bud's head turned and he stared, unbelieving, at the machine.

"You know you miss me, too," Emil's voice went on. "Can you come over tonight? I can send Yver for you. We could go to a movie. You always want to go to the movies. And then get a bite. And then we can eat things we enjoy a lot more. Call me." And then the click, whirr and bleep-bleep-bleep that meant the calls were over.

Bud stood up slowly and stared at Jessie with shock. His mouth open, his eyes wide open.

Jessie sank onto the sofa. "I told you about him. I was going with him," she whispered. "A few months ago. He's the alcoholic I told you about. The one that—started drinking again and—became such a pig—as you heard—and I broke up with him."

"When, yesterday?"

"It's not what it sounds like. He can't seem to get it that it's over. I've told him so many times." Her whisper turned into a squeak.

"Well, I can tell that," said Bud, choking. "I—I guess you'd better answer him."

"No. I haven't seen him since that time you knew about. That one night when you were in Chicago. I told you—"

"When I was in Chicago?" Bud shook his head slowly. "I—I'm sorry I bothered you, Jessie. I guess I've made a big mistake. I'll let myself out."

"Bud, it's not what it sounds like. I can't help it. He keeps calling and—" But the door had closed. He was gone.

"Oh, no," she cried. "Oh, no!" And she pushed her face into the back of the sofa and sobbed.

Thirty-one

Jessie staggered into the kitchen where Fran was humming happily as she stirred a pot of oatmeal.

"Must you?" Jessie groaned, ripping a paper towel from the roll and running cold water over it. She folded it and pressed it on her still swollen eyes.

"Sing or make oatmeal?" Fran retorted cheerfully, taking two cups from the cabinet and pouring decaf in both of them. "What about Neil? Does he like his coffee leaded or unleaded?" she asked.

"Who knows? Let Kerry worry about it. If she's old enough to bring her boyfriend home to sleep in her room for a week, she's old enough to make his darn breakfast."

"My, we sound a little grumpy this morning." Fran took the oatmeal pan off the heat.

"Grumpy? I'm devastated. Destroyed. I can't believe what's happened."

"Oh? A little spat?"

"You'd call the atom bomb a firecracker, when you're in this cheerful mood, Fran. It's an annoying trait. This is thirty-five years of dreaming down the drain. Those damned lawyers and their prenuptial land mines. I can't talk about it."

Kerry poked her head into the kitchen. "Hi! Can I join you two for breakfast?"

"Help yourself," said Fran. "Doug still sleeping?"

"He'll probably sleep until noon. Sex wears him out. It gigs me up." She poured herself some decaf, dug one of Fran's bran muffins out of the freezer and popped it into the microwave, and helped herself to some oatmeal.

"Your mother and I are having a heavy discussion here, Kerry. Very important." She turned back to Jessie. "My god! What happened to your face? It's all swollen. Can you see out of those eyes?"

"More or less. I was crying my head off for hours last night."

"You were? I didn't hear a thing," said Kerry.

"You were otherwise occupied," snapped Jessie.

"Okay, so it's serious," said Fran. "So what did you argue about?"

"You and Bud, Mom?" asked Kerry, surprised. "Just like real people? I thought you didn't do that."

Her mother nodded. "The same thing as the last one. He decided everything without asking what I think. He wants me to quit my job. And he thinks he should get buried next to Bitsy when he dies. That's crazy. She had him for thirty-plus years and didn't even make him happy. Almost no sex at all. Now, it should be my turn."

"I don't think either one of you is going to have much sex after you're dead," said Kerry. "So what's the difference? Better get all you can now."

"That's irrelevant," said Jessie.

"Why does he think he should be buried there?" asked Fran.

"I think it's his kids. He's afraid Esme will go berserk."

"Too late. She's already gone berserk. And who's going to tell her?"

"What if she asks?"

"Did he talk to her about it?" asked Kerry. "She's not totally unreasonable. Maybe he should just ask her."

"What do you mean she's not totally unreasonable?" asked Fran. "I think she's impossible."

"Well, I met her in the elevator here, and

I've talked to her on the phone several times. I kind of like her. She's awfully smart."

"Oh my gosh, a spy!" cried Fran. "A mole, under our own roof."

"Oh, get real, Fran. She's a little stiff and all business. But everybody's different. Being controlled is no crime."

Fran shook her head and turned back to Jessie. "Patch it up," she advised. "I'd hate to see you two blow this over something so trivial. Kerry's right. Once you're dead, who cares where you're buried?"

"It's not trivial. It's basic. He can't decide everything in my life for me like he did for Bitsy. She loved it. So long as he gratified her every whim. I'd hate it. And I don't care where he gets buried but I do not want him buried next to her."

"Oh, Jessie, don't be such a stubborn jackass. You'd let such nonsense wreck a glorious love story? Call him."

"I can't."

"Why not?"

"Because that's not all. Kerry, leave us alone for a minute."

"Oh, Mom, save it, will you? What is there that you can't say in front of me? I know the two of you do more than shake hands."

"Not last night. He followed me back from his office and I had just started listening to the phone messages when he got here. First came your call from Saks or wherever, Kerry. And then this call from Emil came on."

"From Emil? But I thought you broke up with him, Mom."

"God knows I've tried. I've told him a dozen times in the last few months. By phone, note and in person. But he's drinking so much, he can't remember anything. He calls at the office. He puts calls on the machine here. He asks if we've got a date this week. Or worse, he says something sexy. Last night's call was terrible. Piggish. Obscene."

"You mean like something about wanting to get in your pants, Mom?"

"Nothing that subtle. He never talked that way when we were going together. But then he was sober."

"So what did he say?"

"I can't repeat it."

"He wants to have a little sex," guessed Kerry.

"Using the word c-u-n-t and talking about eating. And he makes it sound like I've been having orgies with him right along. I've only seen him once since I found Bud. I told Bud about it then. To get it through Emil's head for once and for all that this was it. But when Bud heard that message, he turned white. Absolutely white."

"Oh, Jesus!" said Fran. "He must have thought —"

Jessie nodded. "I'm just sick over it. He didn't let me explain. He walked out. I think we could have gotten past these other things. But if I was him and I heard that message, I'd think the same thing."

"Gee, Mom," said Kerry. "That's awful."

"There must be something we can do," said Fran. "There's always an answer to any problem. Well, most of the time, anyway."

"Well, I can't think of any. And I've got to get dressed and to work. If I'm not going to be Mrs. Gotrocks, I've still got to pay the bills. And maybe if I keep busy, I won't think so much." She blinked back her tears. Kerry hugged her and walked her back to her room.

Fran slipped into her own room and dialed Webb's number. "Webb, this is Fran. Can you meet me for breakfast somewhere as soon as possible?"

"The deli on seventeenth? Unshaved, fifteen minutes. Shaved, about twenty-five."

"Unshaved. Us field hands can take anything."

"See you there."

She grabbed her purse and started for the door, then stopped dead and came back to her dresser. Sighing, she put on a little pancake and lipstick and lined her eyes. It did make a big difference, she had to admit. "See you later, Kerry," she called on her way out.

As soon as Fran closed the front door, Kerry picked up the phone and dialed Esme's number. She would not tell her about Emil's call, she decided. But the graves, yes. That would give Esme a chance to get back into her father's good graces. And maybe help with the patching up. Worth a try, anyway.

A maid answered. "This is Kerry Moore," Kerry told her. "I have to speak to Mrs. Pearlman. It's very important. About her father."

Esme was on the phone in ten seconds. "Esme, something came up I thought I should tell you."

"Is my father all right?"

"He's fine. Nothing like that. But he and my mom have been arguing. Pretty serious, I think."

"Really? About what?"

"I guess partly because he decides everything without asking her for any input at all, which really blows her cork. She's been making all the decisions for us for five years now and so that really frosts her."

"Like he did for my mother. Only she liked it. My mother didn't want responsibility. She could decide on clothes and wallpaper and decorating but she made such terrible decisions on those that it was just as well my father made the rest."

"And two other things. He doesn't want her working. And she wants to work."

"Any woman should have the right to work, in this world. It's the only real security she has, no matter how rich her husband. No matter how rich she thinks she is. You never know what happens to money. Look at my grandfather. Rich one day. A pauper the next."

"But the other thing is wild. It's about who gets buried where when they die."

"But who's dying?"

"Nobody. But someday everyone will. And your dad has a place next to your mother. And my mom has a place next to my dad. You'd think two people who didn't have such fantastic marriages wouldn't feel all that compelled to sleep next to their firsts but they do. Even though they'd both rather be buried next to each other. And they're both jealous of the other one doing that. Your dad thinks you'd blow up if he didn't agree to be buried next to your mom. And he doesn't want to piss you off any worse than you are now."

"Well, that's ridiculous. What difference does it make once they're dead? I don't like graves anyway. Needle and I plan to be cremated. It's in our wills."

"Well, maybe you have to let him know it

doesn't matter to you. So they can stop arguing."

"How can I tell him anything? He hardly talks to me, he's still so angry with me. I think he really might be cutting me off."

"Well, maybe if you helped them work it out about the graves, and you gave him encouragement in this marriage, and said something about how satisfying it is for a woman to work—he'd see that you really care about him being happy. You'd be back in his good graces just like that, I bet."

"You know, I still think it wasn't right of my father to jump right into an affair so fast. Now that you've told me the whole story, how they loved each other all those years—I understand a little better. But he could have told me. Doesn't he think I have any capacity for understanding feelings?

"And let me tell you, I'm not so eager to help your mother and her roommate when they pulled such a number on me when I came down there."

"Oh, come on, Esme. What would you have done in their shoes? Mom says everybody has to think what they would have done in the other person's shoes or nothing's ever going to work out. You pulled a number on them, too, showing up with no warning like that. I know my mom and I know Fran and they wouldn't either one do anything so awful. You all three had your motors overheating. Fran was looking out for Mom and Mom was trying, no matter how hard it was, to do what Bud said. I mean she's told me fifty times how terrible she felt that morning, and she's been after your dad to make up with you ever since."

"Well, you may be right. I'll talk to Needle and see what he thinks. And I'll call you back. It might take a day or so."

"You eat all the wrong food," scolded Fran after Webb ordered.

"Sorry, ma'am. Oatmeal and a bagel with sliced tomatoes is not my idea of a big breakfast."

"But all that fat and cholesterol. One of these days, you'll drop over with a heart attack."

"So then the story's over. Everyone's story is over one day. Would you care if I did?"

"I'd go to your funeral and say, 'I told you so,' to your casket. But that's not why we're here. Bud and Jessie had a big blowout, a double-header. One, while they talked to the lawyer—over her right to keep working and who gets buried where and over him making all the decisions."

"He's used to that. Been doing it for over thirty years. I guess it's hard to turn off."

"But I can't just let this beautiful story fizzle into nothing. I think they're both at such an emotional pitch that they're reacting all out of proportion."

"Jesus, if they can't make it, is there hope for anyone?" Webb shook his head. The waitress brought their coffee. Webb stirred his for a moment in silence, and then said, "Remember when I asked about your marriages. And the one who really hurt you? And it took you two times to tell me about it."

"It's not easy to talk about. I just want to forget it. It's not easy to forget, either."

"Yeah. Well, now I'm having trouble forgetting it, too."

"Sorry."

"I'd like to kill the S.O.B. How could anyone hurt you? So tough on the outside. So feisty. But you don't fool me, kid. Inside, you're soft. Scared."

"No, I'm not! I'm not afraid of—" she began. But when she looked him in the eye, she couldn't finish. "Well, anyone is a little scared, sometimes."

"I know this is crazy. But I keep feeling like I've got to see that no one ever hurts you again, Fran. That's how I feel. I can't explain it. I don't understand it. I'm a five-time loser; so are you. Maybe six would be lucky."

Fran's mouth dropped open. "Lucky?" she repeated. "You can speak plainer than that."

"I'm saying, do you wanna get married? And I haven't had a drink."

"Oh! Wow! You sure it isn't just that you feel you have to make an honest woman out of me after our little slip in San Francisco? That wasn't your fault. You didn't seduce me. I seduced you. It was driving me crazy that you didn't seem at all interested, even though I was so sure I could feel something—some vibes."

He grinned. "They were there, all right, weren't they? No, that's not it. But I can't forget that night, either."

"Sure you're not just doing this to change the subject? I really want to help Jessie and Bud."

"We'll help them. I'll call him. I've got a meeting at noon. I'll see him right after it. I'll insist. I never tell Bud what to do. I never interfere. But this once, I think you're right. They can't get out of their own way. They're wound up like tops. We'll get them back together if we have to rope and tie them. But first, us. Are we worth a bet?"

Fran nodded, looking across at him with eyes glowing like candles. she reached for his hand just as he reached for hers. And said softly, "It's a long shot. But I'm game if you are. I thought you'd never ask."

Thirty-two

When the phone rang, sounding so loud in the quiet apartment, Kerry pounced on it and said, "Hello?" Doug was still sleeping. How could anyone sleep so much when there were so many good things they could be doing?

"Hello, is this Jessie Moore's residence?" It was a male voice. Deep baritone with a bit of huskiness. Sounded a little like Bud. But it wasn't Bud.

"Yes. I'm her daughter Kerry. But Mom isn't here right now. Would you like to leave your name and number?"

"You're Kerry? Well, that was a bit of luck. This is Benjie Wellman. I think your mother and my father are — you know —"

"I think they are too," Kerry laughed. "In fact, I know they are."

He chuckled at that. "Actually, you're the one I was hoping to talk to. My sister Esme says she got a clearer picture of what's going on there after talking to you. And that's why I'm calling."

"Because you want to know what's going on?"

"Well, kind of. I tried to call my dad several times yesterday, but I kept getting Miss Mary and she kept saying my father didn't want to talk just then. He'd call me. But he never called back. Same thing today. And that's just not my dad. And I thought maybe you knew something."

"All I know is it's like an Arthur Miller play around here the last couple of days. Heavy. They had a spat about something, and like I told Esme, they take everything so seriously, like it was the end of the world or something. I don't know what's with them. My mother isn't like that at all normally. And Esme says, neither is your dad. They waste all that energy being so dramatic and then they make up anyway."

"And that week he just evaporated—"

"We still don't know any more about that than you do."

"I didn't know where to reach him, either, but whenever I've called the office, he's called back pretty quickly. That's how we always work it when he's out of town and hopping from one place to another pretty fast. But yesterday and today, no call-backs. My dad can take care of himself and it's probably nothing. But I was just a little uneasy."

"Well, I don't know much more than you do, Benjie, but if I hear anything, I'll let you know. If you want to leave a number. Are you coming down for the wedding?"

"Wouldn't miss it."

"Unless nature staged a spectacular mudslide or avalanche?"

Benjie chuckled. "Who's been telling you tales on me? But, yeah, that would be a hard one to call."

"Oh, sure. You can't let nature put on a show like that and not have anyone watching. When Esme told me some of the projects you've been in on and some of the research, all I could think of is where do I sign up. I mean, how great it must feel to know that you're doing something that really needs doing. You're finding out things that add one more little chip of knowledge in that huge mosaic of the universe and life and how it all fits together."

"You know, that's just how I feel sometimes," said Benjie. "Like there's so much out there we don't know about that we need to know about. And I'm just helping pull back the curtain a tiny little bit at a time. But while I'm doing it, the only problem is, I don't get to be with my family as much as I'd like. But, listen, Kerry. If there's anything I should know—"

"I'll call. Or I'll tell Esme, and she can call you."

"Good enough. I'll see you at the wedding. Oh, and got a pencil? Here's my number."

Doug came staggering out of her room just before noon. "I thought you were going to just sleep the whole day away," said Kerry grumpily.

"Don't blame me. You wear me out, woman."

"The newspaper's in the kitchen. You want some breakfast?"

"I don't need the paper. Everybody gone?"

"Yes."

"Okay. Then let's have some breakfast first, to keep up our strength."

"And after breakfast, you want to go to the beach," said Kerry. "But before the beach you want to jump into bed with me."

Doug laughed. "You read my mind."

Kerry smiled and sighed. Yes, sometimes it was just too easy to read Doug's mind. Aloud she said, "Well, what do you want for breakfast?"

Thirty-three

They pulled into the small lot and parked next to a pile of boxes and tires below the sign, Runaways. The squat, patched stucco building huddled beneath a large overhang. There were no windows or openings in front, but at the side was a door marked by a neon entrance sign. "Maybe I'll wait in the car," said Fran.

"No. You wouldn't be safe out here alone," said Webb, helping her from the van. "You insisted on coming. You wouldn't listen. So now, dammit, stay with me." She nodded and followed him inside. While he bought two bags of potato chips, she looked down the bar and over at the tables. Bud wasn't there. They hurried out and scrambled back into the van, locked the doors and started the motor. Fran threw the chips in back with the rest. There was quite a pile of them by now. "I think we're wasting time," he said. "There must be dozens of these places. If only I could remember exactly what he said. Just that it was on Sunrise or Oakland Park, I think and west of U.S. 1. Hell, most of the city is west of U.S. 1. And he doesn't know shit about these joints. Or what could happen to him, drunk, in the wrong one."

"How do you know he's in one of them? He might just be off playing golf somewhere."

"No way. Not in his state. And nobody knows where he is. Bud never does that. There's always at least one person at his office who knows. And I can always find out. Just like Bud can always find out where I am, from my office. Even if I'm not letting anyone else know. That's how we operate. We cover for each other. We look after each other. And he's been stewing over that lousy phone call from Jessie's friend—former friend—for two days. He'd be out of his mind enough to do something really stupid."

"Okay. Makes sense. But how do you know he went back to the same place?"

"I don't. But we can't prowl every bar in the county."

"Can't you remember anything else about it? He didn't mention the name?"

"No, except there had been a big accident when he was there. But, wait a minute. I think

411

he said something about road repair. And a lot of equipment and materials. Only that was weeks ago. It might not still be there."

"There's road repair going on all over I-95 and the cross streets."

"But this must be some local stuff. Otherwise why would he mention it?"

"It's worth a try. Let's look for local road repair stuff."

"That he didn't get rolled and mugged last time was a seven-day wonder. Probably the only reason was because the place was crawling with cops and cop-cars because of the accident."

"What time did Miss Mary say he left?"

"Around six. She said he slept until noon, which he never does. He prowled around the whole afternoon, very upset. Wouldn't take calls. For two days, he's been saying yeah, he'll talk to me in a day or so. But today, he wouldn't even take my call. I tried every hour or so. Finally Miss Mary told me he was gone. She said he's been upset for three days. Didn't even shave yesterday, looked awful, and obviously had something on his mind. That's all she knew. But she was frantic with worry."

They rode on in grim silence. Then, west of I-95, they both spotted it at once.

"There," cried Fran.

But Webb was already slowing down. He

eased onto the gravel in front of a low flat-roof building with a sign atop reading "The Double Eye." The lot next door was jammed with heavy road equipment.

Inside, they found Bud standing at the bar, staring morosely down at two glasses in front of him. One a shot glass. One a tumbler, and behind them a small bottle of diet Coke. "Once a drunk always a drunk," said Webb, taking the stool to Bud's left. Fran took the one on the other side, curious to see how Webb would handle this.

"If I don't end up one, ish not caush I din' try," said Bud.

"You're drinking it with fucking diet Coke?" hooted Webb.

"I can't shtand the taste," said Bud morosely.

Webb grabbed the bills on the bar in front of Bud and stuffed them in Bud's pocket, pulled a couple of twenties from his wallet and put them down. The bartender came over. "Three diet Cokes," he ordered.

"Make mine a double. With lime," said Fran.

"It's not the greatest way to figure things out, Bud," said Webb. "Unless you want to get your head caved in and everything but your socks stolen."

"Mine your own fuckin' business. I don't really give a fuck."

413

"I should," Webb snapped back in a terse whisper. "I should just walk out and let someone grind you to chopped liver to get at that watch and wallet. Any jackass who does such fucking stupid things really doesn't deserve to be helped. Anyone who can't take five minutes to hear both sides of something—anyone who's got to be bossing people around like a goddamn Castro—anyone who stomps off to sulk like a spoiled brat, is a fucking loser in my book."

"Now, lissen, Webb," Bud began. "I've been lied to and cuck-a-doodled. No cuckholed. No, wait. What'sh that word?" The bartender brought their Cokes. Bud reached for his, fumbled, and sloshed it on the bar. He took his napkin and wiped back and forth clumsily in the puddle.

"You're supposed to drink that—not clean the bar with it," said Fran.

"Now, lissen, Webb," Bud began again.

"No. You listen to me, Buddy. We're walking out of this hole. For old time's sake I'll do this just once. I'm taking you home. Fran will drive you in your car and I'll follow in mine. And if you want to come back tomorrow and finish what you've started here, fine with me. But first, tomorrow morning, when you sober up and you'll remember it, I'm going to tell you again what a fucking prick you've been. And you're gonna listen. I'm gonna tell you how that damned Emil character has been harassing Jessie for two months and driving her nuts. And you never did anything to protect her. If she had an affair with him before, so the fuck what? What was she supposed to do, just keep her legs crossed forever waiting for you to come along? Get real.

"You never ask a lady what she's done before she met you, Buddy. Or with who. It's none of your fuckin' business. Any more than it's any of her business where you've been puttin' it. Your business is what happens after."

He tossed off his Coke. Fran took a big swallow of hers. They stood up. "Now, walk out of here. Straight out," Webb ordered. Bud turned and walked, unsteadily but upright, with Webb on one side and Fran on the other, through the door. Outside, Webb felt Bud's pockets and pulled out his car key, and quickly scanned the parked cars and found Bud's. They half walked, half dragged him over. Fran opened the doors, and while Webb pushed Bud in on the right, she hurried around and took the driver's seat and started the engine. "Look, the hood emblem's gone already," Webb snorted.

"Lock the doors and get out of here," he ordered Fran tersely. "To the Hammock. Don't stop for anything. Don't look back. Now!" he ordered, slamming the door. Fran nodded and started the engine. As she eased out of the parking slot and then headed for the road, three men emerged from the bar. Webb sprinted for his Mercedes. The men spotted him and turned toward him at a trot. Webb fumbled a second with the key, opened the door, jumped in, slammed it and locked it. Just as he turned on the ignition, one of the men reached the car and jumped on the fender while another threw a rock at his window. It hit the jamb. Stomping on the gas, Webb zigzagged from the lot, fanning gravel and finally flinging his passenger into the culvert. He peeled on two wheels onto the side road. At the corner, he ignored the stop sign, plunged right out onto the road like a hot-rodder, and headed east, toward I-95 and the Hammock.

He was breathing heavily and his back was wet with sweat. And fear.

At the Hammock, Miss Mary was appalled when they half dragged, half carried Bud in the door and down the hall to his room. "He'll be okay by morning," Webb assured her. "Miss Fran and I will be here for breakfast. Figure about eight." They pulled Bud's shoes off, pulled a cover over him and crept out.

* * *

In the hallway, Webb kissed Fran long and hard. "You were wonderful," she said. "I saw. In the rearview mirror. When the men came out. I was terrified."

"We could all three have been worked over. I shouldn't have taken you. Damn fool thing to do."

"I'm sorry I insisted. I never will again, I swear. You really meant it, didn't you?" she said with wonder. "Like you looked after Bud. You really will look after me, won't you?"

"I'll try."

"But then, it only seems fair that — well, that I should look after you, too."

"No feeding me granola."

"That's not the kind of care I was thinking of. I was thinking of some things I need to tell you, that I only know one way to say. Your place?"

Webb grinned. "We have to be back here by eight in the morning. I guess we can make it. If we get right to the point."

Breakfast the next morning was not a festive affair. Bud was still unshaven, his eyes were bloodshot, his stomach queasy. As soon as Miss Mary placed a platter of bacon and eggs on the table and retired to the kitchen, Webb laced into him, repeating everything he had said the night before, and more. Then it was Fran's turn.

"I don't care if you and Jessie get married or not —" she began. "No, wait. That's not true. I do care. I thought you two were Cinderella and the prince. I hate to see a beautiful love story have such a half-assed ending. But if it could, you're not the guy for her, anyway. Only I can't let you think anything so bad of Jessie. She's not a sleeparound. She's so straight she's silly sometimes. And only a jackass would react like she was a hooker just because she went with someone else, before you.

"And you're not invited to our wedding, if that's what you think of people just because they've messed around a little bit sexually. Webb and I certainly have."

Bud looked up. "What was that about a wedding?"

"Fran's and mine," said Webb. "We're going to give it a try."

"You're kidding. But after so many times —"

"Not that many. Only five each. We figured we'd make it an even half dozen."

"When did this happen?"

"We decided a couple of days ago. Right after you and Jessie blew up. It's been incubating for a while."

"But you don't even like each other."

"No," agreed Fran. "But we tried that already—marrying people we like. It doesn't work."

"Huh? Uh—well, when are you doing it?"

"We thought we'd do it with you two," said Webb. "We thought maybe because the notary or the judge or someone was out already, he would give us a cut rate. But now that you're not doing it, we wondered if you had made any arrangements yet. Maybe we could take them over."

"I hadn't told her yet. But yes. At Burt and Jack's. A week from tomorrow. I had Edgar set it all up."

"Good. That will save us the trouble. Could you just switch it all to my name? Or give me all the dope and I'll do it." He turned to Fran. "Maybe we have to invite them. Separately. After all, it's their wedding we're using."

"I suppose," Fran nodded. "I wanted Jessie, anyway."

"God, how could this all happen?" Bud moaned. "I always thought if I ever found her again, it would be slick as butter. We'd hit it right off again and get married and ride into the sunset. First, I'm afraid to meet her. And trying like crazy to make it happen sort of by accident. And when I do meet her, she's got this damn job that comes first. Then that thing with Ginny. Jessie knew something was funny there. Then my daughter raises hell. Then Jes-

419

sie says I'm bossy. And she wants to keep work-ing. And then some tart from her office hints that Jessie's had a pack of men after her. And then this other guy pops up. And it looks like she's had something going on the side all this time. Only I still can't believe Jessie would do anything like that. But that call . . . And then—"

"And then you start acting like an asshole. Don't leave that out, Bud. Anyway, don't cancel any arrangements. Fran and I will take over everything but your license and blood tests."

"And we better tell them to change the name on the cake," said Fran.

"I feel like an asshole," said Bud, pushing his untouched plate away and taking a long swal-low of coffee. "Stupid, I guess, thinking you can go back to the wrong turns and take the right ones. It just doesn't work."

Miss Mary came back in with another pot of coffee. "This is hotter and fresher, Mr. Bud," she said. "And you just had another call from Miss Esme. If you want to talk to her now, she's hanging on. Or I can tell her you'll call later."

Bud looked at Webb and Fran and said, "What more could happen? I'll talk to her now, Miss Mary. I'll pick it up in my room."

Thirty-four

"Hello, Sess?"

"Yes. Is that you, Webb? What is this Jessie told me—it's off with them?"

"For now."

"I don't believe it. We had just gotten our tickets when she called. That's not my brother. What's wrong?"

"I think it's all knocked him silly, Sess. Bitsy, Jessie, all the excitement. He was scared out of his bird that Jessie might not be interested or they wouldn't feel the same. And he just had another little thing that came up that really got to him. And Jessie's had a life before him. That's not easy for him to handle, I guess. And somehow they're both as fussy as two old hens, all of a sudden. Scrapping over nothing."

"Bud never scraps."

"He does now. Well, I can't tell him what to do. But Fran and I are trying to at least get them together to talk. Maybe they'll patch it by then. Maybe not. But come down anyway. Fran and I are gonna do it. You know — Jessie's roommate. Same day. You might get two weddings for the price of one but at least we can guarantee you one."

"You're kidding! You and Jessie's roommate? Getting married? I don't believe it!"

"Believe it. Bud had all their arrangements made but he hadn't told her yet. He just called Burt and Jack's and tied it all up. We hated to waste all that. And like I say, it could end up a double. I wouldn't hold my breath, but it could."

"Webb, is there anything I can do? I want so much for Bud to be happy."

"Talk to him. Talk to her. They both are crawling around on their stomachs, lower than a couple of snakes."

"I will. Oh, Webb, are you really trying matrimony again? Anyway, we'll be there. With two wedding presents. Just in case."

"Hello, Esme? This is Webb."

"Webb? What's going on down there now? It sounds from here as though my father is running his own soap opera."

"Funny, that's exactly what it looks like from here."

"First I get a note from his girlfriend inviting

Needle and me to their wedding. They haven't even set the stone for my mother and he's getting married. And the note comes from her, not him."

"He's been a little wound up and agitated, Esme. He's really been upset about the break with you."

"Well, he doesn't show it. He doesn't call me. The only way I keep on top of what's going on down there is I talk to Kerry every few days, his girlfriend's daughter. And she called to tell me it was off."

"Kerry! How do you know Kerry?"

"I met her in the elevator one day. She's a nice little person. Rather good insight for her age. She's told me a few things I was unaware of that explain my father's behavior. If only he had confided in me, we could have avoided all this misunderstanding."

"Well, anyway, Fran and I would like you to come down, because Wednesday at noon when your Dad and Jessie were supposed to get married, we're getting married—same place, same time. If they patch it up by then, you get two weddings with one stone. Their problems don't amount to a pile of buffalo chips. If not, it'll just be Fran and me."

"You're getting married again? I don't believe it."

"Yeah, Nobody does. But I am. And you're invited."

"Oh, I don't know, Webb. This Fran, the roommate, we didn't exactly hit it off that one morning."

"Well, put yourself in her shoes, Esme. Try to understand."

"That's what Kerry said."

"She's right. Your dad and Jessie will be there. Good chance to iron things out."

"Well, they certainly need that. Let me say, I think we might come. I thank you for asking us. I'll talk to Needle and let you know in a day or so."

"Decide to come, Esme. If your dad marries Jessie that day, you should be there. If he was marrying Godzilla, you should be there. If you boycott the wedding, it will look like a protest. And you'll never be able to undo it. Don't make the strain any worse."

"If I thought he wanted me there, I certainly would be. I mean, he hasn't invited me. And even Benjie couldn't get through to talk to him for a couple of days."

"That should tell you, Esme, it isn't you. It's him. Of course he wants you there, whether he says so or not. He's just not himself. He's been through a lot. And whether the stone is set or not doesn't matter. Your dad isn't very religious, Esme. You know that. Neither are you. Besides which, Jessie is a living doll. He's very lucky."

"That's what Kerry says. But now it's so awkward. After that scene in their apartment. And my father practically disowning me."

"He hasn't disowned you. He loves you. He thinks you're the one that's pulled the rug out. But he's feeling very low right now, Essie. You'd really be doing him a mitzvah if you helped him get this straightened out. He'd appreciate it. It would be the first step in making up."

"But how can I help him? I haven't a clue. Kerry told me one of the problems is he just makes all the decisions without asking her mother. My mother liked it when he made all the decisions. This lady doesn't. I don't blame her for that. I wouldn't either. But if I tell my father that, it will hardly help heal the wound."

"But I'll see you at the wedding?"

"Well, I think so. And I will call my father again."

"Hello, is this Mr. Pontchetrain?"

"Speaking."

"This is Fran Dimitri, Jessie Moore's roommate."

"Do I know you?"

"No, but I have some information for you, Mr. Pontchetrain. Did you know that Jessie has become engaged to a very wealthy businessman. He owns Well-Tech Labs, and Medi-Quip Supplies, and I don't know what all else."

"Oh, shit," cried Pontchetrain. "You mean that rock she's been wearing the last couple of weeks is for real? I thought it was Cubic Zirconia."

"It's real."

"My word! Just how rich is this man?"

"Jessie won't have to worry where her next diamonds are coming from. Or her next Mercedes. Every single woman here and in Chicago would give her eyeteeth just to meet him. And Jessie's got him."

"You mean I'm going to have to replace her? And it's so difficult to find anyone who can write worth a poodilly-woot."

"Maybe. Maybe not. I have a hunch that if you could cut her hours and make them a little more flexible, she'd stay."

"At the same salary?"

"I don't think money will be a prime concern for her anymore, sir. But having a little time to spend with her husband, to take little business trips with him when necessary—that would be."

"Well I guess we could let someone else do the cut lines and proofing, if we could pay them minimum. Jessie ask you to call me?"

"Are you kidding? She'd throttle me if she knew I was poking my nose into this. But I know how much she enjoys her writing. She doesn't want the writing to get in the way of her marriage or the marriage to get in the way of her writing. Seems like a compromise should be possible. If you suggested it, it might make all the difference. And you wouldn't have to replace her."

"Well, I thank you for the information, Miss—"

"Dimitri."

"Yes. I'll mull it over and see what I can do. By the bye, is she having a very large wedding?"

"No. I think it's going to be very luxurious, and very small. But it might be that we could wangle an invitation for a friend."

"Would you look into that for me?"

"I'd be delighted to."

"Hi Esme. It's Kerry. I just had this brainstorm. Sometimes I am so smart I frighten myself."

"I know. I've often felt the same way, Kerry."

"Here's my idea. I think you should call your dad and tell him that you and your husband have been approached by a grave salesman, and you discussed buying lots from him. But because you knew he had those three lots left in that cemetery where your mom is buried—"

"Beth Sharon."

"Yeah. Whatever. For your brother and you and him. So you wonder if your husband could buy your dad's lot so you and your husband would have a pair. Because you know he'll probably want to be buried next to his new wife if anything ever happens to him and this way you can still be buried next to your husband, because if your dad doesn't sell you the lot, you'll have to buy another pair somewhere because you and your husband want to lie next to each other for eternity."

There was a long pause on the other end of the wire. "What a complicated plot," Esme said. "Actually, Needle and I want to be cremated, but my father doesn't know that yet."

"Well, none of this is cast in concrete. You and your husband aren't going to die for eons yet, so once you get that lot, you can change your minds. Or have your ashes buried there. But the thing is, it would let your dad know you understand if he wants to be buried next to my mother. And it kind of says you've accepted the marriage, you know?"

"Hm," Esme murmured. "You may have something there."

"Great idea, huh? Then you say that you heard they're getting married next week and you want to be sure and be there for it so please tell you the exact day. You might add that you'll call your brother. I know my mom said there's no way they should do that wedding without you two there. That's why she sent notes to you both."

"But isn't it off now?"

"They've been scrapping over such silly stuff.

Prenuptial nerves, I guess. But I'd bet my Lionel Ritchie records they'll be standing up there with Webb and Fran next Wednesday."

"But why do I have to do all the making up?"

"Get real, Es. Sometimes, that's the way it works. All that really counts now, bottom line, is that you and your father get back to being buddies again. Right?"

"Bottom line."

"So do it. Call him."

"Hm. I guess I will."

"Are you keeping Benjie up-to-date? He said to call if there was anything and I couldn't get hold of you."

"I talk to him every couple of days but I hardly know what to tell him."

"I just thought maybe I shouldn't put a long-distance Alaska call on the phone bill just now."

"That's probably true. Anyway, thanks for everything, Kerry."

"De nada. I'll save your neck anytime. And there'll probably be times you'll save mine. What else are stepsisters for?"

"This is Mrs. Pearlman. May I please speak to my father?"

"Just a moment, Mrs. Pearlman. I believe your father is just heading into a meeting, but let me try his desk."

Two rings and then, her father's familiar voice. "Hello? Bud Wellman."

"Daddy, it's Esme."

"I'm just heading into a meeting, Es."

"I know you're awfully busy Daddy, but there were a couple of things I needed to tell you and ask you, if you have just a minute."

"Just one."

"The first is about the graves. I don't want to upset you or anything, bringing this up just now Daddy, but you know those three graves at Beth Sharon? Well, this salesman called Needle . . ."

"Jessie? This is Sess — Bud's sister. I got your note and then I talked to Webb and I had to call and tell you I'm flabbergasted. My advice is to be patient, dear. He's the best guy in the world. But he's been through so much in the last couple of months. Bitsy, and you."

"If he'd only just stop deciding things without ever asking me what I think. I suppose a few years ago I would hardly have noticed. Harry decided a lot, too. But now, it drives me crazy."

"I know. It would me, too. But you just have to remember where it's coming from. All those years of practice. So it's ingrained by now. He had to make all the decisions for Bitsy. By herself, she could hardly decide to get up in the morning. But I'm sure that talking to him

430

about that will help. He's a rational man. He's beginning to understand that a normal person wants a little input. It's just habit."

"Oh, Sess, there's so much more. We all have habits from our life before. But he heard a telephone message from this guy I used to go with. Emil was drunk and talking about going to bed with me. I haven't seen him in months but to Bud it sounded like I was still seeing him on the sly."

"Well, that he'll have to figure out for himself, Jessie. Or you'll have to explain to him. Nothing wrong with that, either, my dear—just talking things over. Anyway, when we come down for Webb's wedding, I hope it'll be a double."

"Bud? It's Sess. Have you got a minute?"

"I've got a meeting but I'm late already. I'll just have to be a minute later. I'm glad you called. I just had a call from Esme that I can hardly believe. She wants to buy my cemetery lot so she and Needle can be buried together and she said she figured that Jessie and I would want to be buried together somewhere else, anyway. Can you beat that. And I thought she'd be so upset."

"Wonderful, Bud. I told you these things have a way of working out without the tiniest bit of interference. All by themselves, if you give them a chance."

"And she wants to come to the wedding! She said Jessie had sent her a note inviting her, only she understood it was now being delayed and would I be sure to let her know when it would be, no matter how small or spur-of-the-moment it was, so she and Needle could be there. She said she heard that Jessie is very nice, but that after all, even if I was marrying Godzilla, she should be there. I practically dropped the telephone. But why didn't Jessie tell me she was inviting Esme?"

"I told you Esme should be there. If Jessie hadn't invited her, I would have. But you, dear brother, should call and confirm it. How does it feel with the shoe on the other foot, brother?"

"What shoe? What do you mean?"

"She decided this without asking you. The same way you keep deciding everything without talking it over with her."

"Yeah, she gets really ticked about that."

"Well, who wouldn't? Bud, you are a wonderful person and the best brother in the world, but I have to tell you this. I would have been upset, too. That's treating a grown, capable woman like a ten-year-old."

"But Bitsy—"

"Bud, Bitsy liked being treated like a ten-year-old. She was a ten-year-old. But to most people that's insulting. If Dell did that to me, he'd sleep alone for a week."

"I have."

"Well, anyway, I've never told you what to do in your personal life, Bud. And I never will again. But I had to tell you that. We'll be down for Webb's wedding. And all I want for you is the very best, Bud. What makes you happy. Whatever you decide, I'm on your side. I love you, Brother."

"Emil Worth, here."

"Mr. Worth this is Kerry Moore, Jessie's daughter."

"Ah, yes, Kerry. And what can I do for you? Is Jessie all right?"

"Well, yes and no, Mr. Worth. My mom has become engaged to a Mr. Bud Wellman."

"What a surprise."

"But the other day, Mr. Wellman came by while my mom was listening to our telephone messages and this call from you came on. A terrible call. Suggesting you get together for certain activities. And I don't mean tennis."

"You don't mean—"

"Yes. Sex. Very explicit. You might say obscene. You made it sound like you and Mom were still hanging out together."

"Oh, dear. I must have been—in my cups," said Emil lamely.

"Bud was so shocked he marched out. I think you may have caused them to split up. And my mom is totally wiped out."

"But the attachment could hardly have had very long roots, so to speak, Kerry. They couldn't have been seeing each other for very long."

"Oh, no? Well, get this. She met him when she was in high school and had a big crush on him then. And he had this thing for her. They married different people but they still had this crush all these years. And when they met again after all that time, it was instant commitment. Very serious."

"Well, I'm very sorry. I wouldn't hurt your mother for the world. I was rather attached to her myself. Still, I am a gentleman. But I don't know if an apology would do more harm than good."

"No, it would do a lot more good than harm. I should send you a copy of your message. I taped it. And you'd see how totally gross it was."

"Oh. Well, then, I suppose we have to face the consequences. I'll call him."

"Better do it right now before you get all boozey and forget."

"But of course. Do you have his number handy? And what was his name again?"

"A Mr. Emil Worth on the line, Mr. Wellman? Shall I tell him you'll call him back later?"

"I don't think I know any Emil Worth. Wait a minute. Emil? Could it be—? Oh, hell. I'm so late now. Put him on and then tell Ambry to apologize to the section heads and tell them I'll be there in a couple of minutes. Tell him to go ahead and start serving breakfast. I'll be right in."

"Yes, sir. I'll connect you now."

"Hello?"

"Hello, is this Mr. Bud Wellman?"

"Yes."

"Mr. Wellman, my name is Emil Worth. I'm a friend of Jessie Moore's. Or perhaps I should say, a past friend."

"So I understand," said Bud curtly.

"No, sir, you don't understand, and that's why I am making this very awkward phone call. Please let me explain."

"Go ahead. But make it short. I'm late now for a meeting that began twenty minutes ago."

"I'll be brief. I began seeing Miss Moore several months ago, after having been interested in her for some time. But I happen to have this drinking problem, you see, and Miss Moore was not interested at that time. Until I went on the wagon several months ago. And then we began seeing each other. I must say our relationship was delightful and we certainly enjoyed each other's company. Until I—I began drinking again. At any rate, we broke up, as they

435

say. Only Miss Moore had to tell me several times before it sunk in. And to tell the truth, when I've had a few, I forget, and I telephone her. She did call and tell me she was seeing someone else and to please stop calling and leaving messages. She called me several times to tell me that, as a matter of fact. And that my messages were too — intimate and — embarrassing.

"But I'm afraid I may have sent her a couple of messages even after that. I can only apologize profusely, with sincere regret. For any of these foolish acts I have committed, on the sauce, as it were."

"You sound perfectly sober now, Mr. Worth."

"Oh, yes. I am always sober mornings, Mr. Wellman. I never drink until after lunch. My sincerest apologies, Mr. Wellman. And I thank you for your time."

"Hello, Bud?"

"Jessie! Uh, gee — were you trying very long to get through? This line has been tied up for half an hour."

"No. I just now decided the best thing to do was to call you. I want to give you back the ring. It's the most beautiful ring I've ever seen, but I —"

"No, that's yours, Jessie. I'm not an Indian giver."

"Oh, no, I can't keep it, Bud. If we were

still — you know — together — I'd never take it off. But now — And I want to give it to you in person. I don't want anything to happen to it. I want to put it right into your hand and know you've got it."

"Well, I'd like to see you in person. I mean, even if you're pissed at me we don't have to be enemies."

"Oh, no! I'm not pissed. I understand what a shock that must have been. I haven't seen him and there's been nothing like what the tape sounded like. Nothing. But even if you don't believe me and you hate me, we can still be — well — friends, can't we?"

"How could I ever hate you, Jessie? I think we still ought to — uh — keep in touch. Maybe see each other, sometimes. And try to get things straightened out in our heads."

"I'm so glad you said that."

"I mean like maybe tonight —"

"I can bring the ring."

"Oh, yeah, the ring. We could have dinner or something."

"Yes. Whatever you like."

"Uh — was all so abrupt. We should have talked. My fault."

"Well — yes, it does seem we should at least clear the air, doesn't it. A kind of farewell visit."

"If it's not too late."

"No. In fact, it would be sort of a terrible thing for us not to be close, even, just once more."

"Why don't I get a room for us tonight?"

"Oh, yes. I mean, I guess so. And could we just not even mention our problems, at first Bud? Could we just pretend everything is fine and we're just so in love we can't wait to be alone?"

"Yeah. Right. How soon will you be free?"

"I've got an American Cancer Society meeting at the Pier. I'm heading there now. And then I've got to go home to be there when Doug leaves."

"He's leaving today?"

"Yes. He really wanted to go yesterday, but Kerry's giving him a lift to Palm Beach and her car wasn't going to be ready in time so they changed his tickets. And she's supposed to go from there to Vero Beach to spend a few days visiting our old neighbor's housekeeper from fifteen years ago. A sweet lady. They've stayed friends all this time."

"Are you sure her car's in good enough shape for that trip?"

"I think so."

"We should have gotten her a new car, Jessie. Why didn't you remind me? I don't like the idea of her driving that far in a bad car."

"I guess I just don't think in terms of new cars right away. I think they'll be okay."

"Meet you at the Marriott after they leave?"

"Okay."

"Don't bother to dress. I mean, nothing fussy. Whatever you've got on now. Would it cause you any trouble with your job if we meet about three?"

"Funny thing. Pontchetrain came over to me about half an hour ago and said that he heard I was engaged and if I planned to keep working he would cut down some of my chores and be very flexible about my hours. So I wouldn't have to quit when I got married. Wasn't that nice? Out of the blue? I didn't tell him yet that it was off. I thought I'd enjoy the flexibility for a few days first. And I kind of need it. I'm not functioning too well. All these dramatic changes and emotional wring-outs. It all takes a lot of adjusting to."

"That makes two of us," said Bud. "I can barely tell up from down by now. Well listen— I'll see you over there about three."

"Make it three-thirty, Bud to be safe."

"Okay, three-thirty. In the lobby, next to the escalators."

"Miss Halloran?"

"Yes, Mr. Wellman?"

"I'm going into that meeting now. But first I want you to take care of a few things for me. Book me the biggest suite they have open at the Marriott Harbor Beach, for this afternoon. Has to be ready by three. Flowers, fruit, hors d'oeuvre tray, ice, snacks, sodas and all that. And I want to transfer title of my cemetery lot to my daughter. Call Cromwell about that. Call Neiman Marcus and get me a wedding present for Mr. Webber and Fran Dimitri. Something major. Have them call me with suggestions. Send it to Ms. Fran Dimitri, same address as mine, only apartment G770. Oh, and if I have any appointments for tomorrow or next Wednesday, change them."

"Mom, it's Kerry."

"Hi, honey, I'm just leaving for that luncheon. I'll whiz in and out and be home in about two hours."

"I know. That's why I'm calling. Doug is out on the terrace getting his last bit of sun and I might not get another chance to talk to you in private."

"Anything wrong, Kerry? Why in private?"

"Because, Mom, I think I'm going to break up with Doug. I'm going to tell him as soon as I can after he gets back up north. But I wanted to run it by you, first."

"Break up with Doug? I thought you were going to get married. What's happened?"

"Nothing much, Mom. I still think he's just a dear. I hope we'll be friends forever. But I can't marry him, Mom. He's just too young for me."

"Kerry, dear, it's your life — your decision. But why did he suddenly become too young?

When?"

"Maybe it's just that I'm growing up, Mom. Or maybe it's that I'm beginning to realize what a crazy place that world out there is. I don't want a boy, Mom. I want a man. Someone I can really look up to. Someone who makes me feel safe and looked after. Someone who has done some heavy thinking about life and stuff."

"I'm stunned, honey. I thought you and Doug—"

"Everybody did. But I guess I was in love with love. I still am. I'd love to be as charged about a guy as you are about Bud. How wonderful that must be. I mean, I have been, of course. But never for more than a week."

"We'll talk when I get home."

"No, I don't want Doug to have a clue till I figure out how to tell him. I don't want to hurt him, Mom. He's been too good a friend for that. I mean, we almost got pregnant together."

"Maybe in a few years, he'll grow up enough—"

"I don't think I can wait. I'll call after we get back and tell you how it goes."

"Okay, honey. You know I love you to pieces."

"I know. I love you to pieces, too."

"Is Mr. Wellman there?"

"Yes, but he's in a meeting. Oh, no, here he is now. It must have just broken up. I'll connect you."

"Bud Wellman, here."

"Fran Dimitri, here."

"Oh, hi, Fran. What's up?"

"Just checking that you'll be there Wednesday. We hate to think we'll be all alone."

"Why? Who's not coming?"

"My mother for one. She's a kind of senior hippie. Lives on this little commune in Georgia with her lover, Ivan Nadazhski, that crazy Russian poet who predicted the crash of Communism about five years before it happened and had to defect. Remember him? They're in the middle of radish planting or radish harvesting, or something and she says they need her. She says that with my track record, she doesn't consider this a very unique occasion and she'll try to make the next one."

Bud laughed. "Nothing like a vote of confidence."

"Webb's mother isn't coming, either. She's very old. She says she has a cold and feels terrible and says it isn't as though she won't ever get another chance. It's not like it was a Bar Mitzvah or something that you only do once. And next time give her more notice. But Esme and Needle are coming. And Kerry. And Sess and Dell. Benjie probably. And Jessie, of course."

"Well, that's a handful."

"And we want you and Jessie to be our witnesses. Just like we were supposed to be for you two."

"That's okay with her?"

"She said yes, if it's okay with you."

"Oh, sure. Glad to do it. Wonderful."

"We got through our prenuptial agreements."

"That's where we got hung up. What did you agree to?"

"Probably not the same kind of stuff you hung up on. Webb asked me to agree to haircombing and makeup and stockings with reasonable frequency, whatever that means. And I made him agree that if we ever get divorced, he has to give half of everything to Plants for the Planet and several other ecology groups and the like. I figured then he'd stay married this time. I can't bear the thought of another divorce. Changing my name again? Moving again? Forget it. If he ever wants a different wife he'll just have to commit bigamy. I'm thinking of putting my brand on his forehead. And elsewhere. Oh, and we have a clause that neither one of us is allowed to brag about past lovers."

"Queer sense of humor you two have."

"Who's being funny? That can cause a lot of jealousy and feelings of inadequacy."

"Where will you be buried if someone dies?"

"Well, I don't ever plan to. And with all my

oat bran and bee pollen and jogging, I probably won't. But Webb probably will, the way he
ODs on cholesterol all the time. Like you. But
if such a thing should come to pass, we both
want to be roasted and our ashes dumped in
any convenient landfill. Unmarked."

"I think you deserve each other," said Bud
with a rueful chuckle.

"Why, Bud, what a lovely thing to say.
Thank you, so much. So anyway, we can count
on you?"

"You can count on me. I wouldn't miss this
for anything."

Thirty-five

He was waiting at the escalators when she came rushing around the corner of the lobby, carrying the attache case she had been using as an overnight bag. She hurried up to him, then stopped awkwardly.

"Hi," he said.

"Hi. Am I late?"

He shook his head. "I just got here a little early to check out the room. Well, we might as well go right up and settle in, though. Don't you think? Too early for dinner. Did you have lunch?"

"Sort of," she nodded.

"There's some stuff upstairs. We can order whatever you want. Unless you feel like getting something down here."

"Oh, no," she said quickly. "Upstairs is fine."

He took her case. And her arm. They headed for the elevators.

* * *

At the room, he had trouble with the key. "I guess I'm a little nervous," he said when he finally got it to turn, and swung the door open.

"Me, too," she said, walking in. "Oh, Bud, what a place. It must be their best suite. And the flowers! They're beautiful."

"So are you. I've missed you. It's been a rough week. God, I've been angry and felt put down, and mixed up and just plain miserable. Wanting you. I've never had so much trouble sorting anything out."

"Listen, Bud. If anyone's hurt and put down, here, it's me. I haven't done a damn thing wrong, and you were too quick to believe that I had. And I thought we were just going to set it aside for tonight. You need me. I need you. We both need to wrap up something we started. There are a million women out there who would be happy to be with you tonight or any night. But I think you still want me. And I know I still want you."

"Right. And I'm glad you're here, honey," he said.

"We said we weren't going to talk about the last week. If you want to talk about it another time, okay. But not tonight. Please?"

"You're right. Come here." He held his arms out. She walked into them and he closed them gently around her. "I'm so glad you came," he repeated.

She slipped away. "No. Wait. I want to put on my slinky gown. I bought it the day you first talked about us getting married. I thought I'd wear it on—on our wedding night. But I want to look pretty for you, tonight."

"I'll just take it off you."

"That's okay. Let me wear it for sixty seconds and feel sexy. Besides, I thought you were going to get me some lunch, first. Do you do this with all your dates?"

"Oh, yeah. I'm sorry. What would you like?"

"I'm only teasing you, Bud. I want you for lunch. Where's the loo?" He pointed and she picked up her attache case. At the door she turned and said, "Don't just stand there, sir. Take your clothes off. I'll only be a minute."

It was black. Sheer, with panels of lace. Tiny lace straps. Cut low front and back. And full. It twirled and floated when she waltzed out of the bathroom. Bud watched. Then followed her into the bedroom. He reached for her but she held him off with one arm. "Not yet. I have this all planned," she said. "And I didn't ask you for any input. Turn the radio on. WLYF, I think. Easy listening stuff. Very softly."

Bud did as she asked. The yearning strains of "Unchained Melody," filled the room. He turned down the volume. "And the light should be very low. Turn them all off and pull the drapes," she ordered. He did so. "Yes. That's lovely. Very romantic."

"I, of course, don't need all this," said Bud, pulling the spread and sheet back from the king-sized bed. He lay down, propped his head up on one arm and watched her.

"I'll be right there," Jessie said, humming to the music and twirling as though she were dancing in a ballroom. "I can't resist. I feel like a princess at a ball."

In the gauzy light, he watched the sheer, frothy folds turn and whirl about her silky white limbs as she glided gracefully around the room.

The song ended. She made a final turn and stopped. He clapped. She curtsied so low her breasts almost fell out of the top of the gown. And then she crawled in beside him, put her arms around him and pulled herself close.

"Oh, Jessie!" He ran his hands down her back, her buttocks, her thighs and up again. "So silky. You feel as silky as you look in that thing." He leaned over and rubbed his face against the fabric on her breast and tummy and pelvis. "I'm glad you wore it. Oh, honey, you are so sexy."

"I feel so sexy," she whispered. "I wouldn't be anyplace else in the world right now. Let's forget the idiotic world. It's not here."

"It's not here," he agreed, sliding the pretty gown up and lifting her to pull it over her head. He took her hand to guide it. "Touch me Jessie. I want you, now. Now!"

"Yes, now," she repeated.

"Oh God, I want to grab you everywhere." He moaned with the intensity of his pleasure and his moans brought her quickly to the brink. They thrashed at each other with a frenzy out of control, pushing, pushing until her body grew rigid, clenching like a fist wrapped around him to squeeze out every last bit of delight as he came deep within her.

And then they clung together, gasping, murmuring together, wordless sounds of love, as the pleasure softened like a beautiful scene blurring out of focus.

They lay there, limp, as the pounding of their hearts slowed, and their gasping faded into a lovely, languorous stillness. And after long moments of this still and gentle bliss, slowly, very slowly, he eased to one side, took her in his arms and held her as tenderly as a newborn baby, gently kissing her cheeks, her eyes, her neck — and she, kissing him as sweetly as he kissed her — his forehead and the top of his head, as one might kiss a child.

"I knew when I saw you in that gown, it would be something amazing," he said.

"I wanted it to be wonderful for you, tonight. It might be the last time. But I don't want you ever to forget what we had."

"My Jessie, my little Jessie." He buried his face in her neck. "It can't be the last time. We're just getting started."

"But we've broken up, Bud. We're going our separate ways."

"Well, I don't know which way you're going, Jessie, but I'm going the same way. I'll never get enough of you."

"I'll probably never get enough of you, either. I may wear myself down to a nubbin trying to. But that doesn't mean—"

"It means that whatever we have to work out, we can work out. It means that things aren't always what they look like and if I'd just keep loose and take a close look sometimes instead of exploding right away, I'd save us all a lot of misery and trouble. Good thing your Pontchetrain said you could have flexible hours. We can start there, figuring things out."

"I guess we have to start somewhere. And I can bend a little more on that. And I don't have to work there forever. Maybe long enough to ease into freelancing. But we don't need to start solving everything tonight. I think what we need tonight is probably stamina. Maybe we ought to have a little something to eat."

"Between every installment?" asked Bud. "Don't worry. We can. There's enough stuff out there to feed Massachusetts. But first, put your pretty gown on again, will you Babe?"

They found a tray of seafood in the refrigerator and Jessie made some coffee. And after nibbling the shrimp and stone crabs, they fed each

450

other bites of pastries from the pastry tray.

Jessie leaned over on the couch to put her head in Bud's lap. He stroked her forehead, then lifted her up to slide down beneath her so she was lying on top of him. He lifted her up to kiss first one breast and then the other, teasing them with his tongue.

"That's only going to make me want more," she said, closing her eyes and savoring the sensation.

"That's the idea."

"No rush, though."

"No. We'll go slowly. We've got all the time in the world. And we can keep holding each other and loving each other until we grow sleepy. Or hungry. Or you grow a callus."

She smiled, savoring his touch and whispered, "You promise?"

"I promise."

She forgot all about giving back the ring.

When three Pier 66 valets rushed up to help them out of the limo, Jessie couldn't help giggling. "What's so funny?" Bud asked, taking her arm to escort her inside for the Tiara Ball.

"I was thinking what a difference the car makes. The service. Three valets right there falling all over us."

Bud laughed, too. "Yeah. Everything but shining your shoes."

"You didn't have to get a limo, sweetheart. I

451

wouldn't have cared if we came on a bicycle. I was just so pleased that you agreed to come with me on one of these and see what it's all about."

"I know what it's all about, Jess. Bitsy lived for this junk. She had to get a social fix a few times a week or she'd break out in hives."

"Hives?"

"Her allergies would get worse when she was upset. Yeah, if she didn't get invited or didn't get a good table at something, she'd actually get a runny nose or hives."

"Well, I just want you to know I don't cover many events that are this grand. Ponchie only sends me to things where we get comped. That means a lot of ribbon-cuttings and receptions and meetings. More community things than social events. But the comps for this came two days ago after I'd sent regrets. Actually, I wish we never took comps. I always feel like a moocher."

"You should have let me get the tickets. We buy a certain amount of charity tickets all the time in cities where we have a lab. Anything you ever want to go to and you're not invited, just let Miss Halloran know. She'll get you tickets. Say, I don't know about you," he grunted, as they walked through the entrance, "but I'm almost kind of sore. You know where."

"You're sore?" retorted Jessie. "I can hardly walk. Someone's been attacking my privates the last couple of days."

"What a coincidence. Mine, too. Feels a little bit like it's been caught in an old-fashioned washing machine wringer. Whatever we do, tonight—please don't ask me to dance. Or if we must, please don't press up too close."

"Not a chance," she shook her head emphatically. "My panties feel like the crotch is made of Velcro."

He laughed and led her onto the escalator up to the ballroom. "We don't have to stay very late, do we?"

"No. But don't pester me to go home. You know that the minute we get back to that hotel, the first thing you'll want to do is put your privates back in the wringer. Another time, we'll make an evening of one of these things. But tonight—just long enough for me to get my story. We've already missed most of the cocktail hour, fortunately. I really appreciate your coming with me like this, Bud. Especially on such short notice."

"Oh, hell, I'm kind of interested to see what you do at these things. And then too, if I go, you can't take anyone else."

At the check-in table, Mercy Magoo handed them name tags and told Jessie she was at table twelve. And then she smirked, "Another new escort, Jessie? Where do you find all these men?" And putting her hand out toward Bud, she simpered, "I'm Mercy Morgan Magoo, a close

453

friend of Jessie's."

"Mercy, meet Bud Wellman," said Jessie.

"I'm delighted. I've heard so much about you," leered Mercy. "Every speck wonderful and interesting, of course. We're glad to have you joining us tonight. If Jessie gets tied up and you need a dance partner, I'm at the table behind yours—number fourteen. Oh, and Jessie, Lacy Pride and her date are at your table. She asked to switch there once we found out you were coming, and you know—she underwrote the band and the cocktail hour. We couldn't say no."

"Delighted," Jessie lied graciously.

"What was all that supposed to mean," said Bud, as they turned into the ballroom to look for table twelve.

"She was letting you know she was available, and cleverly making me sound like a runaround, and like a date who's too busy to dance with you, and one who blabs about you endlessly. And telling you she's a dear friend—that's such an exaggeration, it's called a lie. Such tactics. And Lacy's husband, Jock, died last year and left her loaded and lonesome. So she keeps telling everyone how much she loved him and that she wouldn't think of dating anyone and that she attends these things only to help the causes and only with longtime friends, no romances. But it seems that every single guy in southeast Florida above a certain age, is a longtime friend of hers. And meanwhile she's coming on strong at everyone else's dates and her neighbors are buzzing over the cars that are parked in her drive all night. Always splitting at dawn, they say. Oh, the stories that are going around."

"My god, it sounds like the Hammock Gazette," said Bud. "And who actually cares?"

"It's really none of their business. And probably no one would give a darn if she weren't professing her celibacy so loudly and constantly. People don't really care if someone messes around a little. But they don't like to be deliberately misled. And they resent it when someone polishes their own halo that way, so publicly. Anyway, be warned. She probably heard you would be with me and that's why she wanted to sit here. She's certainly never been that friendly before."

"I don't know if I can take many more of these predatory females," Bud sighed. "Thank God, after Wednesday I'll be just another married guy, and they'll go pick on someone else."

Their tablemates were already seated. "Hi, everyone," Jessie greeted them. "Ed and Maryjane DeMet, R.T. and Bess Lassiter, Humberto and Maria Manuela, Lacy Pride and Daryl Dukane—Bud Wellman."

Everyone else nodded and the men half stood, but Lacy—dressed in black as always since her husband died—slinky lace and sequins for this affair—rose quickly and came around to Jessie and Bud. She gave Jessie a hug and then took Bud's hand in both of hers. "I understand you lost your wife a very short time ago, Bud. I am so sorry. We have that in common," she cooed. "I lost my beloved Jock just a few months ago, too. I'll never get over it. I know just how you feel. I don't date. I just come to these things with very old friends like Daryl here, because it upsets the seating if you come alone and I wouldn't cause any trouble to anyone for all the tea in China. But I know just exactly how you feel right now. I'm simply desolate, too." She wiped a nonexistent tear and smiled bravely at him.

"Thank you," said Bud, pulling his hand free and turning to seat Jessie. Before he could, two women charged at them, kissing Jessie on the cheek and both talking at once. "Oh, Jessie, we're so glad you could make it." "Darling, we're so glad you could bring someone and stay for a while." "Jessie, don't you look pretty tonight." And turning to Bud, one said, "I'm Melody Zack, and this is Pattie Whipple. We're good friends of Jessie's. And where has she been hiding you?"

Jessie repeated everyone's name again, and Melody and Pattie launched into a lengthy and seemingly pointless story about the cocktail hour, interrupting each other and giggling a lot until they were replaced by a new set of women, a trio this time, who slipped around them and began a similar routine. Two more women came over and somehow squeezed in front of them, and then two more on the other side. At which point Bud said, "Oh, will you excuse us please — we were just going to dance," and grabbing Jessie by the arm he strode quickly to the dance floor, with her skipping to keep up, behind him.

"What are we doing out here? I thought you didn't want to dance," teased Jessie as Bud began to execute a very conservative and pedestrian fox-trot.

"Don't talk for a minute until I get the hang of this again. I'm counting," he said. "One slide two and three slide four. One slide two and three slide four. There, I think I've got it."

"I didn't know you danced."

"I don't, much. You can see I'm not Beau Jangles. I can get around the floor. I'll do it whenever you want me to. If you ever want me to after this sample," he chuckled. "But I had to get away from that mob of women. I felt like one of them was going to grab my zipper any minute."

"It's just because you're the new bachelor on the block," Jessie sighed. "And handsome and rich too. They'll let up after we're married."

"I can't wait until Wednesday," Bud grumbled.

"You're so romantic," she giggled. "It's touching to know that you think of me in terms of a

457

fortress that will protect you from those women."

"God, I hope so." The fox-trot segued into a hot rock number—"Dancing On The Ceiling." "Oh, Jesus, I can't handle this," groaned Bud.

"Look. Those women have all gone back to their tables."

"Good! Let's hurry and sit down before they come back," he said, again taking her hand and striding almost at a run back to the table with Jessie trotting behind him. But he had no sooner pulled out her chair when Lacy stood up and hurried around toward him.

"Oh, Bud darling," she cooed. "You must dance this one with me. It's my favorite rock number and Daryl's back has been out for days." She grabbed his arm, ignoring his protests that he didn't do rock and began pulling him in the direction of the floor.

Bud looked helplessly back at Jessie as he followed Lacy. Once on the floor she threw her arms around his neck, jammed her pelvis against his and began writhing sinuously to the music. "Oo, I like dancing with you. It feels so good. Move those hips, Bud. I know you know how. Let yourself go."

"Okay, let's really rock," he cried, reaching up and pulling her arms from around his neck, stepping back and leaping into the air. He dodged behind the couple next to them, jumping, stomping and twisting furiously in no recognizable steps, more or less to the beat. As

Lacy, following him, closed in, he moved again, still leaping and hopping and flailing his arms and legs and head frantically, ducking around one couple after another. Any time she nearly caught up with him he tucked himself behind another couple or hopped to another part of the floor. It was hide-and-seek rock until the song ended. Then he said, "Thank you very much, Lacy, that was great," and grabbing her hand, he all but dragged her behind him as he strode back to the table, much as he had dragged Jessie out to the dance floor ten minutes before. He yanked out her chair with one hand, pushed her onto it with the other, and shoved it so hard the edge hit the back of her knees and she collapsed onto it. "Thank you," he said firmly. "That was my one and only dance with anyone but Jessie for the whole night. That's all I'm allowed." He smiled broadly and hurried around to his own chair and dove into it.

"Well that was some performance, start to finish," whispered Jessie in his ear.

"She jammed herself against me with her hips pushing at me, and she meant business," explained Bud.

"I warned you. She has eyes for you. But I thought you eluded her pretty successfully. You looked like you were playing tag."

"We were. Or she was. I was just trying to keep away from her and that was the only way I could think of. God, I'm exhausted. That was too gymnastic for this old man. And if anyone is going to make this pecker sore, it's gonna be you."

"Except look at the way she's eyeing you now, Bud. She's wired. She's ready to explode. If she tries to dance with you again, I'm going to tell her to go to the ladies' room and masturbate."

"Jessie," he hissed into her ear, "this isn't funny."

"What are you two whispering about," laughed Lacy, leering at him across the table.

"Oh, I'm just whispering romantic nothings in her ear, ha-ha-ha," said Bud aloud. And then he hissed to Jessie, "We have to go. Tell them we have to go."

Just then Ann Ransome came fluttering over and Melody and Pattie were right behind her, taking a second shot. "Tell us what's so secret," asked Ransome.

Bud just grinned at her and turned back to Jessie's ear. "Tell them we have to go."

"Oh, Bud, they just served the salad."

"That broad is going to try again. And now there are three more, here."

"If we say we're leaving, thirty people will want to say goodnight and shake your hand and we'll never get out of here anyway," Jessie hissed. "And I still have to run around for a few minutes here and get some names and quotes and all the essential poop."

"Okay. Here's what we'll do. I'm heading for the men's room. I'll stay there for exactly ten minutes. Then I'll poke my head out and see if you're close by. If not, I'll go hibernate back inside for two minutes more. And try again. I'll keep on taking a look every two minutes until I see you."

"But that's terribly rude of us to just duck out without saying good-bye. The other people at our table are very nice. So are most of the people here. Those pesky ones don't even belong to the Royal Dames."

"The royal what?"

"The organization running this ball."

"They're whispering sweet nothings," Ransome explained to Melody and Pattie, who were now standing there, staring at him expectantly.

"Got any better ideas?" Bud asked Jessie.

"Yes, we could stay."

"I mean any better ideas of how to make an exit."

"No. Okay, Bud! We'll do like you say. Only I'll have to not only get some names and stuff. I'll have to come back here to say good-bye to everyone and tell them — and tell them —"

"Tell them I'm expecting an important call. Tell them I suddenly felt horny. Tell them I've got a toothache."

"I'll tell them something. You've got a migraine. Or I have. Okay, you go first." Jessie sat there for a minute after Bud excused himself and headed for the men's room. Then she grabbed her notebook and started across the room.

She stopped at the table of the chairman, Doris Logan, and got party parameters there— headcount, amount earned, etc. She scribbled a few notes on the decorations, took the names of guests at three nearby tables, and picked up a few quotes. She took hasty notes on the decorations, cornered the maître d' and checked the menu. In exactly fourteen minutes she was on the way back to her table to pick up her wrap, her program and her purse.

"Sorry, everyone. My toothache is back. I just had a root canal done yesterday," she lied. "Oh, it hurts so much. Bud insists we have to go and said to ask you to excuse us if we just rush off. No, don't get up." And pressing her hand against her jaw dramatically, she turned and walked quickly toward the ballroom doors.

Outside, she made a beeline for the men's room. He emerged a minute later. "Let's go," she said. "I already did the good-byes. I told them I had a root canal done yesterday and I'm in great pain."

"Some fun evening," Bud said as they waited for his car.

"Well, it couldn't have been too much of a chore. We were only in there about forty minutes. I'll have to call someone tomorrow to find out if anything unusual went on. And here's another case of your insisting on something—our leaving early—and not really giving me any input."

"Well, you could have objected."

"And argued right there in public? No thanks. It was bad enough we whispered together for so long planning our escape."

"Well what else should we have done? Asked the table to vote?"

"No. But you could have asked me to. But, when you don't let me have any input at all, you make me wonder just what kind of partnership I'm getting into here."

"Now, no more backing down. We decided to go ahead with it Wednesday and that's that."

"Oh, is it?" Jessie shot back. "Well, we'll see about that." And she went marching ahead of him to the escalator and down towards the hotel entrance.

Thirty-six

She left the office at noon, picked Bud up at the Hammock and drove him in silence to the deli on 17th St. "You want just tomato and onion?" he asked. She nodded. "On a salt bagel this time. And lots of pickles."

He went up to the counter and ordered while she poured their coffee at the coffee-makers. When he brought their sandwiches back to the table, he smiled ruefully. "Is it okay if I sit with you?"

"Oh, Bud, you know it is. I guess I don't really blame you for last night, in a way. It is a drag being pestered like that. But gosh, are you ever going to get so you let me decide anything? And then giving me a lecture on neatness on the way home. I'm a grown-up now. So what if I'm not as neat as you?"

"Now that's the understatement of the year," he laughed.

"See? Look how important it is to you. The understatement of the year," she repeated. "And to me, it's a matter or priorities. I have more important things to do."

"If you'd let me get you a maid, Jessie, the whole thing would evaporate. We're going to have help after we're married. Why not now?"

"Well, now it's sort of a moot question. If we're getting married Wednesday."

"But it's another example of one of the things we've got to work out. Okay, I should ask your opinion on things. But then I should get some input with you, too. We can't be always sparring over who's in control. And I will be the man of the house, Jessie."

She hooted. "Oh, gosh, don't tell me you're a chauvinist, now."

"Maybe I am. I don't want you taking anyone to anything you're covering for that rag you work for anymore."

"I don't mind going alone daytimes, Bud. I almost always do. But at night, I don't feel safe alone. And you don't want to go."

"I might, if the predatory females let up after we're married. And you can always take a girlfriend. But what I'd rather do if you really must stay there, Jess, is send you with a driver to get you to these events and home safely, and to hang around to look after you."

Jessie put down her coffee cup and looked

up in surprise. "Would you do that for me?"

"Jessie, don't you understand? We can afford maids. We can afford drivers. We can afford anything that makes our lives a little better, safer and easier. Why not take those steps?"

She shook her head. "I guess I just don't think in terms of that kind of money," she said. "But you're right about my cutting down, Bud. I've been thinking about it. I'm going to have more flexible hours. And there's no reason I can't go with you most of the time when you go out of town. I can just take a computer with me and write while you're busy. I can send copy in by phone. I can take different kinds of assignments—stuff I can do that way. Yes, I will get a maid. I'll hire people to do everything I don't absolutely have to do myself, so I'll have more time for you and more time for writing. Where there's a will, there's a way."

"Best news I've had all week," said Bud, squeezing her hand. "Now, we're going back to the office to meet with Edgar again in about twenty minutes, Jessie. I've gone over everything with him this morning, and dumped the dumb questions. And if you want us to be buried together, that's fine with me. Esme said she thought we would want to do that."

"Esme said that? Then you're talking to her. That's wonderful."

"So just remember, no matter what jackass thing Edgar might say—he means well but he might—let's just keep calm and cool and discuss it like two intelligent grown-ups."

"But I've got another ribbon-cutting this afternoon."

"Can you cancel it? Can you get the info later from someone?"

"Well, actually, I could. I've got a detailed press release. I'll just have to check and see if everything happened the way it tells."

"Okay. Then let's go to my office and get this taken care of."

Just then Bud's beeper went off. The office. He went to the phone. Two minutes later he was back. "Sorry, Jessie. We'll have to meet with Edgar maybe tomorrow. I—uh—something's come up."

"Like what?"

"Like—well, it's hard to explain. But it's something I must take care of. Just drop me back at the Hammock and I—I'll call you later, after your ribbon-cutting."

"The last time you said that and got that look on your face, you ran off and disappeared for four days. And I still don't know why."

He ignored the jab. "You're going to be at your office all afternoon?"

"After the ribbon-cutting, yes."

"I'll call you there later. Come on. Let's go."

Thirty-seven

Jessie tried not to think of that almost guilty look on Bud's face when she had dropped him off at the Hammock. She tried to keep her mind on her work as she slit open envelope after envelope from the stack of mail on her desk. She read her messages, made calls, scanned the negatives from her last two assignments and ID'd them and wrote cut lines. But it was like someone else was doing her thinking for her. Her mind was trapped by that look on Bud's face. Thank goodness Cynthia was tied up with layout and Heloise was out of the office. She didn't have to talk to anyone, thank goodness. When she finished, she called to leave messages for Bud. "Although for all I know," she told herself, "he could be on a plane to Nebraska or somewhere by now." At his apartment her message was, "Heading for that ribbon-cutting. It's about two-thirty. I'll be back here at the office by four-thirty at the latest. If you're through with your emergency by then, call me here. Or I'll be home by about seven."

When his office switchboard answered, she asked for Miss Halloran. But she got someone else. "I'm Patsy, the new girl. Miss Halloran's in a meeting."

"This is Mrs. Moore. I wanted to leave word for Mr. Wellman."

"Oh, I think they said to say he's not here. I don't know for sure. I haven't met him yet," said Patsy.

"Well, when Miss Halloran comes back, tell her Mrs. Moore said to tell Mr. Wellman she'd be at her office from about four-thirty to seven-ish and home after that."

She grabbed her notebook and camera and stomped out of the office. She's supposed to say he's not here? What did that mean? That he really was? What the hell was going on with him now?

When she opened her car door, she saw Bud's briefcase. Damn. No point in just bringing it home tonight. He might not be there. He might need it now. Should she go back in and call his office? No, she'd be late for the ribbon-cutting. His offices were only about five minutes from the new museum anyway. She'd drop it off. If he was gone somewhere, he was gone. At least she tried.

At the new Oldtime Davie Museum, a private institution dedicated to Davie's history, and built and endowed by the wealthy and horsey Oslander family, she stayed just long enough to ask twenty people their names, and to get more enthusiastic and colorful quotes than she could possibly use. She shot a great picture of Gene Oslander on his horse beside the magnificent Eric Troutman sculpture of a bucking rodeo bronc in front of the Museum entrance drive. As soon as the short speeches were over, she ran in to take a quick spin around the inside of the new museum before the crowds began to pour in for the refreshments — pastries and coffee. And then she headed for her car. If he was at the office, she'd surprise him. If not, she'd just drop the case off and let them worry about how to get it to him, if he needed it. She tried to concentrate on her driving, but Bud's face, with that uneasy, almost desperate expression, was right there on her windshield the whole way.

Exactly six minutes later, she pulled into the lot at Bud's offices, spotted two spaces near the office doors on either side of a minivan, and turned into the first one. But just as she pushed open her door, a company car pulled into the lot. My gosh, was that Bud driving? And was that a woman in the front seat beside him? The car pulled into the space on the other side of the van.

Jessie grabbed her purse and Bud's case and had one foot out of her door when she heard the doors on the other car open. And then a woman's voice. "I don't know what to say to you, Bud. Except that I love you. I always will."

"I know, Ginny."

"You're so special. We won't do anything like this ever again. We won't need to."

"Well, we hope not. But we never say never, Ginny. Just let me run in and put all this in Edgar's hands, and I'll be right out to bring you back to the hotel."

Jessie shot out of her car and stepped quickly around the back of the van. "And let me put this in your hands, Bud Wellman," she wailed, shoving the case into Bud's surprised face. "You left it in my car. I thought I'd better bring it here in case there was anything in it you needed for this emergency. But it sure doesn't look like that kind of emergency. I thought I'd surprise you. And it looks like I sure did."

Bud grabbed the case, sputtering, "Jessie, I— it isn't what it looks like. Oh, God! Jessie, I—"

"Oh, don't bother to explain. It's all pretty obvious. I should have called first so you could have been warned I was coming. But I never thought—I never expected—I'm not very smart, am I?" Her voice broke.

"It's not what you think, Jessie."

"I believed you. Even though you looked guilty as heck when I dropped you off. Just like you sounded guilty when you took off that last time. To see this same lady, I assume."

"Jessie, listen to me. This is Virginia Oakley. Virginia, this is my Jessie."

"*Your* Jessie," Jessie cried. "Think again, Bud. I belong to myself, from now on. I would never belong to anyone who would lie to me so—" She stifled a sob. "I—excuse me. I guess I've just blundered into the wr-wrong place at the wr-wrong time."

"Jessie," Bud cried. "Please, let me explain. Yes, it was the same woman. I had to go to her then. But you don't know—"

"No, I don't know. I don't know why you had to lie to me then. Oh, Bud, you're the last person in the whole world I'd ever expect—to lie to me. I've loved you so much. For so long—" And with tears rolling Jessie rushed back, jumped into her car and slammed the door. And while Bud and Virginia Oakley watched—openmouthed, stunned—she backed her car out to the road like a rocket, shifted with a sickening screech, and shot forward on her way home.

"Oh, God, she didn't understand. Oh, Bud, I'm so sorry! I thought she knew about me. Why doesn't she know? She thinks—"

"Well, she knows that we'd been—you know—seeing each other years ago. I told her that when we first started seeing each other. I told her it was over. Ten years. I never expected to see you again. But I didn't tell her when I came there to help you when your husband died. I meant to tell her. I wanted to. But I didn't know how she'd take it. I didn't want to lose her. I thought I'd wait until after we were married. I lied to her while I was there. Kept telling her I was in other towns and states."

"Why on earth, Bud—?"

"I was determined to help you through that, Ginny. And I didn't know if she could handle it. And I had to grab some clothes and get out of there fast to make the only plane that day I could get a seat on. So I just said it was business. But I'd already told her about you being from St. Charles. I was afraid that if I mentioned the town, or even Chicago, she might put two and two together. So when I called, I told her I was calling from San Diego or somewhere."

"And after that first fib, there was only one direction you could take," said Ginny.

"Right. More lies. Each time, it made me half sick. I'd choke up. All those years we were seeing each other, I didn't have any trouble lying a little to keep it all secret."

"Me either. But that was so justified in a way. We were just solving a problem, the best way we could."

"Today, when I called in and got your messages—that you were on your way here, there wasn't time. I picked up some cash, came right over, told Edgar what was going on so he could figure the best way to handle it, called the hotel to get you a room, and headed for the airport. Bang, bang, bang. I wished I could tell her. No time. I meant to tell her—like maybe tonight. Maybe after the wedding. I didn't want to hide it from her, exactly."

"I shouldn't have come. I never thought I'd ever see you again. After all those years. But when Ned died, I just fell apart. I didn't have anyone to turn to. You took care of everything. And now this. I didn't even think of calling when I had the accident. But with three operations and no insurance—it's taken every penny. I've sold everything I could sell. There was no one who could help me except you. And I just couldn't face losing my house, too. It's all I have. I had no idea—"

"You did the right thing. I'll take care of it. I have more goddamn money than I know what to do with, and I'm glad to put some of it somewhere where it does some good."

"I don't know how to thank you, Bud. I'd do anything for you. I owe you. I wouldn't make trouble for you for anything in the world."

"You owe me nothing. I'm the one who owes you. You did so much for me back then, Ginny. Helped me to see things. Jessie and I have both been far too sensitive with each other. Too ready to pop off. I went crazy when I heard that phone message I told you about. From a drunken nut. Stupid? I never gave her a chance to explain. Just exploded. And stewed for three days and got drunk."

"Yeah, it does sound like you're both touchy as firecrackers. Almost like you're looking for things to get hurt about. So dramatic."

Bud nodded. "I don't know why."

"Sounds like a typical teenage romance," she said with a rueful smile. "All passion and the highest highs and lowest lows. Maybe you both have to get that out of your systems. Maybe because you never let it run its course when you were kids. Maybe it has to do that sooner or later. I don't know about her, but I know you. There's a grown-up there, behind all this fussing. Maybe if you can get through all this courtship garbage, you'll have it made."

Bud gave her a grim smile. "That's if she ever talks to me again. Come on, get back in the car. I'll take you to your hotel as soon as I give these papers to Edgar. It'll take me two minutes. And then I'll go back and try to find Jessie. And see if she'll give me a chance to explain."

When the guard called from the gatehouse to announce that Mr. Webber had arrived, Fran gave her sobbing roommate another pat on the back and said, "That's Webb, downstairs. I have to go down for a minute, Jessie, but I'll be right back up."

Jessie looked up. "Back up? Why back up?"

"I'm not going to leave you alone in this state."

"Don't be silly, Fran. G-go with him. I'm okay. I j-just needed a g-good cry."

"No, you're not okay, Jessie. I've never seen you like this."

"No. I'm all right. I don't want you to stay. I just want to be alone, Fran. Please. That's all I want. To be alone."

Fran nodded, grabbed her keys from the table and let herself out the door. In the hallway, she sprinted down toward the elevator, pressed the call button, pressed it again impatiently, and when the door opened, darted inside. Webb would understand. They couldn't just leave Jessie like this. He would know what to do.

His car, the Jag this time, was pulled over into a guest parking area just outside the G entrance. She ran to it, and let herself in. Webb reached for her and kissed her. "Hey, where's your stuff? Not even a handbag?"

"It's still upstairs. We can't go yet, Webb. Something awful's happened. Jessie is upstairs hysterical. She says to just leave her alone. But I'm afraid to."

"But what happened? Why is she upset?"

"Some misunderstanding, I'm sure. But she said Bud was with another woman. Today. At his office. Jessie came by to drop something off and caught them together. And she says that when he disappeared right after they started see-

477

ing each other that time, it was to go to the same woman."

"Oh, Christ," snorted Webb. "I knew something would happen. I told him he should tell her."

"Tell her? Tell her what? We knew something peculiar was going on then, Webb. A business emergency? Oh, sure. But all that business of not being able to say where he was or where she could telephone him. Come on! Who was he kidding? But Bud never told Jessie the real story, and you never told me. You were both kind of evasive when we tried to find out. And this woman was part of it."

"It wasn't my story to tell, Fran. Hell, I wanted to tell you. Lies are too much trouble to keep track of. But I couldn't because Bud didn't want Jessie to know. He was wrong. Jessie would never have objected, if she knew what happened and why."

"Well, what? Why?"

"With the seal of the confessional?"

"Anything. Just tell me. But fast. I think we better get back up to Jessie."

"Okay. Here it is. Bud had an affair going for many years with a woman whose husband was a paraplegic. It was very discreet. I never had a clue that Bud had anything going, ever. But he stopped about ten years ago and they never exchanged a word all that time. When Bud lit out of here like his tail was on fire right after you two got together, it was because her husband had just died. In a hospital, after some kind of surgery. And while he was half delirious near the end, he was calling out about how he wanted to die and had wanted to for so long. She suddenly felt guilty for keeping him alive. Like she'd been causing him to suffer. She totally fell apart. And called for help. Hysterical. Bud couldn't refuse."

"But he was scared for Jessie to know."

"Right. So he pretended it was a business thing. He asked me to come there and help him. He didn't want anyone, including Ginny, getting the wrong idea. I couldn't refuse, either. He's my best friend. He'd do it for me. So I met him there the next day. She was a mess. Feeling like a criminal for working so hard to keep him alive all those years. So we did it all. Set up the funeral for her, and stayed for it. Paid off all her outstanding bills. And helped her with all the crap and legal stuff.

"And then I flew home and he flew to Arizona first to take care of something real there, that came up at the same time. Some leases we have. And then he flew home. He wanted to tell Jessie. I urged him to, and I never give advice like that. That's why he had me come to the airport with Jessie. I was going to help him explain. But he just couldn't. After lying to her about where he was for five days, he didn't know how to start. And he was afraid of losing her. So he put it off."

Fran nodded. "And to us it just didn't add up. If it was anyone else, we would have been sure it was another woman. But Bud seems like such a straight arrow. You just can't think of him cheating on anyone. I don't know how he managed it with Bitsy."

"I don't either. He's not a good liar. He stumbled over his words. I heard one call he made to Jessie from Ginny's and it was pathetic. He said he was in Alaska, and then he hung up without saying good-bye, like he'd been cut off."

"Well, now it all makes sense," said Fran. "Jeez, you men can't get out of your own way half the time." She opened the car door. "Let's go back upstairs, Webb, and make sure Jessie's okay. Maybe you could tell her what happened. Before she tries to kill herself or something."

But upstairs they found the apartment empty. The light was on in Jessie's room. But Jessie was gone.

"She's not here," cried Fran. "But look, there's her purse. And her keys. So she didn't drive anywhere. She's gotta be here, somewhere. Where would she go all upset and crying like that. Oh my God, not the roof? Oh, please, God, not the roof." She and Webb sprinted for the door and out of it. Down the halls they ran to the C building, with its stairway up to the roof patio high above the lobby, bordering its atrium.

"But Jessie wouldn't do anything crazy—" huffed Webb as they raced up the steps.

"I don't know. I've never seen her like this. And where is she? Oh, Lord. That little fence up here would be so easy to climb over. Can you kill yourself if you jump from just seven stories? No, up there would be like eight."

But the roof patio was empty. They tore back down to the seventh floor, and took the elevator to the lobby, scanned it, and hurried out to the pool area.

She wasn't there.

They poked their heads into the card room. The billiards room, the library, the gym, the loggia and the large meeting room. They jogged around the whole courtyard, the bar, over to the shuffleboard courts, the gazebos and the barbecue patio.

"Maybe she's just taking a walk, to clear her head," suggested Webb. They jogged around the whole perimeter road.

No Jessie, anywhere.

"Let's go back upstairs," Webb said. "Maybe she slipped back in while we were down here. Maybe she was in the bathroom while we were upstairs. Maybe she was just taking out the garbage. Don't panic."

* * *

They checked the apartment again. No Jessie. Webb picked up the phone and dialed Bud's number. Bud answered. "Listen fella, I don't want to worry you or anything. But we can't find Jessie. Is she there with you?"

"No. I only wish she was. And I just called her office for the fifth time. I drove over, before. She didn't go back there after — after — oh, Webb. I've really blown it this time. And she's not in her apartment. I just called."

"That's where we're calling from. She was here just a little while ago, crying torrents, Fran says. She told Fran about what happened at your office. And when I got here, and Fran came down to explain what happened and we both came back up to see Jessie was okay, she was gone. But her car keys and purse are still here. We've looked everywhere here. Fran is very worried. What was Ginny doing here?"

"Long story. Car accident. Operations. She's losing everything. Charged airfare and came to ask for a loan. She could have done it by phone. But she panicked. She can't get one anywhere and she's about to lose her house. I hadda help her. I had Edgar work it out."

"Jessie probably would have understood, if you'd just told her," said Webb.

"I know. I know. I was going to. I'm coming over there."

* * *

Bud was at the door a few minutes later. "You looked everywhere here?" he asked as he walked in.

Webb nodded. "Her car's still here. So where could she be?"

"Maybe we should call 911," said Fran.

"We have nothing to tell them. She's been gone twenty minutes," Webb said. "Hey, are we absolutely certain we've looked everywhere here? Is there anyplace we haven't thought of?"

Fran shook her head. "We went everywhere except out to the pond garden and nobody ever goes there. It's too buggy. The path is practically overgrown—"

"The pond garden?" repeated Bud. "What's that? I never heard of it."

"There's a little path to it off the perimeter road on the west side. Near that big clump of ficuses and gumbo limbos and stuff. You can hardly see the path anymore because hardly anyone uses it."

"And it goes toward the pond?" asked Bud.

"Yeah. There's a little clearing and some benches and a concrete table on this little stone patio right at the edge of the pond. When the channel is high, sometimes it's flooded. So it gets awfully buggy. It's really pretty, but no one uses it much."

Bud and Webb stood up at the same time. "Let's go," said Bud, and the three of them headed for the door.

The smell on the path was strong — fruity scents of tropical foliage and the blooming orchid trees. Half way down it they spotted her through the sea grapes, sitting on a stone bench, staring out at the pond, framed by a sky drenched in glorious pinks and golds from the setting sun. To the north the lavender dusk was moving in. Bud held up his hand and they stopped. He pointed back the way they had come and Fran and Webb nodded, understanding. Bud wanted to handle this alone. They turned and headed back toward the perimeter road. And Bud made his way toward Jessie.

Thirty-eight

He approached her slowly. She appeared not to hear his footsteps crunching on the path. Even when he stood to one side of her only about six feet away, she seemed not to know he was there. Her face, so pink in the rosy, fading light, had a look of melancholy. Her eyes were still puffy from the tears that had washed all her makeup away. She never had looked more beautiful to him.

"What are you doing down here by yourself, Jessie?" he asked, quietly.

She started, then looked up and shrugged. "I guess I'm wallowing in my sadness, or something like that," she said, with the barest hint of a smile.

He sat on the second bench. "Sadness, honey? We've had three days of the best loving any human being could have. We've found some answers we've been looking for and we'll probably find more. We've been so happy and so close, until today. And I have an answer about today, too, if you'll listen. I should have told you before, I know. I should have known that you'd take it for what it was. And you'd understand. I guess I was expecting too much, thinking that you'd just know there was an explanation no matter how things looked. And that you'd just wait forever for me to get around to giving it to you. I reacted the same way about your phone call."

"But if there is an explanation, Bud, why didn't you give it to me? Why didn't I know?"

"Because I couldn't think of how to explain it fast enough, when Ginny got in touch with me the first time. I hadn't talked to her or anything for all those years. I never expected to again. And I had to move fast. She was hysterical. Babbling. Talking about how she deserved to die for trying so hard to keep her husband alive when all he wanted to do was die. I called our travel agent and got him busy. The only plane I could get on for sure was leaving in thirty minutes. I didn't have time to figure out what to do. And I was afraid to tell you without enough time to really explain everything. So I fudged. And I had my office get hold of Webb and send him out to help me in St.

Charles. I had no idea what I'd find there. What I'd have to do.

"I swear, I fully intended to tell you on the ride home from the airport when I got back. That's why I had Webb come too. so he could help. And back me up. And I felt so bad for lying in the first place, I didn't know what to say. So I just punted. I put it off. But I'm telling you now. Honey, our relationship wasn't a romance in any way. It was a practical solution for two physically needy people. We both had a big sex drive and no outlet. But I did get to know that she was a good person. That she loved her husband passionately. We talked a little sometimes. I told her about you. She was there when I needed someone, Jessie. I had to help her when she needed help."

Jessie nodded. "Yes. You're right. You did the right thing. And I can understand how you got kind of fuddled and then why you were so nervous about it."

"And then, except for a thank-you card, I haven't heard a word from her until yesterday. A letter was delivered to the office. And then there were two phone calls saying she was flying here and she was desperate. She was losing everything. I had to go. I got her a room, met the plane, bang-bang-bang again. Put Edgar on it. We'll pay off the mortgage. I gave her some money. I wanted to set up a little trust or

487

something and she said no, just get her out of this hole and she'll be able to work, now, she thought."

"She thought? Was something wrong?"

"She was in a bad car accident right after the funeral. She had just quit her old job about a week before her husband, Ned, died. And taken another one and planned it so she'd have six weeks off in between before starting with the new place. She was planning to fix up their house and stuff. But she didn't extend the supplemental insurance from her old job and that from her new one wouldn't take effect until a couple of weeks after she started working. Big mistake. The accident happened—hit and run—a week after her insurance stopped. Demolished her car. She had all kinds of internal injuries. She was in the hospital for three weeks. And needed lots of surgery. Medicare helped but she still had a lot of bills. And while she was in the hospital all kinds of junk hit the fan. She found out her husband had shorted some stocks and wiped out their investments. The IRS was questioning some returns and wanting money. Her husband used to handle all that stuff. He couldn't move much, but he could talk and think. She finds out he'd taken a loan on the house. Everything crashing down at once. I had to help her. She has no one. And that's the whole story."

Jessie nodded. "Yes. You had to help her. I understand."

"Honey, we have so much. We both have to learn not to take everything so hard. To trust each other."

"I do trust you, Bud. Down deep. Even when I was weeping buckets up there, most of the reason was because I was so frustrated. Because no matter how clear the evidence, I kept thinking there must be a reason. An answer. That just isn't you. But why didn't I know about it?"

"I should have told you right away. I always will, honey, from now on. We'll both try not to go crazy over every little thing."

"I was thinking: look at us. Now, I know how good love can be, and I'm still afraid of it." She traced the pattern of the flagstone with her toe. "Maybe I'm afraid that I just won't fit. In your world. I've never hobnobbed with really rich people before. I don't know how to live that way. Maybe I won't be able to learn. What if we do get married and you get exasperated with me over that. If you ever gave up on me again, I don't know if I could bear it. I still feel so battered inside about this afternoon. I blew up without giving you a chance. Almost like I was looking for an excuse to get out of this."

"Time will help us, honey. We're both healing. And we'll help each other."

"I'm almost afraid to try again. It's opening the door to the possibility of so much pain. I'm not cut out to live so grandly. I'm just a simple person."

"So am I, Jess. I sure don't need the trappings. We can live as simply as you like."

"I need to work a little. It's almost as if I'm afraid to give up my work altogether. Maybe I'm too old to change. Maybe we just can't make it."

"We can. We will. If we can just talk about things and settle them before they get too big."

"Yeah, and once we get in that office again with your lawyers and those papers, you'll get nervous—I'll get nervous, and everything will hit the fan again. When people who don't have anything get married—they don't have to go through such hassles."

"I told you all we have to do is take the damn things and sign them. I had them cut out everything they possibly could, Jess. We have to sign that stuff, Jessie. I have to see that you're protected. Listen, honey—I don't like lawyers either. And I don't trust them. Most of them work for themselves, not you. Ben taught me that a long time ago. He said most of them were just hired guns on sale to the highest bidder. He said the very nature of litigation work breaks down their integrity pretty quickly if they have any to start with. But you have no choice. You've got to use them. They turn the world today. I try to find the most honest and honorable ones I can. There are some. And I keep 'em on a short rope. But we have to use them."

"Or Emil will pull another dumb thing or someone I've gone seriously with before will turn up and you'll go crazy again. Something will ruin it."

"That's up to us, Jessie. We have so much. We're so lucky. All we have to do is enjoy it. And not take anything so seriously. All the other stuff doesn't matter. Being together matters. That's all. Now let's get upstairs, honey. We've got a lot to take care of and only a day and a half to do it in, if we're getting married Wednesday."

"If we go through with it."

"We will. Well, let's say, just in case we decide to, if that makes you feel better. But we are getting married. We are not going to do anything foolish."

"Look who's talking. The dude who went cruising in the gin mills practically begging to get mugged."

"Yeah, I know. I've pulled some real jackass tricks the last couple of months."

"Right. Me, too."

"But no more. If Emil calls again, I'll tell

him to get lost. If Ginny or someone else out of my past crawls out of the woodwork, we'll handle it together. Webb's right. Whatever we did to get through our lives before — that was then. This is now."

Jessie nodded. He pulled her to her feet, hugged her and felt her hand. "You're wearing your ring again."

"Yes. I think it's safer on my finger than left at home in a drawer."

"Good. Now, what else do we have to do to get ready for Wednesday? And what are we going to do on Wednesday."

"What do you want to do?"

"You know what I want to do. You?"

She nodded. "I think so. It's just that —"

"We have to sign the stuff no matter what, Jessie. I mean, even if we don't get married, I have to see that you're looked after. And Kerry. You know damn well we're not going to let each other go. We'll be living together. In court that's like being married. So why not do it right? So let's tell Edgar we'll be over in the morning and get stuff signed and out of the way. It'll only take a few minutes. Okay?"

"Okay. But remember, you said we don't have to live very grandly. Once I thought that would be fun. Now, it scares me."

"We'll live however we please. In a trailer park if you want to. I really don't give a damn.

492

And don't worry. You'll get used to having money. It's easier than you think. If I could do it, anyone could. Let's not worry about it until it happens."

"Well, I guess we can sign the papers."

"And then we don't have to commit ourselves until Wednesday morning. We've got everything we need — the license and the blood tests. A judge will be there anyway. Someone Edgar dug up. We can redo it with a rabbi, later, if we want to. I just want you to be mine, honey."

"And I want you."

"Then why the hell not do it and get it over with?"

"Okay, I guess. But why do I keep feeling like I'm going in to take an important exam and I've never cracked the book?"

Thirty-nine

"I just love weddings. Isn't this jungle absolutely totally boffo?" crowed Kerry, eyeing the masses of beautiful blossoms and greenery that now transformed Burt and Jack's party room into a lush blooming bower. "And look at that pretty little flowered arch. Is that where you do it?"

"It's called a chuppah," explained Bud. "In Jewish weddings, that's where you have the ceremony."

"Is this going to be a Jewish wedding?"

"Halfway," he laughed. "My half. And we're not having a rabbi, but the judge is Jewish."

"Is it sort of like a bar mitzvah?"

"Not nearly as fancy, but similar."

"It looks like the Botanical Gardens in here," said Fran. "But I'll tell you, this business of getting married, it isn't as easy as it used to be. All those agreements!"

"Yeah, they really messed up Jessie and me for a while there," said Bud. "She felt like she was giving up her U.S. citizenship. So did I."

"I wanted my granola rights and Webb wanted his cholesterol rights," said Fran.

"She fought me tooth and nail on that but I was unbudgeable," grinned Webb. "And if she ever tries to leave me, I get custody of the yogurt-maker. I've got her hog-tied. She'll never abandon her yogurt-maker."

"I'm so sorry Miss Mary couldn't be here," said Kerry. "For a really ancient person, she's kind of neat."

"She and her sister had already booked this cruise," said Webb. "And it was so iffy for Bud and Jessie. What if we pulled Miss Mary off the cruise and then they didn't get married? So we just left it that way. She won't be back until the weekend. She'll understand."

"And don't you just love this place?" Kerry went on. "Sitting right here on the water and looking out and seeing all the yachts and cruise ships and tugs go by? The fireplaces and the little arches. It's like you guys are getting married in a darling little home. If I was still planning on committing marriage with Doug, I'd want to do it here."

"It was here or the Pump Room," said Webb.

"In the Pump Room you have to give everybody a little card that slides in a slot and opens the door."

"Oh, how darling," cried Kerry. "Kind of like getting married in a speakeasy."

"Say, where's your mother?" asked Webb. "I don't see her anywhere."

"In the ladies' room," said Kerry.

"Where's Benjie?"

"Oh, is Benjie going to make it?" cried Kerry. "I'm actually going to get to meet the Adorable Snowman?"

"I expect him any minute. He said he'd be here if he had to ski down," said Sess.

"I'm dying to meet him in person—the body that goes with the voice," said Kerry. "He's got a great voice. You can tell he's got hair on his chest."

"You've talked to Benjie?" asked Sess, surprised.

"Just twice, on the phone. The second time was yesterday. He wasn't sure yet if he could get here on time. I told him to hijack a helicopter if he had to. But get here."

Just then a portly, white-haired man stepped tentatively through the arch. "The Moore-Wellman-Dimitri-Webber weddings?" he asked. "I'm Judge Perlmutter."

"I'm Mr. Wellman's sister, Judge," said Sess, taking his hand. "You're in the right place. Of course, it all changes from day to day—the time, the place, the cast. But you do have the latest cast right, I think."

"Make the ceremony short and sweet, Judge, if you want to get all the way through it without any dropouts," advised Dell.

Esme and Needle poked their heads in, saw Webb, Bud, and Kerry, and joined them. "I was sure we were in the wrong place," said Esme. "It's not easy to find." She came over to greet her father and her aunt with little kisses in the air, then noticed the chuppah. "Oh, a chuppah! How nice, Daddy. I didn't know you knew what one was for." She shook hands with Fran and Webb, and nodded as Webb introduced the judge. Needle shook everyone's hand enthusiastically and then found the hors d'oeuvres table and got down to business, while Esme pulled a little package out of her purse and handed it to Kerry.

"Pearls and a charm bracelet," she said when Kerry looked at it puzzled. "For you. The bracelet is the one my father got me. Piece by piece. He bought all of those charms himself, all over the world. And the pearls are from Needle and me, to our new stepsister."

"But I didn't get a present for you," wailed Kerry, tearing off the wrapping.

"You've already given me one," said Esme. "Are you feeling better about you know what?"

"You mean Doug? Breaking up? Yes, I guess so. I'm resigned to it. We're still friends but I'm just too old for him, I guess. Women grow up faster. I love him dearly. But he's such a boy. And I think I need a man, now."

"No doubt," Esme said.

"Oh Esme, I love them!" Kerry cried, pulling the pearls and bracelet from their box.

"Wear them in good health, dear," said Esme, and she took the bracelet, looped it around Kerry's wrist and closed the clasp. And then she hooked the pearls' clasp. Over at the hors d'oeuvres, Needle stopped chewing long enough to nod agreement, and then asked, "Did Benjie get here?"

"No," Kerry shook her head. "Not yet. I didn't even know he was coming for sure. But Sess just said she expects him any second. I can't wait to see what he looks like."

"Where's your bride?" Needle asked Bud.

"She'll be here in a minute," he answered. "I think. If she doesn't change her mind again, as she has four times in two days. She's in the ladies' room. Unless she's crawled out the window and gone home."

"Well, everything certainly looks beautiful," said Sess, glancing about the room.

Judge Perlmutter cleared his throat. "I think we can start arranging who stands where," he said. "Is anyone giving anyone away?"

"I thought that I could give away my mother," said Kerry. "And my mother would like to give away Fran but she's going to be busy enough getting married so I thought maybe Sess could do that, as Mom's proxy."

"Good idea, Kerry. I'd love to," said Sess. "I've never been a proxy at a wedding before."

"And are you having a best man or matron of honor or any such?" asked the judge.

"We're having everything," nodded Kerry. "I thought that Needle and Dell could be best men," said Kerry. "In proxy for Bud and Webb, who would be each other's best men if they weren't doing a double-header here."

"Good thinking," Sess and Esme said together.

"Except I think we need a scorecard to keep the players straight," said Webb.

Just then a man who was a stranger to most of the company came through the arch. Mr. Pontchetrain. "Oh, hello. I'm here for Jessie Moore's nuptials," he said. "Am I in the wrong place?"

"Ah, Mr. Pontchetrain," called Fran. "No, you've got the right place, sir. I'm Fran Dimitri. Jessie's roommate. Come and join us." And then to Bud, she whispered, "I invited him. I didn't want him to think Jessie was just gold-bricking today. He wanted to be invited and I figured you never know when you'll need a marker to call in. Or an extra man."

"For what?" asked Webb. Fran quickly whispered to Kerry who Pontchetrain was and how she had invited him.

"Well, good thing you came, Mr. Pontchetrain," said Kerry. "I'm Kerry, Jessie's daughter. And as a matter of fact, you're just in time. We need two matrons of honor. Esme could be one but everyone else is used up. And Benjie could be a proxy but he's not here yet. You can be the backup proxy matron of honor to Mom for Fran, and Esme, you can be Fran's matron of honor, the proxy for my Mom."

"I've never been a matron of honor before," said Pontchetrain dubiously. "Not even a backup proxy. Is that done?"

"Not many men get the chance," said Sess.

"Kerry always did think outside the lines," noted Fran.

"And if this Benjie does arrive in time, I'm not the matron of honor?" asked Pontchetrain.

"No," said Kerry. "And we're about out of major roles. I don't see you as a flower girl. Even proxy. But if Benjie does get here, you can be the ring-bearer."

"Who's on first, again, Kerry?" asked Webb.

"I'm getting confused," said the Judge.

"That's okay, Judge," Kerry assured him. "I've got it all in my head. Here, I'll write it down for you. So you get everyone married to the right partners on the certificates."

"That would be nice," nodded the judge. "Hmm. We have two grooms in the room, but we only have one bride."

"The other one will be in when you're ready to roll," said Kerry. "But my mom has been so busy changing her mind back and forth, she didn't have much time to get ready. So she's still finishing up."

"What's she doing in there? Giving herself a permanent?" asked Pontchetrain.

They all looked at the arch. And as they did, Benjie strode through it. And Fran, Webb, Sess, Esme, Dell, Needle and Bud heaved a collective sigh of relief. "The Adorable Snowman," cried Kerry. "Bud, Webb, give your rings to Mr. Pontchetrain."

"Am I on time? That plane was circling for twenty minutes. I was ready to put on a parachute and jump," Benjie said, grinning broadly.

Esme and Sess ran to hug him and Benjie bent down to hug them back. Webb, Dell and Bud came to hug him, too, and shake his hand. "This is my bride, Benjie," said Webb, introducing Fran. "The last Mrs. Webber."

"I bet he says that to all his wives," said Fran.

"And this," said Bud, "is your new stepsister, Kerry. Jessie's daughter."

"Wow," said Benjie. "Hey, they

them pretty here in Florida. You look just like your voice sounds."

"Funny, I was just going to say the same thing to you. They grow 'em pretty good up there in Alaska, too, I'd say," Kerry retorted, looking up at her new stepbrother and blushing. "Uh — how's the mud up there, these days?"

"Slippery," laughed Benjie. "I'm not feeling very friendly toward it lately."

"Oh, I'm so glad you made it," cried Kerry. "When we get this ceremony over with, I have to talk to you. See, I was planning this paper on — on — Eskimo life-expectancies. Maybe you could help me with some sources."

"Oh, yeah? Sure thing. In fact one of the studies on a project I worked on last year was the Eskimos' diets. I could probably come up with some really good stuff for you, if I put my thinking cap on. We can talk about it right after we get everyone married off."

Fran poked Webb and whispered, "Did we just see the start of something big, here? Eskimo life-expectancies? Where did she g_ _ that from? She's majoring in English Lit."

_ _ed and whispered back, "Well, I
_ _'s going to wear black over
_ _if she still remembers his

_ _stand in front of the

chuppah, from where he carefully instructed each member of the small group where to stand before him. "Can I stand next to my pretty new stepsister?" asked Benjie. "I think I'm finally beginning to understand what they see in incest."

"Doug who?" Fran giggled into Webb's ear.

"Wait. I'll come over there and stand near you, Benjie," said Kerry. "You'll get the judge confused if you move, and I have something to take care of first." Esme and Sess exchanged meaningful glances. Was Benjie just being polite?

"But where's the other bride?" asked the judge.

"Oh, waiter, would you check if anyone's sneaking out the back door," asked Bud. "But what she said was that she had to change."

Kerry winked at Sess, who winked back. "I'll get her," she said. "Don't start anything without me."

Everyone turned to watch the arch expectantly. In a few moments Kerry returned. "Okay, Sess," she said. Sess took a tape recorder from her purse and punched a button. The sounds of the "Wedding March" filled the room. And through the arch stepped Jessie, wearing a long white lace gown, white satin slippers and a veil cascading from a pearl tiara, and carrying a trailing bouquet of dozens of tiny white orchids.

Everyone gasped. Bud's eyes opened wide and he broke into a euphoric smile. He blinked a few times, almost as though he were fighting a happy tear or two. Kerry took her mother's arm, and in measured steps in time with the music, led her up to where Bud was waiting, then turned and marched back toward Benjie. Bud reached for Jessie's hand with both of his, and held it to his cheek.

"Dearly beloved—" began the judge.

"Jessie," Bud almost choked, "you did it. Oh, honey, you're beautiful."

"You said you wanted me to wear one. So when we decided to go ahead, I called David's and told them I needed one right away. This one was my size so I took it. Then I canceled it. Then I took it again."

"It's perfect."

"It really looks neat, Mom. You can't even see all the pins."

"Or I'd have been tripping—it was much too long," said Jessie. "They couldn't get it hemmed in time so Kerry told them to just send it over with the hem still pinned. Who cares?"

"Dearly beloved," began the judge again.

"I'm really tickled pink that you did that, Jessie."

"I have never been so utterly upstaged in my

life," said Fran.

"Are you kidding? You look like a movie star, when you wear shoes and stockings, like this," laughed Webb, hugging her.

Just then, Cynthia and Heloise twinkled through the arch in lame pants outfits. "Jessie, are we too late? We had to get everything proofed before we left—"

"No, we're just getting started," said Jessie.

"The dress is wild, Jessie," hooted Cynthia. "Oh, Mr. Pontchetrain! We didn't know you'd be here."

"Well, I didn't know you'd be here, either, so we're even," he snorted. "But now that you are, would you please just stand back there and be still. They're trying to run a wedding here."

"Who are they?" Benjie whispered to Kerry.

"They work at Mom's office," she whispered back. "Aren't they wild. They're called Sin and Hell. And boy are they sexy!"

"Those pants are pretty tight."

"Yeah, the kind that either feel good or hurt. Read-my-lips pants, we call them." And she and Benjie struggled to keep from laughing out loud.

"Dearly beloved," began the judge once more. "We are gathered together—"

"Oh, we should have pictures," Kerry cried, interrupting the judge once more. "Who's got the camera? Mom, did you forget the camera?"

"I have a camera," said Mr. Pontchetrain, digging one out of his shoulder bag. "Being a publisher, I never go anywhere without one. Will someone take one of me being ring-bearer? I'd like to send it to my mother. She'll get such a kick out of it."

"Do you suppose we could get on with this wedding?" cried the judge. "You may get pictures, but nobody will be married if we don't."

It was a charming little ceremony, everyone agreed afterward. Very short. Once the judge got them all quieted down, he raced through it like a tobacco auctioneer, skipping all the non-essentials, and quickly pronounced both pairs man and wife.

He had barely finished when a three-man combo arrived. Waiters removed the chuppah and the musicians took its place and began playing very hip music. "Yo, Snowman!" called Kerry, who was sitting with her mother and Bud, over to Esme and Needle's table, where Benjie was sitting.

"Yo, stepsister, what's up?" Benjie called back.

"Do you rock?" she asked.

"Do I rock?" he cried. "Do I rock! Like a cradle. Bring that little bod over here and I'll show you." He leapt up and met her on the floor and the two of them began gyrating wildly. They hardly sat down again long enough to eat the wedding feast.

"I thought the brides and grooms were supposed to waltz together first," said Webb.

"Only in the movies. And normal weddings," said Fran.

Sess heard them. "And if my brother tried to do a waltz he'd tie himself in a knot," she explained, laughing. "He probably forbade the band to play one. If you two want to do a wedding waltz, we'll put in a special request."

The wedding dinner featured Australian lobster tails, with fresh vegetables—Fran's and Jessie's heart-healthy choice—macaroni and cheese—Bud's favorite—and peanut-butter cookies—for Webb.

After dinner, the maître d' wheeled out a table with two wedding cakes. "I thought we were going to share yours," said Jessie.

"Nope. Fran insisted we order a separate one for you just in case."

The two couples cut the huge carrot and Black Forest cakes and fed each other the first bites. They toasted each other, and made their way around the tables, hugging and kissing everyone. "Be happy, Daddy," Esme said. She couldn't quite bring herself to hug her stepmother, but she took Jessie's hand and squeezed it wordlessly.

"Okay, enough of all this mush," said Kerry. "You can go off and honeymoon now." Jessie threw her bouquet at Kerry, and laughed when she caught it.

"Thanks for your permission," she said.

And a few minutes later, amid a barrage of rice supplied by the waiters, the two couples ran through the arch and out the door.

The rest of the small group hung around for an hour or so, laughing, gabbing and drinking champagne, before deciding it was time to head over to Bud's apartment for one last coffee together before they all headed their separate ways.

Kerry offered Benjie a ride. And he accepted quickly. "You'll have to get Dad to bring you up to Alaska next time he comes," he told her. "It's God's country all right. Fewer and fewer really pristine places like that left all the time."

"Oh, I'd love to," said Kerry. "Would you show us around?"

"Sure. Take you out to a couple of the other camps, too, if you like, and show you some of the stuff we're studying up there."

"Oh, that would be wonderful," cried Kerry. "I can't wait!"

"Meanwhile, you live in the same place as my dad, don't you?"

Kerry nodded. "Right down the hall. Only I

just went back to school last week. I flew down for this but I'm going back tomorrow."

"Well, I'm going to be here a couple of days. So we could work on your paper first. Do you have it with you?"

"You mean now, right after the party?"

"I guess we're all going over there from here, but no one will mind if we do a little homework."

"I don't have it with me. It's barely started. But I can tell you pretty much what I was thinking of doing."

"Glad you have wheels," he said. "I took a cab from the airport."

"I've got my mom's car. And I've got the key to your dad's place."

"Let's go now, then," said Benjie, "and beat everyone back. The faster we get there, the sooner we can get started. And the sooner you can get it done. And you know, if you want to come up by yourself if there's anything I can help you with up there, Dad can probably hitch you a ride with someone. He's got all kinds of friends with private planes and they come up to fish and hunt."

"Oh, that sounds wonderful. And you're absolutely right," Kerry said. "The sooner we get started the better."

"When you're ready for Alaska, just tell me and I'll take care of getting you there."

The two of them slipped out a moment later, laughing over some anecdote of Benjie's.

"Did you catch all that?" asked Dell. "Maybe it's because romance is in the air. I've never before seen Benjie give that much attention to anything that wasn't on a slide or in a test tube."

"Brotherly concern?" suggested Needle.

"Kerry took one look," said Esme, "and turned on her vamp engines. Do we have something developing here?"

"Who knows," said Sess. "Romance is like hurricanes. All you can do is sit back and watch."

"Kerry," said Esme, "is not the type to just sit back and watch. I've gotten to know that young lady rather well," she said, chuckling. "My advice to Benjie would be, 'Look out, brother; here comes another mudslide.'"

CATCH A RISING STAR!

ROBIN ST. THOMAS

FORTUNE'S SISTERS (2616, $3.95)
It was Pia's destiny to be a Hollywood star. She had complete self-confidence, breathtaking beauty, and the help of her domineering mother. But her younger sister Jeanne began to steal the spotlight meant for Pia, diverting attention away from the ruthlessly ambitious star. When her mother Mathilde started to return the advances of dashing director Wes Guest, Pia's jealousy surfaced. Her passion for Guest and desire to be the brightest star in Hollywood pitted Pia against her own family — sister against sister, mother against daughter. Pia was determined to be the only survivor in the arenas of love and fame. But neither Mathilde nor Jeanne would surrender without a fight. . . .

LOVER'S MASQUERADE (2886, $4.50)
New Orleans. A city of secrets, shrouded in mystery and magic. A city where dreams become obsessions and memories once again become reality. A city where even one trip, like a stop on Claudia Gage's book promotion tour, can lead to a perilous fall. For New Orleans is also the home of Armand Dantine, who knows the secrets that Claudia would conceal and the past she cannot remember. And he will stop at nothing to make her love him, and will not let her go again . . .

SENSATION (3228, $4.95)
They'd dreamed of stardom, and their dreams came true. Now they had fame and the power that comes with it. In Hollywood, in New York, and around the world, the names of Aurora Styles, Rachel Allenby, and Pia Decameron commanded immediate attention — and lust and envy as well. They were stars, idols on pedestals. And there was always someone waiting in the wings to bring them crashing down . . .

Available wherever paperbacks are sold, or order direct from the Publisher. Send cover price plus 50¢ per copy for mailing and handling to Zebra Books, Dept. 4064, 475 Park Avenue South, New York, N.Y. 10016. Residents of New York and Tennessee must include sales tax. DO NOT SEND CASH. For a free Zebra/ Pinnacle catalog please write to the above address.